hannon McKenna i ... *ODAY* bestselling aut ... ranging from roman ... romance and even to pa... herself to the magic of a story. Writing her own stories is ... dream come true. She loves to hear from readers. Visit ... r website, shannonmckenna.com. Find her on Facebook ... Facebook.com/authorshannonmckenna, or join her ... wsletter at shannonmckenna.com/connect.php and ... k for your welcome gift!

obia Bryant is the award-winning and nationally b...stselling author of fifty romance and mainstream ...mmercial fiction works. Twice she has won the RT ...viewers' Choice Best Book Award for African ...erican/Multicultural Romance. Her books have ...eared in *Ebony*, *Essence*, the *New York Post*, the ...*r-Ledger*, the *Dallas Morning News* and many other na...ional publications. One of her bestselling books was adapted to film.

Discover more at millsandboon.co.uk

HOW TO MARRY
A BAD BOY

SHANNON McKENNA

THE PREGNANCY
PROPOSAL

NIOBIA BRYANT

MILLS & BOON

1 London Bridge Street, London, SE1 9GF

www.harpercollins.co.uk

HarperCollins*Publishers*
1st Floor, Watermarque Building,
Ringsend Road, Dublin 4, Ireland

How to Marry a Bad Boy © 2022 Shannon McKenna
The Pregnancy Proposal © 2022 Niobia Bryant

ISBN: 978-0-263-30388-9

0922

HOW TO MARRY
A BAD BOY

SHANNON McKENNA

One

"You're pranking me, right?" Marcus Moss demanded. "Tell me it's a prank."

Gisela Velez, his office manager, clucked her tongue. "Any woman on my list could easily play your temporary wife. Please. Consider it."

"What do I have to do to make you all understand?" he roared. "I will not play this game! I refuse! Get it through your heads!"

"You're not the only one in the game, Marcus," his sister-in-law, Tilda, reminded him. "A lot of careers are on the line."

Marcus Moss, chief technical officer of MossTech, shot to his feet with a murmured obscenity, shoving his chair back from the huge, cluttered desk.

Afternoon light filled his big corner office. He glared around at his sister, Maddie, Tilda and Gisela, all of whom were breaking his balls today. Ruthlessly.

Gisela had been with him since he began working at

MossTech, before he made CTO. She was knowledgeable and competent, and managed his Seattle office with an iron hand when he was out of the country dealing with the far-flung MossTech satellite labs. He had great respect and affection for her, usually. But not today.

Gisela folded her arms over her large bosom, frowning as if he were the unreasonable one. "We're not asking you to fall in love on command. We're asking you to cut a deal."

"You don't have much time before the ax falls," Maddie said. "Your thirty-fifth birthday is in seven weeks, and if you're still unmarried, controlling shares go to Uncle Jerome, and MossTech is screwed."

Marcus closed his eyes, cursing under his breath. The specter of his great-uncle Jerome Moss getting a controlling interest in MossTech was the price of noncompliance with his grandmother's ill-conceived marriage mandate. Even after retirement, Jerome still itched for executive power over MossTech. He'd wanted it ever since he and his brother, Marcus's grandpa Bertram, had founded the company. It had been an uneasy power struggle for the past fifty years of the company's existence, and Gran was using that fact now, ruthlessly. At the risk of hurting herself and Moss-Tech, a company she co-owned, and where she had been chief executive officer for decades. Getting them married, at all costs, meant that much to her.

But it was a nightmare for her three grandchildren. Or rather, just for him, at this point. Caleb had gotten lucky last year. Maddie, only a few weeks ago. They were home free, by the grace of God. Good for them.

"So?" Maddie prompted. "Earth to Marcus. Pick up the pace, buddy."

"What do you think I'm doing?" he protested. "I'm trying to protect as much of our work as possible before Jerome trashes everything we've built over the last several years since we took over. Stop distracting me!"

"Our suggestion buys you time," Tilda urged. "Make a mutually beneficial arrangement with someone from Gisela's list. You don't have to pretend it's a real marriage. Gran knows better than to complain at this point."

"Like it's so easy," he retorted. "But I'm not like Caleb, Til. I've made it clear to everyone I ever hooked up with that I'm not interested in long-term commitment. I don't want the real thing. And I *certainly* don't want a fake thing."

Tilda's green eyes narrowed. "Come on, Marcus. Women drop at your feet like overripe fruit. You snap your fingers, and they jump."

"For a hot weekend fling, sure! That's *not* what's on the table!"

"You're sulking because the burden of Gran's marriage mandate has fallen on you now, right?" Maddie said. "You hoped Caleb and I would crash and burn before you, and you'd be off the hook. But no. Amazingly, it worked out for us."

"That's great, and I'm glad for you, but you shouldn't have indulged Gran like that. Now she thinks she's solved your lives. That it's my turn for her magic touch."

Tilda and Maddie exchanged guilty smiles. "I wasn't calculating Gran's wishes when I fell in love with Jack, Marcus," Maddie said. "I was suiting myself."

"Same here, with me and Caleb," Tilda added.

"Yeah, and so will I," Marcus snapped. "I won't comply. You knew I wouldn't, Caleb knew it, and Gran should have known it, too."

"She's trying to compensate for past mistakes," Tilda said. "She thinks she's helping you, in her clumsy, bossy way. She's really not trying to punish you."

"She's been trying to manage me since I was a toddler," Marcus said. "She could never do it then, so what makes her think that I'd behave now?"

"Do you remember that video call you made from that

rice paddy in Indonesia?" Maddie asked. "The screaming argument heard round the world?"

"The one where Gran tried to pick out my date for your wedding? Oh, yes. I remember that conversation all too well."

"You said that you'd pick someone randomly out of a hat before you'd go with one of her choices," Tilda said. "And guess what? It gave us an idea."

"I was joking, Til," he said through his teeth.

"Yeah, well, we're not. Draw a name, Marcus. See who comes up. C'mon. It'll be fun."

"I started with the MossTech personnel and narrowed it down to women who've been hired for temporary special projects," Gisela told him. "They're smart and ambitious. They have already signed NDAs for the company, and we can write a specific contract for this. They aren't permanent MossTech employees, and we're making the limits clear. They can also refuse without any harm to their jobs. I even checked it out with HR. I wrote an algorithm to sort out eligible single women of a certain age, and I asked around to make sure they weren't engaged or living with their boyfriends. It's the best networking opportunity that they will ever get. It's weird for everybody, I admit, but desperate times call for desperate measures, right? And who wouldn't want to be the MossTech Hottie Dreamboat's temporary wife?"

"That's Caleb's title, not mine," Marcus growled.

"Nope," Tilda informed him. "You inherited the title when Caleb married me. Now poor Caleb is just a regular harried family man, frantically juggling family and career. Earn the name, Wonder Boy."

The smiles she was exchanging with Maddie and Gisela set his teeth on edge. "Do not yank my chain," he warned them.

"Lighten up, bro," Maddie soothed. "I know from experience how hard it is to power-shop for a spouse with brutal time constraints. Caleb only had a month to find someone last year when Gran came up with this mandate. We're trying to give you a jumping-off point."

"Yeah, right off a cliff!"

"Speaking of cliffs, if Jerome takes over, he'll do serious damage to the terms of the merger with my dad's company, which will hurt Riley Biotech's employees," Tilda said. "Help me out here, Marcus. Please. It's not just about you anymore."

"Talk to Gran," he said through his teeth. "I didn't create this mess."

"Buy us time," she pleaded. "Eight hundred people in Riley Biotech are counting on me to protect their livelihoods. Make an effort. Keep Jerome guessing. You have an escape route, remember? The marriage won't be forever. I'll show you the contract Caleb and I used. Use it as a guide. Tweak it however you like."

"No. I won't turn cartwheels for Gran. It's humiliating."

"So's getting your ass fired," Gisela said sourly.

"Come on, Marcus," Maddie coaxed. "You never intended to marry anyway, right? It's not like you're giving up anything real."

"My pride, my dignity, my integrity?"

Gisela rolled her eyes. "Pah. My cousins set me up with Hector at Uncle Luiz's wedding, and we were engaged two days later. It's been thirty years, and it worked. Aside from his snoring, anyhow. How is this any different?"

"At least you can be sure that any person contracted to do a special project for MossTech has been vetted for smarts," Maddie encouraged.

"Did Gran demand a DNA swab? Inspect their teeth? Request their medical records?"

"I didn't speak to Mrs. Moss about this at all. And they're all nice, respectable young women, so be polite."

Gisela's gaze challenged him as she pulled a spreadsheet from a file and plucked an empty gift bag made of brocade-textured midnight blue paper out of her purse. "I don't have a hat, but we can use the bag from the Dior J'adore perfume you gave me on my birthday. I simply love the stuff, by the way."

"Glad to hear it," Marcus said grimly. "It wasn't enough to keep you on my side, though, was it? What do I have to give you, Gisela? Emeralds? My own heart's blood?"

"It's in all of our best interests to stave off the apocalypse," Gisela lectured. "You know that Jerome will fire your administrative staff the minute he fires you, right? We've been sending out résumés for weeks. The stress is very bad for morale."

Marcus had not, in fact, thought of that. He was appalled. "No way!" he said blankly. "Why would he do that? He'd be shooting himself in the foot to fire you!"

"Jerome's never been known for his good sense," Maddie observed.

"You know this place inside out," Marcus said to Gisela. "Our operations, our engineers, our history, the labs worldwide. Jerome would be insane to cut you loose!"

"He'll never trust me," Gisela said, her voice resigned. "I'll be out the door the day he fires you. And I'd really hoped to get all the way to retirement with this job. I don't want to roll the dice again at my age. So you're not the only one with skin in the game, okay? Sebastian!" she bawled through the door. "Bring me some scissors!"

A young assistant scurried in with a pair of scissors clutched in his hand, eyes wide and curious behind his glasses.

Gisela handed him the spreadsheet. "Chop those up, drop them into the gift bag."

Sebastian scanned the list as he snipped names. "Is this for the bride drawing?"

Marcus winced. "The whole admin staff knows about this circus?"

"That's none of your business, Sebastian," Gisela said sternly. She gave Marcus a guilty glance. "I had to ask around for the candidates' relationship status, so word got around. I was as discreet as I could be, but…"

"Right," Marcus growled. "I get it."

Sebastian waved a scrap of paper. "Nix Barb Jennings," he advised. "She met a guy at a conference in Vegas. Now she's got stars in her eyes and can't stop giggling."

"Thanks for the tip." Gisela twitched the scrap from him and tossed it in the trash.

Sebastian stuffed the strips of paper into the bag and placed it on the desk in front of Marcus, his eyes bright with anticipation.

"Out you go, Sebastian," Gisela said briskly. "Chop, chop."

Sebastian slunk out, crestfallen.

"You're telling me, with a straight face, to pick a name out of this bag, walk up to some random woman I don't even know, and ask her to marry me," Marcus said.

The women all spoke in unison. "Yes."

"Bro," Maddie said. "If anyone in the world can, it's you. Not to be crass, but you're rich, you're smart and you're smoking hot. Whatever this woman's professional aspirations are, you can sweeten the pot. She'll say yes. Unless she's in love with someone already, in which case, no harm, no foul. Just draw again."

"You enjoy the thrill of uncertainty, right?" Tilda said. "Aren't you the guy who loves extreme sports? This will break the spell. Get you moving in the right direction."

"Yeah. To another continent, maybe."

Gisela sniffed. "I've always gone over and above for you, Marcus. You owe me this. Just try before you kamikaze all of our careers, okay?"

"Do not guilt-trip me," he snarled. "I'm not the one piloting the death plane!"

Gisela held out the gift bag. "That changes nothing for the rest of us. And I'm not afraid to piss off my boss, since I'm about to be fired anyhow. Pick a name."

Screw it. He was outmaneuvered, and they all knew it. He shoved his hand into the bag, rummaged around... and around.

"Stop stalling," Maddie said.

"Stop nagging," he retorted, yanking out a strip of paper.

"Who is it?" the three women all demanded, all at once.

He gazed at it, frowning. "Eve Seaton," he told them. "Never heard of her."

Tilda let out a gasp. "Oh! I know that name! Caleb was talking about her. Everyone wanted her, but she'd only accept a short-term contract. Caleb would mortgage the farm to get her on his team, though. He's still hoping that she changes her mind."

"What's her specialty?"

"Genetics." Gisela sat before his computer, typing with blinding speed. "She's brilliant, they say. They hired her to lead a team that's genome sequencing some kind of fast-growing root-rot fungus. Let me...yes. Dr. Eve Seaton. Here. Take a look."

Marcus circled behind Gisela and leaned to look at the personnel photo on the screen. The shot had been snapped for her lanyard. She was brunette, and her dark, wavy hair was scraped back severely into something, a bun, a braid, a ponytail, who knew. The observer was given no clues about the rear details from that squarely frontal pose, just a faint fuzz of curling wisps around her forehead. She wore harsh, black-framed glasses, a white lab coat that blended in with the white background in the overexposed shot so that her hands and face seemed to float in an otherworldly sea of white.

He leaned closer. Her eyes pulled him, in spite of the glasses that somehow did not obscure them at all. Big, deep-set, a bright, light-catching gray. Full of calm challenge.

He leaned closer and inhaled a choking whiff of Gisela's J'adore. He teased what oxygen he could out of the air and tried not to cough.

Eve Seaton's other features were too washed out to make much of them, but she looked serious, prim. She had a heart-shaped face, delicate points to her jaw. Her lips were pressed tight, so it was hard to tell their true shape. In this picture, her eyes dominated.

After a moment, he realized that the women were exchanging smug looks.

"I bet this one's as smart as you, bro, if not smarter." Maddie had that little-sister nyah-nyah taunting tone. "Maybe you should draw again."

"Don't jerk me around," he growled. "I outgrew that garbage in kindergarten."

Their smothered giggles put him over the top. He was done with this interchange.

"Ladies, it's been real," he said curtly. "Talk to you later."

"Wait!" Gisela clicked with the mouse. "She's in the genetics lab on the fourth level of the Rosen Building, and her office number is 450. Take this." She rummaged through files and held one out. "This is everything I could collect on her. Educational bona fides, CV, professional organizations, scientific articles. You can make her dreams come true...in exchange for this insignificant favor that costs her nothing. Hmm?"

Marcus took the file. There was no way to remove those women from his office other than throwing them out bodily, so he left himself, striding through the cubicles outside. Their occupants looked away quickly as he passed, sensing his volcanic seething.

Unfortunately, the hapless Sebastian hadn't gotten the memo. He jumped up from his desk. "Hey, Mr. Moss! So how did it go? Who'd you pick?"

Marcus jabbed his finger in Sebastian's direction so savagely the kid jerked back, though he was ten feet away. "Not. Another. Word."

Sebastian recoiled, blinking rapidly. "Um, ah, yeah. Sorry. Sorry."

Marcus strode on, ashamed at himself for snarling at a bumbling dweeb like Sebastian. He headed straight for the door to the courtyard in search of air, sky.

It's not just about you anymore.

You're not the only one with skin in the game.

Just try before you kamikaze all of our careers, okay?

Goddamn Gran for dumping this mess on him. If he had only himself to consider, he'd walk away from MossTech without a care. Even if it had been his brother Caleb's career on the line, he'd have cut loose. He was confident that Caleb would thrive. His brother was doing great. Wildly in love with Tilda and his newly discovered little daughter, Annika, high on the euphoria of getting his best friend Jack Daly back from exile. Jack's name had been cleared of all wrongdoing, thanks to Maddie, who was Jack's new true love.

And all the love and devotion around here was putting him in a sugar coma.

But the thought of Gisela and the rest getting fired… damn. And there were Tilda's people from Riley Biotech as well, all of them hanging on his conscience. It would be a bloodbath.

Marcus stopped in the center of the garden courtyard at the enormous fountain. Water ran smoothly over a huge, gleaming black granite globe.

Marcus opened the file. It was full of articles from scientific journals, co-written by a group of researchers. Eve Seaton's name always led the list.

He was caught by a photo of Eve Seaton on a stage a few years ago, receiving an Oskoff Prize for excellence in biotechnology. Smiling, surrounded by beaming colleagues, holding a crystal plaque. She wore an embroidered charcoal gray silk gown with a high Chinese collar. It fit her body like a glove. Nice body.

The prize had been for the genetics in a project called Corzo. He scanned the documents. She and her team had engineered a fast-growing perennial grass that never needed to be aerated, and was genetically tweaked to sequester huge amounts of carbon from the atmosphere. After two years, a field planted with Corzo could suck more carbon from the atmosphere than a similar-sized plot of primeval rain forest, while also producing a very protein-rich seed that could be eaten by humans and livestock alike. Endangered honeybees also thrived on its flowers. Nice touch. Corzo multitasked like a boss.

The articles Gisela had gathered touted Corzo as being not only edible, but tasty. There was one about how Eve Seaton and her team had partnered with local bakers to develop Corzo recipes. A local magazine touted the Corzo Holiday Tasting Basket with an article entitled "Merry Christmas! Toothsome Treats for a Hopeful Future."

There were photos of her and her team in the article, next to a huge table with an array of baked goods, baskets of pasta, cakes, cookies, pastries. One picture showed Eve dipping a Corzo cracker into a cheesy dip. In another, she wore a little black dress and bright lipstick, laughing as she lifted a piece of what looked like a cinnamon roll.

Lovely smile. Pretty, soft, full lips. Nice figure. Tall, willowy. Stacked.

He pulled out his phone, hit Gisela's contact. She answered. "Boss?"

"Does Eve Seaton's Corzo project have funding?" he asked.

"It did, but it fell through last year for some reason," Gisela said promptly. "Great project, huh? You could get Caleb behind that in no time. He'll want her on board for the Greenroofs urban planning projects he's doing with Maddox Hill Architecture."

"Yeah, right. Bye, Gisela."

The other phone in his other jacket pocket rang, and he cursed under his breath. He should have left it in the drawer where it wouldn't bother him. It was the phone he kept for his sex life, which was rigorously separate from his work phone. Lately, with all the gossip about his need for a wife, he was being hounded by everyone he'd ever slept with.

The display read Teresa Haber. A weekend fling from several months ago. Not someone he particularly wanted to talk to again.

Might as well nip it in the bud right now. He put the phone to his ear. "Hi, Teresa."

"Hello, Marcus." Her voice was low and seductive. "I heard some shocking gossip about your grandmother forcing you to find a bride. Is it true?"

"Yes, but it's covered," he assured her. "Have a good evening, Teresa."

"Oh, so you found someone? Who did you—"

He closed the call. None of her damn business.

He looked at the article in the file, at Eve Seaton's laughing face. On the other side of the fountain was the Rosen Building, and in that the genetics lab. Office 450.

At this hour, the courtyard was nearly empty. People with families were hurrying home to their personal lives. Eve Seaton had probably left the building. Maybe she was out getting a drink with girlfriends, colleagues, who knew. But his feet carried him inside, to the central elevator bank. He got inside, hit the button for the fourth floor.

The elevator opened, and several people got onto the elevator he'd vacated. He strolled through nearly empty halls until he saw Office 450. Locked.

He continued on to the lab Gisela had specified. Inside, a tall Asian guy was emerging from clean room airlock.

Marcus approached him. "Excuse me. Is Eve Seaton still here?"

"Yeah, in the clean room." He pointed at a lone, heavily swathed figure at the far end of the clean room, visible through layers of protective glass beyond the airlock.

"Thanks." Marcus walked over to the window.

Eve Seaton's back was to him. She was slim, she had regal posture, and that was all he could tell about her, dressed in all that protective gear. She could have been an astronaut, with the gloves, the booties, the hood, the goggles, the mask.

Which made it harder to justify to himself. He was staring at a person swathed in a coverall, peering into a microscope. A person who had no idea he was there.

As spectacles went, it was as interesting as watching paint dry, yet here he stood, contemplating his possible future wife.

Not bored at all.

Two

Eve stowed her gear in the bin to have it freshly sterilized, and rolled her stiff shoulders, exhausted. She should have gone home hours ago. Cooked a healthy dinner with vegetables in it. Done some yoga. But no, instead she was clocking in ridiculous hours on the MossTech genome sequencing project. All in a vain attempt to keep herself too busy to dwell on that bastard Walter. If not for him, she wouldn't have needed this job at all. She'd be doing her own start-up, bringing Corzo to a world that badly needed it.

It had been months, and she still could barely believe it. Walter had been so supportive, so admiring of her mission. He was an accountant by profession, a natural money-man, and that was what she needed to shore up Corzo, and compensate for her weak points. Right?

Yeah, he was a money-man, and no mistake. She just hadn't understood quite what kind. Not until he stole her inheritance, plus every last penny she'd saved over the past several years, and ran off, with his side piece in tow.

Stop it. If she started thinking about how far Walter had set her back, she got into a toxic feedback loop and got so angry, she felt sick.

A glass of wine and a sandwich would help. Some sleep would not suck, either. She saw herself reflected in the glass, and winced. The synthetic hood plastered her hair down, made her scalp damp and her glasses fog. She should go back to contacts, but they made her eyes itch. Besides, Walter had preferred the contacts. He found her sexier without glasses.

Ha. Screw sexy. Screw Walter. She pushed the glasses up on her nose and twisted her hair into a careless bun as she emerged from the airlock.

"Excuse me."

The low, quiet voice behind her made her spin around with a gasp, heart pounding.

"Sorry if I startled you," the owner of the voice said. "Are you Dr. Eve Seaton?"

Eve tried to form words, but the vocal mechanism wouldn't engage.

Marcus Moss. In the flesh. He was the secret reason she'd chosen a job at MossTech, over other equally prestigious options. A dizzy, girlish part of her brain had hoped she might run into him sometime. Like a fawning groupie.

He took a step forward. "I didn't mean to startle you. I should have introduced myself. I'm Marcus Moss."

Oh, but she knew. CTO of MossTech, brilliant engineer and master of all that he surveyed, who played a starring role in her dreams. The X-rated ones, anyway.

Hoo, boy. He was so fine at close range, it verged on the indecent.

Moss waited for a response, a polite frown of puzzlement between his dark, well-shaped brows. He was biracial, and she'd heard that his father was Japanese, or maybe Korean. And damn was he attractive.

His sensual mouth quirked in a small smile. He was used to this. Speechless, open-mouthed girls who forgot their mother tongue when he smiled at them.

"Sorry I scared you," he said gently. "I promise, I'm not dangerous."

She almost laughed. *The hell you're not, buddy.*

"I'm MossTech's chief—"

"Chief technical officer, yes. I'm aware of that." Thank God, her voice functioned again. "Sorry, my voice got stuck for a second."

"So you know who I am."

"Of course. Everyone knows who you are." *But they don't have feverish, erotic dreams about you. They don't set Google Alerts for any scrap of news about you.*

If she let herself think about how weird that was, she'd scare herself, so she'd decided that her crush was a private, harmless coping mechanism. Like collecting saltshakers, bird-watching, tai chi.

"You're working on the fungus genome sequencing, correct?" he asked.

"That's right." She aimed for a professional tone, but it came out breathy and high-pitched. "So, Mr. Moss? What can I do for you?"

"I'm not sure yet," he said. "But I have… I guess you could call it a business proposition to put to you."

Eve brushed a wisp of hair off her forehead. "Business? Me? What kind?"

Marcus Moss opened his mouth and then closed it again. He looked almost nervous. "Could we go someplace to talk?" he asked. "I need a drink. And some dinner. Have you eaten?"

"Ah…well…" She glanced at the leggings and tee she wore under the coverall. "I'm not dressed for going out."

"We'll go someplace quiet. I'm not dressed formally, either."

Ha. The hell he wasn't. His impeccable designer clothes looked amazing. Fresh, crisp, perfectly cut, loose where they needed to be loose, deliciously snug where they needed to be snug.

That body would look amazing in any clothing. Or none at all, if it came to that.

Eve pushed that distracting thought away before it could mess her up.

"So?" he prompted, after she'd stared blankly for too many seconds. "Dinner? Steak, seafood, Asian, fusion, sushi, Mexican, Turkish, Vietnamese?"

"Um…okay," she said faintly.

"Which one? Got a preference?"

"After twelve hours in here, I'm incapable of making decisions," she said. "Anything's fine. You're the executive. Making decisions is your job description, right?"

His dark eyes narrowed. "Yes, but I try not to throw my weight around."

"That's thoughtful, but tonight, you'd be doing me a huge favor if you took this burden from me, because I am fried. Excuse me, while I grab my purse."

She hurried off before she could do any more nervous babbling. Dinner with Marcus Moss, after twelve hours of genome sequencing? She looked like a wet rag. Why couldn't she be one of those women who were always put together? Their makeup stayed put, their clothes didn't crease, their hair stayed smooth. Her mother had been one of those, for all the good it did her. Mom had always looked perfect, even if the sky was falling. Which it frequently had, for her.

Hanging in the closet of her office was a burgundy merino dress she'd left there one day when it proved to be too hot. Shape-wise, it was the equivalent of wearing a flour sack, but at least she didn't look like she'd just come out of the gym. She ran a brush through her hair, debating between hair loose or messy bun.

Messy bun won the day. A neat bun would be better, but at this hour, with low blood sugar and shaky hands, a neat bun wasn't going to happen.

She pawed through cluttered drawers until she found a patterned silk scarf. She knotted it around her neck and fished mascara and some eyeliner out of the depths of her purse. She hadn't worn makeup in months. The Walter debacle had put a damper on her urge to decorate herself. See what happened when she risked love and romance? She handpicked another parasitical user, just like her father, and the others. She'd be better off focusing on her mission.

But this was Marcus-freaking-Moss, damn it, and she was putting on mascara.

Sadly, she had nothing to cover the purplish shadows under her eyes, nor was there lipstick in her purse's miscellany. She bit her lips, to get some color. Slicked on lip balm.

Marcus Moss was waiting outside her office when she came out. Something inside her chest went ka-thunk. Beautiful things happened to that man's face when he smiled.

"So?" she asked. "Where to?"

"There's a steakhouse near here. Do you know Driscoll's?"

"I haven't been there, but steak sounds great."

The cool September evening was rather drizzly and damp. They must have talked about something on the short walk through the streets of downtown Seattle to the restaurant, but when the maître d' ushered them to a table, she had no memory of what they'd said.

They knew him here and treated him like royalty. The place was hushed, low murmurs mingled with soft clinks of cutlery. She was dazzled by the spectacle of Marcus Moss, tasting wine. The splash, the sensual swish, then he held it to the light to admire the color, then he sniffed the aromas, eyes closed…and then, oh, God…he sipped it.

She practically orgasmed on the spot.

Marcus nodded his approval to the server, who poured out wine, laid out their menus and vanished.

"So," she said. "It's a steakhouse, so I guess it's silly to ask what's good here."

"After a twelve-hour day, I suggest the entrecote, the salad of fresh greens topped with char-grilled fresh artichokes, olive oil and Amalfi lemon, and a side of herbed potatoes," he said.

"God, yes." She pushed the menu away. "Go no further."

"Not even to the desserts? They're very good."

She tasted the red wine, which was deep and aromatic. "One thing at a time," she told him. "First, tell me why I'm here. I'm burning with curiosity."

His gaze slid away from her face. "It must seem strange, for me to bother a complete stranger at work after a long day."

"Actually, we have met before," she said.

His eyebrows rose. "We have? When? Where?"

Oh, crap. She regretted putting him on the spot. "The first time was five years ago. I saw you and your brother at the World Agri-Tech Innovation Summit. I also saw your talk at the Prescott Institute. And I was at the Future Innovation trade show last year. My team planned to rent a booth, but my funding fell through, so I just came as a spectator."

She'd also come to admire Marcus himself, but he didn't need to know that. Better go easy on the wine, or she'd blurt out things that would make him uncomfortable.

"I'm sorry I didn't recognize you," he said.

"I was one out of a huge crowd of fans," she assured him. "Your project was amazing. I was rooting for you, though the Bloom Brothers' project was also spectacular. I'd love to collaborate with those two. I've been working on a project for a few years that I think would interest them, a grain that's engineered to sequester carbon. I have various strains for different climates and growing seasons."

"Corzo, yes," he said. "I'm familiar with it."

Her jaw dropped. "You are?"

"Of course," he said. "It's an impressive project. You'd be a good fit with the Blooms. You have a holistic mindset similar to theirs. I could organize a meeting. I'm very good friends with their publicist."

Eve was startled. "Really? That would be amazing."

"Sure," he said. "So what happened before the trade show? Why didn't you get a booth and take part in the contest? Did you have a setback in your research?"

Eve choked on her wine, dabbing her mouth. "Not in the research, no."

"Sorry," he said swiftly. "None of my business."

"It's okay," she told him. "It's common knowledge, after all. I have no secrets."

"Okay. So…?" He waited.

Eve set aside her wineglass and organized her thoughts. "I was engaged last year," she admitted. "To my financial manager. People told me at the time that wasn't the greatest idea, but I pooh-poohed them. The first of my many mistakes."

He winced. "I think I know where this is going."

"Yeah, everyone saw it coming but me. Walter was part of the firm that had managed my mother's estate, upon her death. What was left of it, anyway."

"Left of it?"

"She was the heiress to the Travis retail fortune, before she married my father," she explained. "He cleaned her out. Stripped everything he could before he left for good. All that was left was the real estate he hadn't been able to liquidate. After my mother died, I intended to sell that property, and use the cash to launch my start-up."

Marcus waited patiently, his eyes intent on her face.

"I'd gotten involved with Walter in the meantime," she went on finally. "He was an account manager at my mother's investment firm, though I didn't know that when we started dating. He'd researched my assets, extensively. And then he asked me out."

"I see," he murmured.

"My team and I were planning our start-up," she said. "Walter offered to lend us his skills. It seemed perfect. But as soon as the property sales were finalized, and the money deposited in my account, Walter disappeared. With all my money."

He hissed through his teeth. "What an asshole."

"Yeah," she agreed. "To make it sting even more, his twenty-four-year-old female administrative assistant disappeared along with him. The fair Arielle."

"Have the police made any progress in finding him?"

"Not yet," she said. "He's smart. Methodical. Ironically, that's one of the things I found really attractive about him. He must have been planning this before he even met me."

"Slime," Marcus said forcefully.

"Yes," she said. "Romantically, I'm over him. Nothing could be more unsexy than a bloodsucking thief. But the money, oh, that hurt. It wasn't a vast sum, but it would have gotten us going."

"Us?" he asked. "Going where?"

"Me and my Corzo team," she explained. "That was our seed money. Money management is not my strong suit, so Walter's promise to help us was very seductive to me. I'd fantasized being free to geek out on the science, and leave the bean counting to him. I should have known it was too good to be true."

"Luckily for you, Walter is shortsighted," Marcus said.

"Corzo has incredible commercial potential. I confidently predict that Walter and Arielle will watch your stock prices skyrocket, and see you start making nine figures right around the time their stolen loot runs out, and they have to downgrade from their luxury hotel to cheaper lodging. Where they will start arguing about money. What should they pawn first? His motorcycle, or her emeralds?"

She laughed out loud. "What a great image. Thanks for that. So, that happened not long before I had to send the money for the booth at Future Innovation. We'd been selected as finalists, but my life fell apart, so I withdrew the project and came as a spectator. Trying not to feel sorry for myself."

"You're entitled to feel angry," he said. "I hope they nail that asshole and his girlfriend both. They can rot in jail and ponder their character flaws."

"Me, too. But even if I got that satisfaction, I'll never get the money back," she said. "They're eating it, or driving it, or snorting it up their nose as we speak."

"Even so, this is a blip in your screen," he said. "You'll get past it."

"I intend to," she told him. "That's why I took this job. We're all working at other places until we scare up seed money again."

"Is that why you'd only agree to a temporary contract here at MossTech?"

Eve was startled. "For a CTO of a company as enormous as MossTech, you certainly know a lot about the terms of my very recent employment."

Marcus shrugged. "Us executives. We know things. It's our job."

She laughed. "Well, yes, that's why. We need a stroke of luck. Even with all of us saving, we'll need outside investors. My mycologist, Sara, arranged a meeting with some investors from Hong Kong last week, but they made me nervous."

"What are their names? I know a lot of the players."

After a split second, Eve decided there was no reason not to tell him. "The Yueh Xiang Group."

He shook his head. "I know the Yueh Xiang," he said. "Shady as hell. They'll eat you alive and spit out your bones."

Her heart sank. "Well, hell. Maybe I'm developing a nose for sleaze. Too late to sniff out Walter, but better late than never."

"Definitely. Which brings me to the reason you're here."

At last, his mysterious agenda. She was so dazzled she'd almost stopped wondering why he'd asked her out. "I'm all ears."

"I was impressed by Corzo. Have you considered partnering with MossTech?"

"We've considered every option," she said. "But my team and I want to maintain control of the patent."

"I could help you find investors independent of Moss-Tech," he said. "The idea sells itself. I mean, feeding the honeybees? Get out of here."

She laughed. "I know, right? Corzo honey is delicious. It has an exotic flowery aroma like no other."

"I'd love to try it sometime," he said.

She saw it in her imagination. Her finger dipping into the glass jar of luminous, pale Corzo honey. Lifting it to his lips. The swirling pull of his lips against her fingertip. The flirtatious twist of his tongue, licking away every drop.

She pulled herself back to reality. "Ah, yeah," she said, distracted. "I'll…get you some. To taste. It's great in tea. Or, um…yogurt."

"Love to." His deep, resonant voice was caressing her senses like a brush of fur.

"But why?" she demanded. "I appreciate the interest,

but if I decline partnership with MossTech, why interest yourself in Corzo?"

He took a sip of wine. "I need a favor from you."

Tension built inside her. "I'd be happy to help any way I can, but what could I possibly do for Marcus Moss, the CTO of MossTech?"

He looked her right in the eyes. "I need for you to marry me," he said.

Three

Ouch. Not smooth. But there was no good way to slip a zinger like that into a dinner conversation. It was like throwing a lit firecracker on the table.

Eve Seaton gazed at him, her pink mouth slightly open. A puzzled crease between her elegant dark eyebrows. Waiting for the punch line of the joke. Because it had to be a joke, right?

She sucked her lower lip between her teeth, then let it go. It gleamed, soft and pink, in the candlelight. "Excuse me?" she asked faintly. "I'm not following."

"Just temporarily, of course," he said hastily.

Eve shook her head. "I don't understand," she said. "I don't even know you."

"I'm sorry. This is very awkward," he said. "I'm proposing a business arrangement. For complicated legal reasons, I need to be married before I turn thirty-five, or suffer consequences I'm not willing to accept. There isn't anyone that I want to marry, nor have I ever wanted marriage in the first place. One solution to this dilemma could be to approach someone who has a project I could support, and in return, she'd consent to being my wife for a limited period. To solve my problem."

He paused for a moment. She just stared. The silence was absolute.

"In name only," he added carefully. "Of course."

"Ah...yes." Eve lifted her glass of wine and took a gulp. "Of course."

As she set it down, he noticed her well-shaped, unpainted nails. Her slender fingers. Her hand was trembling.

That alarmed him. "I didn't mean to scare you. I wouldn't ask something like this of just anyone. It had to be someone for whom I could return the favor in some concrete way. I picked you out because I thought I could help you with your project wholeheartedly, and wouldn't find doing so a burden. But if this upsets you, forget I said it."

"You didn't scare me," she said. "You surprised the living hell out of me."

He let out a relieved breath. "Do you know about this marriage requirement? The way people gossip, I figured you might."

"When I'm in work mode, I don't think of anything but work," she said. "Besides, I'm new here. I don't really know people well enough to participate in gossip."

Huh. That was refreshing, after all the whispering, giggling, sidewise looks and the exhausting tsunami of ex-lovers and flames like Teresa, some still unmarried, others freshly divorced, filling his voice mail with seductive come-ons.

Eve wasn't like that. She had a mission, and she was committed to it. Her priorities were out there in blazing neon, for all the world to see.

"How did you get into this fix?" She sounded fascinated. "It sounds so antique."

"It is," he agreed. "My grandmother decided that my brother and sister and I are too driven and work-focused, even though she was the one who drove us to be that way. She was the previous MossTech CEO, and she was the one who wanted us to take over management of the company, about eight years ago. In her mind, she raised us and she warped us, so now it's her sacred duty to fix us. Like knocking the dings out of a dented car, and her strategies are about that subtle. Blunt force."

"Oh, dear," she murmured.

"My brother and I have to be married by age thirty-five, and my sister by age thirty."

"Or else…what?"

"Or she gives controlling shares of MossTech to my great-uncle Jerome. He's wanted to be the big boss from the beginning, but my grandparents always kept him in check. At least, up until now."

Her wince showed that Uncle Jerome's reputation as a grade-A asshole had spread far and wide. "That seems a rather extreme punishment."

He let out a short laugh. "Oh, ya think?"

"But I thought your brother was married," she said. "With a daughter, even."

"Yes, but it's recent. Caleb got lucky. He hooked up with an ex that he was still in love with. Turned out that she'd had his child years before. Gran frothed with joy. In fact, this whole mess started because Gran got wind of Tilda's kid being Caleb's. It flipped a switch inside her. She really wanted her great-grandchild. And not just Annika. She wants more. A whole dynasty of them. So here we are."

"Wow," she said. "Drama to the utmost."

"Oh, always," he said. "We Mosses excel at drama. My sister, Maddie, did okay, too. She's getting married to Jack, who she's crazy about, in ten days, on the eve of her thirti-

eth birthday. She's timing the ceremony to sign the paperwork at eleven fifty-nine."

Eve laughed. "Just to mess with everyone's head?"

"Yeah, she and Jack think it's hilarious," he said grimly.
"Ha. Ha. Ha."

"But the joke's on you, right?"

"Exactly. They can afford to laugh. If MossTech goes
to the dogs, it won't be their fault. There are a lot of jobs at
stake, not just mine and Caleb's. Jerome would clean the
place out of everyone loyal to us."

"That's awful," she said.

"Yes," he said. "I hate being jerked around. But I hate
hurting all those people more. And handing MossTech to
that bastard while he cackles and rubs his icy hands together, God, that stings. Caleb and I worked hard to build
this company up. Not to brag, but we brought MossTech
into the third millennium. All that work, for nothing."

"I see," she murmured.

"Anyway, that's what's driving this bizarre proposal," he
concluded. "Gran's paperwork stipulates that I stay married
for five years. We can of course keep our own private living spaces, and conduct our private lives however we like,
as long as we're discreet and put on a good show on public occasions. That's all I need from you. In return, I'll do
everything in my power to help Corzo launch and thrive."

"Um…wow."

The server arrived with their meals. They fell silent as
plates of food were arrayed before them. Steaks sizzled on
their platters, but Eve didn't pick up her fork. She looked
pale.

"If it makes you uncomfortable, forget it," he urged. "I
didn't mean to offend you."

"I'm not offended," she said quickly. "On the contrary."

"Try your steak," he urged her. "I should have waited
until you'd eaten before springing this on you."

He started into his own food, but he couldn't relax and enjoy it until he saw her take a few dainty bites. Her reaction worried him. She'd been so sparkling before, quick to laugh, readily telling him all about herself, and his offer had quenched all that. Now she looked colorless, subdued. He missed how she'd been before.

He refilled her wineglass. "I think I've made a mistake," he ventured in the strained silence. "I wish I could take it back. I want you to enjoy your meal."

"I'm sorry if I give that impression," she said. "But my last attempt at matrimony made me swear off the institution for life. So I don't know what to say."

"You're like me," he said. "I never wanted it, either, and not wanting it makes you a uniquely perfect candidate. You won't be sacrificing anything important to you, so you have nothing to lose and everything to gain."

"You make a strong case for it," she said. "You don't think your grandmother would sense that the marriage was fake?"

"I don't care if she does or not. I don't think she'll give us a hard time. At this point, she'll be grateful if she can save face without destroying the company that she helped my grandfather found."

"Am I the first person you've asked?"

"Yes," he said. "The situation is embarrassing, but I wouldn't mind getting behind something like Corzo. The world needs it. My brother and I wanted MossTech to be all about service to the world. Uncle Jerome doesn't share our philosophy."

She laid aside her fork and knife, steepling her slender hands together. "Just to be clear. If I were to agree, how would it play out?"

His spirits shot up. "It would have to be soon," he said. "We'd meet with my lawyers. Bring your own lawyer, and I will foot the cost for whatever you're billed for having the contract reviewed. If the terms are acceptable, we apply for a marriage license and get married as soon as possible. I want to present my new bride at my sister's wedding. Surprise, suckers."

She snorted with laughter. "Sounds fun. When's that wedding, again?"

"Ten days. We have to move fast. Jerome will be there, so there will be drama."

"What kind of drama?"

"He's a foul-tempered asshole," Marcus said. "He'll be aggressive and rude and inappropriate. He was to Tilda and to Jack. You are, of course, free to tell him where he can stick it, which Tilda and Jack both did. Are you conflict-averse?"

"I don't actively seek it out, but I don't let people walk over my face, either. Walter was a special case."

"Screw Walter. This is a great way to get back everything he took from you and more."

Their conversation paused as a server came to take their plates. Eve leaned forward. "Do you need an answer right away, or can I take some time to think about it?"

Marcus realized he should have thought this through. "Not too much time," he said. "The time I have to put this deal together is running out, so if you decline, I have to move fast to find someone else. Could you give me an answer by tomorrow?"

"Seems fair," she said.

"I'll put my number into your phone. Call me if you have questions."

Eve passed her smartphone to him. He entered his name and number into her contacts and returned it. "There," he said. "Done."

The server reappeared behind them. "Can I tempt you with any of today's dessert specials?" he asked. "We have a fruit trifle with crème Chantilly, a blackberry millefoglie tart with vanilla cinnamon ice cream and chocolate lava cake."

"Sounds delicious, but not tonight," Eve said. "Could you call me a car? I usually grab a bus to get home."

"Of course." The server turned to Marcus. "And for you, sir?"

"No dessert." He turned to Eve. "I can call a MossTech car to take you home."

"I'm fine with a car service," she assured him.

He could well imagine that she wasn't ready to give her home address to a strange man. Particularly one making offers as strange as his. "Use Egret Cars," he told the server.

"Don't you need one, too?" Eve asked.

"I'll walk," he told her. "My apartment isn't far from here."

"Must be nice, to live so close to work," she said.

"I'm out of the country a lot. When I'm in town, I don't like to waste any of my time commuting. So I bought a place that's minutes away by foot."

"That's great," she said. "I love this city, and I do have a car, but the traffic exhausts me."

The server appeared again. "Miss, your car is here."

Eve stopped by the cash register, but Marcus waved her onward. They stepped out into the chilly breeze and stopped next to the idling Egret sedan.

"Did we walk out of there without paying?" she asked him.

He shook his head. "I have an account. I'm not a bad cook, but after a long day, I'm too tired to deal with it, and this place is right on my way home."

"I get you," she said, with feeling. She pulled her jacket close against the wind, her bright silk scarf fluttering. "Thank you for a very…unique evening."

"You're welcome," he said. "I try to keep things interesting."

"Well, then." Eve looked flustered. "I'll let you know my decision soon."

He held out his hand, and she took it—*whoa*.

Sensations flashed through him, like wind lifting his hair except it was everywhere. A caressing, whole-body rush of startled awareness. He was hyper-conscious of every detail of her. The curl of her lashes, the sweep of her brow, the curiosity in her bright eyes.

Her lips looked like they would be so soft to kiss.

She pulled her hand away and got into the car. He shut the door after her, maintaining eye contact until the car pulled away, and her eyes were lost to sight.

Dial it down, Moss. This wasn't about emotion. That was the point of picking out a random stranger for this. No feelings. Simple. Controlled. Detached.

But his eyes followed the red taillights until they turned. A deep, tingling hum pervaded his whole body. Eve Seaton made him feel intrigued, challenged, tempted. Aroused, just by a brief timid handshake.

He couldn't help but wonder what effect a kiss might have.

Four

Marry Marcus Moss? What in the actual *hell*?

Eve wanted to bounce and shriek, but the driver was a grizzled older man who looked tired. He did not need any overwrought silliness inflicted on him, so she held it in, but she was still rocking back and forth, her hands over her mouth. She still caught some nervous looks from the guy in the rearview.

Omigod. Marcus Moss's number, in her phone. She half expected the device to burst into flames. He was brilliant, gorgeous. She'd actually had a good time. Laughing, talking, drinking, nerve endings caressed by his resonant voice, his aftershave tickling her nose. A more distilled kind of fun than she'd ever had.

And after all the sensory overload, he'd proposed. Holy…freaking…*cow*.

It was a marriage proposal, turned inside out. She'd been chosen specifically because he didn't love her, want her or envision her in his future. That made her perfect, for his purposes. Her lack of desirability made her desirable.

Oof. Put that way, it stung a little.

Not that she blamed him. He'd never seen her before. The only problem was her Godzilla-sized crush on him, which would disqualify her, if he knew about it, emotional intensity being precisely what he did not want. The driver reached Sara's apartment. She leaned forward, hand in her wallet. "What do I owe you?"

"It's paid for, ma'am," was his laconic reply.

"But...but I told him he didn't need to—"

"Done deal," the guy said.

"At least let me give you your tip," she said. "How much was the—"

"Tipped already, twenty-five percent. Don't sweat it, ma'am. The gentleman took care of it."

Did he, now? After she'd specifically told him not to. She murmured her thanks and made her way up the two flights of stairs on the outside of the house to the top-floor apartment where Sara lived. She texted with her phone instead of knocking.

Sara! Please be awake.

Sara didn't take long to respond. What are you doing up at this hour?

I'm outside your door, she texted.

?? her friend replied.

A light flipped on a minute later, and Sara's slim shadow moved behind it. She twitched the curtain aside to peer out onto the porch.

She pulled the door open. "What the hell, Eve? Is something wrong?"

"I have news," she said, as she entered her friend's apartment.

Her best friend, Sara Cho, was a brilliant mycologist. They had met at CalTech and done postgraduate work together. Sara was her dream colleague. Smart, creative, a sense of humor, rock-solid principles.

Sara, too, currently worked at another lab, at Ballard ChemZyne. She was recently and bitterly divorced, not long before Walter had made his escape. She and Eve had already been friends, but the wretched perfidy of men was a great bonding agent.

Sara beckoned her into the kitchen. Her long black hair was twisted into a thick glossy braid. "So?" she prompted. "What happened? Are you okay?"

"I… I don't know," Eve said. "I think I'm about to do a really crazy thing."

"Really? Fun crazy, or scary crazy?"

"I'm not sure, but I'm scared right now," she admitted.

Sara flipped on the lights and studied Eve's face. "Spill it, girlfriend."

"Marcus Moss asked me to marry him," she blurted.

Sara's face went blank. "Hang on. Marcus Moss, celebrated billionaire CTO of MossTech?"

"Yes," she squeaked.

"The gorgeous studmuffin you've had a sloppy crush on ever since you shared an elevator with him at the Agri-Tech Summit five years ago?"

"The very one," she said.

"But you've never even been introduced to him! Though I know you only went to MossTech because you were hoping to scope him from afar."

"Wrong! I went there because it was the best job offer!"

Sara rolled her eyes. "Sure it was. I didn't blame you, after Walter. You deserved to indulge in some eye candy. But marriage, Eve? How in the hell?"

"A temporary marriage," she explained. "A fake marriage. Sorry, I should have led with that. His grandma insists he get married before his thirty-fifth birthday or else he and his brother, the CEO, lose control of MossTech to their great-uncle. Jerome Moss."

Sara made a face. "Ouch. That won't go well."

"Exactly. So that's it, Sara. I'm the lucky girl. He never wanted to marry, so he's picking out a stranger that he doesn't give a damn about, who will expect nothing from him. A marriage in name only." She paused. "So, uh. It's not like I have to have sex with him, or anything."

There was a brief silence. Sara let out a burst of smoth-ered laughter. "*Have* to have sex? Get real. It's me, Sara. Say, 'get to have sex,' and I'll buy it."

Eve snorted. "If you must. It's not like I 'get' to have sex with him. Happy now?"

"Not quite," Sara said. "Because if you're not getting hot, sweaty, pounding sex with Marcus Moss out of it, what the hell *are* you getting out of it?"

"Corzo," Eve said.

Sara's jaw dropped. "No way!"

"For real," she said. "He'll help us launch Corzo if I do this for him. Favor for favor. If I stay legally married to him for five years, he'll help us find more investors, et cetera. He thinks Corzo has loads of potential."

Sara pressed her hands to her mouth. "Eve. Oh my God."

"I know, right?"

Sara grabbed her shoulders. "So? Have you said yes?"

"I have until tomorrow night to decide," she said.

"So what's stopping you?" Sara asked. "What's the catch?"

Eve bit her lip. "You know the catch," she said, in a small voice. "It's my dumb crush on him. I get all flustered and red in the face, and I talk too much, and you know he's going to notice, sooner or later. It's exactly what he's going to these insane lengths to avoid. And when he does notice,

I'll feel so stupid and small. I'm just not sure if I can survive feeling that small again. It might break me."

"Oh, honey." Sara pulled her into a hug. "I bet the spell will break as soon as you get close enough to smell his pits."

"I was close enough tonight," Eve said, her voice muffled against Sara's hair.

"Yes? And?" her friend prompted.

"He smelled delicious," she admitted. "I could have eaten him up with a spoon."

"Yikes," Sara murmured. "You, my dear, are a sad case."

"Oh, I know," she agreed.

Sara hugged her again. "I'll tell you what. There are a couple of different ways this can go. Option one, you play it cool. Stay distant, fulfill your side of the bargain like the professional you are. Take what he has to offer and squeeze him like an orange."

She laughed soggily. "Okay. And option two?"

"In option two, you take this opportunity to seduce the hell out of him, get him to fall in love with you…and squeeze him like an orange."

That cracked them both up.

"Me, seducing him," Eve muttered. "As if."

Sara looked disapproving. "Why the hell not? You've got the looks. You're just too busy and distracted to exploit them. You've got the brains. You're highly motivated. You'll have the opportunity. The guy will be your husband, for God's sake. It's doable."

"Sara, I love you, but you're a very bad influence," Eve said.

"I know," Sara agreed. "And I'm very excited about what Marcus Moss's help could mean for Corzo. But truthfully? I love you, babe. You've already been through a lot of shit, and your happiness is more important to me. Only do this if you can do it without hurting yourself. Maybe even have some fun with it. Otherwise, we'll muddle on as we have so far."

Eve gave her a misty, tearful smile. "I'm going to do it."

Sara jumped up. "Omigod! Omigod! For real?"

"Yeah." Eve pulled out her phone and found the contact. She glanced at the kitchen clock. It was past 1:00 a.m., but it was his fault she was awake so late. She hit Call.

He answered quickly. "Hello?"

"Mr. Moss? This is Eve Seaton."

"Eve." There was a smile in his voice. "Call me Marcus. Have you come to a decision?"

"Yes, I have," she said. "I'll do it."

"Excellent. I'm so glad. Can you meet me tomorrow afternoon, at my lawyer's office? The legal department at MossTech is in the Kobe Tower, eighth floor."

"I can find it," she said.

"Great. I'll text you the exact time when I talk to their office tomorrow."

"I'll be there. Thanks for this opportunity. My team will be thrilled."

"I'm the one who should thank you. You've just saved MossTech's ass."

"We'll thank each other," she said. "Good night."

She looked at the phone in disbelief. "We draw up the contract tomorrow," she said to Sara.

They grabbed each other, dancing with joy.

Sara pulled open the fridge and took out a bottle of champagne. "I was saving this for my birthday, but if this doesn't call for a toast, I don't know what does. Get out the champagne flutes."

Pop, the cork yielded, hitting the ceiling and bouncing off the table and to the floor. Pale foam fizzed sensually from the bottle. Sara poured the cold, pale wine into the delicate champagne flutes Eve had set out on the table and handed her one.

"To the success of all of our endeavors." Eve lifted her glass.

They drank, and Sara promptly refilled them to the brim.

"To squeezing the sex god like an orange," Sara said. "No matter what comes out."

They exploded into giggles, clinked glasses and drank.

"I can't believe I'm doing this," Eve said as Sara filled her glass a third time.

"You'll crush it," Sara said firmly.

Eve set her glass on the table and wiped away an embarrassing rush of tears. "Sorry," she quavered. "I'm a little bit drunk."

"On two glasses of champagne?"

"And the wine I drank with Marcus," she explained.

"That has a nice ring to it," Sara encouraged. "'The wine I drank with Marcus.' I like the sound of it."

"So do I!" Eve wailed. "But it would be so stupid to get all intense about him—"

"Babe," her friend said wryly. "You already are intense about him."

"I know. And if I did as you said, and tried to seduce him, I'd melt like ice cream all over him and make a big sticky mess."

It took a while for her to stop shaking. Sara handed Eve a napkin to dab her eyes, and blow her nose.

"Interesting," Sara said thoughtfully. "You never showed this emotional intensity about Walter. Even when he robbed you blind and slithered off into the tall grass with Arielle."

"Oh, come on, Sara," Eve muttered. "I don't even know the guy."

"Well, babe," Sara said philosophically. "For good or for ill, you're gonna know him now."

Five

Marcus was glad that he'd worn the black Versace suit when he saw Eve enter the room at the Seattle Municipal Court. She looked good. He was glad he'd requested this room, too. True, this was a business arrangement, but why conduct important business in an unattractive setting?

Hence, the corner room, with floor-to-ceiling windows. Too bad they couldn't have used the roof terrace, but it was drizzling. Besides, he had to be careful not to overdo it.

Eve looked amazing. She was wearing a knee-length fitted burgundy dress of some textured fabric that hugged every dip and curve. Hair twisted into an elegant French roll. Sexy black pumps. Her heavy, black-framed glasses looked like a bold and fearless fashion choice in the context of that outfit. Or maybe that was just the way she held herself. Chin high, eyes meeting his, proud and regal. Elegant.

Her silver-gray eyes silently said, *let's do this.*

His cousin, Ronnie, stood next to him, blue eyes full of curiosity. She was his great-uncle Jerome's daughter, but she was five years younger than him, and she'd been raised with Marcus and his siblings for much of her childhood. She was as close to him as a sister.

He'd asked Ronnie to be his witness because he couldn't bear either Caleb or Maddie in that role right now. They were floating on cloud nine, with the condescending vibe of two lucky bastards who'd been kissed by fate. They'd found rapturous happiness and fulfilled their familial obligations, in one blow.

Woo-hoo. Yay for them, but it stuck in his craw.

Ronnie had dressed up for the occasion in a minidress of black-and-white-checked wool, black tights, black pumps and glittering jet earrings, her red hair in a high braided bun. When he and Eve had met with the lawyers, they'd agreed to keep it simple and private. The officiant, and one witness apiece. No one else needed to know until Maddie's wedding. Just Ronnie herself, who was sworn to secrecy.

Eve had brought a friend for her own witness, a small, beautiful Asian American woman who looked him over with bold interest.

Marcus stepped forward, taking Eve's hand. "You look beautiful," he told her.

"Thank you. I wasn't sure how much I should dress up, but I figured, a woman doesn't get married every day of the week."

"You look perfect." He turned to her friend. "How do you do? I'm Marcus Moss."

"Sara Cho," the friend said. "I'm glad to meet you."

"Sara is a member of the Corzo team," Eve said. "She's our mycologist."

"Then I'm sure we'll be seeing a lot of each other," he said to Sara, smiling.

Marcus gestured at Ronnie, who came forward. "This is my cousin, Ronnie Moss."

Eve shook Ronnie's hand. "I didn't know Marcus had close relatives, besides his brothers and sisters."

"None but me," Ronnie told her. "My dad was their grandpa Bertram's little brother. If it hadn't been for them and my aunt Elaine, I wouldn't have made it through my childhood intact at all." She rolled her eyes. "Insofar as any of us can be considered intact. I'm Jerome Moss's daughter. How intact could I be?"

Eve gave him a startled look, but Ronnie caught it and spoke up. "Don't worry," she assured Eve. "I'm on Marcus's side."

"Ah… I didn't mean to imply—"

"And it's completely my dad's fault that we're talking about sides at all," Ronnie went on. "Dad has an ego the size of Texas. I genuinely wish that Aunt Elaine's marriage mandate included me, too. I'm turning thirty in a few months. There's nothing I'd like better than to get married at the eleventh hour, like Maddie's doing, and throw it right in Dad's face. He deserves it."

"Sounds unnecessarily risky," Eve said carefully.

"Not for me. I'm already engaged." She held out a spectacularly large diamond ring. "I'm a sure thing. It would be a moral slap to my father. We're not on very good terms. If you haven't noticed." She looked embarrassed. "Sorry. Didn't mean to lay my family crap on you."

"That's okay," Eve assured her. "I haven't spoken to my own father in over six years."

Ronnie looked impressed. "You've got me beat."

"Yes, I always perform well in screwed-up-family one-upmanship competitions," Eve told her. "I score very high."

"Then you'll fit right in," Ronnie said warmly.

The officiant walked in, a stern-looking gray-haired man with a no-nonsense air. The officiant began the ceremony.

As the man spoke, something strange happened to Marcus. All sound retreated, as if his mind had floated free of his body. All he could hear was his heart, thudding, pan-icked, deafeningly loud. Marcus focused on Eve's face. She was his anchor. She kept him from floating off to God knew where.

Fortunately, Eve was watching the officiant, and didn't appear to notice his condition. Her beautiful red lips were moving. Then the officiant's lips, too. He heard nothing. Oh, crap, now the guy was looking at him. He needed to respond, but to what, he had no clue. He struggled to tune in. To breathe.

"…to marry Eve Elizabeth Seaton?" The officiant's voice sounded very far away.

They looked at him expectantly. Ronnie, standing behind him, was frowning. She snapped her fingers.

Pay attention, she mouthed.

"Uh… I do," he forced out.

The officiant frowned. "No. We haven't gotten to the vows yet," he said sternly. "I said, are you, Marcus James Moss, free to lawfully marry Eve Elizabeth Seaton? The affirmative response is, 'I am.' Is that quite clear?"

"I am," he said grimly.

Evidently Eve had already declared her lawful freedom, because the guy moved briskly on.

And he was back to the real world. His normal self. Thank God. What the *hell* had happened? Was that a panic attack? This was a fine time to start having them.

He could follow along now, well enough to recite the ap-propriate vows. He could hear Eve's clear, musical voice quietly echoing them. He hoped whatever the hell that was wouldn't happen to him again. It was like being taken over. Extremely unsettling.

The time came for rings, which he'd picked out the week before. He pulled out two thick bands of white gold, rounded, glowing bright. Eve had gotten her short nails manicured. They gleamed with a transparent, pink-tinted glossy sheen. The ring looked good on her. The skin of her hand was velvet soft. Holding it was like having a bird resting in his hand.

"...pronounce you man and wife. You may now kiss the bride." The officiant sounded like he was doing Marcus a big favor.

Marcus met Eve's startled eyes and leaned down to brush his lips against hers.

Or at least, that was the plan. A dry little peck to seal the bargain. But as soon as her soft lips touched his, he was jarred by a feeling he'd never experienced.

The world just...opened up. In a flash, he saw everything, felt everything, sensed everything. There were no barriers between him and her mysterious allure. He sensed the endless possibilities of that kiss with startled wonder.

He leaned into her softness, the tender sweetness of her lips. Eve's hands splayed on his shirtfront, but she didn't shove him away. Her nails dug in, seeking a better grip as her mouth opened beneath his—

A nervous cough, and Marcus froze, remembering where he was. *Whoa.*

He retreated from the embrace. Eve did the same. His face felt hot. The officiant had a save-it-for-the-wedding-night scowl.

Ronnie pressed her lips together. She looked like she was trying not to smile. Sara Cho looked shocked.

"Excuse me," he said softly.

Eve's eyes fell. "It's okay," she whispered.

He was appalled. Control was his thing. He kept his sex life compartmentalized. It never touched work, family, MossTech. But this bargain with Eve was wound up inextricably with all of those things. Sex with Eve would be a disaster in terms of control.

In every other way, the idea yanked him like a tow chain.

"Sorry," he said again, helplessly.

"You already apologized," Eve murmured. "You do that out of sheer habit, right? I won't take it seriously if you don't. But we should avoid tongue-kissing, as a rule. We didn't cover that kind of thing in the contract."

She was smiling, teasing, giving him an out. He tried to match her energy. "Uh, yeah. Absolutely."

They signed the paperwork and thanked the judge, who promised to register the certificate at the appropriate office. The four of them walked outside onto the wide sidewalk outside the building. It was late afternoon, and the misty drizzle of early fall in Seattle had formed a fuzz of tiny droplets on the fibers of Eve's burgundy wool coat.

He was a married man. Eve looked dazed. Ronnie's speculative gaze shuttled back and forth between them. Sara Cho's face was cold. Hostility radiated off her. Eve's best friend thought he was an opportunistic slut. Not a great beginning.

"Could I invite all of you out to dinner?" he asked. "We should celebrate."

"That sounds great," Eve said.

"Sorry, I can't," Sara said, her voice clipped. "I have another engagement."

"I can't either, sorry," Ronnie said. "I promised to meet Jareth, my fiancé, at the airport. He's in from LA for the weekend. But I really do look forward to getting to know you."

"So do I," Eve said warmly.

"Say hi to Jareth for me," Marcus said, out of politeness, though he'd never particularly liked the guy. He seemed the perfect fiancé on the surface, smooth and well-spoken and ambitious, always with a big smile and a hearty, friendly manner, but Marcus had the nagging sense that there was nothing much underneath the pleasant veneer.

But whatever made Ronnie happy was fine with him.

"Would you excuse us for a moment?" Sara's voice rang

out. "I need to speak to Eve in private." She grabbed her friend's arm and dragged her out of earshot.

"Uh-oh," Ronnie murmured. "Eve's best girlfriend hates your guts. And I would, too, after that shocking performance. Good God, Marcus. Control yourself."

His cousin's intent gaze made him uncomfortable. "Don't go looking for drama where there isn't any."

"Don't go pretending it doesn't exist when it's glaring right into your face," Ronnie said. "That kiss, dude? What in the actual hell?"

"Don't make it into a thing, Ron—"

"I'm not the one who made it into a thing," Ronnie told him. "You did that yourself, and it's irresponsible. Confusing, for her. This will blow up in your face if you don't watch it."

"I'm starting to regret asking you here. I should've brought Gisela."

"You think Gisela wouldn't have ripped you a new one if she'd seen what I saw? Gisela has more at stake than I do if you screw this up. Think about Gisela and all the rest of them, and keep that bad boy zipped up tight, okay? I say this because I love you."

"Are you done with the sermon?" he asked, through gritted teeth.

"For now, if you're good. But there's plenty more where that came from."

"Don't you have to run the airport? You don't want to keep Jareth waiting."

"Be good." Her voice was soft but forceful. "Congratulations. I hope this whole thing shakes out well for us all. But watch yourself. Bye."

She took off, calling and waving her goodbyes to Eve and Sara as she passed.

Marcus watched her disappear, still smarting from her reproof.

She was right. He had to keep things cool. He might have known that this would get complicated, full of hidden pitfalls. The classic hallmark of Gran's influence on his life.

Still, he couldn't blame Gran for the kiss. That was his own personal bad judgment. He had to own it.

Bad judgment or no, that kiss was going to haunt his dreams.

Six

"Sara, what on earth?" Eve was startled by the force with which her friend dragged her into the shelter of the courthouse portico. "What's gotten into you?"

"Where does he get off?" Sara hissed. "How *dare* he?"

"How dare he what?" Eve grabbed her friend's hand. "Because he kissed me?"

Sara huffed furiously. "Duh! Does he think you're just his for the taking?"

"Calm down," she soothed. "I think he just did that out of habit. He said he was sorry. Twice. No big deal."

"Oh! Will he nail you, too, out of habit? The first time you happen to be anywhere near a horizontal surface, boom, you'll find yourself with your legs in the air! Oops! Will he apologize then, too? I do not want you to be a notch on his belt, Eve!"

"I won't be," she assured him. "He's a perfect gentleman."

"Ha!" Sara snapped. "Not!"

"I'm bewildered. Aren't you the woman who told me to go for it? To squeeze him like an orange? Now you're all agitated just because he kissed me after being invited to do so by a municipal judge?"

"He didn't just kiss you, Eve!" Sara protested. "He was... sucking face!"

That jerked a startled laugh out of her. "Um, no."

"This is not funny," Sara said. "I know that I said to seduce him. But there is a huge difference between you seducing him, and him seducing you. Vast."

"Is there? I don't see it. It doesn't matter, because I don't intend—"

"It's a power thing, Eve. Don't you see? You're way more vulnerable than he is. I should never have advised you to do this! I was dazzled by the opportunity to get Corzo going again, and now I feel like a bad, selfish friend."

"Oh, no, no, no." Eve seized her friend and hugged her. "You're a great friend. You're panicking over nothing. This is a business arrangement, and we both stand to gain from it. He knows better, I know better. Trust me. We're grown-ups."

Sara snorted. "That's not what I saw."

Ronnie Moss passed by them, smiling and waving. They both waved back.

Sara's eyes brimmed with tears. "Please, be careful, okay?" she pleaded. "Keep that guy at arm's length. Promise me."

"Don't stress about me," Eve urged. "I'll be fine. Put all that energy into figuring out how to start Corzo again. Tell everyone, so we can start planning."

"Okay," Sara said, her voice garbled with tears. "Okay, I'm on it."

Eve hugged her, and they walked back to where Marcus stood waiting. The cold wind flapped his long coat and ruffled his jet-black hair. God, he was tall.

"Congratulations," Sara said stiffly. "Enjoy your dinner. Eve, call me when you're back home, okay?"

"Of course," she said gently. "Talk to you later."

When Sara was lost to sight, Marcus crooked his arm, a courtly, old-fashioned gesture. She took his arm, and they fell immediately into step.

"Your friend is suspicious of me," he said.

"That kiss alarmed her," Eve explained. "She's afraid you'll sweep me off my feet. Give me unrealistic expectations. But it's okay. I'm chill."

"You're lucky to have such a protective friend," he said. "And she was right to disapprove. It was undisciplined on my part. It won't happen again."

Well, shoot. That was well and good, but his promise left her feeling rather deflated. "Already forgotten," she said crisply. "So? Where to?"

"It's early for dinner, but I thought we could find some place near here and get drinks. We haven't really done that part yet."

"What part of what?"

"The get-to-know-you chat over coffee or drinks that you do on a first date." He stopped, looking into a pub window. "This looks good. Beer, wine, cocktails. Shall we?"

She agreed and soon they were seated inside, listening to low-key blues music, studying a list of artisanal beers as long as her arm.

"Do you have decision-making capacity tonight?" he asked her.

"I just made one of the biggest decisions of my life, so by rights, I should be feeling depleted," she said. "But oddly enough, I know what I want. God forbid you should think that I'm a passive pushover."

"You're the farthest thing from passive that I've ever encountered."

"I'm not sure what that means, but thank you. I want a

red wine like what we had at the steakhouse. It was warm and mellow and spicy, like a pine forest in midsummer."

"That's a very clear and articulated decision," he told her. "My compliments."

"Yes, isn't it? I'm getting better at it."

The server passed their table. "We'll take a bottle of Salice Salentino," Marcus said. "Cantine Sant'Agata. Do you have a 2014?"

"I'll check." The woman gave them the menus and left, but not before casting a long, fascinated look at Marcus. It occurred to her that she was going to have to get used to that.

"So," he said. "Remind me how this goes. I don't do first dates very often."

"Really? I thought you got all kinds of action." She clapped her hands over her mouth. "Oh, God. That was rude."

He grinned. "Maybe, sometimes, but my encounters don't usually involve a lot of conversation."

"Ah." Her face reddened.

"So?" he prompted, after a mortified pause. "What do we talk about?"

"I don't date much, but we'd probably start with work," she began. "But we already know the basics. Then there's school, but I expect you and your lawyers went through my academic past with a fine-tooth comb, right?"

His eyebrows lifted. "Yes," he admitted. "But they only told me about the things that might be a problem."

"To be sure I wasn't harboring a dreadful secret?"

He shrugged. "Your life is blameless. Notable only by the fact that it's so productive. I've read some articles. The ones you published in *Nature Reviews Genetics* and *Genome Research*. Amazing work. No discernible bullshit in any of them."

"Thanks," she said, pleased. She'd never been with a

person who understood what she did in her job. Walter had tried for a while, but he'd given up on the pretense very early on.

"What about you?" she asked. "I know you've been CTO for the last several years. That you and your brother took the reins of MossTech together."

"Yes, exactly. Before that, I was working as an engineer in Indonesia, setting up micropropagation labs for NGOs. Troubleshooting lab hardware and software."

"Do you speak Chinese?"

"Yes, and Tagalog, Malay and Javanese. But my Chinese is strongest. I spent a few years there, during college and after. I use Chinese all the time, but I never have the time to drill down and make it better, the way I'd like to."

"That's you being a perfectionist," she said.

"I guess you'd know."

They paused in their laughter as the server arrived with the wine. Eve was all ready to enjoy the sexy spectacle of wine tasting again, but as the server poured wine into the glass, Marcus gestured at her.

"Have her taste it," he said.

"Oh, no, you do it," she urged him.

"I want to watch you while you taste it." His deep voice was silky. "If you like the scent of a pine forest in the summer."

"Oh. Um. If you insist." She felt incredibly exposed for the brief ritual. She swirled, inhaled and then lifted the glass to her lips.

The complex flavor of the aromatic red wine expanded in her mouth. Deep, subtle aromas she'd never perceived before. Bitter herbs and sweet fruits, lavender, berries. Relentless drenching sunshine. She almost felt as if she were performing for him. Something intimate and sensual.

Oh, God, dial it down. It's just a sip of wine. She let out a sigh and signaled her approval. "It's lovely."

The woman poured, cast a final hungry glance at Marcus and left.

"Is it as good as the one we had at Driscoll's?"

"Better," she said. "The heavens opened up."

"I love it when they do that." He took a sip and sighed. "Ah, yes. Nice."

She was overheated. Sensory overload from every direction. And his deep voice stimulated all her tender, secret inner parts, setting everything aflutter.

She had to get this back on track. She'd promised Sara she'd stay cool.

"Okay, so we've covered employment background and educational history," she said briskly. "We should move on to...how about family background?"

"What comes after family?"

"Oh, miscellany. Likes and dislikes. Hobbies. Music, books, sports teams, favorite TV series. If it goes well, maybe you might make it to politics, religion, hopes and dreams, worst fears, greatest heartbreaks, heart's desires."

"For you, the sequence is ass-backward," he said.

"How do you figure?" she asked. "We haven't even started."

"Certainly we have," he said. "Your hopes and dreams and heart's desires are all out there for the world to see. In blazing neon."

"How so?" She frowned, perplexed.

"You're that rare person who never wondered what her heart's desire is," he said. "You figured it out early on, and then you went for it."

"You mean Corzo?"

"Yes. I think I can guess what your worst nightmare is, too. A lot of us share that nightmare, and Corzo is an answer to it. A proactive, powerful, elegant answer."

"Thanks," she said. "That's very perceptive. But your

professional efforts amount to the same thing, on a larger scale. A MossTech-sized scale."

"Scale doesn't matter."

Eve snorted. "Only someone in your position on that scale can afford to say a thing like that."

He studied her thoughtfully. "Maybe we should backtrack," he said, his voice neutral. "Go back to family. Hobbies."

She took a sip of wine, considering it. "Family's sure to hit a nerve."

"True thing," he agreed. "My family drives me out of my skull. And you're in the same boat, right? You told Ronnie you hadn't spoken to your father in years. You told me he ran through all of your late mother's money. Do I remember that right?"

"Yes. I lost Mom three years ago. Heart attack. I think it was years of pining, being hurt, hoping he'd change, always disappointed. It wore her heart out."

"I'm so sorry," he said. "Any other family?"

She shook her head. "I was an only child. By the time I was born, Mom knew better than to have more children with my dad, but she still couldn't bring herself to leave him. She was an only child herself. So sad to be all alone in the world and all that. My solitary state was definitely part of the opportunity that Walter smelled in the air."

The pulse of a classic old blues tune filled the silence between them.

"And your dad?" he asked.

Eve held out her hand. "Why, pray tell, are we starting with me?"

Marcus shrugged. "It fell out that way."

"Things don't just 'fall out' with you," she said. "You pilot them. You know in advance the results you want to obtain."

His brows drew together. "Is that a bad thing?"

"Depends," she said. "I want to know you, too. But I bet you prefer to know everything about everyone while remaining unknowable yourself."

His face was impassive. After a couple of minutes of silence, she started getting nervous. She had to suppress the urge to fill the silence with chatter.

"Is there something in particular that you want to know?" he asked. "I'll tell you anything. Shall we go back to hobbies? I could tell you about my passion for extreme sports. Skydiving, parasailing, free climbing."

That measured voice made her toes tighten. She lifted her chin. "No. Just don't manage me. Don't evade or misdirect or flatter me. I'll call you out."

He nodded and poured wine into her glass. "I'll answer any question you want with total honesty, but you might as well finish. Tell me about your dad."

She sighed. "Well, it's like I told you. We're estranged. I don't see that changing. He was a bon vivant. He liked to party, he went on long, expensive vacations that lasted for months. He drank too much, he gambled, he liked drugs and the company of other women. My mother tried to divorce him, but every time, he persuaded her that he'd changed. He was very charming, and he cleaned her out. Once he'd liquefied everything he could, he left. That was six years ago."

"I'm so sorry," he said. "You're lucky to be rid of him."

"I don't know if I am rid of him," she said. "I keep meeting him. In a metaphorical sense, I mean."

"What does that mean?"

She instantly regretted blurting that out. It was the Marcus Moss effect. Ironic, since he was so good at holding things back. "I seem to keep meeting the same kind of man and having the same results, that's all."

"Elaborate," he said. "Now I'm curious."

"Oh, God, this is embarrassing. Can we let it go?"

He gave his head a shake and waited.

Aw, what the hell. "I first identified the pattern when I was an undergrad at CalTech," she said. "I'd moved in with Doug, my boyfriend, into his off-campus apartment. He kept telling me he'd cover the next month's rent if I'd spot him for this month. But the next month, it was the same story. That happened over and over. Soon I was paying groceries and utilities, too, plus cooking for him, doing his laundry and cleaning his cat's litter box. And this all while working in the lab, taking exams and writing my thesis on cell biology. After six months, a light bulb went on in my head. I packed my stuff and left."

"What an opportunistic prick," Marcus said slowly.

"Yes. Then there was my thesis adviser in grad school. We had an affair while I was working on a project under his supervision. I thought I was in love. How lucky to have a mentor so supportive of my research, right? Then he stole my work and published it as his own. He sent me a note, saying thanks for your contribution, couldn't have done it without you, et cetera. As if he could have done it at all."

Marcus's eyes narrowed in disgust. "Hack asshole."

"Yes, he was," she agreed. "That's how I pick 'em."

"What's his name?"

She was startled. "Why on earth do you want to know?"

"I want to make sure I never hire the bastard."

"Never mind," she murmured. "So, about a year ago, I decided, carefully, deliberately, to try again. And look at the card I pulled. Walter. There you have it. That's my reason for swearing off matrimony. I keep falling into the same trap. Walter seemed so different, you know? But then, so did Hugh, my thesis adviser. I should have known about Doug. He was just a good-looking zero, not much else to him. But all of them were opportunistic parasites. I've got a mysterious sign taped to my back that only guys like that can see. It says, 'Step right up. Help yourself.'"

Marcus was quiet for a moment, watching the candle flicker on the table between them. "I'm not a parasite, Eve."

She was horrified. "God, Marcus! I never meant to imply that you were!"

"You didn't. But it's important to state, for the record, that I will always give as good as I get, if not better."

"Yes," she said. "I'm sorry, I didn't mean to—"

"Don't apologize. If I sound like I'm angry, it's because I am. But not at you. I'm angry at Walter and Hugh and… What was his name? Dave?"

"Doug," she murmured.

"Doug. Your dad, too. I despise manipulative users. What a wasteful drain on your energy. I want you to blast off into orbit with Corzo, and shake them off forever."

She smiled at him. "What a lovely thought. I hope I pull it off."

"You will," he said. "I'll make sure of it."

They smiled as the server appeared with olives, little squares of hot rosemary focaccia and tiny knots of mozzarella. Once she'd retreated, Eve nibbled on a fat, savory red olive and gave him an encouraging nod. "Okay," she said. "Your turn."

"For what?"

"Family," she said. "So far, I know you have an interfering, manipulative grandma, a very difficult great-uncle with an ego the size of Texas. Then there's your cousin Ronnie, who is currently engaged, and a brother and sister, both happily paired. Right?"

"That about covers it," he said.

"What about your parents?" she asked. "Where are they in the mix?"

"Nowhere," he said. "My mother died when I was very small."

She was taken aback. "Oh, no. That must have been devastating."

He lifted his shoulders. "I don't know." His tone was distant. "I hadn't seen her for over a year when she died. My last memory was hearing her bitch about me on the phone to my grandmother. I was driving her crazy, evidently. She needed to get rid of me."

"Oh," she faltered. "Ouch."

"So she sent me off to Gran and Grandpa Bertram, where she'd already sent my brother, Caleb, and that was the last I ever saw of her. She never came to see us again. She died in a boat accident, not long after Maddie was born. I then proceeded to drive a series of nannies out of their minds. Gran tells me I was a hell-spawned monster. But to her credit, she never gave up on me. She hung in there, stubborn as a rock. We get that from her."

"You don't seem wild now," she said.

Marcus's gaze locked on to hers, and suddenly, a hypnotic glow of seduction was emanating from him. "Don't I?" he asked softly. "How would you know?"

She held out a quelling hand. "Do not even try to distract me. We're not done. You said I could ask you anything."

"Anything, yes, but not everything," he complained. "Enough, already."

"Anything," she repeated sternly. "How about your dad?"

He shook his head. "I cannot give you any satisfaction on that score," he said. "I know nothing about him."

"Nothing?"

"My mother lived in an expat enclave of beach houses in Thailand, and she was partying hard, with a jet-set crowd. None of the three of us have a name or even a nationality for our fathers. All of that biographical data went down with the yacht."

"Oh," she murmured.

"The three of us got curious, and did genetic tests once, for fun," he went on. "Caleb's mystery half was mostly

Spanish and Portuguese. Maddie's was mostly northern Africa. Mine was equal parts Japanese and Korean. No more leads beyond that, but I don't look like the pictures of my mother that hang in Gran's house, so I must look like some guy she rolled around with one night almost thirty-six years ago, and then never saw again. She was not a careful woman."

Eve was silenced by the bitterness in his voice. "I see why you evade the subject," she said. "Sorry I lectured you about it."

"I've never talked this much about my past to anyone."

"Then I'm honored," she told him.

The painful confessions had loosened them, somehow. They both finally relaxed into the conversation. They drank wine, ate finger food and worked their way through the more frivolous items on her impromptu first-date list. The appetizers were tasty, so they continued with entrees. A flaky vegetable pastry for her, a grilled lamb dish for him.

The time sped by. When a dessert cart rolled by, Eve shook her head. "I'm too full, and even if I wasn't, who could choose?"

"We can bring a sampler," the server offered swiftly. "You could try them all."

"Great idea," Marcus agreed. "Bring the sampler."

"And then I have to get home," she told him. "I need to call Sara, or she'll go into a tailspin, thinking that I'm… well. Never mind."

"Sacrificed upon the altar of my insatiable lust?" he suggested.

"Well, yeah," she admitted.

"I'll prove that my intentions are honorable. Oh, before I forget. I have an account at Federica Atelier. You'll need an evening gown for Maddie and Jack's wedding."

"Federica Atelier?" She was startled. "Marcus, get real!"

"She's a friend. She'll do it as a favor to me."

"But... But a Federica is one-of-a-kind wearable art! There's a waiting list six months long for a fitting with her! I have plenty of nice dresses, Marcus."

"This expense is on me," he said. "It's our first public outing as a couple, and I'm your husband now, remember? I can buy you a dress. It's not weird at all. Really. There was even a clause in the contract covering a clothing budget."

"But it's not necessary," she protested.

Dessert was laid before them, a tray with six little plates, each with a small serving of dessert, even a mini-ramekin of crème brûlée.

"A woman with great strain burdening her decision-making capacities should not be forced to choose between her pleasures." Marcus's voice had taken on that dangerously caressing tone that stroked something deep inside her, something that tingled and glowed. "She should taste them all."

"That's a very decadent mindset," she said.

"Decadent and luxurious, that's me," he said.

She gazed at him with narrowed eyes as the thought formed in her mind. "You let people think that," she said slowly. "You do it on purpose."

His eyes narrowed. "Meaning what?"

"It's a mask," she said. "You hide behind that persona."

"Many can bear witness to my decadence. It's heavily documented."

She let her spoon crack through the fine sugary glaze of the crème brûlée, and scooped up a bite. "Just because you play the part well doesn't mean it's not a part."

"I don't hide who I am," Marcus said. "Don't project fantasies onto me, Eve."

"I'm not," she told him. "I'm following my instincts."

He shook his head, his eyes cool again. "Maybe you're right. In any case, we should get you home. Sara will worry."

"Okay, but after two bottles of wine, we should both take a cab."

"I have a driver waiting," Marcus said. "He's outside."

"Since when? I never saw you call anyone."

He held out his watch, which had a digital touch-screen face. "If I push this, my phone texts a pickup request and my GPS location to my driver. I'll take you home."

"Oh, no. I'll call a car service, so you can—"

"We just got married. We're husband and wife, and we've never even seen each other's living spaces. Please?"

She threw out her hands. "There's no need."

"It would be my pleasure."

It was a reasonable offer. She'd been having a really good time with him. But the sexual awareness was a constant, rumbling hum in her mind. She had no idea what he would do if they were alone. Or, more to the point, what she would do.

If he started turning on his devastating, seductive charm, oh, Lord.

She was toast.

Seven

Marcus couldn't take his eyes off her. The rest of the world faded into the background. He wanted to know every detail. Her stories, her thoughts and opinions, and all the subtle, mysterious things about her that he had no name for yet. Being with Eve woke up new senses, new longings. New hungers.

He couldn't stop flirting. It was involuntary. He couldn't be any other way with her, unless he shut his damn mouth and sat there like a statue. With other women, he was good with seductive blather, but it was calculated, a means to an end. If he behaved in a certain way, he achieved a desired result. His technique had never failed him.

With Eve, there was no technique, just a sharp, clawing desire for something he couldn't even define.

Sex, of course. That was a given, but he wanted more than sex. Much more.

And he couldn't plan it or control it, or even describe

it. He was hooked on her eyes, the tone of her voice, the curved lines at the corners of her mouth when she smiled.

Alvarez was waiting outside the restaurant in the black Porsche Cayenne SUV. Marcus opened Eve's door and without thinking, gave Alvarez her home address.

Then he looked at Eve's face, realizing how creepy that might seem.

"Is my street address one of those things you know because you're an executive?" she asked.

"No, I'm just a details nerd," he confessed. "I read your work file. I have a steel-trap mind for info like that. But I should have let you tell Alvarez your own address. That looked bad. Sorry."

"It's okay," she murmured. "A man probably shouldn't be blamed for knowing the street address of the woman he's married to."

"I appreciate your understanding," he said. "While I have you here in my clutches, can you schedule an appointment with Federica tomorrow? I think crimson would look amazing on you. I want you to make a splash."

"Alarming thought," she said.

"Why? You're gorgeous. I want to flaunt you."

She looked flustered. "Um. Fine. I'll, ah, arrange an appointment."

He was overdoing it. But damn… Eve, dressed in a sexy red evening gown that was exquisitely tailored to her pinup-girl body—how could any man not be openly enthusiastic about that prospect?

Damn, what were the odds, when he stuck his hand into Gisela's gift bag, that he'd pick out a stunner? Brilliant, too. Funny. Challenging. Intriguing.

But he felt like a clumsy adolescent. All this embarrassing intensity. He had to keep a lid on it, or it would blow up in his face, like Ronnie had warned.

"I'm sorry to drag you to hell and gone all over Seattle," Eve said.

"No trouble," he replied. "Kind of a long commute for work, though, isn't it?"

"Yes, it is. I got the apartment to be close to the first job I got in Seattle. The MossTech job is much more recent. I was going to get Corzo established, and then buy something out in the suburbs, with a big lawn where I could have a garden. But that fell through."

"Not for long," he said. "Things are changing for you."

The traffic wasn't bad, so they made good time. When the car pulled in front of her apartment building, they sat there silently for a moment.

"Would you, ah...like to come in?" she asked shyly. "You mentioned wanting to see my living space."

His heart rate spiked. "I'd like that very much."

Marcus followed her into the building, past the curious gaze of the doorman. She was on the eighth floor, and he could tell the second she unlocked the door of her apartment that the place was full of plants. He smelled flowers, the humidity, the rich scent of earth. Plants sweetened the air.

Then she turned on the light, and he almost laughed. The place was a jungle of hanging plants with long, dangling fronds, burgeoning and beautiful. Spider plants, hanging ferns, begonias, succulents. In front of the entire length of the picture window was a long, raised wooden box, bursting with a tall, luxurious grass.

"Is that Corzo?" he asked.

"It is. The latest iteration. I like to live with it day by day, so I can observe it."

He stroked a blade of grass with his fingertips. "It looks tough and enthusiastic."

"Oh yeah. It's the best," she said. "I'm fond of it. It's flexible, it's unfussy. It adapts to all environments. It's a

champion of a plant. A really good sport. A farmer planting Corzo would have to go out of her way to screw it up."

"Great qualities," he said.

She looked abashed. "I love my plants. They're like
friends, to me."

"I'd love to see a big planting of it."

"I can take you to some plantings nearby," she said.

"Great. It's a date." He wandered through her place and
saw antique prints of botanical drawings decorating the
walls. He leaned closer. "These are really beautiful."

"I have a thing for nineteenth-century lady botanists,"
she told him. "If I'd been born back then, that would have
been me. Gardening, painting flowers, studying nature. If
I'd been born into the ruling class, that is. Otherwise I'd
have been hauling wood and dipping candles like all the
rest. I'm so glad I was born in a time when I can be a scientist. And those lady botanists paved the way for me."

"Everyone should have the chance to develop their tal-
ents," he said. "We need all of our human capital to survive.
The Moss Foundation supports educational programs all
over the world. From early childhood education to college
scholarships. We believe in it."

"I'm glad we're on the same page about something so
important," she said.

"About this, too," he said, gesturing at her plants. "You
said you liked plants and gardening, back at the restaurant when we talked hobbies, but you're as nuts about it as
I am. I breed flowers, too, in my greenhouse at home. It's
the only thing that relaxes me."

"I'd love to see them," she said.

"You will," he promised.

"How do you take care of a greenhouse when you have
to travel so much?"

"My assistants, Sven and Aram, come in to check on my
babies while I'm gone. And I have an automated system.

Watering, misting, humidity, plant food. Cameras, so I can monitor them remotely." He paused. "But I think they like it when I'm home. Probably I'm flattering myself."

She laughed. "I feel the same way. Let's go ahead and flatter ourselves. The plants don't mind our nonsense."

"Good thought," he said.

They smiled at each other. She was shorter now, having stepped out of her high-heeled shoes. She was padding around on her wool rug in her black-stockinged feet.

Her feet were very pretty. Small, narrow, arched.

"Would you like a glass of brandy?" she asked.

"That would be great." He followed her, through the living room and into the kitchen of the open-plan apartment.

Eve took two small brandy snifters from the cupboard, and pulled out a bottle of Camus. "It's been a while since I got this stuff out."

She poured out some brandy and passed it to him. Her hands brushed against his, and the brief contact reverberated through him like a rung bell.

He lifted his glass. "To our new partnership."

"To the fulfillment of our wildest dreams," she added.

"Amen to that." They clinked glasses and drank.

The brandy had a deep, mellow burn. He was intensely aware of her nearness. The sheen of her hair, brought out by the hanging lamps over her kitchen bar.

It was happening again. That secret heat, igniting. Her smile faded, replaced by caution. "Marcus," she whispered. It was probably meant to be a warning tone, but it was so soft, it sounded like an invitation.

Back off, Moss. Don't.

He clenched his hands into fists, tearing his gaze from her face.

It landed on her bar, where a tea tray was displayed. It held packs of teas in a mug, a sugar bowl and a crock of pale golden honey. A distraction. He seized on it.

"Is that Corzo honey?" he asked.

Eve glanced around. "Yes, it is. Only kind I use."

"Can I try it?"

"Of course." She opened the pot. The honey shone, limpid and backlit, like a gem. She dipped in a coffee spoon and held it out to him. "Here."

He reached for it. Her hand flashed forward, catching the errant drops that fell from the spoon.

"Oops," she murmured. "It never crystallizes."

Marcus dipped his finger in the spoon and tasted it.

Aromatic. Exotic. When he opened his eyes, Eve waited expectantly.

"So?" she prompted. "What do you think?"

"It's complex," he said. "Flowery. Delicate, but strong." *Like you.*

She looked pleased. "I think so, too."

Marcus tried another dab. "I'm tasting the culmination of all your hard work," he said. "Distilled into golden drops of sweet elixir."

She laughed. "I just tweaked some details. The plants, the sun and the bees did the heavy lifting."

"It only exists because of you."

The impulse overcame him. He took her hand, lifted her honey-smeared fingertip and pulled it into his mouth. Images thundered through his mind of licking honey off all of her secret female parts. Leaving no part unlicked, unkissed.

She didn't pull away. She was flushed, eyes dilated, with a dazed glow of arousal. His heart galloped.

"Sorry," he said hoarsely. "The honey. It got to me."

Marcus swirled his fingertip into the sticky spoon and lifted it to her lips. Painting them with honey until they shone, parted, pink. Glossy.

Her breath was ragged as he leaned closer. His lips inches from hers. She could feel his heat. He waited for the sign, alert for any subtle form that it might take. That countermove from her that said *yes, go for it*.

Her hand came up, settling on his chest, fingers digging into the fabric. Pulling him closer. There it was. It unleashed him.

He pulled her close and kissed her.

Eight

The tangy sweetness of Corzo honey on Marcus's mouth melted all her barriers. Her mouth opened as her body leaned into his. Twining, clinging. Arms, legs. Clutching his nape, sliding over his jacket, gripping his shirt. Buttons, scraping against her knuckles.

She wanted to rip them open. Feel hot, bare skin.

Her skirt was stretchy but too snug to wrap her legs around his. That problem was swiftly solved when he shifted her around and moved her toward the couch.

Her legs hit the cushions. She sat, abruptly. He knelt in front of her, still kissing, stroking the sides of her thighs. Every stroke released a torrent of excitement.

She glowed, melted, opened. She didn't remember pushing her skirt up, but up it went.

He shifted her again, and she was on her back. He arched over her, his mouth hot against her throat. Her legs wrapped around him without hesitation. She arched, pressing her chest against his, wriggling to get him right where she desperately wanted him to be, with the hot bulge in the front of his pants pressing her intimate parts. Caressing and teasing. Promising more.

More. She'd never hungered for it like this. His lips felt so good, every sensual kiss and touch leaving a trail of bright pleasure in its wake. Excitement cascading through her body at every caress, every stroke.

His body covered hers. He ground his weight against her, making her squeeze him closer. She was so enthralled, she forgot everything. He filled her senses.

Marcus pinned her body into the cushions with each sensual pulse of his hips. Pleasure bloomed and surged, more intense every time, until it reached a tipping point and overflowed, flooding her with delight.

Long, wrenching, utterly perfect. It left her speechless. A soft, liquid glow.

Sometime later, she drifted back to conscious awareness. Marcus was poised on top of her, nuzzling her throat. Sara's words echoed in her head. *Will he nail you out of habit?* He could, and she would love it. It would rock her world.

Then he'd get up, straighten his clothes and walk out the door, heading back to his ordinary life and his stable of lovers, which he had every right to enjoy. And she would have officially added her name to that long list. One of the many.

She'd signed a piece of paper the other day, formally stating that she would be fine with him conducting his private life as he pleased.

But if she did this, she would feel bereft and stupid and used. She couldn't do that to herself.

Marcus finally spoke. "Beautiful."

"Marcus," she faltered. "I...that was...my God."

"I know, right?" His hand cupped her bottom, tracing the edge of her lace panties with his fingertip. "You go up like a torch. It's amazing." His slow, dragging kisses made her catch her breath. "Of course it's your choice, but my hottest fantasy right now would be to watch you come, oh, maybe eight or ten times more. Each time wearing fewer and fewer articles of clothing, until I finally get to the hot, sweet, wet, secret parts. When they're completely bare, I'll paint them with Corzo honey and lick them clean. It would take a very long time to get it all off."

The image made her weak with arousal. The man could sweet-talk her into a state of quivering surrender without ever touching her.

"Do you have a playbook you follow for this kind of thing?" she asked.

He lifted his head, a frown in his eyes. "In a general sense, yes. I take care to be sure my partner is satisfied. Why does it sound like you're judging me for it?"

"I'm not. I just… I just can't believe this happened. That it went so far, so fast. My brain can't catch up with my body."

"I followed your cues, Eve." His voice was guarded.

"Of course you did. But I'm having second thoughts. About how smart this is."

He lifted himself off her body. "I'm sorry if this was a disappointment," he said. "It seemed like you were having a good time."

"I was. You didn't misread anything. But I'm not the type who can, ah…do this."

"Type?" He got to his feet, tucking his shirt back in. "What type is that?"

"You know," she faltered. "Someone who can have casual sex for the pure enjoyment of it. There is nothing wrong with that, believe me. I truly wish that I could. I'd have so much more fun. But I'm the kind of person who…" Her voice trailed off.

"Who what?" He had his back to her as he shrugged his jacket back on.

"Who takes it all so damn seriously," she said.

"Whereas I'm the type who takes nothing seriously?"

The controlled anger in his voice chilled her. "You go through women very fast," she pointed out. "My understanding was that you married me so that you could fulfill your grandmother's requirement while still being free to continue that lifestyle. That was the substance of the paper that I signed the other day, anyway, right?"

He made an impatient sound. "We had to cover all contingencies."

"I know that. But we didn't cover the contingency of becoming lovers ourselves."

He shook his head. "It flashed through my mind, but I decided not to say it out loud in front of a bunch of Moss-Tech lawyers. It seemed presumptuous, and potentially embarrassing to you."

"Um, yes, it would have been embarrassing," she admitted. "But whether we stipulated it or not, I'm just not wired that way. I just can't do it."

"Then what happened here?" he asked. "It seemed like you wanted this."

She shook her head. "It's confusing. When you start your sexy hoodoo routine—"

He let out a bark of laughter. "Sexy hoodoo?"

"Sorry, but that's how it feels," she said helplessly. "And I just can't."

"I'm sorry I put you in the position of having to say that," he said.

"It really was a great evening," she said. "I'm sorry if I made you think—"

"Don't apologize," he said. "I stepped over the line. I said it wouldn't happen again, and it did. That's unacceptable. But I've learned my lesson."

Her chin tilted. "Good night, then. Don't keep your driver waiting. Though no doubt he's used to it."

He spun around. "What is that supposed to mean?"

"Don't they drive you to your trysts and wait outside until you're done? And then drive you home? I bet you never stay the whole night."

"I don't see what my past trysts have to do with you," he said.

"They don't." She was ashamed of herself for scolding him. "I'm sorry we hit this wall. But maybe it's better we hit it sooner than later."

"Maybe." He pulled on his long coat. "I'll keep my distance. And my word. Unless you've changed your mind. I hope this doesn't change our agreement."

"No," she said. "I'm still ready to do my part."

"Thank you." His tone was stiff. "You'll have to accompany me to Jack and Maddie's wedding, but I'll stay away from you before that."

"Marcus, I didn't mean to—"

"I'll text you the details. And book you a room at the Lodge. Can I order a car to take you to Triple Falls? It's a two-hour drive in the mountains, so it's probably best."

"I prefer to come in my own car," she said.

"As you like. I'll give you all the space you need."

The front door clicked shut behind him, and Eve sank onto the couch, her knees too weak to hold her up. She could see her reflection in the picture window, over the tufts of Corzo. Her hair all wild and lopsided. A curl stuck to the side of her face. She tried to brush it away and realized that her hot face was sticky with honey.

Salt mixed with the sweet as she melted into startled tears.

Nine

"Here's the key fob for your room door, Mr. Moss." The Triple Falls Lodge concierge passed him the device. "Hold it to the sensor until the light turns green. Have a wonderful stay and congratulations."

"Thank you," Marcus said. "Could you tell me if my wife has checked in?"

The guy blinked, unable to process the question. "Ah…"

"We arrived separately. I booked adjoining rooms. Eve Seaton. Has she arrived?"

"One moment." The man had recovered his professional aplomb. His fingers flew on the keyboard. "Yes, she has. Ms. Seaton checked into the adjoining room two hours ago. Shall I, ah, call her room to tell her that you've arrived?"

The guy still looked puzzled, as well he might. Why hadn't Marcus texted the woman, like a normal husband would? A simple *Hey, babe, have you checked in yet?*

What was wrong with him? Did he have no phone? No fingers?

Nope, just no nerve. He was afraid to send a text message to his own wife.

He'd tried. He'd composed countless messages. *I'm so sorry about what happened. Could we have a do-over? I hope we can still be friends. I promise it will never happen again.*

Yeah. He'd made that promise before. It scared him that he'd been unable to keep from breaking it.

He stabbed the button on the elevator with a muffled obscenity. He didn't blame her for avoiding an awkward two-hour car trip with him, or for wanting her own car in case she needed to make a quick escape. He had only himself to blame.

It was hard to look forward to celebrating his little sister's wedding under these circumstances, but lucky for him, Maddie and Jack were both too madly in love with each other to notice if her brother was sulking. He unlocked his room door and entered his luxurious hotel room, eying the connecting door as if a tiger lurked behind it.

He hung his coat, and moved toward the bathroom, which shared a wall with the bathroom of the adjoining room, and stood still. Listening. What was that humming sound? The shower? He leaned forward. No, not running water. That was the roar of a blow-dryer.

The images took over his brain. Eve, pink and damp and naked and seductively beautiful, in front of a foggy bathroom mirror, her luxurious dark hair flying around her head like a flag. All her bottles and lotions spread out over the bathroom counter, adding their sweet scents to hers. It aroused him to the point of pain.

A knock on the door startled him, and he jumped back as if he'd been slapped.

"Who is it?"

"Your bags, sir."

His heart was galloping, and his face was as red as if

he'd been caught peeping. He strode to the door, jerked it open and dug out a generous tip, shutting the door on the young man's effusive thanks.

He had to coordinate with Eve. To talk to the woman. Or at least text her, since she was probably still naked. And rosy. And wet. God help him.

He sat on the bed and opened her contact.

The wedding starts at six. There's a processional to open the party, then dinner, dancing and then the ceremony at 11:30. Can we go down together?

He sat there, staring at his phone like an idiot, until he saw the dots that indicated that she was typing back.

Of course. Shall we go meet at 5:45? Earlier?

Let's go at 5:35, so I can introduce you to my grandmother, he replied. I'll knock when it's time.

I'll be ready. See you then.

Less than an hour from now. He tried to relax in the shower. Took his time with the shave, aftershave, deodorant.

He examined his tux-clad self in the mirror, hoping his inner agitation would not show. He looked the same as always, but the constant struggle to control himself had turned his face into a mask.

He looked stiff, humorless, tense. No fun at all.

He glanced at his watch. Four minutes. The seconds crawled by. He pulled the box out that contained the gift he'd bought for Eve. He was nervous about that, too. If she'd think that he was stepping over the line once again by offering it.

Enough waffling. He slid the key fob and phone into his pocket, went into the hall and knocked on her door.

"Marcus? Is that you?"

"Yes, it's me," he replied.

"Be right there. Just a second… This damn thing is driving me wild."

He was jealous of whatever drove her wild. That should be his job. He'd do it so wickedly well. He stomped that thought as best he could.

Then her door opened, and so did his mouth.

Eve looked spectacular in a strapless crimson gown that rustled and gleamed. A tight-boned corset-style top highlighted her perfect breasts, accentuating the luscious valley of cleavage between them, and the dress had a full, poufy skirt. The deep scarlet color made her glow like a pearl. She wasn't wearing glasses, and her big gray eyes seemed even more striking, highlighted with shadow and shimmer and those insanely long, thick lashes. Her lips were a hot red, and her ringlets had been blown out into a glossy, luxurious mane of long, loose curls.

"Marcus?" The way she said his name sounded like it wasn't the first time she'd said it. "Marcus, are you okay? Earth to Marcus?"

"Sorry," he said. "I was just… You look incredible."

She gave him a luminous smile. "Thank you. I decided, no specs tonight, I'm bringing back the contact lenses, but only for special occasions."

"You look great either way," he assured her.

Another gorgeous smile was his reward for that comment. "The dress is a winner," she said. "I absolutely love it. And Federica was wonderful. She wouldn't tell me how much it cost you, but I priced some comparable ones, and oh my God, Marcus."

He tried swallowing, but his throat was dry. "Worth every last penny."

"Insanely extravagant," she said. "On the plus side, I feel like a princess from an old fairy tale on my way to the king's palace."

"That's exactly how you look," he said. "And the hair, whoa. You can make it look like that by yourself?" He almost reached out to touch a gleaming lock. Stopped himself in time. *Boundaries.*

She laughed. "Blowouts are hard to do. I called the hotel last week and tried to schedule a hairdresser before the reception. First, they told me everyone was booked. Then, I pulled the 'I am Mrs. Marcus Moss' card. Everything changed. Hell of a thing."

He reflected that the cat could be out of the bag at this point, regarding his married state, if the concierge or the hairdresser mentioned anything to his family members. But whatever. "Good," he said. "Use that card anytime you can. It's yours for the using."

"Cool. So the woman they recommended did a great job." Eve tossed her hair, which gleamed as it slid over her shoulders, the curls bouncing at the small of her back. "I should have asked her to stay a little longer to help with the dress, which is a pain in the ass to fasten on my own. I got the hooks into the right place, but this dress has thirty silk-covered buttons, and I am not a contortionist. I was wondering if you could, um…" She tilted her head, looking up from under her lashes. "…help a girl out?"

Ha. He'd pay in blood for the privilege. *Play it cool, Moss. Breathe.*

"Happy to," he said, with rigid self-control. "Turn around."

She spun around, shaking her hair forward over her shoulders, presenting him with a new series of sensory dilemmas. He was inches from the glossy, fragrant hair, the smooth expanse of her bare back. Her elegant shoulder blades, her delicate spine, the velvety shadows cast from the overhead lamp, throwing every perfect detail into sharp relief. He could feel her body's warmth with his face. See the down on her nape. The crimson fabric was warm. He got to work, trying to keep his stiff fingers from fumbling. Button after button. Not rushing it. Thirty tight little buttons, thirty tight little toggles.

It took a long time. That magic thing happened to the air. His breath got trapped inside him, the air started vibrating and that intense awareness of her swelled into something unmanageable.

He fought it. His jaw ached. When the buttons were finished, he stepped back.

"Looks perfect," he said.

She turned with a smile, tossing her hair, and took a red taffeta stole, luxuriously lined with black velvet, and draped it around her shoulders. It was trimmed at the ends with a long fringe of black crystal beads. She draped a black evening bag on a beaded strap, also trimmed with fringe, over her wrist, and dropped in her lipstick, room key and phone.

"There," she said. "Shall we go forth and conquer?"

"One last thing," he said. "I double-checked the colors you chose with Federica, so this goes with the dress." He pulled the box out of his pocket and opened it.

Eve gazed down at the square-cut ruby and diamond pendant, shocked. A heart's-blood ruby, set off by the glittering diamonds. "Oh…my God, Marcus. Is that a…"

"A ruby? Yes. I wanted something bold for you. Fiery."

"It's too much," she protested. "I can't accept this."

"Why not?" He held it out. It spun and glittered on the end of the delicate golden box chain. "It's the least I can do. You should have a proper engagement ring."

"Oh, get real," she said, as he moved around behind her. "I'm not really your wife, so this is excessive, as far as theatrical props go. The dress was bad enough."

"The dress is very good, and so is this," he told her patiently. "Go with it, Eve."

"Ha," she murmured. "Famous last words."

He held it in front of her, nestling it in the hollow of her collarbone and fastening the clasp. He lifted her hair free, taking his time. Watching it slide, soft and slippery as silk, over his wrists and forearms. The backs of his hands. So warm.

He resisted the urge to clasp her waist, press her against him. She didn't need to feel that bulge, pressing against her luscious backside. Instead, he slid his palms along the outsides of her arms, which made a jolt of intense energy surge between them.

She met his eyes in the mirror. They looked soft. Dazed.

"Thanks," she whispered. "It's lovely. But you're doing it again. The sexy hoodoo. Please don't."

He lifted his hands away, stepping back. "Sorry. I don't know what it is that I'm doing, but I'll try really hard to stop. Shall we go?"

"Sure," she murmured.

In the corridor, he offered his arm. The swish and rustle of her skirts as she walked was subtly erotic.

Doing it again. Doing what? How was he supposed to stop doing it, when he had no clue what it was? They paced toward the elevator. He tried not to stare at himself or at her in the elevator's mirrored walls. The air felt thick. Hot.

His instructions from Maddie had been to get off at the mezzanine level, and make their first appearance into the great hall down the big central staircase. It was embarrassing, but the bride always got her way.

But considering how great Eve looked, it seemed appropriate that everyone should gawk at her beauty, perfectly framed on the sweeping, late nineteenth-century staircase. He'd wanted to make a splash.

They stood together at the top of the staircase, looking

over the crowd that filled the large, lavish art deco–style hall. It had a wall of huge arched windows that showed off the glow of the setting sun over the mountains. There had been over three hundred people invited. It was the wedding of the year, after Maddie finally cleared Jack's name of every last shadow of wrongdoing.

Everyone wanted in on that spectacular and highly publicized happy ending.

But the murmuring roar of the crowd's chatter quieted as people looked up. Everyone stared, and jaws dropped as Marcus and Eve started to descend the steps.

Eve glided down the stairs, head high, as if she were floating. Chin up, back straight, regal as a queen, charismatic as a rock diva. All that was missing was some stage smoke, some mood lighting and a wind machine to lift her hair. And here he was, feeling smug about it, as if he could take any credit for her splendor.

He took in Gran, Caleb and Tilda in a glance, all gaping at Eve. Then Ronnie, giving him a finger-flutter of a wave and a secret smile. Gisela was beaming, arm in arm with her big, stolid husband, Hector. Gisela looked satisfied with herself.

Uncle Jerome scowled with Scrooge-like sourness, on high alert for whatever or whoever was going to try to rip him off. Tonight, Marcus was that lucky guy. His uncle would go to bed disappointed tonight, and that fact made Marcus savagely glad.

He went straight toward Gran, the source of all this drama. "Gran," he said. "Allow me to present my wife, Eve Seaton."

An audible gasp sounded from everyone within earshot, at least forty people. A murmur rose as the information spread via a wave of chattering whispers.

Jerome was close enough to hear it firsthand. He pushed to the fore. "What the hell?" he bellowed.

"Nuptial bliss, Uncle," Marcus said. "Love is in the air."

"From under what rock did you dig up this girl? You think I'll fall for this garbage?"

"Jerome." Gran's voice was sharp. "You are here on sufferance. This is my grandchild's wedding. Keep your ugliness to yourself, or be escorted out."

Marcus turned away from his sputtering, positioning Eve so her back was to him.

Gran had seized Eve's hands and gazed into her face, her white hair seeming to stick straight up with excitement, though the spikiness was certainly the work of carefully applied styling mousse. "How can this be?" Gran's voice shook. "Why didn't you tell me? Or invite me?"

"It's a very recent thing for us," Eve explained. "Marcus told me it would solve some big logistical problems for him if we anticipated what we both knew was inevitable. So we went for it."

"I wish I could have been there, even for a civil ceremony." She cast Marcus a reproving look. "Heartless boy, cutting me out of that!"

"Sorry, but a guy can't get everything right all the time," Marcus said. "Particularly not when he's being shoved around with legal mandates."

"Oh, pfft. Stop your whining." Gran flicked her fingers at him, and turned to Eve. "Why, look at you! You're perfectly lovely. Where on earth did he find you, my dear?"

"The clean room of the genetics lab," Marcus interjected. "She's a geneticist, working on genome sequencing. A brilliant geneticist. Caleb recruited her."

"So I did." It was Caleb's voice behind them, Tilda at his side. He looked as startled as Gran. Good for Tilda, keeping his secret even from her adoring husband. "I didn't know she knew you."

"We've met, over the years," Eve offered. "Forums, conferences."

"If I'd known you two were close, I'd have leaned on you to help recruit her." Caleb gave Marcus an accusing look. "We could have snagged her for MossTech years ago."

"I was in Sumatra when you hired her," Marcus said. "Plus, don't get your hopes up. She's got entrepreneurial plans of her own."

"Really?" Gran's eyes brightened with curiosity. "What are these plans, pray tell?"

"That's a conversation for another time," Eve said. "But I'll be delighted to tell you all about it when we have a free minute."

Tilda pressed forward, looking as lovely as ever in a dusky rose-tinted gown. She gave Eve a hug. "Welcome," she said. "I'm thrilled beyond measure to meet you."

"Is it true?" Marcus's niece, Annika, Tilda's pretty little nine-year-old daughter, appeared. She folded her arms and frowned at Marcus. Her long dark hair was pulled back with a lace band, and she wore a white, filmy pouf of a dress with a floating tulle skirt, and white-silk ballerina shoes. She held a bouquet of brilliant blue hydrangeas bigger than her head. "You got married without telling us? And didn't ask me to be the flower girl? What's the use of having an uncle if you can't be the flower girl?"

"It was just a meeting at the courthouse with a judge, to sign documents," Eve explained. "No flowers or anything. So sorry about that."

"I'm Annika," the girl said. "So are you my new aunt, then?"

"I suppose I am," she said and laughed in surprise as Annika lunged for her and hugged her around the waist.

"You're pretty," Annika announced. "I like your dress. It's a princess dress."

"Your uncle got it for me," Eve told her. "Yours is also extremely princessy. I'm sorry about the flower girl thing, but we'll try to make it up to you, okay?"

Annika gave Eve a gap-toothed grin. "All right." She slanted an assessing glance at Marcus. "She's okay."

"Glad you approve," he murmured.

At that moment, trumpets blared. A brass quintet started with a loud baroque fanfare.

"Annika, run along with Daddy and Gran!" Tilda said. "They're about to start!"

Annika scampered away, holding Caleb's hand and spilling rose petals right and left from her overfilled basket. Caleb escorted Gran with his other arm, and the crowd was expertly herded by the staff to make way on the red carpet for the entrance.

Marcus tucked Eve's arm into his. He'd been so sick of Maddie's preaching and lecturing, he'd resisted her pleas that he join the wedding party. Now he felt a pang of regret. This was the marriage of his only sister, and he'd batted it away, out of spite.

He needed to be a better man than that.

After a few minutes, Jack Daly, Maddie's bridegroom, emerged at the top of the staircase, his face alight with happiness. The brass quintet blared the processional as he descended the stairs, and then turned around, waiting for his bride.

A beaming Annika appeared at the top of the stairs. She started down the steps, flinging petals with great energy.

Then Maddie appeared at the top of the stairs, swathed in her long, voluminous veil, flanked on one side by Caleb, and the other by Gran, who looked jubilant.

Maddie looked stunning. Her wild halo of black curls was crowned with a flowing wreath of daisies and odd bits of glitter that caught the light, and she wore a slinky dress of creamy ivory silk that set off her golden-brown skin and clung lovingly to her body. When she reached the bottom of the staircase, she kissed her grandmother and Caleb, and then turned to Jack, and took his hand. Her eyes shone with joy, which made Marcus fiercely glad. Maddie was a top-of-the-line human being. She deserved all the happiness in the world.

Jack had better treat her like a goddess.

That dazed-with-happiness look on the bride and grooms' faces did something to him that he didn't expect. A strange, shaky heat, blooming in his chest and his throat. Like something was melting down.

Eve shifted beside him, making a murmur of protest. He realized that he'd been squeezing her hand too hard.

"Sorry," he muttered.

She smiled, eyes sparkling with tears. Which ratcheted his problem up even higher.

Look away. Marcus forced himself to focus on Annika, hurling her rose petals to the left and the right as she followed the red carpet through the crowded room, preceding Maddie and Jack. Gran and Caleb followed them as they made their way toward the ballroom.

Marcus was not the sentimental type. He usually assumed that tears were a manipulative act, because they certainly never came out of him. Now look at him. Fighting tears with all the strength he had. And losing.

When Maddie and Jack reached the ballroom entrance, Maddie turned around, calling and beckoning for everyone to follow her into the enormous ballroom.

The ballroom was amazing. Vaulted ceilings, gilded columns, crystal chandeliers, beaux arts decor, and a band was already set up on the platform at the end of the room. Someone had done a complicated light installation, sending a moving, spinning show of colored lights moving around the walls.

Jack escorted Maddie to the bandstand, and she grabbed the mic. "Good evening, everyone!" she called out. "Thank you for coming to our wedding! As you have no doubt guessed, we are organizing things differently tonight. We open with the processional, then we dance, eat, drink and make merry, and then, almost at the stroke of midnight, when we're all loosened up, we tie the knot for real!"

The room erupted in cheers of raucous approval.

"To that end, let's get dancing!" She put the mic back in the stand.

Jack lifted her from the dais into his arms, and they swept into the middle of the ballroom as a slow, romantic ballad began. The lead singer came forward, a burly bearded guy. He seized the mic with a silver-and-black prosthetic hand. "Congratulations to the lucky newlyweds!" he called out. "Since this is a backward wedding, we thought we'd open the dance with a brand-new original tune, written by yours truly! This is 'My Backward Love,' debuting tonight! Maddie and Jack, this one's for you!"

The instruments swelled, the lights dimmed. The sun had fully set outside, but the sky still glowed a dull pink. A spotlight lit the stage, and a bigger one settled onto Maddie and Jack, swaying together alone in the middle of the room as the one-armed man began to sing in a rich, scratchy bass-baritone croon. The words sliced straight into his mind, somehow.

I loved that girl before I knew her
She spun my foolish head around
Now all my lies have gotten truer
What once was lost is found
I tried to start things at the start
The way the good guys do
But you ran by and stole my heart
Now all I want is you, baby.
Just my one and only backward love.

Marcus looked at Eve. He could see from her eyes that she was following the lyrics. He leaned down to speak into her ear. "They stole our song."

Her lips curved. Other couples were spilling out onto the dance floor, so he took her hand, tugging. "We've been backward from the start," he said. "May I have this dance... wife?"

She laughed. "You may, husband."

Just a dance, he reminded himself, as they came together. Her arms circled his neck and his arm cradled her waist. He held her hand in his as they swayed to the plaintive, compelling voice of the singer. After all, it would be remarked upon if they didn't dance.

And he never wanted the music to stop.

Ten

Just chemistry. Cold, hard chemistry.

Eve repeated that to herself as she swayed in Marcus's arms, thrumming in reaction to his nearness. His body felt so dense and strong. In absolute control.

Every shimmering hot rush of fresh pleasure and sensual awareness could be explained, if one went to the trouble. It was a fizzy cocktail of dopamine, serotonin, adrenaline, pheromones. Her glands were overexcited by the nearness of Marcus Moss.

Cold, hard chemistry. But it didn't feel cold. It felt wildly hot. Her whole body was yammering that she do her part to propagate the human race. That she use the most desirable male specimen she'd ever seen. Biology, dragging her by the hair, insisting that she give her children this man's genes. *Do it, girl. Nail that guy down right now, while you can.*

Never mind that doing so would destroy her emotionally. Hell, it might destroy her professionally, too. Biology didn't care. It wanted what it wanted.

And it wanted Marcus Moss, stark naked, in a locked room, all night long.

It was a constant struggle to keep her mind functioning in the face of his sexy sorcery. It was blasting at her full bore, at point-blank range. His body felt so good. He moved lightly for such a big man. Catlike grace.

After the dance, the band started the opening chords to another song. He looked as dazed as she felt, and she was glad he felt it, too. But that made it even more dangerous.

Biology was dragging him, too. Both of them. Right over a cliff.

After a couple of dances, he got her a glass of champagne, and started introducing her to people. His first stop was a stout, beaming sixty-something lady with jet-black hair and sharp black eyes, magnificently arrayed in a silver sequined gown.

"This is Gisela Velez, office manager and miracle worker," he explained. "And her husband, Hector. Gisela and Hector, this is my bride, Eve Seaton."

Gisela pumped her hand, beaming. "Glad to meet you." She turned to Marcus and patted his cheek. "That wasn't so hard, was it?" she stage-whispered. "You two look good together! She's so pretty!"

"Gisela," he growled. "Have mercy."

She patted his cheek again. "You done good, Marcus," she said indulgently. "Go on, now. Dance with your beautiful bride."

Eve leaned in close when they were out of earshot. "She seems more like an aunt than an employee."

"Yeah, that's because she is," he said. "I've known Gisela since I was a little kid. She was Grandpa Bertram's secretary, back when MossTech was much smaller. She watched us all grow up."

"She loves you like a son," she said.

"Yeah, and I care about her, too. It's a complicated dynamic for a corporate office, but we make it work."

"More human," she said.

"A little too human, sometimes. Come on, there are people you have to meet."

The next few hours were a whirlwind of networking. She met a stunning blonde named Ava Maddox and her husband, Zack. Ava was six months pregnant, barely showing in her empire-waisted bronze dress. Marcus explained that this was the publicist and bosom friend of the Bloom Brothers, so she talked Corzo to Ava. She met Ava's handsome older brother, celebrated architect and CEO of Maddox Hill Architecture. They discussed the sustainable housing projects, his urban greening project, the Mars project and Corzo in the context of all three. She was introduced to executives from biotech companies, to lobbyists, to venture capitalists and journalists.

When she talked to them, it was clear that Marcus had been working on them beforehand, priming them all to be curious and excited about Corzo.

When she met the bride and groom, Maddie gave her a hug. "You're awesome," she said. "You guys look great together. Stick around. You've got my vote."

Eve looked into Maddie's eyes and instantly understood two things. One, that Maddie understood that the marriage was fake—and two, that she was hoping that somehow, it might become real.

That was gratifying, as well as terrifying. It forced her to acknowledge that she hoped that, too. Hoped for it so hard, no matter how she tried not to. Hope made her so vulnerable. This pull she felt toward Marcus couldn't lead anywhere other than heartbreak.

Then again. She would never know unless she risked it.

"Thanks," she whispered. "You're very sweet. You and Jack seem great together."

"I'd say the same about you and Marcus," Maddie said. "Fingers crossed."

Over Maddie's shoulder, Eve saw Uncle Jerome approach. "Trouble on the horizon," she murmured.

Maddie turned. "Ah, yes. Jerome, in attack mode. Don't let him rattle you."

"He won't," Eve assured her.

"Marcus!" Jerome's voice rang out, making all nearby heads turn. "Congratulations. My compliments. She's very shiny and bright. What acting or modeling agency did you rent your pretty dolly from? And how much did she cost?"

"She's not a doll, Uncle. Nor is she an actress or model. Not that I have anything against acting or modeling, but Eve happens to be an accomplished scientist."

"Is she?" Jerome's cold eyes raked Eve. "She can't be that bright, or she'd have researched you more carefully and sent you packing before you even got started. Does she know how short your attention span is?"

"Dad, stop!" Ronnie scolded. "We talked about this!"

Jerome leaned into Eve's face. "Did he even remember your name the morning after your wedding night?" he sneered.

"Give me some space," Eve told him coolly. "You're too close."

"Dad!" Ronnie grabbed his wrist. "Just stop!"

Jerome yanked his arm free. "They are baiting me!" he hissed. "Out of nowhere, he trots out this scarlet tart and passes her off as his wife?"

"The marriage is registered at the municipal courthouse," Marcus said. "We have multiple witnesses."

"Of which I am one," Ronnie said.

Jerome's face went from red to purple. "You're participating in this? To spite me?"

"Dad, please. My cousin was getting married, and he asked me to be his witness. Of course I agreed. You don't have to take everything so damned personally."

Jerome turned on Eve. "Accomplished scientist? More like a high-priced escort, if you ask me."

"Dad!" Ronnie looked horrified. "Stop it!"

"Keep this in mind about your bridegroom, young lady," Jerome snarled into her face. "Whenever you're not looking directly at him, he'll be rolling around in a bed someplace with one of his side girls. Count on it."

"Dad. You're making a scene!"

Jerome turned his glare onto Elaine Moss, making her way toward them. "You and your grandchildren turned this event into a spectacle to humiliate me. And you, Veronica? Playing along with them? I did not expect that of you. Maybe you should spend your energy holding on to the man you have, rather than meddling in your cousins' messes. I don't see him around here, right? Is Jareth slipping through your fingers, girl?"

Ronnie's mouth was tight. "Go to hell, Dad."

"You'll guarantee it." Jerome stomped away, shoving through the gawking crowd.

Eve let out a sigh when the man was at a safe distance. "The dress worked," she said. "All that's missing is a scarlet *A* stitched onto the front."

"Sorry," Marcus said. "He outdid himself."

"It's fine," she assured him. "It's your Moss stuff. It doesn't touch me. Still. Scarlet tart? I kind of love it. I think I'll get it printed on a T-shirt."

But it had bothered Ronnie, whose shoulders hunched as she pressed her face into her hands. "There's nothing I could ever say or do that he would approve of," she said. "Nothing."

Elaine pulled her young niece into her arms. "Sorry," she murmured. "I may have set him off, but I don't understand why he takes it out on you. You don't deserve it. If there's anything I can do—"

"Oh, there is." Ronnie straightened. The smears of mascara made her brilliant eyes look even brighter. "Put me into your marriage mandate. I want to look at his face while I personally slam the door on his fantasies of taking over MossTech. Let me be the one to do that."

Elaine looked startled. Her grandchildren exchanged horrified glances.

"Oh, honey," Elaine said. "I've been walking this tightrope for months. Tonight, by the grace of God, it looks like I can finally step off it, and now you want me to jump back on? I can't handle the stress any longer."

"It's not a tightrope," Ronnie coaxed. "No stress at all. I'm marrying Jareth in a few months. He's asked me three times to go to Vegas and tie the knot early. He'll go whenever I ask him to."

Elaine's eyebrow tilted up. "But he couldn't come to your cousin's wedding with you, though?"

"He couldn't, Aunt. He was in talks for casting a new film. Please, give me this. I admit, it's vengeful, but Dad deserves it. I intend to cut all ties with him, but he won't give a damn about that. The only thing he cares about is MossTech. Give me the satisfaction of taking that from him, and he can go to hell."

Elaine harrumphed. "I understand your frustration, but tensions are high. Let's let things cool off."

"Please, Aunt Elaine," Ronnie urged.

"Time for the ceremony, or we'll pass the stroke of midnight and make all this a moot point," Tilda said. "Annika, run and get Daddy. He's lost track of the time talking sustainable urban gardens with Drew. Is the brass quintet around? They need to repeat the wedding march. And where did the celebrant go…ah, yes, there he is."

Maddie took the veil she'd removed for dancing off the

table and turned to Eve with a smile. "Would you help me drape this again?"

With the help of Eve, Tilda and Marcus's grandmother, Maddie was soon ready, lipstick freshened, veil draped, dress adjusted. She gazed across the room at her bridegroom, who waited at an arbor twined with flowers at the far side of the big ballroom. His answering gaze was worshipful.

It made her chest feel soft and unsteady.

Marcus put his hand on Maddie's shoulder. "Hey," he said tentatively. "I've been dickish lately. I've been stressed about the marriage mandate. But I love you. I'm sorry I said no to walking you down the aisle with Gran and Caleb."

Maddie's amber eyes widened. "Really? You've changed your mind?" She leaped at him, crushing her bouquet in the spontaneous hug. "Let's reorganize it on the spot! Gran will walk with me, then Caleb and Tilda, then you and Eve behind them. Annika goes in front with rose petals. It'll be perfect!"

"Me?" Eve was startled. "But I…but you just met me—"

"You're my new sister! You look like loads of fun. I can't wait to hang out. Plus, Gran is wearing pale pink, and Tilda is in that fabulous deep rose, and you're in that stunning crimson, so together, we're like a garden of roses, fading from white to red. I couldn't have planned it better if I'd worked out all the details myself."

"Are you sure? I mean, won't it be weird, to have a stranger—"

"Not at all. I'm thrilled."

Eve was touched by Maddie's expansive warmth. The Mosses did nothing halfway. For good or for bad, they went the distance.

So a few minutes later, she was part of a wedding procession on Marcus's arm as the brass quintet blasted out the wedding march even more triumphantly than they had the first time. The crowd was primed with food, wine and dancing, and the cheering was raucous. The light designer had put on a spinning kaleidoscope of lacy hearts that circled the walls around them, and a warm gold spotlight illuminated the flowery arbor where Jack waited for them to march up the red carpet toward him.

Everyone was smiling. She spotted Gisela, beaming and clapping. She locked eyes with Ava Maddox, who blew her a kiss. Jerome had shoved his way to the front of the throng. Eve looked away from his icy glare. He was a problem for the Mosses to deal with, not her.

The ceremony passed, lit up like a theatrical production. Heartfelt vows were spoken into the mic, voices trembling with emotion. Her eyes watered, and by the time Jack and Maddie exchanged rings, she had to dig out a tissue to mop the tears. She caught Tilda's eye. They exchanged smiles. Tilda, too, was dabbing her eyes and nose.

When Jack was invited to kiss the bride, the room erupted in cheers. The music swelled, the trumpets blared a Bach fugue. The celebrant beckoned the bride and groom over to the table to sign their documents. A leather-bound folder lay on the flower-decked table, next to a gold pen in a penholder. The celebrant opened it, and his jaw dropped.

"They're gone!" he said.

"What?" Elaine asked sharply. "What's gone?"

"The marriage documents! They're gone!" He held out the folder. "They were in here! They were all ready!"

Everyone looked at Jerome, who shook his head slowly, his lips curled in an amused smile. "It wasn't me," he said. "Incompetence, I expect. Or someone else is tired of your theatrics, besides me." He shook his cuff and looked at his watch. "My, my, look at this. Less than two minutes to midnight. Your stunt has backfired, Elaine. Such a dirty shame."

Elaine Moss stepped forward. "You bastard," she said. "You never were afraid to strike a low blow. You always prided yourself on your lack of scruples."

"You put yourself in this position with your own hands. Ah, look…" He checked his watch. "Ticktock, ticktock… and…voila! My great-niece is thirty years old, and legally unmarried! Happy birthday, my dear. Many happy returns of the day."

"You sonofabitch," Elaine said.

Eve glanced at Marcus's face as many thoughts flashed through her mind in quick succession. She was dismayed at such a beautiful, heartfelt wedding being marred. On the other hand, everything might have just completely changed, in a heartbeat. At least for her.

Marcus was off the hook. There was no further need for him to follow the dictates of the marriage mandate. Not if Jerome had already won the game.

This whole thing might already be over. Marcus was free to start divorcing her as soon as his lawyers turned on their cell phones in the morning.

The thought gave her a pang of regret. So she really had been foolish enough to hope that she could be on the cusp of something…well. Real.

"Quiet, everyone!" Maddie took the mic and addressed the room. "I am, as of one minute ago, thirty years old, yes, and you can all wish me a happy birthday later. But Jack and I did not want to leave anything so important to chance, so we were secretly married six weeks ago. The paperwork is registered, and Tilda and Caleb witnessed it. Go ahead and check the validity of our marriage to your heart's content, Uncle Jerome. Tonight's signature was just theater."

Applause started to swell as Maddie stared at her uncle, her smile gone and her golden eyes very hard.

"You lost," she said in a low voice. "Game over."

"Go to hell." Jerome walked out of the ballroom.

Maddie went to her grandmother and hugged her, whispering in her ear. They all gathered around Elaine, who was still visibly trembling.

Ronnie approached. "Put my name on the documents, Aunt Elaine," she said, her voice hard. "Let me hit him where it hurts."

"I'll call my lawyers first thing in the morning," Elaine said.

"For what?" Tilda hissed. "Oh, God. Gran, are you nuts? Tell me you won't."

"Jerome needs to get his knuckles rapped," Gran said. "This is the best way to do it."

"Back onto the funhouse ride again," Caleb said wearily. "God, Gran." He turned to Marcus. "We're safe for now, but I'm guessing that you two will be Jerome's next target," he said. "You're the freshest couple, so he'll see you as the weakest link, and start looking for leverage right away. Watch out for him."

Maddie grabbed the mic. "Crisis averted, people! And now that we've performed our family floor show for you all, it's time to cut the cake and slow-dance! Get in the mood, lovers!"

By the sheer force of her personality, Maddie got the party back on track again. The cake was wheeled out to be admired, and beside it, on a pedestal, a huge square birthday layer cake, blazing with candles.

Maddie blew out her candles. She and Jack took their time with the ritual of cutting the wedding cake, feeding each other bites. The catering staff swept the cake away and emerged shortly afterward, carrying trays of plates loaded with cake.

The band once again began a romantic ballad. Marcus held out his hand. "Dance with me," he said.

She gazed at his outstretched hand…and melted into his arms.

Everything about him felt so right. The way her head fit under his chin. The way he held her. Closely, warmly, but never clutching or pulling her off balance.

This was it. The point of no return. She could not resist his sensual promise. And what was more—she liked the guy, aside from her gargantuan crush on him. He was smart, fun. He "got" her.

But of course he made her feel that way. He was a born seducer. He was herding her expertly into bed. She knew that, and still, she was going to let him do it. Sweet, sweet relief. She would try not to let this irresponsible choice affect her business partners. She had her team to think of. She would try to hold this thing very lightly, but she was seizing the moment. She would not live her life forever regretting that she'd never let Marcus Moss seduce her. That she'd never flown so crazy high above the clouds, straight up into the glittering stars.

Even if afterward, she was destined to dive-bomb into the unforgiving rocks below.

The energy had changed, after that encounter with Jerome. Marcus couldn't put his finger on what had changed, but Eve melted into his arms as they danced, her tension gone. The band played romantic tunes as the nuptial lace heart shadow-show revolved on the walls of the ballroom.

Maybe it was the magic of the night, maybe the champagne. Lights moved over her face as she flung her head back, smiling. He spun her and gathered her close, and when he dipped her, she relaxed into the move with total boneless trust and abandon before he swept her up again. That unguarded moment turned him on intensely.

If he was even so much as a minute alone with Eve, he'd forget all the reasons why he couldn't do this. He kept on grimly repeating the litany. No vibing at her, no sex hoodoo, no flirting. No charged glances, or tongue-kissing or honey-smearing. No explosive orgasms as she wound her strong thighs around his hips and squeezed herself to sweet completion against him.

The song had drawn to a close. He maneuvered her to the ballroom's exit.

Eve leaned against the wall, flushed from wine and dancing.

"Marcus?" she asked. "Are you okay? You look almost like you have a fever."

Damn right, he did. "I think I should turn in. But you don't have to."

She snorted. "I'm not staying here by myself," she told him. "It's just the hard-core lovebirds out there on the dance floor. I'm ready to head upstairs, too. Shall we say good-night to your grandmother?"

"She went to bed almost an hour ago with Annika. They're sharing a room."

"That's lovely." Eve scanned the room. Tilda and Caleb, and Maddie and Jack, all clinched and swaying to a romantic ballad. "Looks like we aren't going to interrupt them to say good-night," she said with a smile. "Shall we?"

He could do this. Walk to the elevator. Stop at the door to her room. Say good-night. No physical contact, no smile, fleeting if any eye contact.

Shut the door. Then sit on the bed, grit his teeth and breathe.

"Sure," he forced out. His voice felt rough and cold.

Eve almost lost her balance on the stairs, and he seized her arm and kept holding it. "Sorry about that spectacle tonight," he said. "Your introduction to the Moss family was a true initiation, complete with intrigue and betrayal. We like to keep things exciting."

"Everyone made a good impression," Eve assured him. "Your family is great. What's not to like? They're fun, they're smart, they're interesting. Except for your weirdo uncle, of course. That guy has issues. What on earth is his deal?"

"They say he was romantically disappointed by Ronnie's mother," Marcus said. "She was a lot younger than him. When she was working in Sri Lanka, she had an affair with some guy who was running a MossTech satellite lab."

"Oh. So they got divorced?"

"No," he said. "It was worse. There was a terrorist attack. The lab was bombed. She died in the bombing, and so did her lover."

Eve looked startled. "That's terrible," she said. "How old was Ronnie?"

"Seven, I think. I remember it pretty well. I was about twelve. It was really awful. And Jerome, well. He was no picnic before, but after that, he totally lost it."

"That's terribly sad. You've made me feel sorry for your mean uncle."

"Trust me," he said dryly. "It passes."

They laughed, and Marcus went on. "Gran made it worse by taunting him with this marriage mandate. She's been dangling this prize of finally having the controlling shares, after decades of wanting to take the company in a different direction, and it's driving him out of his mind. It was just nastiness before, but now he goes for the jugular. And Ronnie catches the worst of it."

"She looked pretty wrecked tonight," Eve said.

"She did, yes. But convincing Gran to prolong this bullshit, just to deliver a moral slap to Jerome? That was insane. On both their parts. We were almost in the clear, and then Gran lost her temper and her self-control. I'm afraid it'll bite her in the ass."

"Ronnie said she was a sure thing," Eve said. "As good as married already."

Marcus grunted. "Yeah, well. Anything can happen."

"I suppose," she said. "I'll keep my fingers crossed for her."

They had reached her hotel room, and their smiles faded.

He couldn't stop staring at her tousled mane of curls. His hands clenched with the need to stroke that hot silkiness.

Eve's eyes were wide, dilated. Her lips were parted, like

she was working up to something. Whatever it was, she probably shouldn't say it.

"Good night." He kept his voice clipped, turning toward his own door.

"Wait."

That breathless word made the universe stop spinning. He turned. "What?"

Eve licked her lips, so that they gleamed. "The hotel staff left a bottle of champagne in a bucket of ice in my room," she said. "Did they leave one for you, too?"

"I didn't notice," he said.

"Do you want to come in for a glass?"

He took a moment to reply. "You told me to stop whatever happens when I look at you," he said. "If I go into your hotel room, I'll do it again. You know I will."

"Yes," she whispered. "I do know it."

"We've got something between us, Eve. And drinking wine alone with you in a hotel room late at night? That will not help me control it."

"So don't," she said softly.

He stared for a stunned moment. "Don't what? Don't come in? Don't say it? Don't control it? Orient me, Eve. Help me get this right."

A couple of female guests from the wedding came stumbling by, giggling and casting fascinated glances in their direction, and Eve pulled her key fob from her evening bag. "Come in," she said. "I don't want to discuss this out in the hall."

Fair enough. He followed her into the room.

Eve let her stole slowly drop from her shoulders, like a bud emerging from protective leaves. She kicked off her heels. Crimson nail polish peeked out from the bottom of the gown. Her fingernails were the same shade. He wanted to see her in only nail polish, lipstick and the ruby. That would be a great look for her.

Her eyes slid away from his, her face pink. "So, ah…"

"I know, I know. I'm vibing at you again. I'm not going to apologize this time."

"I didn't ask you to," she said.

"You've changed your mind?"

She tossed her hair back. "I've decided I want to experience…that. With you."

"That," he repeated slowly. "By 'that,' I assume you mean sex. Are you sure?"

"I've been processing since last week. And I think maybe I can pull it off."

"Pull what off?" he said, bewildered. "What is this, a heist? A magic trick?"

She waved her hand impatiently. "The emotional choreography. I want to enjoy you without getting wound up about you. I need to…to take this lightly."

He realized he wasn't altogether pleased by this development. "Take it lightly," he repeated. "So you don't want to care about it?"

"Well, I suppose," she said, uncertain. "Isn't that how it's done? A lot of my women friends can amuse themselves with men without tying themselves in knots about it. Maybe it's the kind of thing that one gets better at with practice."

"You want to practice casual sex. With me."

A puzzled frown appeared on Eve's face. "Why do you sound so disappointed about that? I thought you were the reigning king of casual sex."

"That's an exaggeration," he growled.

"Then why do you sound so judgy? I'm trying to both indulge myself and protect myself at the same time. To keep emotions out of it."

"No," Marcus blurted out.

She bit her lip. "So… You don't want to do it?"

"I want you," he clarified. "But I want you with all the emotions in. I don't want you to put up walls to keep me out or go to great lengths to not care. That's not what I want."

Eve looked confused. "But how does this even work if I don't protect myself?"

"I don't want a measured slice of you, with all the rest behind a locked door," he said. "That would drive me nuts."

"I thought you didn't want to get involved emotionally," she said.

"I said that before I knew you," he said. "I hadn't talked to you, or kissed you, or made you come. I want to risk us. I want you. I want…more." The words came out roughly. "I want to know you. Really know you."

Her lips twitched. "In the biblical sense?"

"Of course, but not only. I want more from you."

"I want it all, too," she said simply. "But I'm risking more than you are."

"It doesn't feel that way to me." His voice felt raw. "I'm on uncharted ground here, Eve. I have no idea what I'm doing. What might come next."

"One thing," she said. "If you want me to let down my guard, we have to be exclusive. That's a deal breaker for me."

"Is this about what Jerome said about me?"

"Not at all. I spare no thoughts for him. This is a fundamental change in our original understanding. If you want to be with me, you have to commit to being only me. Are you willing to do that?"

"Yes," he said without hesitation.

She blinked. "Just like that?"

"Just like that. I can't think about anyone but you. I don't want anyone else."

"I hope you're being straight with me, you seductive bastard," she said. "Because if I get this wrong, I'll hate myself for a fool." Her eyes blazed with emotion.

"You won't," he assured her. "I want you. All of you."

She opened her arms, with the sweetest smile he'd ever seen. "Then take me."

Eleven

Eve had half hoped that he'd sweep her off her feet and expertly ravish her on the spot, but he did no such thing. He just stood there, eyes burning with emotion.

"Are you sure?" His voice sounded hoarse.

"Yes," she said. "Life is short, and I'm going for it."

The energy buzzing between them was more exciting than any lover's touch she'd ever felt.

"How do you want this to go?" he asked.

"You are the last person in the world I would ever have expected that question from," she said. "Marcus Moss, famous Don Juan, with all the slick moves?"

"You keep throwing that in my face," he said.

"Sorry," she murmured. "I talk too much when I'm nervous."

"I'm nervous, too," he said. "I don't have any moves. I feel like a clueless teenager with you."

She couldn't help wondering if his intensity, his uncertainty, were acts meant to put her at ease. If so, they worked

like a charm. It made her want to soothe and reassure him.
Make him feel utterly welcome.

Who knew. Maybe it was a line, maybe it wasn't, but
she might as well let his clever magic work on her without
fighting it. It was all part of the game.

"One thing you could do would be to unfasten these
damn buttons for me," she suggested. "They're as hard to
manage now as they were in the beginning."

"I'm on it," he said.

She turned her back to him, and found herself right in
front of the mirror, looking into his reflected eyes.

It was a shock to see herself that way. She shone from the
inside, her parted lips hot red, her cheeks flushed. The ruby
glowed at her throat. The bodice showcased her breasts.
That billowing skirt was from a princess in a fairy tale,
ready to run away on bare, vulnerable feet. Her naked toes
were curled into the carpet fibers, trying to anchor herself
so that she didn't waft away like a Chinese lantern.

She shook her hair forward as Marcus started in on the
buttons. The corset bodice was closed by hooks and eyes.
He tugged at the bodice, just enough so that her nipples
poked over the pleated red frill at her décolletage. Her nipples were puckered and tight. Her breath came fast. The
effect was intensely erotic, like a painting of a seventeenth-
century brothel. The handsome aristocrat, taking his pleasure with his chosen courtesan.

Marcus made a tormented sound in his throat and swept
her hair to the side to kiss her neck. Whimpers of pleasure
felt wrenched out of her. She pressed against him, eager
to feel the hard bulge against her bottom. She shook with
excitement.

He scooped up big armfuls of her skirt and stroked his
hands along her thighs. He lingered at the bare skin at the
top, stroking the thin film of her panties while he nuzzled
and kissed her neck. She moved against his hand, squeezing

her thighs around it, making those sounds that she could not control. He stroked her breasts with exquisite skill, the other hand busy between her legs, getting every sure, tender touch exactly right, until he slid his fingers beneath her panties and stroked her.

A thundering wave of pleasure rolled through her.

When her eyes opened, her hands were braced against the vanity, her breasts hanging out of her dress, and the ruby pendant dangled, swinging like a glittering pendulum. Her hair hung loose, hiding her face. "My God, Marcus," she whispered.

He met her eyes in the mirror. "So?" There was a note of challenge in his voice. "Are you going to panic, like the last time?"

"No," she said. "I want this."

He let out a sigh. "Thank God. I didn't bring condoms with me, but I'll go find a machine."

"About that. Just so you know. When I found out that Walter was unfaithful, I got myself tested for everything imaginable. And I have no issues."

"Me, too," he said. "I'm always careful to use latex, and I've always tested negative. And I've been tested recently."

"Well," she said. "In that case, I have a contraceptive implant, and it's good for a while yet. So we can just, um. Go for it."

Marcus looked electrified. "Really? You'd be okay with that?"

"I'd love it."

Marcus kissed her throat. "That's the most exciting offer I've ever had."

He pulled the sheet and coverlet off, and started in on his necktie and tux jacket.

Eve reached back, straining for the hooks. "Could you finish opening this dress?"

He unfastened his pants. "No," he said. "The dress makes me rock-hard. It stays."

She stroked the expanse of her crimson skirt with her hands. "This dress cost thousands of dollars, Marcus, even if you refuse to tell me exactly how many," she said sternly. "I intend to use it again the first chance I get. This dress is not a sex toy, you get me?"

He kicked off his shoes. "I won't hurt the dress," he assured her. "At worst, it might get a few creases. We'll get it cleaned, and it'll be ready for use. Pinkie swear. Besides, I'll buy you more dresses. Lots more."

"Don't be silly. I'm not a kept woman."

"No," he said. "You're my wife." He wrenched his tux pants down over his long powerful legs, along with his briefs. Then he shrugged off the shirt, tossed it away and stood there, stark naked.

His naked torso was all lean, powerful muscle. His chest broad. A prodigious erection jutted from a tangle of black hair. Thick and eager-looking.

He waited, letting her look, as if he needed a sign from her to start.

She seized his hand, dragging him closer. She put her hands around his shaft. Hot, hard. She felt the pulse throb against her hand. He made a low, harsh sound deep in his throat.

"Is that okay?" she asked.

"Best thing I ever felt," he said, his voice strangled. "But how about you play with me afterward? I want to make you come again before I lose it completely."

"Okay," she said. "Lay it on me, Marcus. All your mad skills. I'm not afraid."

Marcus pried her fingers loose and sank to his knees, tossing her skirt up. "I've made you come twice by feel. This time, I want to see what I'm doing. And taste it. Can I?"

"I...ah...yes," she faltered, knees weakening, barely able to focus on holding her dress out of his way.

"I love touching you." His voice was a dreamy rasp. "So smooth and silky between your legs. Like the petals of some exotic flower, full of nectar. And inside, oh, God. So hot." He slid a tender finger along the quivering seam of her folds, reaching inside. Wherever he touched, she was glowing with eagerness to be stroked, licked.

He was so good at it. Masterful, gentle, patient. The sensations swelled, endlessly bigger. She would lose herself and never be found, but there was no stopping the wild pleasure that shuddered through her once again.

When she could breathe again, she found Marcus unfastening her dress. "We can lose the dress now," he said. "I want to see you in just the stockings. And the ruby."

She tried to help, but she was boneless, unraveled. Fortunately, Marcus was equal to the task by himself. He tossed the dress away and moved them both so he was on top of her.

"You're sure this is what you want?" he asked.

Eve splayed her hands against his chest, winding her fingers through his silky black chest hair, arching her back. She wound her legs around his hips, giving him a tug.

Now. Her lips formed the word, and he surged forward, filling her.

So sensitized. The slick glide of his body made her shiver and moan.

Eve moved against him as he sought the perfect angle that would hit every spot inside her. They found their rhythm. Just panting breaths, her whimpering gasps. Every stroke was unimaginably good. Every one that followed even better. There was no end to it. Her climax was approaching again; they felt it on the horizon. He waited until she tipped over the edge and let go himself.

Sweet, pulsing obliteration. It swept through them both.

Sometime later, he felt her shiver. "You're cold," he said.

"I'm fine." Her voice was dry from yelling.

Marcus retrieved the sheet and coverlet and fished the forgotten pillows from the floor, slipping one under her head. She lay there, enjoying how his body moved. Bending and stretching and twisting as he tucked her in.

And then, the crowning pleasure, as he slid back between the sheets. He felt so good, so hot and solid and delicious. At close range, his face was even more outrageously beautiful. Every hair, every eyelash, every line. His sensual lips. His erection pressed against her belly. Their foreheads touched as he stroked her face.

"Look at you," she whispered. "I thought you'd be the kind of guy who withdrew emotionally after sex. I was braced for that. But look at you. A cuddler."

"I usually do withdraw," he admitted. "I usually feel awkward and flat, after sex."

"And… How do you feel now?"

"Excited. Happy." He hesitated. "Scared," he added.

"Me, too," she admitted. "All of the above."

She reached out to stroke his erection, squeezing. Sliding her hand along his length. She gripped his shoulders and tugged at him, pulling him on top of herself.

His eyes narrowed. "Aren't you tired?"

"No. You?"

He grinned. "What do you think?"

She shifted beneath him, clasping him with her legs. "I think that you're entirely capable of serving my voracious desires once again," she told him, canting her hips to take him in.

A twisting move and he was lodged deep inside. "So do it," she demanded.

"At your command," he said.

He explored her body, taking his time, using his clever fingers in tandem to bring her to climax again and again as they rocked and surged. After a few rounds of that, she was drenched with sweat. Shivering uncontrollably. Taken apart.

"Are you ready for me to finish?" he asked.

She nodded. Marcus started again, driving her into a perfect storm of chaotic pleasure.

After, she lay there, feeling incredibly soft and relaxed. Clear and bright. Full of light.

They wound around each other, as he kissed her throat, her shoulder.

Damn. So much for keeping it light and keeping her heart barricaded.

She was madly in love with him, and she had been from the start. She was in wildest-dreams, most-extravagant-wishes territory, and she never wanted to leave it.

God help her now.

Twelve

Marcus felt so different when he woke, he barely knew who he was.

He was a bad sleeper, usually. A clenched knot of tension most of the time, and the knot didn't loosen when he woke. The only thing that helped was strenuous exercise, so he ran, or lifted weights, or did kung fu forms every morning, until he'd eased his tension enough to start the day.

This morning there was no tension, just an expansive glow of physical well-being. He felt stupid even formulating the thought, but he felt, well…happy.

Now was not the time to get sappy and vulnerable. But the feeling wouldn't stay down. It kept springing up like a Labrador.

Eve stirred. Her soft, silken heat pressed against his body sparked instant, throbbing arousal. He played it cool, turning to meet her eyes with a smile. "Hey."

She rolled to face him. Her leg was draped over his, and

that made his heart and various other connected parts go nuts. He brushed her hair off her face.

"Good morning," she said. "Would you say that this was our wedding night?"

He wasn't sure where she was going with this. "I guess so," he said cautiously. "Why?"

"Then the moment of truth has arrived," she said. "Do you remember my name?"

He laughed out loud at that. "You said you weren't listening to Jerome!"

She giggled. "Just messing with you."

Hey, two could play that game. "Give me a second to dig around in my overloaded database," he mused. "So many women's names. It started with a vowel, right?"

"Oh, shut up." She swatted his chest.

"I'm thinking, an *E*, definitely," he told her. "Edith? Edwina?" He paused, frowning. "Eloise? Ethel? Elspeth? Wait, I'm getting something. Floating up from the depths. It's something biblical, and it has to do with the garden of... is your name Eden?"

"Very funny," she said with a snort.

Marcus stroked her cheek with his fingertip, memorizing the incredible softness. "I remember every last thing you've said to me. Since we first met."

Her eyes widened in alarm. "Gosh. I certainly don't remember everything I said to you. I did a lot of nervous babbling."

"Maybe, but I listened to it," he told her, kissing her throat.

"Um, thank you?" she ventured. "I think?"

"I love your name," he said against her throat. "It suits you on so many levels."

"Yeah? How's that?"

"The original Eve was curious, like you," he said. "She couldn't just accept what she was told. She had to know firsthand. She had to experiment. I'd call her the first sci-entist. She knew there was a price to pay, but she tasted the apple anyway. It was worth it to her."

Eve laughed. "I never thought about it that way before."

"It's also a story about temptation," he said, rolling her on top of himself, settling her right where she needed to be, her hot, delicious weight against his stiff shaft. "Desire." He kissed her hungrily. "A silver-tongued serpent, leading her astray." He arched his hips, nudging inside. Sliding the tip of his penis up and down...around her clitoris, until she gasped with pleasure, lifting herself.

Slow, hot, exquisite. A heavy, pumping rhythm. Perfec-tion, slick and deep. Eventually, it turned frenzied. Hands clasping, fingers clutching.

They exploded together.

In the giddy high that followed, she snuggled closer. "I tease you about being a heartless seducer, and you respond by seducing me," she observed.

"I'm very suggestible," he told her.

They laughed, with what breath they had left.

"Oh, by the way," Marcus said suddenly. "There's a big post-wedding brunch happening downstairs."

"Oh, God." Eve sat up. "Now you tell me?"

"Sorry, I got distracted. It should be in full swing by now."

"So we should hurry, right?"

"Or we could play hooky," he suggested. "Get breakfast delivered. Paint each other with strawberries and cream, maybe maple syrup. Not as good as Corzo honey, but it'll do."

She laughed at him. "Today is not the day to blow off your family, Marcus. Your grandmother is down there, and everyone you know is watching."

Marcus let out a sigh. "I guess," he said with bad grace.

"I'll shower first." She slid out of his arms and pulled

a black velvet scrunchie out of her toiletries bag, twisting her hair into a topknot. "Actually, we have two bathrooms, so you don't even have to wait."

"We could shower together," he suggested.

"We'd never get downstairs, and we'd probably flood the place. Next time."

"I have a hot tub on my rooftop terrace in the city," he told her. "We can go there tonight, take a long soak, look at the city lights as we sip cold champagne."

"That sounds fabulous," she said. "I offered you champagne last night, but we got so distracted, we never got around to opening it."

"Let me distract you again," he coaxed.

"No! Out with you!" She shooed him away, laughing.

Marcus gathered his tux and went to his own room. He hurried through the routine of showering and shaving, eager to see her again. All the time. He'd never felt like this before. He had to be careful not to overdo it and seem needy.

He knocked on her door once he'd dressed.

"Come in," she called. "I'm putting on my boots."

She looked stunning in a clingy knit dress of fading shades of dusty rose, pink, purple. A narrow black belt accentuated her slender waist, and high-heeled black boots jacked up her height, so her eyes were at his chin level. Her hair hung gloriously loose, but her eyes were made up, her lips that hot, sexy red. The ruby pendant looked perfect with this dress, too. It glowed with its own light, nestled at her collarbone.

"You look gorgeous," he said.

"You're looking very smart yourself," she retorted.

Marcus glanced at his dark suit and silver-gray dress shirt. "I have to stay sharp if I'm standing next to you. You were the most beautiful woman in the room last night."

"Oh, please. Nobody outshone the bride. Your sister is a real showstopper."

"True, Maddie's a looker. I know that objectively, but I always see my smart-mouthed, goofy little sister with the braces."

"Lucky you, having her and Caleb," Eve said. "I always thought it would be wonderful to have brothers and sisters."

"I'm glad to have them," he admitted. "And I'm glad that they're happy with their new spouses. It still blows my mind. Out of nowhere, they got lucky and struck gold."

Marcus stopped talking as they got into the elevator. His own words echoed in his head. He may have struck gold, too, but that by no means guaranteed that he could hang on to it.

And whether Eve had struck gold in him still remained to be seen.

Walking into the dining room, he saw Gran held court like a benevolent empress at the head of the largest table. Two places were empty to one side of her. On the other side was little Annika, then Tilda and Caleb. Maddie and Jack were nowhere to be seen. They had done their duty, and they were excused. Free to run away and play.

But instead of resenting them, as he usually would have, it occurred to him that it sounded like a hell of a lot of fun.

He could do that. He and Eve could shift around their work schedules a little, carve out some time and run off together. Somewhere Eve would like. And just play.

People did that, but he never had. It hadn't occurred to him. But being with Eve…well, damn. That changed his point of view completely.

"My dears! At last!" Gran wagged a scolding finger, but her eyes were smiling. "Sit by me, Eve." Gran patted the chair next to her.

Marcus took his seat on the other side of Eve. Marcus met his sister-in-law's eyes, then his brother's, as the server poured out their coffee. Both were smiling in a way that made him feel like he'd walked into the dining room naked. "What?" he demanded. "What's the look?"

"You look so relaxed." Tilda and Caleb smiled at each other like fools.

"I'm half asleep," Marcus said defensively. "Late night."

"I bet it was," Caleb murmured.

"Do not embarrass her," Marcus said in soft, menacing tones.

"We would never," Tilda told him solemnly. "Just let us be pleased for you, okay? Is that so much to ask?"

He checked to see if Eve was following, but she was leaning toward Gran, deep in conversation. "It's not too much to ask, no," he said. "It's just too soon to ask. Don't jinx me."

Caleb nodded. "Gotcha."

Marcus stood. "I need fuel," he said. "Can I get you a plate?"

"Sure, thanks," Eve said. "Anything is fine. It all looks good."

"Yes, run along, Marcus. Eve was telling me all about Corzo," Gran said. "What a marvelous project. Go on, dear. Honeybees, you were saying? Good heavens. That's delightful."

"Yes, that part was a real surprise, at first." Eve turned to his grandmother.

Marcus left them to it, and headed toward the lavish buffet, loading both their plates. Artichoke and egg pastry, buttermilk pancakes, link sausages, bacon and a bowl of fresh raspberries with a dollop of cream. A good beginning.

A server took the plates away as soon as he finished loading them, and accompanied him to the table, but Teresa Haber stepped suddenly into his path.

She smiled brightly, feigning surprise. "Oh, Marcus! It's you!"

"Good morning, Teresa."

Teresa wore a tight leather miniskirt. A low-cut, fluffy white mohair sweater clung to her lush figure and showed a lot of cleavage.

"You look well, Marcus," Teresa said. "Married life suits you. Where on earth did you find that girl?"

"In a lab," he said.

"Oh, I see! So you fell in love with her brain, then? Aw. That's sweet."

Marcus let his polite smile fade to nothing and kept calmly looking at her, long enough to make her uncomfortable. "Enjoy your breakfast, Teresa," he said.

She tossed her hair and flounced away.

Caleb joined him. "She looks pissed," he said. "Drama?"

"Why would there be?" Marcus said. "I never led her on. Who invited her?"

"Beats the hell out of me. She wasn't on Jack's or Maddie's guest list. Maybe she was somebody's plus-one."

Back at the table, Eve looked at her plate, startled. "Wow, yum. Decadent excess!"

"Always," he murmured. "It's just who I am."

She met his eyes, and he gave her a teasing smile. "Okay, fine. You got me," he said. "That's just a mask to hide my tender inner self, but don't tell anyone. Let it be our little secret."

She giggled and took a bite of pancake. "I've never been so hungry in my life."

"Eve's been telling me how she developed Corzo," Gran said.

"Yeah, I was impressed by Corzo, too," he said. "Where are Maddie and Jack?"

"They left early to catch a plane. I think they were heading to Brazil. That enormous waterfall, you know the one?"

"Oh, yes!" Eve's eyes lit. "Iguazu Falls? I would love to see that someday!"

"Let's go," Marcus said on impulse.

She looked startled. "Uh… Are we maybe getting ahead of ourselves?"

"That's our shtick. Backward love, right?" He hummed the refrain to her.

"Marcus," Gran murmured. "Look at you. Giggling. Humming, for goodness' sake. You're positively giddy this morning."

"Gran, please," he said wearily.

"I'm thrilled to see you having a good time. Why don't you two have your own honeymoon? You cheated us all out of a proper wedding, so at the very least, you should take a proper honeymoon. Organize it right away!"

"Well, it's not so simple," Eve said. "I need to work, and so does Marcus, right?"

"I could probably clear my schedule," Marcus said blandly.

"Maybe you could, but I've only been in this job for a couple of months, so it seems a bit presumptuous."

"Eve," Gran said delicately. "I love you to pieces for making me say this. But Caleb and Marcus are your boss's boss's bosses. You can go wherever you like, whenever you like. Discreetly, of course. Without rubbing it in anyone's face."

"Ahhh…" Eve dabbed at her lips with a napkin and shot a panicked look at Marcus. "We'll talk about this later, okay?"

"Sure," he said. "Iceland would be fun. The Galapagos. The Andes. Or Europe."

"Don't leave quite yet," Caleb told them. "I was talking to Galen Landis yesterday, like you asked me to." He looked at Eve. "The Landis Forum. You know it?"

"Oh, yes," Eve said. "We were going to present Corzo there last year, but things went south right about then, so I didn't get the paperwork in. I was hoping for next year."

"Nope," Caleb said, with satisfaction. "You and your

team are going. Landis wants you to present Corzo at the forum. Yours is the very first presentation."

Eve's jaw dropped. "But we missed the deadline! We can't possibly…"

"Do you have a presentation prepared?" Caleb asked.

"Of course!"

"So go," he said. "They're waiting for you. It's all set."

"I'm sure you can get your team together in time," Marcus said. "Why not?"

"It's all happening faster than my brain can keep up," Eve said faintly.

Tilda patted her arm. "Welcome to the Moss family," she said. "Like being run over by a train, but in a good way."

"Where is the Landis Forum this year?" Gran asked.

"At the coast," Caleb said. "At Paradise Point."

"Great." Marcus looked over at her. "Paradise Point is a luxury resort on the Washington coast designed by Drew, my architect friend that you met last night," he said. "It's beautiful. It has a Michelin-star restaurant, too."

"And since you'll be going to Paradise Point, there's no reason not to take some time to enjoy your new beach home right near Carruthers Cove, right?" Gran said with satisfaction. "At long last, I can get rid of that last property!"

Eve looked around at them all, bewildered. "What property?"

Marcus rolled his eyes. "Gran bought three houses on the coast, as future wedding presents for the three of us. Up on the bluff. Ocean view. Private beach."

"And that sulky ingrate hasn't even been to see his!" Gran scolded.

"It didn't belong to me, Gran, and I figured it never would, so why torture myself?" Marcus told her. "At the time, I had no intention of playing along."

"And then you found this treasure." Gran leaned over to

kiss Eve's cheek. "You've been saved in the nick of time, in the best possible way."

"We took a look at your house," Tilda told them. "It's really stunning."

"Yeah, we peeked!" Annika said. "It's pretty. Totally different than ours or Aunt Maddie's, but just as nice. Well, almost. Ours is definitely the best."

"Annika," Tilda said sternly. "That's rude."

"Why?" Annika asked, her eyes innocently wide. "They never even saw it yet!"

"Still rude," Tilda insisted.

"Sorry," Annika said cheerfully. "But it really is pretty. It's definitely got the best trees. The trees are, like, huge."

Eve turned to Marcus, startled. "A beachfront house? As a wedding present?"

"Gran's just like that. She shoves her grandkids face-first into matrimony, and showers them with luxuries as a reward. It's very twisted."

"Hush," Gran said crisply. "It's an investment, and part of your inheritance. It's also an investment in your future work-life balance. Caleb and Tilda and Annika go all the time. It's good for them. I'm sure it'll be good for Jack and Maddie, too."

"Convenient that it's ten miles away from the Paradise Point resort," Caleb pointed out. "It'll be the perfect staging area for your team."

Gisela strolled by and patted Marcus on the shoulder. "Good morning," she said. "Great party last night, eh? You danced the night away. Like Cinderella and her prince, except with no pumpkin time!"

"Oh, Gisela," Gran said. "Can the office do without Marcus for a bit? He and Eve need to organize a working honeymoon to present her project to the Landis Forum."

"Gran," Marcus growled. "I'm a chief executive of a

multinational corporation. I don't need a permission slip from my grandmother."

"You certainly don't, honey," Gran said indulgently, patting his cheek. "Just look at you, all grown up! A married man, no less! It makes my heart go soft."

"Certainly we can," Gisela assured his grandmother. "It'll be much easier now that the staff isn't always running off for long lunches to do job interviews. Go and have fun!"

"You are a gem, Gisela," Gran told her warmly.

Gisela winked and waved as she rejoined her husband.

Marcus leaned to murmur in her ear. "The ball-busting is more intense than I anticipated. Can we go? I'll take you back to the city, and we'll head to Carruthers Cove tomorrow. Tell your team to come up a few days before the forum to prepare. Gran, how many people can we comfortably host in the house?"

"At least six, besides you two, if people share rooms," Gran told him. "It's four bedrooms and five baths, and if you need more space, I'm sure your brother and sister can help you out with their beach houses, eh? Convenient, isn't it?"

"Spectacular, Gran." Marcus bent to kiss his grandmother. "Couldn't be better."

"No, it really couldn't be." Gran gazed at Eve with a misty look in her eyes. "Let me give you a hug," she said, holding out her arms. "Welcome to our family."

Eve leaned over and embraced Gran, whose eyes were suspiciously shiny.

Time to sweep Eve out of harm's way before things got weepy. "We're taking off," he announced. "Have a great day, everyone. Let's head home."

"I have my car," she reminded him. "I'll follow you."

Caleb saw his younger brother's alarm and stepped in swiftly.

"I'll drive her car," he offered. "Carlo drove Tilda and

Annika here, so he can drive them home, and I'll leave Eve's car in your garage."

"I can drive my own car back, guys," Eve protested.

"That's perfect." Marcus gave his brother a grateful glance. "Thanks."

"But…" Eve looked at Caleb, alarmed. "I don't want to put you to any trouble!"

"No trouble at all," Caleb assured her.

Marcus didn't want to watch Eve in the rearview mirror. Having her right next to him, where he could hold her hand, stroke her leg, smell her perfume…yes.

That was more like it.

Thirteen

Well, look at that. Swept off her feet by a man whom she was officially head over heels in love with, and there was nothing she could do about it except try not to be uptight.

Gisela had said it was like Cinderella and her prince, but with no pumpkin time. Too much to hope. Pumpkin time always rolled around, and the little voice in the back of her head kept on yapping at her to not forget it. The voice had her best interests at heart, of course. It wanted to protect her from disappointment. And make sure that when this bubble popped, she acted with dignity and grace. She would continue to hold up her end of their bargain, as if nothing had happened.

But until that time, she was going to enjoy the hell out of Marcus Moss.

The ride back to the city was fun. There was no lack of things to talk about, things to laugh about together. The wedding, then last night's erotic bliss, it all felt like a dream. And now a luxury beach house in Carruthers Cove? And the Landis Forum, for her team? And Marcus was so beautiful, it almost hurt to look at him.

She made a call to her boss to arrange the time away. Helen had already been apprised by Gisela, but the woman was reeling to learn that Eve had married MossTech's CTO. She agreed to the time off with no complaint. It would take time to get used to this new reality. Or, well. Maybe she shouldn't get too used to it. Maybe it wasn't reality at all.

But she wasn't going to think about that right now.

When they pulled into the garage in Marcus's apartment building, her car was parked next to his sports car, leaving ample room for the SUV he was driving.

"I'll need to go home and pack for the coast before we leave," she told him.

"Let's get an early start and drop by on our way to the coast," he suggested as he led her to a dedicated elevator. It shot them to the penthouse and opened into his foyer.

Marcus's two-story apartment was huge. It featured a two-story ceiling, with tall French doors and towering solarium windows that opened onto a vast terrace. She gazed at the wood-plank flooring, the curved gray marble accent wall, the big comfortable gas fireplace that Marcus turned on with a tap of his phone. It gave out an instant, cheerful warmth and cast flickering shadows on the walls of the living room.

The furniture was beautiful, in various warm earth tones. An arrangement of comfortable couches were grouped around a low mahogany table.

There was a floating industrial steel staircase with a bronze railing leading to the next floor, where the bedrooms were presumably located. She spotted long hanging bronze lamps, gleaming wooden paneling. And at the far end of the room, she saw a huge kitchen, and a massive dining room table. A breakfast nook with glass on three sides.

"What a gorgeous place," she said.

"Thanks," he said. "Gran and Maddie helped with the

interiors while I was working in Asia. But I like how it turned out." He took her suitcase. "I'll run this up to the bedroom and then give you the grand tour."

He returned moments later, phone in hand. "Let me order some groceries for later. How do you feel about a steak for the grill? I don't want to do anything complicated, and steak is easy."

"I'm still full from breakfast," she told him.

He gave her a devilish grin. "We'll burn off all of our breakfast. Count on it."

That promise ignited the air between them. The surface of her skin tingled, as if the wind was rushing over it.

She was flustered, her face hot, and her eyes seized on the first thing she saw on the coffee table. In a simple gray ceramic pot, a fiery, speckled orchid seemed to float, as if it was illuminated from within.

"The orchid is stunning," she said. "Where did you find it? What kind is it?"

Marcus looked pleased. "It's one of mine."

"You bred that yourself?" she asked, impressed.

"Yes, it's a Cattleya crossed with Laelia. It took me forever to get it right, but I love the way it turned out. I call it 'Firedrake.'"

She admired its ethereal beauty. "It's amazing."

"Wait till you see what I've got in my greenhouse." He sounded like an excited boy when he talked about his flowers. "Come on, I'll show you around."

She followed, freshly stunned by an exquisite view of city, mountains, Puget Sound, from every window. She was freshly reminded that this man was wealthy beyond her imagination. Her own mother had come from money, before her father's excesses had reduced it to nothing, but not this kind of money. This was another level entirely.

Finally, Marcus pulled her out onto a terrace. "There's the hot tub I mentioned," he told him, pointing at the wooden platform and deep sunken tub. "I have prosecco chilling in the refrigerator. But I wanted to show you this."

He opened a glassed-in space and pulled her into the fragrant warmth and humidity of a high-tech greenhouse, lit with the glow of artificial grow lamps.

The part she could see was ablaze with orchids of every description. She moved closer, delighted. "Marcus. This is wonderland!"

"I figured a woman who channels nineteenth-century lady botanists would enjoy my hybrids," he told her.

"Show me everything," she said eagerly.

For the next hour, they went from plant to plant, geeking out about nitrogen, microbiomes, water drainage and the challenges of orchid root rot.

"Tilda has trouble with that," he told her. "I have to go regularly to visit the orchid that I gave her to make sure she doesn't accidentally kill it."

"You gave your sister-in-law a bespoke orchid?" She was intensely charmed.

"Yeah, as a late wedding present. I named it 'Love Reborn.' For their story."

"Very romantic," Eve said.

"The one I gave Maddie I called 'Torch of Truth.' The blossom is yellow, fading to white on the top, and it stands up straight, like a candle flame. 'Torch of Truth' is perfect for them."

"Are you going to tell me their stories after all this buildup?" she asked.

"Maybe in the hot tub, after some prosecco has loosened me up. My siblings' love affairs are stories best told half-drunk."

"I'm so intrigued," she told him. "I won't let you forget."

"Great. Come on and see my hibiscus flowers. This is the latest bloomer."

Eve bent to admire the blossoms. They were transparent

pink in the center, fading to deeper red, and finally to a frill of burgundy around the border, so deep a red, it looked black.

"I call this one 'Persephone's Secret,'" he said.

"Sexy," she commented. "So did other girlfriends respond to your seduction by flower, or is it just me that's melting down, getting all hot and bothered?"

"I wouldn't know," Marcus said. "Only family comes in here. And my assistants, when I'm traveling. I don't entertain."

"You mean, you never brought your girlfriends to this ultra-mega babe lair?"

"No. This place is my private refuge."

"And yet, here I am," she said.

"Here you are," he agreed. "I wanted you to see my flowers. It's my private thing, separate from the work hustle, MossTech. They're just for me. No masks."

She smiled, tears prickling her eyes. "I'm honored to witness them. Pure magic." Her eyes fell on a luxurious hibiscus plant, one with no flowers. "What about this one?"

"She won't bloom," he said. "She's holding out on me. Making me wait."

His low voice rumbled tenderly. Then he gently tilted her chin until their eyes met. His warm lips came so close. Still closer.

Closeness turned to touch, and all the sensual promise of voluptuous hothouse flowers exploded between them.

He lifted her onto the table, pushing at her skirt, stroking her thigh. She fell back, propped on her elbows as he slid her panties off, leaving her thigh-high stockings on. She was bare below, naked to his fascinated gaze. He stroked her tender folds, her sensitive, sweet spots, circling, caressing. His touch made her shudder and gasp.

"You're so beautiful," he said. "So hot and wet and sweet. Can I taste you?"

"Yes," she gasped out. "Oh, yes."

He sank to his knees and put his mouth to her with devastating skill. He took his time, flicking and circling with his tongue, swirling and lapping. Driving her relentlessly into a frenzy of helpless delight.

When she focused her eyes, he had unbuckled his belt and was stroking her slick, sensitized folds with the tip of his penis. "Is this what you want?" he asked.

She nodded, and they both groaned as he surged forward, filling her. He leaned over to drag her neckline off her shoulder, kissing the curve of her breast as he pumped in, out. Deep, slow, heavy strokes, expertly petting every glowing hot spot inside her.

So good. So intensely sweet. Every thrust made her wild, rising and straining for the next one. She clutched him, demanding more, breathless. Incoherent.

Marcus resisted for a long time before the pace quickened, but eventually the table was rattling on the tile floor. The hibiscus planters tottered and shook on the tabletop as he pumped himself against her, holding back until she reached the edge.

An exquisite flash of communion fused them. The sweetest sensation.

She could get so hooked on this. Destroyed, when it was finally wrenched away.

Eve pushed the thought away, but Marcus lifted his head, sensing it. "Are you okay?"

"I'm incredible." Her voice was dry, cracked. "I can hardly move."

He pulled her upright. Eve slid off the table, pulling her skirt down. "A quick shower might be in order," she said.

"I have lots of bathrooms, but the one with the huge glass shower cabin and six different jets of water is right off my bedroom."

"Sounds luxurious," she said.

"Yeah, and there's plenty of space for two."

Marcus led her up the staircase and into his room. A king-size bed dominated a vast room with floor-to-ceiling windows on two walls. She admired the red-and-crimson silk Persian rug that adorned the hardwood flooring.

The shower was everything he'd promised. His bathroom was bigger than her living room, holding an antique tub, a vast shower stall faced with shiny black slate.

Being naked under rushing hot water with Marcus Moss ended up as she might have expected. Three explosive orgasms later, she could barely stay on her feet.

He rinsed her, wrapping her in a fluffy silver-gray towel, and rummaged through the bathroom cabinet. "Hang on. I think I have a spare…yes!" He yanked out a white terry cloth shower robe triumphantly, and wrapped her in it. "Hey, I'm hungry. You?"

"I could eat," she admitted.

"We can throw that steak on the grill," he said. "There's fresh bread, salad."

"Sounds great," she said.

Soon they were sipping prosecco while the aroma of sizzling meat rose from the grill. They feasted on fresh, crusty bread, salad and tender Florentine steak. For a final treat, they devoured cinnamon-apple cream tarts as the city lights began to glow. They had whiled away the entire day canoodling.

They weren't finished, either, Eve realized, as he lifted the lid off of the steaming hot tub and topped up her wine. "Shall we soak?"

"Sure, but you promised to tell me about Maddie's and Caleb's adventures."

He tugged her sash loose. "Those are tales best told naked. Hot. Wet."

She set aside her wine, and shrugged the robe off, shivering in the chilly wind. Nipples taut in the cold. "I'm ready," she said softly. Displaying herself to him.

Marcus helped her into the tub, fully erect. Then he sat across from her.

"So far away?" she asked, putting her feet on his lap.

"If I touch you, I'll lose my train of thought. I won't be able to tell the stories."

His brother's and sister's adventures were intensely romantic, even delivered in Marcus's laconic, understated style. Perfect entertainment for a naked girl in a hot tub, overindulging in wine and sex. She listened in fascination all the way to the end.

"Amazing," she said. "So will they really reboot Jack's company, do you think?"

"We'll see. It's still up in the air. Caleb hasn't been sure what was going to happen with MossTech. Too many variables. We're waiting for the dust to settle."

So was she, she reflected. "I love it that everyone got what they were most longing for. Love, trust, friendship. Justice. Redemption. The truth."

Marcus lifted his muscular arm, slicking his hair back with a wet hand and showing her the shape of the silky black armpit hair and the tight muscles of his abs.

"Yeah, they sure did," he said. "I'm glad to see them happy and fulfilled." He hoisted himself onto the side of the hot tub. His thick phallus jutted out. Steam rose from the gleaming planes and angles of his body. "I'm hot," he said.

So was she. Hot and moved by his sensual generosity, his passionate, focused lovemaking. She floated across the big tub, splaying her hand on his belly and trailing it down, grabbing his thick shaft. Squeezing boldly.

It stiffened and lengthened instantly in her hand, flushed and throbbing.

"Eve, you must be tired," he said.

"You provoked me, displaying yourself like that," she said. "Now deal with the consequences. It's my turn to drive you crazy."

She drew him into her mouth, making him gasp in pleasure, and did exactly that.

Fourteen

"There it is," Eve said. "Number 1204. The directions say, turn into the main driveway, and then make the very first right."

Marcus slowed to turn into the driveway and took the first right. The paved road meandered off through rippling emerald grass and towering rock formations.

The drive to the coast had been as much fun as the drive from Triple Falls Lodge. He'd always avoided getting involved with women he knew through work, so this was the first time he'd been able to talk about his job and be fully understood.

More than understood. Debated, challenged, informed. The woman knew her stuff. It was very stimulating, in every sense of the word. Huge turn-on.

Carruthers Cove left them awestruck. The road curved around outcroppings of granite that protruded from the luminous green turf and then wound up and around into a stand of towering pines and firs. The driveway ended below a ski-chalet-style structure, large and luxurious. Understated, the kind of house you would not see from a distance because it blended discreetly into the trees. A big A-frame window faced the ocean, with decks on the ground and second floor. The first-floor deck had been built around various rocky monoliths that poked through like sculptures, indigenous flowers carefully landscaped around them. They got out, gazing around, and without thinking, their hands clasped. They climbed the steps together.

The place was stunning inside as well. He would expect nothing less from Gran, who had refined tastes and a loathing for compromise. It was paneled with fine, rosy cedarwood, filling the house with its subtle woodsy perfume. The living room had a big stone fireplace, comfortable couches in deep, rich colors, piled with pillows and cashmere throws. Huge windows showcased spectacular views in every direction. In the big kitchen, there was a large white cardboard box on the granite-topped central island.

"What's in the box?" Eve asked.

"Fixings for lunch and dinner," Marcus told her. "I asked the caretaker to deliver some things. The red wines, pasta and bread are in here, and his note says that the white wines, champagne and prosecco are in the fridge, along with the fresh food."

Eve opened the refrigerator door, which revealed heaps of cheeses, fruit, sausages, pastry boxes, take-out containers filled with salads, and packets of white-paper-wrapped fish. "Wow, that looks appetizing," she said. "You certainly don't mess around."

"With food, never. We'll start with cedar-smoked salmon, then fried calamari, fresh clam chowder and pan-fried scallops. There's swordfish steak for the grill tonight."

She looked impressed. "Lots of protein."

"We're going to need it," he said.

"Lay it on me. Shall we look around this place?"

The primary bedroom had an enormous attached bath. Three more magnificent bedrooms also had bathrooms. The wraparound deck seemed to float in a wavering sea of trees. There was a hot tub on a side deck and it released an inviting puff of steam when he lifted the cover. Seagulls and pelicans wheeled overhead.

"I'm afraid to think of how much this place must've cost her," she said. "With private beach access, too. And the landscaping."

"Better not to speculate," Marcus advised. "Gran has decided that being happy and enjoying life's many pleasures is now required."

She laughed at his tone. "Oh, poor, poor you!" she teased. "So put-upon."

"The only reason we're laughing is because I got incredibly lucky," he told her. "It could have gone any way, but I ended up with you."

Her eyes sparkled. "Do you think some things are destiny?"

Marcus shook his head. "I'm an engineer. I rely on what I can measure. Even luck is just a mathematical construct. But I'm glad I had some of it this time around. A lot of it, actually."

That look in her eyes was seductive temptation. "I'm a scientist, too," she said. "And I value logic and reason. But this thing between us…it can't be quantified by any unit of measure I'm familiar with."

He slid his arms around her, nuzzling her hair. "We need to examine the phenomenon more deeply," Marcus said. "Gather more data. Repeat, until our results are statistically significant. You know the drill." His hand slid under her shirt to unhook her bra.

Then both of their stomachs rumbled, and they laughed.

He reluctantly withdrew his hand. "After I feed you, of course."

Eve followed him into the kitchen. "We don't want the fish fry to get soggy," she said. "Shall I put it on a baking sheet and into the oven?"

"Good idea. I'll turn on the stove and open a bottle of white."

They savored smoked salmon on artisanal crackers, bowls of fabulous clam chowder, a platter of tender, crispy fried calamari and four different side salads, and a chilled white wine with a wonderful, flowery depth to it. After their feast, they went out to stroll over to the edge of the bluff, where they could look down at the beach, and glimpse what had to be Maddie's and Caleb's houses.

The dilemma of what to do next was no dilemma at all. They headed upstairs and soon their clothes were scattered over the floor of the bedroom.

Marcus had never had sex like this. He'd had plenty of it since his early teens, but he'd never felt the way he felt with Eve beneath him, on top of him. Her bright gray eyes alight with pure emotion, her beautiful, soft lips flushed red and parted with pleasure. Her slim, luscious body wound around his. Pliant, eager. Exquisitely responsive.

It made his soul shake with something that felt like awe.

The afternoon was waning when they showered and gathered their clothing. Eve shot him a smiling glance as she retrieved her long wool sweater from the newel post at the foot of the stairs. "We've broken the house in, don't you think?"

"Not a chance," he said swiftly. "We have miles to go before we sleep. We have to inaugurate every single room."

Her eyes widened. "Ambitious. This place has a lot of rooms."

He gave her a grin. "So we exert ourselves."

There was enough light left to hike to the pathway that led to the beach. They took the staircase that zigzagged to the beach below, and waded in the frigid surf together, looking into tide pools at the starfish and anemones, their tiny, delicate tentacles waving underwater like petals of green and pink flowers.

When the sun was low and the clouds tinted pink, they made their way up to the house, rinsing their feet with a hose at the base of the deck.

The hot tub was caressingly warm, the tub positioned so that two could sit on the bench under the hot water and admire the spectacular sunset over the ocean.

Floating in the hot water with Eve had a predictable effect upon his body, and soon Eve was straddling his lap, water sloshing heavily around them as her body undulated in his arms and her tight, slick depths caressed his aching length. Paradise.

Afterward, Marcus turned on the gas grill and got to work on the swordfish. They dined on that, accompanied by the salads and sides the caretaker had left. Then it was time to light a fire and curl together under the fuzzy cashmere blanket with Eve, legs tangled, talking as they watched the flames flicker around the chunks of wood.

The cuddling under the blanket transformed seamlessly into passion. He took his time, making her shivering and wet and yielding before they stumbled up the stairs.

In the darkness, he felt complete, clasped in Eve's arms.

Deep in the night, with Eve asleep, his nose buried in her silky hair, he put a name to the feeling that had been dogging him. He felt stupid, arriving at something so obvious so late. He'd heard the word all his life, from hopeful girlfriends, books, movies, songs.

Love. He'd always flinched away from the word. He wasn't flinching tonight. He was still and calm inside, observing the phenomenon. The way he felt about Eve. The person he was when he was with her.

The feelings opened doors in his brain, and memories flooded out. Other beaches, long ago. Warmer, sunnier ones. Making sandcastles with Mom, when he was three or so. Laughing and giggling and playing with her. Eating noodles and fried shrimp at her favorite restaurant. Swimming in the rippling blue water over the pale sand, his skinny arms wrapped around her neck.

The memory was achingly beautiful, bursting with happiness and love, but it made his heart hurt. For the other memory, brutally superimposed over it.

He's driving me crazy. I have got to get a break. For his own safety, understand?

That had been his first experience of love ending. Like the end of the world, like death. Being unwanted, unwelcome. He hadn't let himself feel it in years.

Which might explain why he so often felt nothing at all. Until now, anyway. He'd been rattled by all those unexpected feelings since the moment he met her. Every interaction felt amplified, significant, poignant. Full of wonder. Charged with meaning, and danger for his heart.

Eve rolled over, murmuring, "What are you thinking about?"

"You," he said.

She waited and finally spoke again. "That's lovely. What else?"

"Why? What do you mean?"

"You were thinking about something that made you sad."

Whoa, that was unnerving. "What?" he said warily. "Are you reading my mind?"

"No, I just recognized the frequency," she said quietly. "What else were you thinking?"

He relaxed his shoulders, slowly. "About my mother."

Eve cuddled closer, her face facing his. She had no trouble waiting for him to articulate the feeling. The silence got bigger, settling into a deep stillness that gave him the time he needed to find the words.

"I had good memories of her," he said, his voice halting.

"I blocked them. I was so angry at her sending me away. And then for dying. Being with you brings them back."

"What kind of memories?"

He shrugged. "I adored her. She was wonderful. She was my playmate. She swam with me, built sandcastles with me. She took me out to fancy restaurants. She let me sleep in her bed, when she didn't have a lover in it."

"It sounds wonderful," she said.

"It was," he said. "Until she got sick of me."

Eve shifted in his arms, pulling him into a tight embrace. "I'm so sorry."

"It was over thirty years ago. It's a wonder that I can remember her at all. But tonight, I can hear her voice. I can taste the papaya and the rice noodles."

"Are you okay?" she asked.

"I'm fine," he said. "It made me think about how I've always been with women. Expert at shoving them away. I didn't want to care about anyone that much, ever again. I'd never made that connection before. To my mom. Slow learner, huh?"

"Not at all," she said. "So how do you feel now?"

"All I know is, I don't want to push you away." His voice felt raw.

Eve lifted herself onto her elbow, leaning forward to kiss him. "So don't," she said.

"It's not that simple," he muttered.

"Actually, it is. Simple, but hard. I don't want to be pushed away. I've never felt like this before. I love it. I love…"

You. She had almost said it. But she had stopped herself. Too soon.

"I… I love being with you," she finished, her voice hushed. Uncertain.

Marcus rolled on top of her. "Good. Because I'm not going anywhere."

Fifteen

Eve stared at the ceiling, clasped in Marcus's strong arms. The sky outside the windows was turning the dull gray of dawn.

She'd come so close to letting it slip out last night. Blurting it out would have ruined everything. It was too soon to lay that on him. He would recoil from a strong emotion like that. He was notorious for it.

She'd almost blurted it out, as if the truth had a life of its own. Not that it could be any secret to anyone who saw how she fawned on him, following him around like a puppy, hanging on his every word.

Though, to be fair, he was hanging on her words, too.

Which tempted her to wonder if maybe this affair was different for him. It tempted her to hope for miracles.

She wished she could make herself stop hoping. It would be better if she could just enjoy this for what it was. But emotions wouldn't listen to reason, or consider the consequences. They burned through her, leaving a mess of smoke and ash.

She extricated herself from Marcus's embrace, somehow managing not to wake him. She twisted her hair up, took a quick shower, then dressed and headed downstairs.

The house was brightening with the magical glow of sunrise. So many windows. She made some coffee and slid on her shoes to go outside. She really needed a coat, but she was too intoxicated by the scents to get it. She smelled pine, salt, grass, wind and the sea as she sipped her coffee, watching the surf surge and retreat on the beach below.

Any direction she turned was stunning. To one side of the deck was a gully with a small stream that leaped through mossy rocks as it made its way to the edge of the bluff. The trees and foliage glittered with dewdrops on every surface. The murmur of the sea was mixed with the swish and rustle of the tree boughs.

"There you are." It was Marcus's voice, behind her.

She turned to smile at him as he came out the French doors in loose sweatpants and a waffle weave sweatshirt. He had a steaming cup of coffee in his hand.

"I tried not to wake you," she said.

"You didn't," he said. "I woke and found you gone. I felt bereft, so I went looking for you. I needed to make sure that it was real. Not just a beautiful dream."

"In the morning, I'd never go far without some serious coffee," she told him.

"Why are you awake so early? It's not as if you got much sleep."

"I'm buzzed," she admitted. "Overstimulated by sensual excess. I feel like I've been pounding Red Bull for twenty-four hours."

"I don't see that sensual excess decreasing," he said with a grin. "Unless you tell me it's too much, of course. In which case, I'll back off. In a heartbeat."

"Please don't," she said hastily. "The sensual excess is spectacular. Keep it coming."

"Thank God," he said. "You have no clue what it cost me to say that, but a guy's got to stay classy." He slid his arm around her waist. "Maybe once you get used to the sensual excess, you'll sleep better."

Getting used to it. Wouldn't that be nice, to get used to a thing so delicious. That would require settling into it. Trusting that it was going to be there.

It was too soon for that. It might always be too soon for that. But damn it, she would not wreck this gorgeous interlude in her life by being clingy. Nothing lasted forever. Life itself was temporary, for God's sake. The only real tragedy would be to not live this experience to the fullest. No matter the cost.

At least she didn't have to worry about Marcus being a parasite. He had vast quantities of money. She'd never have to carry him. One anxiety to cross off her list.

But there were plenty of other items on the list to stress about.

"I imagine I will," she said. "I have to relax sometime, right?"

"Is everything okay?"

"Oh, yes," she said swiftly. "It's just, you know. A big deal, for me. All of this."

"But you don't want to dial it down," he said.

She shook her head. "Carpe diem, baby. Seize the day."

"Yeah." Marcus raised his coffee cup. "Carpe diem."

Eve pushed her doubts and fears aside. There was no way to banish them completely, but she still managed to enjoy herself. He cooked a gourmet breakfast for her and then showed her a fabulous game involving raspberries, cream and his clever tongue.

After a long shower, they drove to Carruthers Cove and strolled along the main drag, trying out the fudge and the saltwater taffy, poking around junk shops and trinket shops. Marcus kept urging her to shop for new dresses, one for the final reception at the Landis Forum, another for the gala when they got back to Seattle.

"I brought a dress for the Landis Forum reception," she told him. "I'll model it for you when we get back to the house. It's very pretty. I'm sure you'll like it."

"I'm sure it looks great, but why not let me indulge you?"

"Because it's excessive, and unnecessary," she protested.

"You're very beautiful," he said. "I can afford it. It would be fun to adorn you. I would really get off on it. Indulge me. Please."

She met his eyes, full of patient humor, and wondered why she fought it so hard. As if accepting gifts from him would compromise her, weaken her somehow. God knew, she was already compromised. And she was starting to sound cranky and ungracious.

"Thank you," she said. "I'm…well, thank you. That's all."

"Most women as beautiful as you would invest all of their time and energy cultivating their looks," he commented. "It's a powerful card to play. But you don't seem to care all that much. You're more interested in playing the other amazing cards in your hand."

"Beauty the way the world values it is a huge investment of money and time," she said. "A person only has so much. The day is only twenty-four hours long."

"That's the God's own truth," he agreed swiftly. "So why not outsource some of that money and time and let me drape you in cloths of gold?"

She snorted. "Very slick, Moss."

"Keep in mind, being my wife is very high-profile," he said. "Not to stress you out, but your dresses will be photographed and remarked upon. The designer, the price, where you wore it before. They do it to Maddie, and Tilda now, too."

"Yikes," she murmured. "Is this your way of telling me I need to up my game?"

"No." Marcus rolled his eyes. "This is me pleading for the honor of buying you some hot dresses to showcase your stunning beauty. Tilda told me that the Bon Soir Boutique has good stuff."

"You are a man on a mission!"

"Surrender to my wicked wiles," he coaxed. "Ah! Speak of the devil. We're here."

Eve looked at a painted wooden sign over a walkway that led to a Victorian mansion that housed the Bon Soir Boutique. "We can get ice cream after," he wheedled. "Annika informed me of the best ice cream places and the best flavors. I will share that proprietary information with you, if you give me this one small thing."

She laughed. "You're terrible. Fine, Marcus. Drape me in cloths of gold, then. For the honor of the Moss Dynasty."

Marcus had surprisingly clear ideas and strong opinions for a guy. He also had a keen eye for what would look good on her. Once the shopkeeper realized he'd spend a crapton of money in her shop, she turned the place inside out for them.

In the end, Eve settled on a fitted cobalt blue dress with a tulip skirt that frilled out of the bottom for the Landis Forum reception. Then something caught Marcus's eye.

"Wait," he said, pulling one off the rack. "What about this one?"

He held up a gown of fine, pleated gold chiffon, edged with gold beads. The silk slip beneath was a deep gold, and the décolletage and hem were edged with the same gold-faceted beads. It was gorgeous. "Do you have this in her size?"

The shopkeeper beamed. "It's one of a kind. It might

be a bit big in the waist, but I could take it in. Would you like to try it on? I have a matching wrap and evening bag."

"Let's see it."

In the dressing room, the dress slid over her in a sensual caress, dropping perfectly into place around her, and hanging just right. It draped at the bust to showcase her cleavage, skimmed her hips, and the beaded hem had a luscious sway at her ankles.

She stepped out of the fitting room to show Marcus. "Cloths of gold," she said.

"Wow." His eyes glowed. "That one's for the Moss Foundation Gala."

"I love it," she admitted.

"Me, too." He sounded pleased with himself. "All men will envy me."

They made arrangements for the alterations, and Eve walked out feeling pampered.

"Ice cream?" Marcus asked.

"Oh, yeah," she told him. "Shopping works up my appetite."

They took a long barefoot stroll on the beach as they savored their ice cream. She went with the honey vanilla and chocolate madness. He had coffee mocha and pistachio. Icy salt water rushed over their toes and foamed around their ankles. Even his feet were beautiful. Long, brown, strong. Elegantly arched, with long toes. It had never occurred to her to admire a man's feet before. She had it so bad, it was scary.

That perfect day stretched into a perfect evening and then a perfect night. All five of the days they spent alone together melted seamlessly into a blissful dream. Long drives along the coast, leisurely hikes, trips to outdoor spas with steaming-hot mineral baths. Wild kissing on the couch, wild kissing on the beach, wild kissing in front of the fire.

It flew by too fast, and then it was over, and they were

planning for the arrival of her team. Sara was the first to show up. Marcus waited on the deck outside the front door to greet her, alongside Eve, who felt intensely self-conscious as her friend ran up the stairs, looking her over suspiciously as if scanning for damage.

She gave Eve a hug. "Honeymooning suits you," she said. "You're so rosy. I like it." She glanced at Marcus. "Is he treating you right?"

"Sara!" Eve hissed. "Don't embarrass me!"

"I do my very best," Marcus assured Sara.

The rest of her team trickled in over the next hour. When all six were there, they sat to a lavish catered seafood dinner. Her colleagues were awkward and shy with Marcus at first, but after prosecco and some bottles of pinot grigio, they loosened up, and soon Marcus fit in with them perfectly. Walter had never been able to follow the conversations when it veered into science, but when Marcus didn't understand something, he asked intelligent questions until he did.

He won them all over, except for perhaps Sara, who still harbored doubts.

The next day, they started in full Corzo-focus mode. Marcus stayed mostly out of the way, keeping the coffee flowing and the plates of goodies filled. He unobtrusively ensured that lunch and dinner happened at the appropriate intervals as they worked.

On the opening day of the forum, they met downstairs early in the morning, and piled into three cars. Eve was so nervous, she practically yelped when Marcus reached to pat her leg. "It's going to go well," he told her. "I can feel it."

She shot him a look. "Thanks, but I'm so rusty. I haven't spoken in public since before the Walter debacle, and it's a perishable skill."

"It's about time you got back into it," he said. "They're going to eat it up."

"Quite literally, if the catering company did the delivery of Corzo goodies to Paradise Point on time, that is. Damn, I forgot to call and check if it arrived!"

"I called," he assured her. "It's all there, and the tables are being arranged as we speak. It'll be smooth as silk. Your research is rock-solid, your team is strong, it's a sexy project. You've got this, Eve."

It was so sweet of him, to bolster her up. But the glow in his dark eyes made her insecurity stab deeper.

Yes, she had this. But what she wanted was him.

Forever and always.

Sixteen

"And so, ladies and gentlemen, that is the promise that Corzo delivers," Eve concluded. "Within a few years, rather than decades, the results can be seen from space." She clicked a slide, showing the satellite pictures, side by side. "These are two pictures of the same tract of eastern California desert," she said, indicating with the laser pointer. "This one is from three years ago. In this picture, you see the same place this year."

The satellite photo from three years ago was barren and pale, while the more recent photo was a luxuriant green. The difference was stark.

"This was after a year of even less rainfall than the three years prior," Eve said. "Add to that the effect on honeybee colonies, the carbon sequestering and the rich soil microbiome that makes the ecosystem resistant to disease and climate stress. I invite you to take a Corzo booklet and consider what place Corzo might have in your own plans to transform our planet's agriculture into something vital and sustainable, offering a future of hope and plenty for all. Thank you."

Thunderous applause. People rose for a standing ovation. The room was electrified.

Marcus could take no credit at all for any of her talent, but he was still fiercely proud. That smart, gorgeous, competent woman was his wife. *Whoa.*

"Oh, and ladies and gentlemen!" Eve called into the mic. "One last thing! I mentioned that Corzo's protein profile was as complete as any animal protein, but I did not tell you how delicious it is. That will be for all of you to decide. My team and I would like to offer you a refreshment of Corzo-based snacks! Try out sandwiches, hamburgers, muffins, cookies, pastries, cappuccino made with foamed Corzo milk, even a delicious Corzo beer! Enjoy!"

Laughter and more applause as the catering team whipped silver covers off the platters of food set up along the entire side of the room.

The crowd surged toward the buffet like a hungry herd to the trough.

Marcus left them to it and started pushing his way through the crowd toward Eve. She was shorter than the seething mass of mostly male venture capitalists who had found Eve herself more appetizing than the buffet, so it took some time to fight his way to her side. He kept at it, a pleasant smile plastered on his face as he pushed through the crowd.

Finally, he was right behind her. He laid his hand on her shoulder.

"Hey," he said. "That was amazing. You blew me away."

Eve gave him a brilliant smile over her shoulder, and opened her mouth to reply, then let out a squeak as he captured her mouth in a brief but possessive kiss. "I practically busted out the buttons in my shirt." He pitched his voice to be heard by at least three layers of the men crowded around her. "I kept thinking, damn. I can hardly believe that stunning woman is my bride."

"You guys are married?" said an aggrieved voice.

A tall, bearded guy whom she'd recognized as the CEO of a med-tech company looked crestfallen. "Congrats," he said to Marcus. "I didn't know you were married, Moss. I heard about your brother and your sister, but not about you."

"It happened really fast," Marcus said. "Once I spotted her, I had to snap her up fast. You know how it is. Carpe diem, right?"

"Lucky guy," someone from behind him said.

Marcus gave them all a hard, glittering smile. "Don't I know it." Subtext: *Don't even think about it, dudes. Let it go. For all time.*

His ruthless alpha-dog strategy loosened the crush, but he still ended up lingering like a smiling sentinel for twenty minutes while Eve chatted and networked.

When the tight crowd eased, he escorted her and her team around, making introductions to executives, investors, philanthropists and venture capitalists. They were stuffing their faces with the catered Corzo bounty, which looked very appetizing, especially with lunch still a couple of hours on the horizon.

Trevor Wexford, a venture capitalist whom Marcus knew and cordially disliked, swaggered by, his napkin loaded with Corzo mini-burgers, a cup of beer in his other hand. Trevor was a short, balding guy with a goatee and sharp, close-set dark eyes.

"My compliments for your presentation," Trevor said, his gaze raking Eve lasciviously. "I'd love to get together and talk."

"There's a sign-up sheet," Marcus reminded him. "You can reserve a half-hour slot to discuss partnership opportunities with her team in the afternoon time slots. There are only three slots left, so I'd move fast."

"Actually, I hoped to get you for a meal," Wexford said to Eve, waggling his eyebrows. "Maybe away from here, so we won't be constantly interrupted by all the people who constantly want your attention. Dinner tonight?"

"We're on our honeymoon, Trevor," Marcus said. "It's a working honeymoon, but meals are mine. Download the Landis Forum scheduling app on your phone, and book a slot like the rest of the teeming masses."

"Marcus!" Eve gave him a startled glance.

Whoops. He was overdoing it. He gave Eve an innocent smile. "Are you hungry?" he asked. "I can get you a plate. What's your pleasure? Sweet or savory?"

"I'll handle that myself," she said in a sharp, hushed voice. "I can handle a lot of things myself. From getting my own snacks to organizing my own appointments. I appreciate your zeal, but you're hovering."

"Yeah, don't hover," Trevor said, sneering. "Callista hates when I do that."

Yeah, in fact, Callista did hate that. She'd complained about it in their last encounter. Marcus knew Trevor's beautiful and sexually adventurous wife very well, since they had used each other for hot, no-strings sex on more than one occasion. But that was in the past, and he never kissed and told.

"Sorry," Marcus murmured. "The temptation is strong. But I'll fight it."

"You do that," Trevor said. He turned to Eve. "So? Dinner?"

"Let's start with the appointment schedule, so you can meet my team," Eve said.

Marcus rejoiced inwardly as Trevor shrugged. "If you insist," he said, stuffing another burger into his face and washing it down with beer. "The beer is like a good German weiss. When you went on about the protein profile, I thought the food would be birdfeed, but these juicy little beef burgers are tasty as hell."

"Actually, it's not beef," Eve told him. "That's Corzo. Not just the bread. The burger, too."

Trevor stopped chewing and stared. "Huh?"

"Mixed in with some other plant proteins, but yes."

Trevor stared at the burger in his hand, blinking. "Well, I'll be damned."

"We get that a lot," she said. "Enjoy!"

Marcus swept her off toward the next introduction, before she had a chance to scold him again, and she was quickly distracted by the task of charming another venture capitalist. The guy was camped out next to the beer table, already red-faced on his third glass. While Eve was charming him, Marcus noticed mini-jars of Corzo honey in a basket next to the coffee, tea and cappuccino station. He pocketed a few of them, and then spotted Annabelle Harlow, a middle-aged lady built like a brick wall, with a poufy mane of bright red hair and a Texas twang. She was an heiress to a massive Texas oil and gas fortune. He brought her over to meet Eve, and predictably, Eve charmed her. Annabelle then took Eve under her wing and introduced her to her own contacts.

And on it went. The day was long, intense. Caleb had strong-armed Landis into shifting Eve's Corzo presentation onto the very first day, so she could impress all the participants before any exhaustion, burnout or cynicism set in. Still, Corzo would've impressed them on any day and at any hour. Eve was tirelessly gorgeous and vibrant. Smart, charming, funny. He could watch her forever.

So could a lot of other guys. He couldn't help but notice. In fact, his biggest challenge was in controlling his impulses to be possessive of her time and attention. That would be childish and stupid. This was her moment to shine. It was her job to charm and impress these people, and it was his job to help her do it.

The whole week passed like that. A blur of constant networking and extroversion. Every afternoon session with the Corzo team was booked. By the time they got back to their house every night, it was long after dark, and the team dropped directly into bed.

Eve herself slept little. She was up late every night, tapping away at her laptop until long after midnight. If he were a dickhead, he'd be jealous. As it was, he dealt with it. He was the rainmaker. The magic man who made it all happen for her.

And it happened. By the final day, Corzo's future had been secured. They had more than enough investors to proceed. Eve's team was very friendly with him now, and he got several big hugs that last day before they headed back to the city.

Before Sara climbed into the driver's seat, she gave him a fierce hug and a narrow stare, focusing into his eyes. "Keep it up," she muttered.

Keep up what? Following Eve around, trying to keep her attention? Like he had any choice. He hugged Sara back. "I'll try," he promised.

Once Sara's taillights disappeared into the thick trees, Marcus let out a long sigh.

"Wow," he said. "That was intense."

"It sure was." Eve's hand found his, her fingers twining with his. "Thanks for making it all happen for me. You really delivered on your promise."

"I just facilitated. You're the one with the goods."

"You know damn well it wouldn't have gone that way without you. So thanks."

He squeezed her hand. "It was an honor."

They gazed out at the moon rising. "I'm glad it's just us again," Eve said.

"Me, too," Marcus said. "Even though I love your team. We have a few days before we have to be back for the gala. Shall we stay here until then?"

"That sounds great." Eve headed inside, tugging him after herself.

He followed her through the house, still cluttered from Corzo meetings. Up the stairs into the bedroom. Eve kicked off her shoes. "I'm grabbing a quick shower."

Marcus threw off his coat and shirt, and kicked off his shoes. He was reminded of that moment during their wedding ceremony. The panic attack, or whatever it was. Like pressure was building inside him, energy about to burst out, but he had no idea what it would look like when it did.

The bathroom door opened, and Eve came out in a cloud of steam, wrapped in a towel, her mass of curly dark hair damp and fuzzed with misty droplets. So sweet and fragrant. Her eyes were so bright and deep. Her lips so red.

The words fell out of his mouth. "I love you," he said.

Eve's mouth fell open. Her eyes went huge.

"You don't have to say anything," he added. "I never said that before to anyone. It just…did a jailbreak. I know it's too soon. Sorry."

"Marcus, I—"

"You don't have to respond. I know it's not—"

"Marcus, stop." Her voice was crisp. "Let me respond how I want to. Don't try to control my reaction."

"Okay," he said swiftly. "Respond, then."

"I love you, too," she said.

He stared at her until he could speak again. "You…you do?"

"Ass over teakettle," she said. "Ever since that first dinner with you, when you found me at the lab and proposed to me. I've been fighting this feeling so hard. But you make it impossible. You're so sweet and sexy. Fun to be with. I can't resist."

"That first night here, you, are…" His voice trailed off. "You started to say…"

"I almost blurted it out," she admitted. "But I stopped myself. I didn't want to scare you, or be too clingy. I was trying to play it cool."

"No," he said. "I don't want you to play it cool. I want all the heat. Cling all you want. It'll never be enough for me. I want all of you."

She let the towel drop. "You can have all of me," she said.

Just a split second of unbelieving joy, and she was in his arms. Then she was beneath him on the bed, arms and legs clasping him. Holding him. So sweet. Her skin was flower-petal soft, her scent made him dizzy. He gulped it in.

He got his pants off somehow, kicking and struggling. It was her flowerlike scent that reminded him, and he reached into the bedside drawer until he found his prize. The little jars of Corzo honey that he'd stowed in there, for occasions such as this.

She laughed when she saw them. "What's this? Have you been purloining the swag, Moss?"

"I earned this honey," he told her, as he opened one. "I've been thinking about it ever since that night when I kissed it off your lips. I love the taste of it, mixed with the taste of you."

Her laughter cut off into a moan of startled pleasure as he painted her taut, perfect, deep-pink nipple with honey, smearing it until it gleamed in the dim light. "I love you," he said again, loving the way the words made him feel. "I love you."

He bent to suck the honey off her nipple, and she arched beneath him, gasping. He just kept on saying it, even though the words were muffled by having his mouth full and his tongue busy.

But he didn't stop. He would never get tired of saying it.

Seventeen

"Gran's texting me to rescue her from Joanna Hollis," Marcus murmured into her ear. "Excuse me. I'll be back as soon as I can. That Hollis woman will talk our ears off."

Eve smiled at him. "Okay, good luck with it. Later."

Marcus kissed her, as he did every time he walked away, even just to the next room. She followed his progress helplessly with her eyes as he strode away. So gorgeous.

The world glowed with promise. She was decked out in the gorgeous golden gown he'd bought for her at the coast, and it made her feel so beautiful. She'd given in to her feelings for him completely. She couldn't help it. She was entertaining hopes and dreams and longings she'd never dared to voice before. Like children, for instance. When to have them. How many, what to name them. They were leaving for a two-week honeymoon that weekend, some stunning South Sea island that Marcus wanted to show her. Sugar sand, palm trees, pale blue water.

She was practically living with him, going home only to

water the plants and get fresh clothes, but she still hadn't had time to officially move in, not with Corzo taking off, plus the time that a red-hot love affair took out of her schedule. The genome project was missing her, too. There just weren't enough hours in the day. Busy, busy.

She intercepted a seething glance from the next table out of the corner of her eye. It was Teresa Haber, whom she'd seen at Maddie and Jack's wedding. The woman's eyes slid away quickly. She was probably still pining for Marcus.

Sara sat next to Eve, stunning in a tight red silk sheath. "Just look at that," Sara murmured as she followed Marcus's progress across the room. "He ticks all the boxes. Smart, rich, handsome, affectionate, a kick-ass engineer, he adores you and he's wicked good in bed, right? Tell me the truth, now."

"Sara! People will hear you!"

"It'll be nothing they haven't heard before," Sara teased. "But as long as all of that famous skill is totally at your service, I guess it's okay."

"He assures me it is," Eve said. "And I believe him."

"Well, then," Sara said with satisfaction. "Great. Couldn't happen to a nicer person. All your wildest dreams. You have some big magic, Eve."

"Thanks. I try."

The room fell silent as the emcee quieted everyone before calling on Tilda Moss, Marcus's gorgeous sister-in-law. Tilda came to the podium and started her speech. She talked about the many applications of the FarEye project, and how it could figure into the Moss Foundation's philanthropic projects in the developing world.

Tilda was an excellent speaker, and Eve and Sara were listening with interest, when a man walking past stumbled against their table. It rattled and swayed, and dumped a glass of red wine right onto the front of Sara's dress.

Sara jerked back with a gasp of dismay, grabbing a napkin and dabbing frantically. "Excuse me. I'm running off to the ladies' to fix this."

"Gotcha. Good luck."

The man who had stumbled into the table used it to shove himself upright, making the plates and glasses rattle and shake again, and Eve recognized Trevor Wexford. The guy had pledged to invest a hefty sum in Corzo, which meant she had to be polite to him, even if he was obnoxious, and somewhat handsy. And on this occasion, extremely drunk.

"Good evening, Mr. Wexford," she said, hoping his wife wasn't nearby. The beautiful Callista was always full of snark.

Trevor swung his head around. His dark, close-set button eyes fastened onto her face. "Oh," he said loudly. "So it's you!"

"Yes, it is," she said. "Please, keep quiet. I'm listening to the speech."

"You're telling me to shut up? Hell of a thing, coming from you."

Eve gave him a blank look. "Huh? What are you talking about?"

"I'll tell you what." Wexford lurched forward, catching himself on the table once again. "You're a fraud. Your whole project is a freaking...goddamn...*fake*!"

Trevor was so loud, Tilda paused in her speech, casting a puzzled glance in their direction. When she spoke again, Eve exhaled and turned back to Wexford, wondering how best to manage him. The guy was clearly hallucinating.

She should get this drunken idiot out of people's way before he disrupted the presentation. She'd spent enough time with her father while he was drunk to know that a man in a contentious mood would always follow an argument, wherever it might lead. He'd never just let it walk out of the room unchallenged.

She rose and headed for the exit. Sure enough, Trevor followed right after, spoiling for a fight.

When she was right outside the ballroom door, in the large lobby area, she turned around, crossing her arms over her chest, waiting until he followed her out.

"Okay, Trevor," she said, when the door had fallen shut. "What the hell are you talking about?"

"I know, Eve." He got in her face, forcing her to avoid the blast of his hot breath. "I know all of it. Everyone knows."

She shook her head. "Everyone knows what?"

"That you falsified your research! You were going to take the money and run, but we're onto you now. You're a fraud, and a thief!"

"But I never—"

"Ah, there you are, sweetheart." Callista, Trevor's wife, resplendent in a black, low-cut sequined gown, slunk sinuously out the ballroom door.

"Do you know what he's going on about?" Eve asked her.

"Certainly," Callista said. "We heard that your original research data has been altered to look more favorable than it really is. We've seen the originals, along with the doctored versions, side by side. We can't be fooled any longer."

"I never doctored anything!" Eve was outraged. "Never in my life!"

"In the face of all this evidence, how can we possibly believe you now?" Callista asked sweetly. "You got farther than most would, I'll give you that, but you can't fool us."

"I have never tried to fool anyone! My research is absolutely sound!"

"Well, be that as it may, I'll take Trevor and get back to the gala," Callista said. "Enjoy it while you can, because I have a feeling you'll soon be persona non grata. Have a nice evening!"

Eve watched, aghast, as Callista dragged her husband by the arm, scolding him as he tottered alongside her.

Doctored evidence? Fraud? What the hell?

Eve ran as fast as her heels would allow to the nearest women's restroom, hoping she'd happen on the one that Sara had chosen. The room with the rows of sinks was deserted, so she turned the corner toward the bathroom stalls, calling out. "Sara! Sara? Are you still in here?"

Nothing. She turned the corner toward the sinks again and stopped.

Teresa Haber stood there, hyperextending her impressive backside as she bent to apply fresh red lipstick to her puckered mouth.

Teresa turned. "Ah, there you are."

"Why?" Eve asked, in trepidation. "Were you looking for me?"

"I noticed you tangling with Trevor," Teresa said. "What a slob, right? Getting blind drunk here, of all places. Such a bozo. What did he want?"

"That's no one's business but mine," Eve told her.

"Oh, don't get snippy. I'm trying to help. He was freaking out about the rumor about the Corzo project, right? He hates being fooled."

Eve's blood pounded in her ears. "What have you heard about that?" Her voice sounded far away.

"It's not like I'm surprised." Teresa rolled her eyes. "Corzo was too good to be true, right? I mean, please. It feeds the planet, it saves the bees, and it cures cancer in its free time. Give me a freaking break. You should've eased down a little on the save-the-planet eco-hype. It was way over-the-top."

"I have never misrepresented my research! Whoever is slandering my work is a goddamn liar!"

"Honey. Please." Teresa's voice was condescending. "Ethics are all very well and good, but we all know that the rules change when billions of dollars are at stake."

"No, actually." Her voice rang in the echoing marble

room. "They don't change for me. I don't give a shit about the money. My research is rock-solid. Someone's out to get me, and I have to find out who."

Teresa dropped her lipstick back into her evening bag and studied Eve as she smeared her lips together. "You know what?" she asked, in a wondering tone. "I believe you. Which is miraculous, considering the cynical bitch that I am. You're very convincing. That wild-eyed crusader look in your eyes can't be faked."

Eve studied her, wary. "I'm not sure how to respond to that."

Teresa shrugged. "My point is, I think that the buzz about Corzo is deserved."

"Okay," Eve said. "So what's your point?"

"Ask yourself, Eve," Teresa said. "Who benefits from this?"

"No one!" she said.

Teresa snorted. "You're so naive. If all of your investors bail, who's the knight in shining armor who will pick up the pieces, and fund your amazing, game-changing big idea? You don't think people have been scheming and plotting to get a piece of you ever since the news about Corzo hit? Even if they have to tear you into bloody pieces to get it?"

Eve was still bewildered. "What are you saying?"

"I'm talking about MossTech. Your adoring husband. I've seen this before, Eve. First, he drapes you with gold and gems, kisses your hand and tells you that you're his precious little princess. He always does that when he wants something. In this case, Corzo. I mean, yeah, Corzo is a game-changer, and I'd scheme for a piece of it, too. But he's an ice-cold whoring bastard to use you like that."

In the mirror behind Teresa, Eve glimpsed her own face. It was chalky white, her eyes horrified, her lipstick bright against her pallor.

"No," she forced out. "That can't be true."

"Face it, Eve," Teresa said. "When everything falls to shit, MossTech will be there, ready to save you. They want your billion-dollar idea for themselves. Marcus is a diabolical manipulator. I can bear witness. He takes what he wants from a woman, and when he's done, he tosses her. He did it to me. He'll do it to you."

"No," she repeated. "No way."

"I didn't want to believe it, either," Teresa said. "Of course, my time with Marcus was brief. I didn't have any amazing intellectual property that he wanted. But it's the same pattern. He courts you, he squeezes you, he dumps you. I could find dozens of women who could tell you the exact same story."

"No." Eve kept repeating it, as if she could ward Teresa's words away.

Teresa's eyes widened as a new thought came to her. "Oh! Do you know how he found you? Funny story. It's been making the rounds. The administrative staff in his office like to gossip, you see."

Eve braced herself for a fresh blow. "He said he'd heard about Corzo, and he thought he could do something to help the project," she said. "That's all."

"Nope." Teresa's tone was triumphant. "He drew your name out of a bag, like a party game. It was random, Eve. That's how much he cares. And because he's a lucky bastard, he drew the name of the girl with the billion-dollar idea. You were a lottery number. No more, no less. He picked you, and he played you."

Eve backed away. "Get away from me."

"I've said my piece. I thought you should know. Truth is better, even when it hurts."

"I don't trust you," Eve said.

"Good luck, Eve. I mean that sincerely, from one Marcus Moss ex to a future one." She walked out, hips swaying.

Eve bent over for a couple of minutes to get the blood

into her head, or she would have ended up on the floor. Her insides churned. Her hands were ice-cold.

Come on, Seaton. No smelling salts for you.

She splashed her face with cold water and checked to make sure her makeup was presentable. Eve stumbled out of the restroom, trying to remember which ballroom entrance was nearest her table, but everything in her head had been displaced by this huge, indigestible fact.

Marcus? Playing her...for Corzo?

Impossible. She couldn't have gotten him this wrong.

She saw a red flash out of the corner of her eye. Sara was hurrying toward her.

Her friend grabbed her arms. "Eve, are you okay? Your face is bone white. Are you sick?"

"Sara," she said "We have a problem."

"Damn right we do," Sara said, stealing her over to one of the ornate antique-style love seat benches that lined the walls of the lobby. "I just talked to Richard Martelle."

"Did he say he's gotten a tip about Corzo?" she asked. "Did he say he'd heard that our research is bogus?"

"You too, huh? Yes."

"I got it from Trevor Wexford," Eve said. "And Teresa Haber."

Sara's mouth tightened. "Somebody's lying ass needs a whooping," she said. "And I'm the one to deliver it. As soon as we pin the rat bastard down."

Eve shook her head. "But how...who would do something like this?" she whispered. "Why?"

Sara's fingers tightened, and she pulled Eve toward her, giving her a tiny shake. "Don't look like that, Eve. It's going to be okay. We'll get through this, just like all the other crap we've gotten through."

Someone emerged from the ballroom. It was Henry O'Calloran, another one of Corzo's investors. She leaped up and hurried toward him. "Henry! Stop!"

Henry, a balding guy with rimless round glasses, turned around, a nervous look in his pale-lashed eyes. "Oh. Eve. I'm in a rush, so—"

"You heard that malicious rumor, right? You got the tip?"

"Ah, yes," Henry admitted. "I did."

"Who was it from?" she demanded.

"Eve." Henry backed away nervously. "I don't want to get involved, okay?"

"I'm not asking you to get involved. I deserve to know who is slandering my work. It costs you nothing, Henry. Just tell us who."

Henry huffed. "It was an anonymous text. Whoever did it sent a package to all the investors with hundreds of pages of attached documents. The originals, and alongside, the altered versions that you shared with us."

"That's a lie," she said. "The research results I showed you were genuine. You're being played by someone, but not by me."

Henry looked from her to Sara and back again. "That might be so, but at the moment, I am not in any position to make the financial commitment we discussed before," he said. "Not until I know more."

"Forward me that text message," Eve said.

Henry harrumphed. "It's inappropriate of you to make demands, under the circumstances—"

"Forward me the goddamn message, Henry. I'm not asking that much."

"Fine." Henry pulled out his phone, scowling, and poked at it. "There. I forwarded it to you and Sara. And if you'll excuse me, I need to get back to my wife."

Eve and Sara both pulled their phones out of their evening bags and hunched over them, heads together, clicking open the attachment.

It was just as Henry had said. Page after page of the research they'd made available to all the potential investors. Each page was placed alongside another slightly altered version of the same document, making it seem as if their originals had been doctored to make the results look more favorable. The way it was presented, it looked very bad for Corzo.

"Even if we go around to the investors one by one to prove them wrong, this hurts us," Sara said. "The project will be tainted by doubt."

Eve swallowed hard as she thought about Teresa's accusation. "It was sent from a cell phone number."

"Probably a burner," Sara said. "Whoever did this is a lying coward."

"There must be ways to figure out whose number it is, right?"

"Sure," Sara said, tapping into her phone. "We reverse-search it. I got familiar with that when I had a cheating husband. He kept taking 'work calls' out on the deck, in the cold, for hours. So I snagged his phone. That's when I found Suzanne, Regina, Karen, Kiki, and discovered what a tomcat skank he was. SwiftSearchNet is my favorite reverse-search tool. It deep-searches the entire internet, and it's faster than all the…oh…"

Sara's voice faded away and she looked at Eve, her eyes wide and startled.

Eve wouldn't have thought her insides could drop still lower than they already were, but they did. Like an express elevator. A hard, sickening plunge.

"Who?" she asked, though she already knew. "Who is it? Show me."

"Baby," Sara whispered. "I am so, so sorry." Reluctantly, she turned her phone so Eve could see the screen, and the name in the search box.

Marcus James Moss.

Eighteen

"Are you sure you don't want to call the doctor?" Marcus asked Eve again as they walked into his apartment. "She can come here. She's always on call for us."

"No," Eve said. "I don't need a doctor."

Marcus studied her face, worried. She really did not look good. Colorless and haunted. Switched off. Like a house with all the window shades drawn.

After Tilda's speech, before the dancing started, she'd told him she was feeling sick and needed to go home. She'd urged him to stay. She'd said she could take a car and go home alone.

Hell, no. If she was sick, he needed to take care of her.

"Can I go out to the pharmacy for you?" he asked. "I can get anything you need."

"No," she repeated, taking off her coat. "There's no need."

Marcus felt helpless. "I wish there was something I could do to help."

Eve unhooked the gold chain necklace that he'd given

her to go with the golden dress. "I heard something very upsetting at the gala," she said.

Hairs rose on his nape. "What happened?"

"Trevor Wexford got an anonymous tip that my Corzo research was falsified."

Marcus's jaw dropped. "That's a huge lie!"

"I know," Eve said. "But someone is trying to sabotage me."

"Trevor Wexford, you said?" Marcus asked. "He's an asshole and an idiot. I'm guessing that whatever he saw won't affect the other investors."

"Wrong. They're pulling out, one after another. Henry O'Calloran, Richard Martelle, both gone. And in the car going home, I got a text from Annabelle Harlow. She's putting a hold on her investment, too. The others will follow. They're spooked."

"We'll fix it, Eve," he said. "I'll talk to them. All of them."

"Will you."

Her flat tone was so unlike her usual voice, it alarmed him. "What the hell is that supposed to mean?" he demanded.

"I'm just wondering. How do you propose to fix this dilemma? Corzo, tragically orphaned once again. What's your brilliant solution, Marcus?"

"I definitely will try to find a solution, but I don't understand your tone," he said.

"Never mind my tone. It's been a rough night, and I'm miserable. I want to know how you would solve my problem."

"First, I find out who spread the rumor," he said. "I expose him, or her. Then I talk to the investors and offer my personal guarantee as to the authenticity of your research."

"Ah," she said. "Very generous of you."

He stared at her. "The hell? Why do you sound sarcastic? What is it with you tonight?"

"No, please, go on. What will you do if they're still too scared to commit?"

"If they have any brains, they'll get over themselves and jump back on board."

"And if they don't have brains? A lot of people don't. And even smart people make poor decisions when they get scared."

Marcus shrugged. "Then we find new, smarter investors who have more nerve."

"Everyone will have heard the rumors," she said. "The project will be irreversibly tainted. Corzo will be damaged goods. No one will want to touch it."

"We'll fix it, Eve," he insisted. "We'll rebrand. Worst-case scenario, you could always count on MossTech. We could provide the funding to develop Corzo, if you don't find any other options you like better."

Her eyes fixed on him, bright and searching. "So, Moss-Tech buying my idea and owning it? That's your solution?"

"That's 'a' solution," he said grimly. "Let me work on it, for God's sake. I just wanted you to know that there are always options."

But she wasn't listening anymore. Her eyes were bleak, faraway.

"So it's true," she whispered. "I did it again. With the pinpoint accuracy of a guided missile. Just like Walter or Hugh, or Doug. I hooked up with another guy who wants to rob me blind. I swear to God, it's like I'm under a curse."

Marcus sucked in air, horrified. "What? Are you talking about me?"

"The tip was sent from a cell phone registered to your name," she told him. "I don't recognize the number, but it's registered to you. Sara reverse-searched it."

"Let me see that number." He held out his hand.

Eve took her phone from her evening bag, opened the message and handed it to him. Marcus opened it, read the opening message.

Did you think Corzo was too good to be true? You were right. See attached.

He paged through some of the attached documents. "I've never seen this message before," he said. "I certainly did not send it."

"Do you recognize the phone number?" Eve asked.

He hesitated for a second. "Yes," he admitted. "That's a number that I used before I met you. Mostly for hookups. That phone's been missing for weeks."

"Missing," Eve said. "That's convenient. You never gave me that number."

"Of course not," he said. "That phone was for people that I didn't want to take calls from during my working day. I made a point of keeping my sex life completely separate from work and family. Until I met you."

"What became of that phone?"

"I don't know." He was feeling hunted. "It disappeared. I lost it."

"Lost it?" she repeated slowly. "Marcus. You're the most careful, meticulous, uber-controlled person I know. You never lose things."

"I lost that phone," he repeated. "I didn't think about it much, though. I didn't need it after I met you. It barely crossed my mind. I was very occupied with you."

"I suppose I should be flattered to get the main number and not the one for the side girls and the one-offs," she said. "Quite the honor to be singled out like that."

"You believe I would do this to you? If anyone, it was Jerome. Caleb said he would come after us. But I did not see this coming."

She slipped off her heels and headed upstairs, shoes dangling from her fingertips. "It's easy and convenient to blame Jerome. He's already cast himself as the bad guy."

He followed her. "Eve, come on. I'm not a damned idiot.

If I had been sabotaging you, I wouldn't have done it from a phone registered in my name!"

"Is that supposed to comfort me?" She headed for the bathroom, where she leaned over the sink and popped out her contact lenses.

He stood in the doorway as she tucked them into their cases and covered them with saline solution. "I would never steal from you," he said. "Or anyone. It's not who I am."

Eve put on her glasses, and pushed past him into the bedroom, unfastening the golden gown. She kept her back carefully turned to him as she hung up the dress. She pulled jeans, a tee and a wool sweater out of the drawer, and dressed quickly, then pulled a pair of white kicks out of his closet. She sat on the bed to pull them on.

He was starting to panic. "Eve, are you listening? Are you leaving me?"

Her eyes were so bleak, it was like a punch to the chest. "I need alone time," she said. "To figure out what is going on. I can't do that with you taking up all the air and scrambling my brain." She tied her shoes and rose, slipping her laptop into its carrying bag and hoisting it over her shoulder. "This marriage thing," she said. "It won't work if you're using me. I can't let myself be used again. I'm sorry."

"But I'm not! You're making a bad call!"

"I'm a scientist," she said. "I make decisions based on the evidence. Wherever it leads me. Regardless of how I feel, or what I might have hoped."

"Bullshit," he said. "This is a knee-jerk reaction to all the guys who screwed you over before. I didn't do that, and I never would. I swear it, Eve. Again."

"I can't stand being made a fool of for the umpteenth time," she said.

"Don't go," he pleaded. "Let's figure this out together. I'll show you it wasn't me. I don't know how yet, but I will. The truth always comes out."

She stopped in the bedroom doorway and turned. "Speaking of the truth coming out, will you tell me something, Marcus?"

"Anything," he said rashly.

"Is it true that you picked my name out of a bag? In front of your admin staff at MossTech? Like a party game. Pin the tail on the donkey. Fish the gullible geek bride out of the hat. Who's the lucky girl? Ha, ha, very jolly."

Marcus stopped breathing. "It wasn't like that," he said. "I hadn't even met you yet. And how is this even relevant?"

"I guess it's not. It just makes me feel even more ridiculous, that's all. Eve Seaton, eternally the butt of the joke. God knows I should be used to it by now."

He followed her out the bedroom door, down the hall, down the stairs. "Eve, let me show you—"

"I've seen enough. I'm done for now. Goodbye, Marcus."

She grabbed her jacket and purse. He reached the bottom of the stairs in time to see tears streaming from her eyes as the elevator door slid shut between them.

He stood there for a long time. Minutes, hours. Eventually he forced his muscles to unlock and wandered from room to room. At one point, he found a chair near the back of his legs, so he sat, clumsily.

Jerome. This was Jerome's doing. He found his phone, and selected his uncle's number.

Jerome answered right away, as if he'd been waiting for this call.

"Marcus." His voice was cool and dragging. "At this hour? I'm an old man. I need my rest."

"You're responsible for this, aren't you?"

Jerome made a scoffing sound. "Throw me a rope, boy. What's this about?"

"Don't deny it," Marcus said. "You sent that tip to Eve's investors with my phone. The one you must have stolen. You want her to think that I'm trying to take Corzo."

"It would be a slick business move, if you had done it," Jerome observed. "I'd congratulate you for it. Corzo would be a jewel in MossTech's crown. I'd respect you far more if you'd own it, and not playact to soothe the little lady's ruffled feelings. But I understand your position. You're whipped, boy. It hurts to watch."

"I'm not playacting," he said.

"No? Is she standing there with you, listening to this conversation? Is this why you're putting on all this touching outrage? For her benefit?"

"It's just you and me," Marcus said. "She's gone."

Jerome grunted thoughtfully. "That's women for you. Flighty, changeable."

"Fuck you, Jerome."

"No need to be crude," Jerome chided. "This might be a blessing for you."

A harsh laugh jerked out of his throat. "Oh, yeah? How do you figure?"

"It's best to learn the truth about women early," Jerome said. "I learned late, and I suffered for it. It always blows up on you eventually, Marcus. You can't let yourself get attached. Keep women at a distance. Enjoy them, certainly, but keep them in their place."

"I'm not interested in love advice from you."

Jerome was undaunted. "She would've gotten tired of you, when she'd gotten what she could get out of you. You'd start looking at the other women trying to get your attention. Face it. You're a rich man. That's all women can see. They don't see you. They might pretend, but they can't pretend forever."

Marcus wanted to shout him down, prove him wrong, but his voice had frozen.

"So?" Jerome prompted. "Maybe this will be the lesson that sinks in. I got mine, years ago. It's time for you to get yours. Let her go. Better to face reality sooner rather than later."

"Yeah, and that works out great for you, doesn't it,

Uncle? You trashed my marriage to get your greedy claws into MossTech. Are you happy now?"

"I wouldn't say 'happy,'" Jerome responded. "But a man takes his victories when he can. It's the only satisfaction one ever gets in this world."

"Cold comfort," Marcus said.

"Maybe. Better cold than nothing."

"I don't want to be like you," Marcus said.

Jerome's low laugh was full of bitterness. "I don't blame you, boy."

Marcus closed the call. How ironic. That conversation, full of hostility and manipulation, was probably the most real and personal interaction he'd ever had with Jerome. Cold comfort for sure.

His phone dropped. Time crawled by. He stared out at the city, a howling ache inside him. Memories were floating up again, from that hurting inside place that he'd never wanted to feel again. Pain and fear. Grief. That endless, sinking cold ache.

He's driving me crazy. I have got to get a break. For his own safety, understand?

Safety. Huh. Like he was so safe now, with that screaming black hole inside him. Hell, maybe it would've ended like this anyway. Love ended. Mom's love certainly had.

He was done with them. Eve and her trust issues, Gran and her stupid mandate, his brother and sister, and their nudging and maneuvering. Jerome's lies and traps. Moss-Tech. To hell with it. All of it.

But first, he'd fix this mess. He'd failed to protect Eve and Corzo from his uncle, so his first task was to save her funding. Afterward, he was out of here. Someplace warm, with a beach. A good natural climate for orchids. Flowers told no lies, nor did they believe any.

They were all that might keep him from turning into Uncle Jerome.

Nineteen

"Yes, I understand." Eve's voice cracked as she spoke. "I'll come in first thing tomorrow to pick them up. Thanks. Have a nice day."

She closed the call, laying the phone on the table. Gingerly, as if handling a loaded gun.

Sara stood there in the kitchen, the pot of steaming French-press coffee she'd been about to pour in her hand. "Who was that?" Sara asked. "What do you have to pick up?"

"The divorce papers." Her voice felt choked, so she coughed to clear it. "I have to take them to Marcus to sign."

"And will he?"

"I guess I'll find out when I call him," Eve said. "We haven't spoken in weeks."

She squeezed her hands together, fighting it until suddenly, she couldn't anymore. Her face dissolved, and the tears slipped out. "I'm so sorry I ruined this for the team."

"Oh, honey." Sara put the coffee down and hurried over

to the table, pulling a chair close so she could wrap Eve in a tight hug. "Don't feel bad about that. We knew it was a long shot. This whole thing sucks. Mostly for you."

"I'm so angry, but I miss him, too," she said. "And I miss who I was with him. The way the world felt. It feels dull and empty and stupid now."

"He's a filthy son of a bitch for doing this to you," Sara said. "You don't deserve it. You really don't, babe. You're the best person I know."

"Thanks." Eve gave her a wan smile. "Sorry I'm such a mess."

"Oh, please," Sara said, rolling her eyes. "When I called Michel to sign the divorce papers, I cried for three days. Michel was a philandering slut, but we shared some great times, and it was so hard to let go. The ninety-day waiting period was a torture of second-guessing myself." She fished out a tissue and handed it over.

Eve gratefully made use of it. "He was so convincing. He made me feel like I was a goddess come down to earth just for him. And it was so great to be with someone who actually got what I do, you know?"

"He might have 'got it' a little too well," Sara said ruefully.

Eve started to laugh, but the laughter swiftly morphed into tears.

"Oh, crap. I'm sorry," Sara said hastily. "I didn't mean to rub salt in the wound."

"I would never have dreamed he'd do that to me." She hid her face in the tissue. "He was so supportive. He busted his ass at the forum. And then he turns around and undermines all the amazing work he'd done. It was all an incredibly expensive, complicated, seductive trap. And I tumbled right into it."

"We might as well take it as a twisted compliment," Sara

said in philosophical tones. "But the lying, scheming bastard has definitely got issues."

"Speaking of scheming bastards, I never dreamed that Walter would rob me, either," Eve said dolefully. "Or Hugh, for that matter. You'd think that growing up watching my dad would have vaccinated me against men like him, but it seems to have had the opposite effect. It left me with a huge blind spot. I'll never be able to trust my own instincts when it comes to men. I should swear off them completely."

"Come on, honey, don't think that way. You are not the problem here. You are enormously lovable. You deserve love."

"But it felt like Marcus loved me," Eve wailed. "It's so confusing. I don't know what to think. Red could be blue, day could be night, for all I know. Who can tell, if you can't trust your own perceptions?"

"You'll trust yourself again someday," Sara said. "But you have a couple of hard tasks ahead of you." She held up one finger. "One, call Marcus about the papers." She held up another finger. "Two, go get him to sign. It'll be awful, but you'll live."

Eve closed her eyes, rubbing them. "God," she whispered.

"Do the first one right now, before you psych yourself out of it," Sara urged. "Cross it off the list."

It was good advice. She reached for her phone and found Marcus's number. Her fingers shook. She hit Call, and it rang twice before the line opened.

"Marcus here," he said.

His voice was so flat, she barely recognized it.

"Hello, Marcus. It's Eve," she said.

"I know."

Of course he knew. His smartphone had told him. Such a stupid thing to say.

She inhaled carefully, taking her time. *Do not babble. Do not stammer. Just don't.*

"I, ah, called because I…" Her voice ran out of sound, like a printer running out of ink.

"Because?" he prompted, after a few seconds.

"I, um, I have the papers ready," she said. "The divorce papers. I'm going to get them from my lawyer tomorrow morning. I was wondering if you would… I mean, if we could…" She swallowed, and tried again, from the top. "We have to meet. To sign the papers. So I can file."

She counted six breaths before Marcus finally replied. "Of course," he said. "Let's meet in the law offices of Moss-Tech tomorrow. Is eleven good for you?"

Like she would quibble. Like she had any kind of gainful occupation. Her life was scorched earth.

"Certainly," she said. "Eleven is fine. See you then."

"Till tomorrow. Goodbye, Eve."

Such finality in his voice. Eve closed the call and stared into space. Her chest ached.

"Is he going to contest it?" Sara asked. "Will he give you any trouble?"

"No trouble at all," she quavered. "He'll be as relieved as I am to have it over with."

Sara pried another tissue out of the pack and passed it to her. Eve pressed it to her eyes, only opening them when an odd thumping sound got her attention.

Sara was setting various items on the table. The pot of steaming coffee. Three bottles of liqueur. A big bar of fine dark chocolate. She filled their mugs more than halfway with coffee, then splashed in a generous shot of Baileys, and other things that Eve's eyes were too tear-blinded to identify. She topped it off with a slug of heavy cream.

"What's this?" Eve asked.

"Today calls for a special coffee," Sara informed her. "You're not driving, because I'm not letting you go anywhere, and you need a Dutch courage to take divorce papers to the great and powerful Marcus Moss."

Eve eyed the doctored coffee dubiously. "And meet with Marcus hungover?"

"Don't wimp out on me, girl." Flakes of chocolate drifted over the table as Sara started grating dark chocolate onto the drinks and then stirred Eve's with a cinnamon stick. She broke off a chunk of chocolate and leaned it against the mug. "I was a bartender back in grad school, remember? This was one of my most decadent creations. Go on. Try it."

Eve took a sip and had to smile. "Wow. It's delicious. And extremely strong. I bet my entire calorie count for the day is in this one mug."

"Probably," Sara agreed. She lifted her mug. "Here's to facing scary, painful obstacles. And to soldiering on in the face of crushing disappointment."

Eve raised her mug. "To soldiering on," she repeated. "And to loyal friends that you can cry on."

That melted them down, and they hugged tightly. By the time they got back to the coffee, it was stone-cold, but whatever.

They just had to make the best of it.

Marcus laid his cell phone on the greenhouse table and returned to pruning the hibiscus. Maddie and Tilda and Annika stood there, watching him as if he were a bomb that could explode at any moment.

"Who was that?" Maddie asked.

He braced himself. "Eve," he said.

After a few moments, Maddie and Tilda exchanged exasperated glances.

"And?" Maddie prompted. "What did she want?"

"The divorce papers are ready to sign. Tomorrow morning."

Maddie gulped. Tilda turned away, her slim shoulders sagging.

"Look, I'm sorry," he said. "I tried. But if I'd known how hard I was going to crash, I would've bailed a long time ago."

"But it's not your fault," Annika said earnestly. "Mommy said that you didn't even do the bad thing Eve thought you did. So why don't you try to explain?"

Marcus controlled his frustration, which was inappropriate to express to a nine-year-old. "I tried that, honey. But she's been burned before, so she won't listen to me."

"But it's stupid!" Annika said rebelliously. "And it's not fair! She's really great, and I really liked her. And she should stay with you!"

"A lot of things in life aren't fair," he said. "We just have to deal with it. Hey, you know what? I think Jocelyn might have left some of those ice cream bars that you like in the freezer. Why don't you see if you can find one. She puts them in the bottom drawer."

Annika's face lit up. "Yum," she said. "Do you guys want one, too?"

"Thanks, not for me, baby," he told her.

Tilda and Maddie also declined, and Annika scampered off into the apartment in search of her ice cream.

Marcus turned to glower at his sister and his sister-in-law. "You two brought Annika here as a human shield, right? That's a dirty trick."

"Depends on how you look at it," Maddie said. "There's only so rude, sulky and self-involved you can be when your innocent and adoring little niece is in earshot. It seems logical to me to use her to bring out your best self."

That jerked a dry laugh from his throat. "Best self, my ass."

"You're going to sign those papers with no complaint?" Tilda said, her voice hushed but impassioned. "That woman loves you, Marcus!"

"I can't take this roller coaster," he told her. "Can I persuade her, can I prove myself to her, can I convince her? So far, the answer is no. She won't take my calls."

"So you're giving up," Tilda said.

"I'm cutting my losses, Til," Marcus said. "I've already lost my job, and my mind, and my career, as I know it. So all of you, for God's sake, back off."

Maddie's face was tight. "I'm so sorry, Marcus. I know you got in really deep with Eve. Can't you try one last time to get through to her?"

"Not without setting myself up to get freshly destroyed. Please stop asking."

Maddie's face crumpled. "It's so stupid! Damn Jerome for wrecking this for you. I thought you'd finally broken through. That maybe you could even be…"

"Be what?" Marcus demanded.

Maddie threw up her hands. "Happy," she said angrily. "It was a long shot, I know. You're uptight, defensive. Always have been, since we were little. But you weren't with Eve. All of a sudden, it seemed like happiness might not be too much to ask for you anymore."

"I thought so, too," he said. "Joke's on us, huh?"

"Don't," Maddie burst out. "Just don't! I hate when you're like this. Brittle and cold. Shutting me out, shutting everyone out. I hate it!"

"Stop hounding me," he snarled. "I can't deal with you on top of the rest of it."

"The rest of what?" asked Annika's bright, piping voice as she skipped back in with her ice cream bar, nibbling on the white chocolate tip.

"Nothing," Marcus muttered.

"You should have some ice cream, too, Uncle Marcus," Annika said, studying his face. "You're thinner, and you've got smudges under your eyes, like Daddy did when he had the flu. Do you have the flu?"

"No, honey," he said wearily. "I'm just tired. Don't worry about me."

Annika grabbed his waist, squeezing him tightly. The hug made something in his chest soften. It hurt. Annika was a sweet little girl. He hugged her back.

"Your new flower is really pretty," she offered.

It was true. The stubborn hibiscus had finally bloomed. Its velvety petals faded from a very pale yellow to salmon to lavender to deep, cobalt blue on the frilly tip. It was spectacular, but he wasn't capable of enjoying it. He saw the world in shades of gray. "It's the first time this one ever bloomed," he told her.

"What's it called?" Annika asked.

"It doesn't have a name yet," he told her. "It's the first one that's ever existed."

"Cool." Annika eyes turned crafty. "You should bring Eve some flowers. Girls like flowers."

"Honey, please. Don't bother him. We talked about this, remember?"

"It's okay." Marcus ruffled her hair. "It's a good idea, but the timing might be off."

"Let's go, baby," Tilda said to her little girl.

Marcus suffered through a series of strangling hugs from all three of the Moss females before he was blessedly alone again. Just the soothing company of his flowers, which did not scold or admonish him. They just existed, glowing with beauty and color, being their generous and radiant selves with no apparent effort.

As he stared at the blossoms, it occurred to him that Annika's naive advice could be the seed of something useful. Flowers were something he and Eve understood instinctively. She wouldn't be on guard against the silent language of flowers.

Of course, he might also end up looking stupid, obvious and blatantly manipulative, but what the hell. She already thought the worst of him. He had nothing left to lose. No matter how she took it, offering her the newly blooming hibiscus would be a classy final gesture.

But he needed to pack his stuff. Have his bags in his car, and a plane ticket and passport in his pocket. From the lawyer's office straight to the airport. It was in everyone's best interests that he put distance between himself and the rest of humanity.

Signing those papers would take all the self-control and class that he had left.

Twenty

Eve stared across the courtyard of the MossTech complex, focusing on the water that ran smoothly over the huge granite globe in the center. Her eyes stung.

Beyond it, next to the lab building, was the soaring, thirty-story Kobe Tower, which housed the legal department of MossTech. It was a handsome building, but today, it loomed over her with a menacing air.

She'd never been so miserable, and it was no surprise, after overindulging in Sara's decadent coffee drinks yesterday. After crashing at Sara's, her friend had rousted her out of bed this morning, revved her up with black coffee and Excedrin, and shoved her out the door to go collect the papers from the divorce lawyer.

She felt a rush of gratitude for Sara, who had stuck by her through all the tears. Starting back with Walter's betrayal. Intensifying exponentially with Marcus's. Sara had offered to accompany her, but Eve had decided that this was a job for herself alone, rigorously dressed in her big-girl panties. Besides, Sara was a spitfire. After Michel, she was angry at men in general, and right now, at Marcus in particular, and Eve wanted to keep things cool and polite today. She'd slide in and out with her signed documents, and move on with whatever the rest of her life would be.

It looked hard and bleak and boring.

"Eve? Eve Seaton?" blared a husky female voice behind her.

Eve spun, heart pounding. "Who?"

"Oh, relax! It's just me! Sorry I startled you." It was Annabelle Harlow, one of the previous Corzo investors.

"Hello, Ms. Harlow," she said, with stiff courtesy. "Good to see you again."

"Oh, hell, call me Annabelle. I wasn't even sure it was you. You're so pale. You've lost weight. Have you been sick, honey?"

Eve smiled politely. True, she didn't look her best. Eating had been a challenge, and she was hungover as hell. She'd tried to salvage the situation with makeup, but clearly her efforts had fallen short of the mark.

"I'm fine," she said. "How are you?"

"Great, now that I heard the news!" The older woman's hearty clap on her back made Eve lurch forward with a cough. "I'm glad I caught you! I was just in a meeting with Caleb and Tilda, discussing partnership possibilities for her FarEye project, and kaboom, I run into you! It's fortuitous. I was meaning to arrange a meeting as soon as possible."

"Fortuitous?" Eve was bewildered. "Didn't you decide to step back from Corzo?"

Annabelle looked blank. "Haven't you been talking to Marcus?"

"Ah...not about that, no," she admitted. "Not lately. I haven't seen him for a while. Last I heard, the investors had pulled out. That was where I left it."

Annabelle blinked. "Young lady, you have some communication issues with your husband!"

Hah. Wasn't that the understatement of the freaking century. "Busy lives," she said, forcing a smile. "You know how it is. Clue me in. What did you want to meet about?"

"To get back into the project, of course!" Annabelle said heartily. "After the Cold Creek Retreat, there's simply no question about it."

"Cold Creek Retreat? What's that?"

Annabelle's jaw dropped. "Sweetheart, you don't know a damn thing about what's been happening lately?"

"Annabelle, just give it to me straight, with no theatrics, please." Despite her best efforts, her tone was getting sharp.

"Now don't get all agitated," Annabelle soothed. "First Marcus called us together, and bought us a spectacular dinner at Canlis, where he proceeded to tell us the tale."

"What tale?"

Annabelle waved an expressive hand. "The marriage mandate, the bonkers uncle, the stolen phone. Such a story! I don't know what was more fabulous, the food or the entertainment. That man is easy on the eyes, eh? And the duck with pumpkin, the oyster emulsion, oh, my Lord! And their apple cake is to die for—"

"Annabelle. Get to the point."

"Sorry. So anyhow, he offered to pay for an audit team of our own choosing to go through the Corzo research material with a fine-tooth comb and judge the veracity of that malicious rumor. So we took him up on it. What the hell, right? It was his dime, and we got to choose our own impartial experts. So the experts did their thing, and then last weekend he had us out for a retreat at the Cold Creek Lodge. For two days, he wined us and dined us while the panel presented its findings. The upshot was, Corzo is truly groundbreaking. An unbelievable opportunity. We were all convinced, except for the Wexfords. They backed out because Callista didn't want drama. My ass, hmm? That snotty little minx lives for drama. But frankly, Corzo is better off without them."

Eve gazed at her, blank and speechless "I... I... That's incredible."

Annabelle patted her shoulder. "We're sorry we ever doubted you. And oh, that Marcus." Annabelle wriggled her shoulders in appreciation. "He believes in your project so passionately. You would've thought Corzo was his own baby, the way he fought for it. Give that fellow a pat on the head, if you know what I mean. It's good to reward them, when they deserve it, eh?" Annabelle tossed her head back with a bawdy laugh.

"Thanks so much, Annabelle," Eve said. "I'm very excited to meet with you. As soon as possible. My team will be so thrilled."

"I'm tickled to death that I got to be the bearer of good news!" Annabelle bubbled. "Such a privilege!"

"Um, yes," Eve stammered. "But please, you'll have to excuse me right now. I'm late for a meeting. But we'll talk again. Very soon."

"Yes, of course we will. Good luck, whatever your meeting's about!"

Eve hurried across the courtyard and into the tower lobby. She took the elevator and walked into the legal department, five minutes late. The lobby was huge and bright and spacious, extremely minimalist and luxe, like all the MossTech buildings.

The elegant woman at the reception desk spotted her and murmured into her phone. Soon afterward, another equally elegant woman appeared to lead her to her destination. The woman's perfectly made-up face made Eve glance around for a reflective surface, just to see how red and puffy her eyes were, and if she had frizz in front of her ears. She stopped herself, with some effort. That way lay madness.

The girl stopped outside a conference room. "Mr. Moss is waiting for you," she said. "And Mr. Cogswell should be along in a few minutes." She opened the door. "Mr. Moss, Ms. Seaton is here," she announced.

Marcus stood with his back to her, looking out the window. He wore an elegant dark gray suit.

He turned. Her breath caught. After a few weeks of not seeing him, the force of his beauty just hit her all over again, with raw force. But he was thinner. There were lines in his face, shadowed eyes, and his mouth looked flat.

"Hello, Marcus," she said.

"Hello, Eve," he replied.

She walked into the room. There was a flowering plant on the table. It was large and lush, and its spectacular flowers were on full display.

She forced herself to break the silence. "I ran into Annabelle Harlow outside. She said she wanted back into the Corzo project."

His eyebrows rose. "Good news," he said. "And? So?"

"Don't play dumb," she said. "Explain this. She told me about a luxury meal at Canlis where you revealed all your private family drama to the investors. An independent audit of my research for them, which you paid for yourself. A luxury retreat at Cold Creek Lodge while the panel walked them through the results. All at your expense, and not a word to me. What the hell?"

"Why should I have said anything? You wouldn't answer my calls. It seemed undignified and creepy to keep bugging you. Besides, I figured you'd hear about it from the investors themselves. I'm surprised it didn't happen sooner."

"Annabelle was shocked that I didn't know."

His mouth twitched. "Annabelle gets off on being shocked."

"Yeah, I guess," she said faintly. "So, um. Thank you. For doing that."

"No need. I couldn't confirm it, but I'm sure that it was my uncle who tried to kill the project. So I considered it my responsibility to clean up the mess. Everything's in place except for the Wexfords and we don't want them anyway. I'm investing my own money to cover the shortfall. My personal funds, to be clear. Not MossTech. I'm not associated with them anymore."

She was startled. "You're not?"

He shrugged. "No. Once I'm divorced, control of the company goes to Jerome anyway."

"Right," she said faintly. "Of course."

"It's good timing, calling when you did. I'm leaving the country, and we needed to take care of this before I go."

That hit her like a punch, deep inside. "Going where?"

"Indonesia. I'll probably settle there. I'll sell the apartment. I'm leaving this afternoon."

She felt light-headed. "This afternoon," she repeated, inanely. "You're not going to...try again? To find someone to marry?"

A brief smile came and went on his face. "No. It's over."

"Oh, God," she whispered.

"We'll be fine without MossTech," he said. "We'll do other useful things with our time. Don't sweat it."

"It's a shame, to let that maniac have MossTech."

"I couldn't agree more, but what can you do," he said. "Sorry to rush you, but I have a plane to catch, so can we get on with this? I'll sign the papers and get out of your hair, and Cogswell can explain the terms of my Corzo investment to you after I leave."

She moved like a puppet. Clumsy gestures. Opening her briefcase. Pulling out the documents. Marcus leaned across the table and twitched the papers toward himself.

"They're flagged," she said faintly. "With, ah, stickers. The places you need to sign. I brought a copy of the prenup

for reference, though I'm sure your lawyer has yours. Do
you need to have your lawyer review the papers?"

He leafed swiftly through the documents from beginning to end. "No need," he said. "This looks like it's all in
order." He leaned over, a pen in his hand.

"Stop." Eve's voice came out louder than she'd intended.

He froze, looking up. "What?"

"Things are changing faster than I have time to catch
up," she said. "I'm confused."

"I'm not," he said flatly. "My position has never changed.
I told you the truth then, and I'm telling it now. All I've been
doing lately is trying to make it right for you."

"But things are different now," she said. "If you kept
your side of the bargain, I should keep mine, too."

He looked away for a moment, and briefly shook his
head. "I'm glad you're convinced now," he said. "But I
wish you'd had more faith in me before."

"Me, too," she said. "I was reactive, and stupid. And I'm
sorry. Like you said, I was making decisions emotionally,
because of past baggage. All I can do now is try to make
it right for you."

He looked up, his eyes keen. "Make it right how?"

She drew in a shaky, nervous breath. "Um. Well. We
could go back to our original agreement, and stay officially
married. If you want to maintain control of MossTech. And
if you, um, still want to be married to me. After everything
that's happened. I'd totally understand if you didn't."

She held her breath. She'd rolled the dice. All or nothing.

"No," Marcus said harshly.

Eve kept her face blank. So it was nothing, then.

Okay. Dignity. Dignity was key.

"I understand," she whispered. "It's all right."

"What I mean is, I'm not doing this half-assed. I won't
stay married to you unless it's completely for real, and we

figure out how to trust each other. One hundred percent. Forever. Till death do us part."

It took a while before his words would penetrate. "You mean…" Her voice faded.

"I want you," he said. "The whole deal. Like we had before, but bigger, deeper, stronger. So strong, nobody could ever push us apart with lies again."

"I'm so sorry about that," she said. "I was wired to expect betrayal."

"So we'll rewire," he said. "I love you, Eve, and there will be no betrayal from me, ever. Please, believe that."

Joy started to glow in her chest. Soft and bright, like the sun emerging from a cloud. "Yes," she whispered, her voice choked. "Oh, my God, yes."

With tear-blurred eyes, she couldn't tell if he ran around the table or leaped across it, but suddenly they were in each other's arms, locked in a desperate, pleading kiss. Trying to make up for the misery and mistakes of the past weeks.

The door clicked open. They heard a gasp, and an embarrassed chuckle. "Sorry," a man's voice murmured. "I take it we're, ah, postponing the appointment?"

"Get lost, Leonard," Marcus rasped.

"Sure thing." Leonard yanked the door shut, laughing.

Marcus reached out to engage the door lock, and then he hoisted her onto the conference room table. The potted plant rattled perilously, almost toppling when their weight hit the table. Marcus reached out to steady it and pushed it out of harm's way.

"I don't remember that blossom." Her voice was choked with emotion. "Is that the hibiscus you showed me? The one that was holding out on you?"

"Yes. It finally bloomed. Annika suggested I bring it to you. She told me girls like flowers, and I thought, hell, yeah. No girl likes flowers like Eve Seaton likes flowers."

"You thought right," she told him. "It's spectacular. What's it called?"

Marcus was smiling helplessly, his fingers wound into her hair, stroking it like he couldn't believe she was there. "I named it 'Eve's Kiss.'"

Anything she might have said in reply was lost against his hungry mouth, but that was no problem at all.

They understood each other perfectly.

* * * * *

THE PREGNANCY PROPOSAL

NIOBIA BRYANT

As always, this one is dedicated to the wonderful thing called love.

One

Sean Cress looked out the window at the streets of Manhattan, New York, from his seat in the rear of a blacked-out luxury SUV. His thoughts were full and he barely noticed the traffic, the New Yorkers walking the streets at a fast pace, or the towering buildings that were either sleek and modern or of stately classical architecture. He was too busy wishing he were headed to the set of one of his numerous cooking shows. As a chef, the merging of his talent in cooking and his innate charm as an on-air personality had created television and streaming gold. Twice he had been named one of *People* magazine's Sexiest Chefs Alive. His extravagant, fast-paced celebrity lifestyle of A-list events added to his allure. He knew that and used every bit of it to his advantage, enjoying the limelight and the ladies.

And he was confident that same popularity and acclaim would secure him the position as Chief Executive Officer of his family's powerful culinary empire. His parents, Phillip Cress Senior and Nicolette Lavoie-Cress, had formed

Cress, INC. after successful careers as chefs with established restaurants, more than two dozen bestselling cookbooks and guides and countless prestigious awards. Their corporation included nationally syndicated cooking shows, cookware, online magazines, an accredited cooking school and a nonprofit foundation. Food was their life and they passed that passion on to their children.

Sean and his brothers all held executive positions in the company and were acclaimed chefs themselves. Lincoln, his father's newly discovered heir born to him in England before his marriage to Nicolette, had been welcomed into the fold as the President of Sustainability. Phillip Junior ran the Cress Family Foundation. Gabriel led up the restaurant division, Coleman oversaw the online magazines and websites and Lucas supervised the cookware line. Sean's duty was the syndicated cooking shows, including those in which he starred.

Their father, Phillip Senior, dangled the succession of one of them to the Cress, INC. throne, pitting them against each other in the past few years—even though they were raised to be loyal and loving to one another. Each had wanted to make their autocratic father proud and steer the already juggernaut company into a bigger and brighter future. But in time, as their father never actually stepped down and several of the brothers made it clear they no longer wanted to be the CEO, the siblings had regained their closeness.

Even if Lincoln, Gabriel and Coleman no longer wanted the position, Sean did.

With the revelation of their father's heart condition and then his subsequent cardiac surgery just a week ago, it was clear their patriarch would not be able to continue the daily grind of managing a massive company. Phillip Junior, Lucas and he were still in the running for the coveted spot. And Sean had big plans for the company by diversifying into owning a food channel to stream their cooking shows instead of having them played on other networks. He felt the success of his division and his popularity and stardom made him the face of the brand and the clear heir apparent. He just *knew* the position was his.

Until this damn scandal.

Sean pinched the bridge of his nose and cleared his throat. Of late, scandal and the Cress family seemed to go hand in hand. First with Monica, their former house-keeper, becoming Gabriel's wife and heir to a massive fortune left behind by her father—an A-list movie actor she never knew. Then the family—and the press—learning that their father had an illegitimate heir back in England conceived just before he left the country to attend college in Paris. The very last thing the family needed was one of Sean's former bedmates releasing a steamy sex tape of him.

He clenched his jaw, remembering the reaction of his mother who loved her family, her cooking and her pri-vacy—and not always in that order.

If not for the scandal ruining the Cress, INC. brand and hurting his position within the company, Sean couldn't care less about the video. It was years old. The woman had been long forgotten. And sex was a natural thing. Besides, the revelation of just how "equipped" he was had increased his popularity—particularly with the ladies.

His family, of course, cared nothing about the upside of the salacious situation.

So far they had kept the news of the video from Phillip Senior who would undoubtedly be so riled up as to cause a physical setback. Lessening the effect of the drama was essential for his father's health, his mother's sanity and his position within Cress, INC.

He'd hired one of the best in the public relations game to get the job done.

Sean looked over at Montgomery Morgan sitting on the

opposite end of the leather rear seat of the SUV. The top-notch publicist was talking low on her phone as she used a stylus to write notes on her iPad before she tucked her bone-straight black hair behind her ear.

"We'll be pulling up any minute," Montgomery said, her voice crisp and clear.

He continued eyeing her and enjoyed himself because the woman looked phenomenal. Jet-black hair brought out the sepia hues in her medium brown complexion. High cheekbones and a slightly square chin were complemented by her full toothy smile, dimples and beautiful feline-like eyes with long lashes. As much as she was a beauty, Montgomery Morgan was also intelligent, levelheaded, cool, reserved and professional. Very straitlaced. In control.

Until she's not.

Two months ago, while attending a dinner party thrown by his brother Gabriel, and her friend/client Monica, he and Montgomery had gotten stuck in the elevator of the couple's luxury townhouse. As the minutes ticked by while they were trapped alone in the confined space, the unflappable publicist had been anything but calm.

Montgomery glanced over and caught his eyes on her. He didn't shift his gaze; instead, he enjoyed the full sight of her face. Her eyes locked with his and her lashes fluttered before she lightly bit her bottom lip.

In that moment he knew that like him, she remembered just what had happened between them on that elevator. Memories of their cries of passion replayed for him. It had been an hour or better of wild abandon before the elevator light came on and exposed their nudity as they rushed into their clothing and agreed it would never happen again.

Best sex ever.

"Hold on one sec," she said before lowering her phone to press the button for another call as she looked away from him. "Montgomery Morgan."

Sean bit back a smile at her formal businesslike tone. Ever the professional.

"What?" Montgomery snapped, sitting up straighter in the seat.

His driver, Colin, slowed the SUV to a stop in front of a midtown Manhattan hotel. Awaiting them was a crowd of onlookers and paparazzi. Sean was more used to the fanfare than the rest of his family, although they were all well-known in their own right. He shifted his gaze back to Montgomery as her jaw clenched and she closed her eyes with a slight shake of her head. "Something wrong?" he asked.

All of the possible emergent situations ran through his mind. An accident? Medical emergency? Death?

He felt concern for the normally stoic woman.

Before their one-night liaison, he and Montgomery had only been cordial when in each other's company at events thrown by Monica and Gabriel. He'd only contacted her last week after the release of the sex tape. Although Cress, INC. had their own publicity and marketing staff, he had wanted Montgomery's expertise in dealing with high-profile clients and had been relieved when she agreed to represent him.

"Montgomery," he said, reaching to touch her wrist when her head lowered.

She stiffened for a moment and then looked over at him. "I'm pregnant," she revealed in a harsh whisper before swiftly turning and opening the door to exit the vehicle.

Sean felt gut punched. "What?" he snapped.

Out the window he watched as she took a deep breath, straightened the Italian cashmere camel trench she wore over a tailored cream pantsuit and slid on oversize shades before walking to come around the rear of the vehicle. And just like that, her facade was back in place, even though she left him completely rattled.

Pregnant?

By me?

His heart pounded.

Knock-knock.

He looked over to his right to find Montgomery had tapped her knuckles against the window. Colin now stood beside her, keeping the crowd back from the vehicle. They awaited his signal that he was ready.

I'm not.

But he took his own steadying breath, slid on his black aviator shades and pulled the latch on the door. Colin pulled it open wide and Sean climbed out, instantly surrounded by the yells of the crowd as he slid his hands into the pockets of the dark gray coat he wore over matching sweater and wool slacks.

"Sean!"

"We love you, Sean!"

"Are you still with the woman in the tape?"

"Sexy Sean!"

"Any statement on the scandal and the effect on Cress, INC.?"

"I saw the tape!"

"We all did!"

Remembering Montgomery's advice, Sean kept his face unreadable as they made their way across the sidewalk into the five-star hotel where she'd set up a press junket. Her strategy was to address the scandal fully, answer all questions and then move on from it. Hopefully.

They entered the building and swiftly moved across the beautifully adorned lobby with its towering gilded ceilings. Aware of the eyes still on them, Sean fought to maintain his composure even as he felt he might just be losing his mind.

A child?

"Are you pregnant by me?" he asked as soon as they turned the corner toward the gilded elevators.

Montgomery faced him. Even with his over six-foot

height, her five foot eight inches and heels brought them nearly eye level. "*If* I'm pregnant, yes it would be yours but let's talk about this later," she said before spinning to press the button for the elevator.

Sean shifted to stand in front of her. "You're just going to drop a bomb on me like that?" he asked, not hiding his exasperation. "And right before a round of interviews, Montgomery?"

She nodded and began to pace. "You're right. It just kind of came out. I was shocked, Sean. I apologize. It's just this morning at my office, my assistant kept nagging me to take a pregnancy test and I finally did it just to shut her up," she said before massaging her temples. "I took the test and left to meet up with you. She called with the results and it shocked me. I honestly did not think I was pregnant."

"Why did she think you were pregnant?" he asked, voicing his curiosity.

"Moody. Sleepy. Hungry. Constantly," she stressed.

"And your cycle?" he asked after hesitating a moment to do so, knowing it was personal.

Montgomery looked affronted. "Really?"

"Considering the situation?" he asked while holding up his hands. "Absolutely."

"I have a highly stressful job and it's irregular at times," she explained. "Look, I feel it needs to be confirmed by a doctor before we flip and lose our minds. Really, I shouldn't have said anything until I knew for sure."

Sean released a breath.

A baby.

I could be a father?

He wasn't ready.

Sean *loved* his life and the freedom to do whatever he wanted. He didn't want to change a thing about it—and so love and settling down with one woman was not a part of his plan. He could easily see himself as The Forever Bachelor. Wifeless. Childless. Enjoying his freedom. Paternity meant sacrifices he was not willing to make, and that was exactly what it took to be a good parent. Not just a sperm donor or sire, but a fully involved father.

It was nothing to take lightly.

The elevator doors slid open and Montgomery stepped on before he followed behind her.

"Damn," she swore as she kept her gaze down on the tips of her polished leather boots as she fidgeted nervously.

Sean turned her to face him again and raised her head with his fingertips to her chin.

Their eyes locked.

She's so beautiful.

That same unseen chemistry surrounded them. It was intense and undeniable.

"This got us into this situation the last time. Remember?" she asked, even as her eyes dipped for a moment to his mouth.

Memories of kissing her made him clear his throat and take a step back before he gave in to the temptation to pull her close and do just that. Again. And again. "Right," he agreed.

Montgomery released a long breath and touched her fingertips to her lips as she turned away as well. "Focus on today. We'll deal with anything else tomorrow," she said, her voice back to authoritative. "Remember everything we went over and stick to the script. Just add—"

"Charm," Sean interjected with his winning smile.

Montgomery looked up at him with a shake of her head and the hint of a smile. "Exactly," she dryly agreed. "Remember this is not to specifically address the scandal but to show you are not shying away from the press because of it. The major topic is your new cooking show and upcoming cookbook, but someone may try to address it with you—whether directly or in a roundabout way."

"I'm disappointed that more respect wasn't shown for a very personal and private moment," he said, remembering the script she crafted for him that was actually very close to his true sentiments. "In my position it's hard to know what is real and staged. That is my biggest regret."

"Excellent!" Montgomery said with a wink and brief nod meant to encourage.

The elevator doors opened and she led him to the suite with a view of Central Park. Her team had turned the room into a set complete with chairs, backdrop, lighting and a few cameras. "Everyone is here and has been set up in the adjoining suite with refreshments and gift bags of Cress merchandise. Either myself or one of my team will check on you between each interview," she continued. "Ready?"

To be a dad? No.

Although he knew it wasn't what she meant, it was all he could think about.

"Yes," Sean said, moving to take the seat she pointed out to him.

The door opened and a petite woman with short, naturally curly hair entered. Her small face was nearly overwhelmed with large, round spectacles. He opened one of the bottles of water on the small table beside him and filled a glass as he watched Montgomery remove her overcoat. She handed it and her tote to the woman he assumed to be her observant and persistent assistant.

He eyed Montgomery's build that was more slender than thick but with curves. The suit she wore was tailored to fit and stylish.

His eyes dipped to her belly.

If she's pregnant she's close to two months.

The thought of a baby made his gut clench. He'd never even been on a date with Montgomery. Never even shared a full-blown conversation on major topics. Now they were expected to co-parent?

"Sean, this is my executive assistant, Hanna," Montgomery said as they walked over to him.

Sean eyed the woman with a nod. "Nice to meet you," he said.

Hanna gave him a nod as well as an up-and-down look. "In person the man lives up to the myth," she whispered to Montgomery.

Sean heard her clearly and bit back a smile.

Montgomery gave her assistant a hard stare and received a helpless shrug in return. "How's the lighting setup on him?" she asked the cameraman.

"Perfect," the man said after taking a test shot.

"Of course," Montgomery muttered dryly.

Sean did give *her* his best smile.

Montgomery turned but not before he saw her roll her eyes.

He chuckled. Even that was a break from the facade of business-only perfection that Montgomery favored and had made her one of the most sought-after publicists on the East Coast. He was relying on her to clear up the scandal and secure his selection as the new CEO of Cress, INC., making her substantial fee well worth the cost.

And if she's pregnant?

Sean frowned as he turned his head to look out the window at Central Park in the distance.

"Are you okay?"

Sean was puzzled by both the male and female voices asking the question. He shifted his gaze from the window to find the cameraman querying him and Hanna looking at her boss. Montgomery and he looked at each other. In her eyes he saw what he was feeling.

Worry.

They both looked away.

"I'm fine," they said in unison.

It was Hanna's and the cameraman's turn to share an odd look.

Sean took another sip of water as his first interviewer was led into the suite. He adjusted his frame in the club chair and stiffened his spine as he prepared himself to try his best to not let the thought of pending fatherhood ruin his chance at redemption.

"This was not a part of my plan," Montgomery muttered as she looked down at the pregnancy test now encased in a clear Ziploc bag before she looked up at her reflection in the mirror of the suite's bathroom. "Damn."

I can't be pregnant. I just can't. Not now. Not yet.

Montgomery had wanted to thrive in her business before meeting her Mr. Perfect, fall in love, get married and *then* start a family. After years of success and building a support system with her business, Montgomery had felt ready to find the man for her and maybe in three to five years have a child. She had become fastidious and a bit dogged in finding the man who checked everything on her list of must-haves. She was on numerous dating apps for professionals and frequented places all the women's magazines said were ideal for meeting men like hardware stores, golf courses, cigar lounges, gyms and churches. She went on blind dates. Prayed about it. And stayed on the lookout.

It had become a part-time job or side hustle. Montgomery was on a mission. She *wanted* companionship, love and steamy sex, but finding "the one" wasn't panning out. Outside of work, her friends and family, she was lonesome and afraid she would forever be single.

And now I might be a single mother.

She balled the plastic-covered test into her grip. In just one night she might have changed the trajectory of her life. Just once Montgomery "Ms. Perfect" Morgan had lost total

control. Quickly and with plenty of fiery passion that had
been undeniable.

More, Sean. Give me more.

Montgomery flushed with warmth at the memory of
the words she gasped before he obeyed her wish. Deeply.
Every pulse on her body fluttered to life.

Just like that night.

In the reflection her eyes widened before she rushed to
shove the baggie into her tote before turning on the faucet
and bending to press cool water to her neck. It failed in
erasing the heat of her desire for Sean Cress.

The man was trouble. Handsome, charming, sexy and
flirtatious, but trouble nonetheless.

As the publicist for The Bridge, Monica's nonprofit bene-
fiting children aged out of the foster care system, Montgomery had soon become the woman's friend, making running
into Sean Cress at both business and family events inevitable. Over the past two years they had always been polite
when crossing each other's path, but there had also been
lingering looks, mildly flirty banter and innocent touches
that created a spark. Montgomery was well aware that Sean
found her attractive, and his smiles let her know that he
was fully tuned in to the attraction she had for him. But
neither acted on it.

Until they both stepped onto the elevator to ride up a
level and somewhere in between the first and second floors,
the sounds of metal grinding echoed around them just before the lights flickered…

*Montgomery instinctively took a step closer to Sean as
her dread kicked into overdrive. "You think you're over
your childhood fear of elevators…until you get stuck on
one," she dryly said as she began to frantically press the
buttons on the control panel.*

Sean reached into the inner pocket of his blazer to re-

move his phone. "I'll call for help," he said, his deep voice echoing in the small space.

Montgomery rested her head against the wall as her normal cool composure began to fade. "Why did I get on this death trap? Why did I get on this death trap? Why did I get on this death trap?" she repeated.

Something pressed to her lower back and she whipped around as her heart pounded. It was Sean's hand and she felt some relief at his presence, knowing she was being ir-rational but unable to fight back her distress.

"There's no signal," Sean said, looking down at her in concern. "But I'm sure help is on the way."

The lights went off.

Montgomery squealed before she flung herself at Se-an's body and wrapped her arms around his neck in panic, squeezing her eyes shut even though darkness reigned. "What if we drop? What if there's a fire? What if—"

"Shhh. It'll be okay," Sean assured her as he wrapped one arm around her body to hold her close. "We'll be okay."

She nodded against his neck, feeling comforted by his strength and the gentle way he rocked their bodies back and forth to calm her as he massaged circles on her lower back. Consoling her. It felt good to rely on someone else. Really good.

Too good.

Montgomery took an extra inhale of his warm cologne. It was enticing.

"Everyone has fears," he said. "I'm sure I'd hit a pitch higher than an opera singer if a snake crossed my path."

She felt a little less crazy about her outburst and man-aged a bit of a smile.

"A little light will help," Sean said. "I'll use the flash-light on my phone."

She still clung to him and enjoyed it. Her heart pounded.

Her breathing was fast. And her pulse sped. Sean's body felt as hard and defined as it looked in his tailored clothing. She felt heady and overwhelmed by him. And her desire.

It was hard to deny in the close quarters with their bodies pressed together.

"Here we go," he said.

With regret, she leaned back and opened her eyes. The light was cast on their faces. She felt transfixed as her eyes flittered over his square-shaped face. His strong chin, cheekbones and jawline were softened by his mouth and sexy downturned dark eyes with long lashes. He truly was handsome. Beautiful even. With his face clean-shaven and his curly hair cut low, he looked younger than his thirty-seven years.

She eyed his soft and tempting mouth as she bit her lip.

His hold of her tightened a bit.

She looked up and their eyes locked.

Chemistry rose quickly and seemed to radiate from their bodies to bounce off the walls.

She felt breathless at the desire she saw in the brown depths of his sparkling eyes.

This was exciting and like nothing she had ever felt before. She nearly ached and trembled from wanting to feel his mouth on hers. And so much more.

"Montgomery," he moaned.

It was her undoing.

"Kiss me," she begged, throwing away any and all inhibitions.

And he did with a groan that revealed he was tired of the torture of not tasting her lips.

The first feel of his mouth touching down upon hers delivered a jolt that was electric.

She tilted her head a bit to the side to enjoy it. Revel in the feel of him and how it made her feel more alive than ever. His tongue touched hers before he suckled the tip into his mouth. Her hands playing with his nape as his strong fingers danced up and down her spine before he began to undo the zip of the lemon corseted satin dress she wore.

She offered no objections.

And when the dress slid down her body and around her matching heels, she was too far lost in her want of him to deny herself the pleasure...

A sudden knock interrupted her steamy recollection. With a gasp of surprise Montgomery looked over at the closed door of the en suite. Even now the memory of the heated moments they'd shared on that elevator made her pulse race. She ran her hands through the length of her hair. "Yeah?" she called.

"You okay, Montgomery?" Sean asked.

Her body instantly betrayed her. Everything worked a bit harder in reaction to him on the other side of the door. Her heart. Her pulse points. Her stomach. The fleshy bud nestled behind the lips of her femininity. The explosive night they'd shared did absolutely nothing to quench her thirst. In fact, it left her parched.

She plastered on her cool, calm and collected expression before opening the door.

Sean was leaning against the wall with his ankles crossed and his hands deep into the pockets of his top-coat. "You okay?" he asked again.

His eyes dipped to her belly and Montgomery instinctively pressed a palm to it. "I'm good," she said, sliding her tote up onto her arm as she stepped into the foyer to stand before him. "And you did great with the junket today."

"I'm glad it's over and hopefully it will be the end of the scandal," he said.

"Hopefully, no other sex tapes from random hookups will appear," she added as she moved away from him to give the now-empty suite one last walk-through.

"Ouch. Judgmental much?" he asked.

Montgomery opened the door to the bedroom and turned on the light before glancing back over her shoulder at him now standing behind her. "Sorry," she said, not sounding like she meant it, before she entered the bedroom to walk around with a cursory look.

"I am an adult who enjoys sex," Sean said, stepping into the room to lightly touch Montgomery's wrist. "And if my memory serves me, so do you."

She looked up at him, all too aware of the feel of his fingertips against her pulse and his deep brown eyes resting on her face. That same attraction between them sizzled. She felt hungry for him. With a shake of her head to break the spell, she looked away but her eyes landed on the bed. She envisioned Sean and her naked upon it. Enjoying sex with each other.

Stroke by delicious stroke.

Montgomery turned away from the mirage with a tremble, wishing she weren't haunted by their rough cries filling the elevator as they climaxed together.

She caught Sean's eyes resting on the bed as well before he locked his gaze with hers.

There was no denying the intensity in the dark depths. Or the way they made her feel hot and a little light-headed. She eased her wrist from his grip and hurried to rush past him to leave the bedroom. Pressing a hand to her throat she felt her pulse pounding against her palm.

Once the lights had returned and the elevator began to move upward, they had rushed into their clothing and emerged to an awaiting crowd as if nothing had happened between them. In the months following they had never spoken of it or even given the slightest inkling that they had done *things* to each other in that elevator. Naughty things.

Until today.

The pregnancy talk unlocked the door they both had seemed to close.

"Thanks, Montgomery."

She whirled. "For the sex?" she asked, feeling the incredulity on her face.

Sean lowered his head with a chuckle before looking up at her.

The move caused her gut to clench.

Why does this man get to me like this?

"No. Thank you for the work you put in to help this scandal die down," he explained with a smile—that smile.

The charming, disarming one.

"It's my job," she said with a succinct nod.

Get it together, Montgomery.

"You're great at it," Sean said. "And the sex."

Montgomery gave him a hard look meant to chastise. "We're not doing that," she said.

Sean looked amused. "Having sex?" he asked.

"Having sex. Talking about having sex. Reminiscing on when we had sex," she said, ticking each off on a finger. "Doing replays on the sex like it was sport or ranking it like I was requesting a score. It was sex, not the Olympics."

Sean bit back a smile.

"Oooh."

They both looked to the door to find it open with Hanna standing in the foyer with her face a mask of shock and then excited approval.

Just great.

"I'll be right with you, Hanna," Montgomery said, rubbing her fingertips over her brows to ease her rising anxiety.

Thankfully, her assistant immediately stepped out of the room and closed the door behind herself. Still, Montgomery walked over to the door and opened it to ensure the little busybody—who was as smart as she was inquisitive—did not have her ear pressed to the wood. With a heavy breath she closed the door and leaned against it, feeling emotional and drained.

"Hey, hey, hey," Sean rushed to say as he strode over to her. "What's wrong?"

In truth, she needed a hug. A tight one. The kind where she could rest her head on a strong chest and let him offer her the strength she felt lacking.

Like in the elevator.

And look what happened.

Montgomery locked her knees and swallowed down all of her feelings. "I'm okay," she lied, stepping back behind her facade.

Just as she had nearly all her life as she grew up the daughter of a devout minister. Every decision, every action, every reaction, was keeping in mind that she was a preacher's kid. The weight of what was expected had felt heavy, and her father had made those obligations clear.

So how do I tell him I'm unmarried and pregnant?

"I gotta go," Montgomery said, sounding as defeated as she felt and needing to be alone to be as weepy as she wanted. "I'll be in touch about the PR and the—the—the—"

"The pregnancy," Sean provided.

She leveled her eyes on his. "The pregnancy," she repeated. "I'll have it confirmed by my doctor and let you know."

"Okay," he said with his eyes studying her.

It made her entire body tingle.

For a moment, as they stood there looking at each other, surrounded by that now-familiar hum of awareness, she could almost believe that everything would be just fine.

Almost.

Two

One week later

Cloaked by the darkness of night, Sean lay on his back in the middle of his king-size bed, looking up at the tray ceiling with its brocade design. The expansive bedroom suite was quiet with none of the noise of his large family breaking through the thick walls or doors of the five-story Victorian-era townhouse in the prominent Lenox Hill section of Manhattan. The entire family had resided in the Cress family townhouse growing up, and although Gabriel, Coleman and Lincoln lived in their own places across New York, it was still a full house. Currently, his parents' quarters took up the entire third floor. On the fourth and fifth floors were three full bedroom suites, and a large den and pantry. Lucas and Sean lived on the fifth, with Sean having moved upstairs to give Phillip Junior, his wife, Raquel, and their school-aged daughter more space on the fourth. Their housekeeper, Felice, who also lived with them full-time, had a suite of rooms and her own entrance in the cellar. Even with nearly ten thousand square feet, five floors, a cellar and the roof garden, it still felt a little crowded with so many adults living together.

He was thankful for the sound structure because he had a lot on his mind.

Sean looked out the glass wall, flanked by gray suede curtains secured by leather ties, that showcased a view of the night landscape in the distance and the snow-covered limbs of the towering tree in the backyard. The view was peaceful, while his thoughts were troubled.

With awaiting confirmation of Montgomery's pregnancy, the blowback from the sex tape scandal, filming new seasons of two cooking shows, working on recipes for his newest cookbook, fighting for the CEO position of Cress, INC. and maintaining his busy social schedule, Sean felt pulled in all directions.

The possibility of becoming a father outweighed them all.

He thought of Montgomery—beautiful with her cool facade that hid a fiery appetite.

More, Sean. Give me more, she had begged.

And there in the dark elevator with only his phone dropped to the floor offering a stream of light up onto the ceiling, he had obeyed her command as he felt for her leg and eased it up onto his shoulder. Her gasp of pleasure echoed around them and he remembered longing for enough light to see her face. Her beauty. Her passion. Her pleasure.

Sean leaned over to pick up his phone from the nightstand. He felt the urge to call Montgomery.

And say what?

That he just wanted to hear her voice and check on her, knowing she was worried.

With a wry chuckle, Sean used his free hand to fling

back the woven coverlet that matched the decor of all shades of gray from light to charcoal. He sat up nude on the side of the bed, thankful for the silk woven rug on the floor under the massive bed to shield his feet from the cold hardwood floors. Leaving his phone atop the crisp white cotton sheets before rising, he made his way over to his en suite to retrieve his black terry-cloth robe embroidered with his initials in white letters. Barefoot, he left his suite. He stopped halfway across the dimly lit den that centered the entire floor with the suites on one side, and the pantry, wrought iron staircase and elevator on the other. He slid his hands into the pockets of his robe and looked out the glass wall running along the entire rear of the house at the magnificent sight it offered.

Growing up only Gabriel and Phillip Junior had the rear suites with the glass wall. They were older and got first choice. Sometimes Sean would sleep on one of three sofas in the den, turning the costly furniture into his impromptu bed so that he could look at the view in the moments just before he fell asleep. He had always been fascinated by its beauty. When he eventually moved out one day, he would miss the focal point most of all.

With one last look, Sean continued across the dimly lit den and descended the stately stairs until he reached the first floor into the living room. Even with just lighting offered by the sconces on the walls, there was no denying the beauty of the modern decor of light gray and steel blue found throughout the entire home. It blended with the features common to its Victorian-era architecture with modern upgrades that were undoubtedly beautiful, luxurious and filled with amenities like its own movie theater with a deluxe snack bar, wine cellar, library, safe room with a secret entry and fully stocked pantries on each level.

And of course, the chef's kitchen.

Sean made his way past the door to the half bath on his

right and down the brief hall to the kitchen with its pale walls and dark cabinetry, complete with an island near the high-end range and refrigerator. The spacious area opened up to the dining room straight ahead and a den to its left, but it was clear which of them was the showcase. Instantly, he felt some of his concerns ease. Cooking was always his safe place and his peace.

Sean checked the pantry and the fridge before deciding to try something he was considering putting in his new cookbook focused on sandwiches from around the world, including sections on bread making and homemade condiments. His team at Cress, INC. had been suggesting various recipes for him to put his own spin on, and he was curious to see just what he could do with their latest recommendation.

He turned on some jazz music very low and got lost in the art of cooking. He lost track of time as he created every aspect of the sandwich from scratch, including the demi baguettes. No detail or extra step was considered unnecessary. Every element was lightly seasoned before being brought together. For the fried meat, instead of standard sausage or beef, Sean used a Cress, INC. cast-iron pan to sear a fine cut of Wagyu beef with a marbling score of twelve that meant the meat would be spectacularly tender by default. For the *frites*, or fries, he chose sweet potatoes instead of white. All of the vegetables were chopped from skills learned during the early days of all of the brothers working in their parents' various kitchens over the years before leaving to attend culinary school. For the traditional sauces he chose to make a robust garlic sauce and then a gentle béarnaise sauce of butter, egg yolks, vinegar, shallots, peppercorns and tarragon.

"Oh. It's you, Mr. Cress."

Sean looked up from thinly slicing red cabbage to find the family's housekeeper, Felice, standing at the top of the polished wood stairs leading down to the finished basement. The middle-aged woman was still in her robe and obviously freshly awakened from her sleep. He gave her a smile begging for forgiveness. "Sorry, Felice. Felt like cooking," he explained before tossing a hand towel over his shoulder and swiftly turning to remove the baguettes he sliced and then pan grilled in garlic butter.

"Of course," she said, covering a yawn with the back of her hand. "I'll stay up and clean up once you're done."

Sean frowned. "No, you won't. I'll clean up, but you will try this for me," he said, taking a baguette and filling it with thin slices of the steak that he let rest so that its juices drawn to the center of the meat during cooking would be redistributed and increase its flavor profile. He topped it with the tossed smoked gouda, arugula, red onion, thin slices of carrots and red cabbage, a drizzle of the garlic sauce and then the sweet potato *frites*, which he topped generously with the béarnaise.

"That does look good, Mr. Cress," Felice said, having watched him intently.

He placed the sandwich on a plate and then the plate onto a tray with a bottle of flavored seltzer from the fridge before handing it to the woman with a nod of thanks. "Let me know what you think. In the morning," he stressed before turning to assemble two more of the sandwiches.

"Good night, Mr. Cress," she said before turning to make her way back up the stairs.

He was alone again. The cooking was complete and his focus instantly shifted back to Montgomery and the baby. Needing a new diversion, he focused on washing the pans he used and then cleaning the stove and countertops.

I'm pregnant, Montgomery had revealed.

He paused in wiping down the large island.

"Sean?"

He smiled as he looked up at his youngest brother, Lucas,

walking into the kitchen in his own monogrammed robe—gifts from their mother. Of all his brothers, he and Lucas were the closest even though they were six years apart.

With the addition of Lincoln as the new eldest brother, it was Phillip Junior, himself, Gabriel, Coleman and then Lucas. As kids he had been as close to Phillip Junior as Gabriel and Coleman were—not just brothers but best friends. As the baby, and the last child his mother knew she would bear, Lucas had become "The Favorite," undeniably. Coleman was "The Rebel." Gabriel reigned as "The Good One" and Sean was "The Star." Lincoln was "The New One" and Phillip Junior, once "The Eldest," was now—in his mind anyway—"The Heir to the Throne."

And he'd felt that way long before Lincoln's addition to their lives, making Phillip Junior more arrogant and unbearable as the brothers got older—especially with their father stepping down from the business one day. It was then Sean began to spend more time with their little brother as adults. Their shared sense of humor made them friends. With Lucas, he could and would discuss anything.

"Couldn't sleep?" Sean asked as his brother came over to look down at the sandwiches.

Lucas gave him a sheepish smile as his stomach grumbled loudly. "I came down for a snack," he said as he rubbed his flat belly.

"Perfect timing," Sean said, motioning with his chin toward the two sandwiches on the now-spotless island.

Lucas gave it a long look and wiped his mouth with his hand as if it watered, but he shook his head. "If I eat like this at two in the morning, I will gain back all the weight I lost," he said. "And that's not happening."

Sean understood.

As a part of their mother's devotion to her youngest son, Nicolette had given him plenty of affection and even more delectable treats as he stuck to her side like a shadow. Until a few years ago, Lucas had carried sixty extra pounds on his tall frame. And being a skilled pastry chef who loved his own treats, he found it had been no easy feat to lose the weight.

"It's not always what you eat but the portion size and the frequency," Sean reminded him, taking a knife to cut one of the eight-inch sandwiches in half. "Plus, I want your take on it."

"For the cookbook?" Lucas asked, giving it another long look before finally shifting his eyes up to his older brother.

"Possibly," Sean said, turning to pull two bottles of beer from the fridge to open both before setting them on the island.

Lucas frowned as he eyed the frosty bottles. "What's wrong?" he asked.

He knows me too well.

Sean attended parties and led a fast-paced lifestyle, but he was typically a light drinker. Thus, reaching for a beer was a tell he was unable to bluff. Besides, he didn't want to. He needed to unload. He walked over to close the door leading to the cellar. "I may have a baby on the way," he admitted.

Lucas stared at him before his eyes widened as if he needed a moment to process the news. He reached for one of the bottles of beer to take a long drink of it. "Details," he ordered before reaching for the sandwich to take a healthy bite.

"What you have, Chef, is a Belgium sandwich—a *mitraillette* or submachine gun," Sean said.

"Seriously, Sean," Lucas drawled.

He smiled at his brother. "I know," he said with a half smile.

"It's delicious, by the way," Lucas added. "But tell me, who's the mother?"

"Montgomery," Sean admitted, as her words seemed to haunt him.

I'm pregnant.

Lucas's eyes widened in surprise. "Beautiful woman," he said.

"Very," Sean agreed, thinking of her.

"But do you want her to be the mother of your child?" Lucas asked as he turned and crossed the kitchen to the cabinets lining the wall to open a drawer and remove linen napkins.

"I'm not ready for *any* woman to have my child," Sean said with a heavy breath before pushing his half of the sandwich away.

Over the past week his appetite had faded.

Lucas picked up the last piece of his sandwich and dragged it through the sauces that had dripped onto the plate. "But if Montgomery *is* pregnant?" he asked before easing the food into his open mouth.

"Then nothing will ever be the same for either one of us," Sean admitted.

"True," Lucas agreed, dropping the napkin atop the plate. "Anyone else know?"

Sean shook his head. "Not yet. She's waiting to hear back from her doctor to confirm the at-home pregnancy test," he explained.

Lucas took a sip of his beer. "Soon?" he asked.

"The sooner, the better," Sean said.

"Whatever you need from me, I'm here," Lucas promised him. "Including a lifetime subscription to condoms."

"Noted."

"At least the drama concerning the sex tape is dying down," Lucas offered.

A small reprieve.

Sean shrugged one shoulder. "And provides evidence

that I do in fact wear condoms," he said, feeling slightly devilish.

Lucas picked up the napkin to throw it onto his brother's face. "That was way more of you than *anyone* needed to see," he said with a wince.

Sean chuckled.

The elevator in the corner of the kitchen slid to a stop. The brothers both looked toward it to see their mother opening the wrought iron gate.

Great.

It was very possible that Nicolette Lavoie-Cress, chef extraordinaire, philanthropist, devoted wife and their mother, might have heard at least a part of their conversation.

God forbid.

She was as beautiful as she was overly protective of her sons—even Lincoln, as her stepson, had been accepted and was doted upon as well. She looked beautiful and elegant in an azure silk robe with lace trim that could almost be an evening gown. Her silver hair only had hints of her once-blond strands, and her favorite color was blue to match her eyes. She was aging well and looked younger than her years. And her love for their tall and broad father born in a small town in England with skin the color of chocolate was unwavering.

"Impossible de dormir?" Lucas asked her in her native French, wanting to know if she was unable to sleep.

"I called the hospital to check on your father and decided I needed something more than the snacks in the pantry for *le casse-croûte*," Nicolette said, her French accent still prominent.

"Try this for a snack," Sean said, offering her the remaining sandwich with a wave of his hand.

Nicolette arched a silver eyebrow as she came to stand beside Lucas, his height nearly two feet above her own. She pulled the platinum-rimmed plate closer before opening the sandwich to inspect it. "A *mitraillette*?" she guessed, eyeing each of her sons with a twinkle in her eyes.

Sean chuckled. "*Oui*, Chef," he said.

"This shall do very nicely," she said with a smile before pressing the sandwich flatter with her palm and then lifting it to take a bite.

Their parents were two of the top chefs in the world, and to watch her take a bite of his food took Sean back to the days of culinary school awaiting the opinion of his teacher. When their *maman* released a soft grunt of pleasure and did a little shimmy, Sean knew she approved. She took another bite and he knew she loved it.

For him that made it a definite addition to the cookbook.

Nicolette looked at him as she used the linen napkin to pat the corners of her mouth. "My wild son," she said. "Charming, handsome, funny, talented and a star. But also, since you were a child, a dimpled rascal who loved chasing pretty little girls and giving them kisses. Women have always been your weakness."

"True," Sean agreed, unable to deny that he had enjoyed seeing just how many ladies he could woo with his dimples.

A lot of times they tried to woo him.

He gave his mother that winning smile.

"Charmer," she muttered, reaching up to lightly pat his face.

When her hand lingered, he knew she fought the urge to put a little more weight into her pat because of the sex tape scandal.

"*Tu es le seul à ne pas t'installer. Allez-vous?*" she asked him softly with her eyes filled with regret.

"You are the only one who will not settle down. Will you?" she had asked in French.

He smiled but it was fake because it hid the guilt and concern he had because settling down or having a child was indeed not what he wanted.

Bzzzzzzzzz.

He and Lucas shared a look as Nicolette reached into the pocket of her robe to remove her cell phone. "It's Gabe!" she gasped, looking up with excited eyes. "The baby is coming. I'm heading to the hospital."

Collette, Phillip Junior and Raquel's daughter who was named after Nicolette, was the heart of the family, but also the lone grandchild. She would enjoy another kid to play with.

Like mine.

"Another Cress grand. What a blessing," Nicolette said, picking up the *mitraillette* before quickly moving to the elevator, presumably to get dressed.

"A blessing indeed, *Maman*," Lucas said with a long look at Sean that was heavy with meaning.

If Montgomery is pregnant with my child, will she be as happy for me as she is for Gabe?

Considering the circumstances, Sean found that hard to believe.

The next morning, dressed in red flannel pajama bottoms, a pink fitted thermal top and woven socks adorned with snowflakes, Montgomery sat on the bottom step of the stairwell of the two-story colonial home she inherited from her grandparents upon their deaths nearly five years ago. She looked around at the brightly lit home. She wished she had the time to strip the paint from the wood to expose the beams and trim. To her, the massive brightly colored area rug that anchored the modern fuchsia sofa would work better with wood than the stark white walls.

Although the home was a classic beauty, it was forever in need of repairs and modernization with closed-concept smaller rooms. Just two months ago Montgomery paid out five figures to replace the roof. A year ago the clay sewer pipes that were commonplace during the era of the home's creation were cracked by tree roots and had to be replaced and their layout shifted to meet current city standards. The memory of its cost still made her flinch. Each and every time.

Her to-do list lengthened. Time, effort and money were constantly being poured into the home.

"You're all set, Go-Go."

Montgomery looked back over her shoulder at her father closing the door to the basement before walking over to her as he cleaned his hands on an old piece of torn cloth. She smiled at his nickname for her. As a baby she was always so active. Constantly moving and on the go.

Go-Go.

"I already feel the heat coming back on, Daddy. Thank you," she said, rising to press a kiss to his bearded cheek.

Reverend Alton "Rev" Morgan was a tall and thin man who was as strict with what he ate as he was with the actions he took in the world. Excess was not his forte.

He shifted his wire-framed glasses on his broad nose but looked over the rim at her. "It's the boiler. You're going to need a new one soon," he said with a booming voice that seemed to shake the rafters of his church every Sunday.

Another bill.

She could almost hear it ring up.

Cha-ching.

She hated it but she would pay it. The five-bedroom, four-thousand-square-foot structure was her home and she loved living in Passion Grove, New Jersey. The town offered a slower-paced, small-town feel but was close enough to midtown Manhattan to allow a daily commute into the city to work. Although her home was on the lower end of some of the estates in the town worth millions, she enjoyed the luxury lifestyle set by her wealthier neighbors. The townspeople enjoyed the holidays with events meant to draw them together. For her, after a long day in the busy and congested streets of Manhattan, coming home to Passion Grove, with its heart-shaped lake and streets named after flowers, was ideal.

Now, if I can only get the house to be perfect as well.

"Waking up without heat was not fun. Thanks for coming to my rescue," she said, wrapping her arms around one of his as she walked with him to the front door.

"Always," he said. "Why did you wait until morning?"

"I was fine, Daddy," she said. "I didn't want to wake you in the middle of the night."

Still, he frowned with disapproval.

Please not a speech.

"Hungry?" Montgomery asked, although she knew the answer. It was a trick to divert him.

He never ate before ten o'clock and it was just a little after eight.

"No. Too early for me," Reverend Morgan said, pausing to look around at the house. "You took down that picture of your grandparents over the fireplace."

"Yes. It's in my office. I'd like to think they were looking over me always and were proud of me," she said.

The real me. Not the act I put on for you.

He grunted.

Montgomery loved her father, but she resented that he wouldn't like the person who she truly was and only the one she pretended to be for him. She often wondered if it would have been any different had her mother not passed away when she was just a toddler. Would she have been free from his rules and high expectations? Allowed to get dirty as a child? Able to hang out with friends? To have fun?

"I better get going," he said.

Montgomery reached around him to pick up an insulated tumbler on the half table in the foyer. "How about coffee to take with you on the ride back to Brooklyn?" she asked. "Dark. Four sweeteners. Just the way you like it."

Her father took the coffee and gave her a smile before nodding his head in approval. "That's my girl," he said. "What are you getting into today?"

Waiting for a call from my doctor.

Yesterday she barely made it to a late appointment and while waiting for it to begin the doctor had been called away to an emergency at the hospital with a patient in labor. Montgomery was given an ultrasound, had had blood work and was asked the routine questions before being assured she would hear from the doctor the next day.

Overnight she was nagged with concerns that if she wasn't pregnant there could be other health issues causing the false negative result.

Like a tumor.

"I have a light workday so I'm going by the hospital to check on my friend who had her baby late last night," she said, able to feel excited for Monica who had become a good friend.

It was seeing Sean again that she dreaded. The awkwardness between them was evident. Just a couple of days ago, as she worked alongside him at a photo shoot for his book cover, it felt strained. Like neither knew what to say as they awaited her appointment with her OB/GYN.

"Which friend? Do I know her *and* her husband?" he asked, his brows creased.

You're worrying about my friend and I might be having a baby of my own.

Montgomery fought the urge to press a hand to her flat belly. "No, you don't know the couple," she explained, seeing him instantly relax at the assurance that Monica was not a single mother. "She's one of my clients."

To see how quickly he imposed his opinion on a stranger just reminded her that his judgment of her would only be tenfold. She hated that she was a grown, successful businesswoman who was self-sufficient, and her father still made her feel like a teenager afraid of being called to the carpet for letting him down. But he did. For her father she had always ensured he thought of her as nothing less than perfect.

Admitting to him that she was unwed and pregnant by a man like Sean Cress—about whom nothing said fatherhood—was daunting for her.

"What's wrong, Go-Go?" her father asked as his eyes searched her face. "You'll have your turn to be a wife and a mother. Be patient. It's all on God's time."

Montgomery stiffened and looked up at her father as she forced a smile to cover what felt to be an alarmed expression on her face. "Be safe, Daddy," she said, reaching past him to open the front door.

She shivered as the cold winds instantly wrapped about them.

"You missed church last week, Montgomery," he said, his voice censorious. "That was disappointing. I hope to see you there Sunday."

"Do you want to know why I missed church?" she asked, feeling that confidence she used every day in her successful career rise up in her.

"Were you sick and shut in?" he asked.

No.

Instead, she said nothing.

"Then nothing else matters," he said with a stern look.

It was pure hilarity that she gave her employees and those she encountered during work the same stare to get prime results. With anyone *but* her father.

Growing up it felt like if she said she was going right, he would demand she go left. And in time, to not feel strangled by his rules, she had learned to be misleading. It was then she found her freedom. While studying at New York University for her double major in communications and marketing with a minor in Spanish, Montgomery had truly found

her wings living on campus and being out from under the
ever-watching eye of Reverend Morgan.

"Yeah, you're right," she said, again relenting to him.

"Be safe. Love you," he said before turning to leave.

"Love you, too, Daddy," she said with a rub to his back
as she gently guided her father out of the house. She looked
out the front window of the living room at him climbing behind the wheel of his Cadillac crossover before he
pulled away.

Montgomery turned and made her way up the stairs for
a hot bath. Halfway up, she took a misstep and stumbled
forward on the steps. She was surprised by her cry of dismay as she quickly reached out to grip the step and prevent
herself from falling onto her belly. She twisted her body
to sit on the step with her heart pounding as she covered
her face with her hands. Tears rose at the thought of accidentally falling down the stairs and causing a miscarriage.

In that moment the idea of that happening flooded her
with fear and misery.

She pressed one hand to her belly and ran the other
through the length of her hair.

She didn't know if she was being foolish to feel so protective of a baby she wasn't even sure existed. Still, it was
possible and that was enough for her to be shaken to her
core. A miscarriage was not the answer. That would fill
her with more regret than her fear of being judged by her
father and left to do it alone by Sean.

Montgomery released a long breath and rose to turn
and make her way up the stairs. In her bathroom she enjoyed a long warm bath. In the full-length mirror, wearing
nothing but her robe opened at the sides, she pictured herself swollen with child. With a shake of the head at herself, she closed her eyes at her own mixed feelings. When
she opened them again, there was a vision of Sean stand-

ing in the mirror behind her with his hands splayed on her rounded belly.

Montgomery blinked to rid herself of the image.

Silly girl.

Sean didn't want children, and Montgomery didn't want Sean. He was only good for cooking and sex—*really* good.

Okay. Exquisite. The man was magnificent in bed and the kitchen.

But not at fatherhood and commitment.

The loud ringing of her cell phone startled Montgomery. She rushed into her bedroom to pick it up from its charging pad on the nightstand. "Dr. Fletch," she said, reading the name of the incoming caller.

"Here we go," she said, sinking down onto the side of the bed as she answered the call and pressed the phone to her ear.

Come what may, I will make the best of it. Just like always.

Three

Sean stood still under the production tent as the stylist arranged the collar of the navy wool peacoat up around his face. The entire team of his show stood outside one of the dozen CRESS restaurants across the world. For each of the dozen shows in the new season, Sean cooked dinner for a celebrity who was connected in some way to each of the cities in which the eateries were located. They were filming the final episode at CRESS XI on the port of Honfleur in Normandy, France.

Sean looked down at the cute brunette with green eyes as she stepped back to eye the matching shirt and dark denims he wore. With a nod, she approved of her work. "Feel good?" she asked, pulling a lint roller from the black apron she wore to swipe at the coat.

"Feel great," he said.

She gave him a lingering look, but Sean looked away to keep it professional. He didn't date in the work pool. Even as a charmer who loved the company of beautiful women,

Sean was not interested in crossing lines at work. He loved his career too much to risk it.

But…had he met her elsewhere he would have gladly accepted the subtle flirtation.

Because of the light rain, the stylist opened an umbrella and handed it to him.

"Ready to shoot, Sean," an assistant said.

The director, Julien Dubois, came up to him. "I actually think the overcast and rain against the backdrop of the harbor will make for a brilliant shoot. *Magnifique!* Yes?" he asked, his French accent heavy. *"Cadre trés intimiste."*

Very intimate setting.

Sean nodded in agreement.

"Let's go," the director said, clasping his hands before turning and walking away.

Sean bit back a smile. Working with the man for the past few days had been a joy. He was in his sixties but had the spirit of a twenty-something lover of life.

Following the instructions of the director, Sean walked up the brief length of the harbor under his umbrella as the camera crew used a track to dolly out away from him. "Welcome to an all-new episode of *Tablemates*, my opportunity to cook a delicious meal of their selection for some of the biggest celebrities across the world," Sean said, walking over to the SUV sitting outside the brightly lit restaurant that seemed to glow against the darkness caused by overcast skies. "Today join me at the beautiful CRESS XI, here at the port of Honfleur in Normandy, France, as I introduce you to my tablemate… Delphine Côté."

Sean stood on his mark, giving a smile and nod to the uniformed driver standing by the rear door holding his own black umbrella to protect him from the light rain. The man opened the door and extended his gloved hand to assist the acclaimed veteran actress from the vehicle. Delphine had been a recluse for the past twenty of her ninety years of life, but accepted the offer to be on the show at Sean's personal invite.

"*Bonjour*, Delphine," Sean said, stepping forward to bend and kiss both her cheeks before extending the crook of his arm to her.

"*Bonjour*, Chef," she said with a twinkle in her eyes.

"Today we'll spend the day cooking and then dining on your favorites—Basque seafood stew, roast duck and *tourtière landaise* or apple and Armagnac phyllo pie," Sean said as the camera recorded them walking together under his umbrella toward the steps of the restaurant.

"Sounds delicious, Chef," Delphine said.

He held the door for her and she entered as he looked back over his shoulder into the camera. "Join me for another episode of *Tablemates*," he said before lowering the umbrella and dashing inside.

"Cut!" Julien shouted.

Sean smiled down at Delphine. "Thank you for today. It will make the perfect finale," he said in fluent French.

"This should be fun," she said with a pat of her hand atop his before turning to follow a production assistant and her nephew, a tall and thin man who obviously doted on his legendary aunt.

Sean allowed his stylist to take the umbrella from him before removing the overcoat. She placed a custom navy apron that matched his shirt over his head and carefully tied it at the waist. He looked around the restaurant whose creation his brother Gabriel had personally overseen. It was stunning with its high ceilings, minimal decor and unique lighting fixtures that all made the views of the harbor the focal point via the tinted glass walls. In every bit of it he saw his brother's love for the project—and perhaps his love for Monica during those early, more tumultuous days of their relationship.

During the shoot, that took the entire day, he enjoyed

himself but his thoughts were on hopping on to the Cress family jet and heading back to New York.

Sean picked up his wineglass and raised it in toast to Delphine where they sat across from one another at a table in the front of house. She raised her glass to touch to his. That was an organic moment. "Thank you for being my tablemate this evening. The company far outshined the meal. *Saluer*," he said with warmth.

Salute.

"Saluer," Delphine repeated.

The cameraman pulled back from their table and then panned up to the sight of the rain against the window.

"Cut!" the director yelled.

Delphine gave Sean a wink before relaxing and leaning back against her chair. "It's been a long time since I allowed cameras in my life. For that meal and your company, it was worth it, Sean," she said before rising to her feet with an agility he hoped to have in his later years.

"Merci," he said.

"Oh my, you're grand," Delphine sighed in pleasure.

Sean smiled bashfully and prepared to thank the woman until he looked up and saw she was instead talking to Gabriel's best friend, Lorenzo León Cortez, a tall, stoic man of mixed Native American and Mexican heritage. His smile faded just a little bit as he was used to being the one to receive compliments.

Lorenzo chuckled deeply. *"Merci beaucoup. Vous êtes assez grand vous-même,"* he said in fluent French although Spanish was his native tongue, thanking her for the praise and bestowing the same upon her as well.

With one last smile up at the man dressed in all black, Delphine followed the production assistant out of the restaurant to her trailer.

Lorenzo and Gabriel had met in cooking school and became fast friends. In time, the family had come to accept him as a close family friend. There had been strain between him and Coleman when his brother assumed Lorenzo was pursuing Jillian before their secret love affair had been revealed. Thankfully, the misunderstanding was cleared and all was well with the men—for which Gabriel had been more thankful than anyone.

"Good show," Lorenzo said. "What I saw of it."

Sean picked up his goblet again to finish the rest of the wine in one deep gulp as the camera crew's talking and actions rose and echoed around them as they began to wrap the day of shooting. "Thanks, Zo," he said. "I almost forgot you were catching me back to the States."

Lorenzo was the head chef of CRESS V on the Champs-élysées in Paris. As the newly appointed godfather of Gabriel and Monica's baby, he was headed to New York to meet his goddaughter.

"I'm all set. Give me a sec," Sean said, rising from his seat.

Lorenzo walked over to the door of the restaurant out of the fast-moving fray.

As Sean thanked the crew for the hard work and nodded in thanks at their applause, he noticed several eyes on his adopted brother before he made his way across the restaurant. He paused to speak to the director, the producers who were on set, and to give the stylist authorization to purchase the entire outfit he wore before he finally pulled on the overcoat and made his way to the door.

"Let's roll," Sean said to Lorenzo.

Both men left the restaurant and dashed out to the chauffeured SUV. There was a couple dozen people waiting in the rain by the vehicle. With a chuckle, Lorenzo got into the rear of the vehicle while Sean took the time to pose for pictures and sign autographs before climbing into the vehicle as well.

"You know, I really need to convince you to do a show

for the streaming service once I get it set up," Sean said. "The ladies couldn't take their eyes off you."

"Oh no. I'll stick to cooking. You can have the fame, superstar," Lorenzo assured him with a deep voice.

"It has its benefits," Sean told him with a mischievous wink.

Lorenzo gave him a steady look. "Yes, I heard," he said, obviously referring to the sex tape.

Sean laughed, but then abruptly stopped. "Please don't bring that up around my parents?" he asked with the utmost seriousness.

It was Lorenzo's turn to find humor. "Trust me, Gabe gave me the heads-up."

Good.

"La Havre Octeville, si vous plait." Sean requested in French for the driver to take them to the nearby airfield. The family's private plane awaited, fueled and ready to jet to America. *"Merci."*

The driver nodded and pulled away, careful of the people still standing near the vehicle to get a sight of the famous and beloved Cress family brother.

Sean gave them all a wave through the glass before reaching for the small locked carry-on already on the seat awaiting him as instructed. In it were the clothes he wore that morning, his briefcase, iPad and phone. He had so many missed calls, texts and emails.

None from Montgomery.

Perhaps I should call her?

He looked out the window at the sight of the rustic medieval town.

Or maybe no news is good news?

He remembered the sight of her beautiful face by the light of his phone in the dark interior of the elevator. The way her feline-like eyes searched his just before he saw her desire for him in the depths of hers. Just before they shared one hell of a kiss.

The memory of it and the sparks it set off made his gut clench.

Montgomery had the type of beguiling beauty that was hard for him to deny. There was something about her that made her stand out in a crowd to him. His eyes would always land on her when they were at an event together. But her demeanor had always been so cool and professional. So unapproachable and formidable.

Until the elevator.

But that version of the woman was gone. He had discovered a new facet to her. The fire. The release. The passion.

His view of her was forever changed.

Sean tapped his phone against his knee before he began to return calls and emails as Lorenzo withdrew a hardcover book and began reading in silence. Soon work became Sean's focus. So much that he was surprised when the vehicle slid to a smooth stop on the paved tarmac of the airfield. He flew in that morning for filming and was headed right back out. As the driver held the door for him, Sean gave him a thankful nod. The men continued across the airfield and up the steps of the sleek black Desault Falcon capable of flying up to twelve people in luxurious comfort.

The uniformed pilot and flight attendant awaited them just outside the cockpit.

"Welcome aboard, Mr. Cress and Señor Cortez," the flight attendant said, accepting their carry-ons. "The sleeping quarters have been prepared for you as requested."

"Thank you," Sean said, striding down the long length of the plane to pass the two leather sofas facing each other, a small conference table and entertainment area to reach the fully made queen-size bed. "You good, Zo? I'm tired as hell."

Lorenzo held up his book before sitting on one of the sofas. "This has my attention," he assured him.

Sean barely took the time to remove his shoes and coat before lying down on his side. In the moments before he fell asleep—without work to distract him—he thought of Montgomery. Again. So many things. Her cries of passion. The feel of her body. The beauty of her eyes. Her possibly being pregnant by him while not ready for fatherhood. At all.

Sean released a heavy breath and welcomed the escape of sleep.

"Mr. Cress. Mr. Cress."

He opened his eyes and looked out the window at the airport. Bright lights broke up the darkness of night. Paris was six hours ahead, so it was early evening in New York.

"We've arrived."

Sean looked back over his shoulder at the flight attendant standing beside the bed. "Thank you," he said, hearing the sleep that thickened his voice.

The smile and the look in the woman's eyes were soft and welcoming.

Sean eyed her for a bit and gave her a grin of his own that he knew was a bit wolfish. She really was appealing, and everything hinted at a night of sexual wonder.

She's no Montgomery.

Sean's eyes widened a bit in shock at that thought.

Since when was Montgomery the epitome of what was desirable to him?

That night.

The attendant's eyes filled with concern. "Is everything okay?" she asked.

Sean sat up and swung his long legs over the side of the bed. "Sorry," he mumbled when she stumbled back to avoid colliding with him.

He slid on his shoes before rising with his coat in hand. He was thankful when she gave him an odd look before quickly making her way to the front of the plane. He pulled on his coat and followed suit. Lorenzo had already disembarked.

"Welcome home, Mr. Cress," the pilot said.

"Feels good to be home," Sean said, accepting his carry-on from the attendant and making his way down the stairs to his awaiting all-black SUV.

The winter winds were crisp and brutal, seeming to reach his bones as he ducked his head and quickly strode across the apron as his driver, Colin, took his case and held the rear door for him. Sean was thankful for the heat of the vehicle as he visibly shivered.

Colin placed their luggage in the rear before moving quickly to reclaim the driver's seat and drive them away. "It's supposed to hit the low twenties tonight. Missing Paris, gentlemen?" Colin asked with a chuckle.

"Yes," Lorenzo exclaimed, rubbing his bare hands together.

"Nope," Sean said without hesitation.

He *loved* New York.

The bright lights and fast pace. Something was always happening in the city. People were always awake. Life was constantly moving. There was an energy—a vibe—that was unmatched.

There was always something—or someone—to do.

"Where to, Mr. Cress?" Colin asked.

"Lenox Hill Hospital."

"Right away," the driver assured him.

Lorenzo dug back into his book.

Sean removed his tablet and began swiping through the list of streaming services and live television stations that might be viable for purchase to become CressTV. He studied each one from their current logo to programming and cost. His team at Cress, INC. had been meticulous in their research and Sean was interested in the streaming service with the easiest transition—even absorbing their employees to not disrupt people's livelihood.

He felt confident that Cress TV would lead to him being appointed CEO of Cress, INC. and afforded the ability to propel the company forward without having to garner the approval of his father who, at times, was against any efforts made to do things differently.

The SUV slowed to a stop outside the hospital.

Sean moved quickly to place his tablet back inside his briefcase. "I'll be a couple of hours. Car is yours. Careful of my case back here," Sean said before climbing out of the rear of the SUV before the driver could leave his seat.

Lorenzo did the same.

Quickly, they made their way inside. Neither man noticed the appreciative looks they drew from the women they passed. After retrieving a visitor's pass, Sean and Lorenzo made their way to Monica's private maternity suite. Sean paused in the doorway at finding Montgomery sitting beside the bed holding his niece. She looked up and their eyes met. And held.

His heart hammered at the very sight of her. And seeing her holding a baby shook him.

"Emme, it's your uncle Sean and godfather Zo!" Monica softly exclaimed from the bed as she leaned over to ease back the baby's blanket. "I wasn't expecting you, Sean. I thought you'd be tired from your trip."

And I wasn't expecting Montgomery.

Sean shifted his eyes from Montgomery with reluctance. "I just got back and came straight here," he said. "I slept on the plane."

"How'd the shoot go?" Gabriel asked from behind him.

Sean turned to find his younger brother sitting at a table in the corner with blueprints laid out before him. "Without a hitch," he assured him, taking another glance back at Montgomery that he couldn't resist as he walked over to look down at the plans. "The new restaurant?"

Gabriel nodded and turned the plans on the table to face his brother. "Cress XIII. Dubai," he said. "Coming 2024."

"Wow," Sean said at the scope and size of the project.

"Go big or stay home," Gabriel said.

Sean nodded. "Damn right," he agreed, turning each page of the blueprint.

"It has me considering leaving Paris to head chef there," Lorenzo said with a broad smile of admiration at the project.

"Oh no, Zo," Monica said from behind them.

The three men looked at her.

"Emme needs all her family and that includes her godfather. Paris is far enough, *Gabe*," she said, giving her husband a meaningful look to stop his friend's contemplation of moving to Dubai.

"He's a grown man, babe" was all Gabriel said.

Sean looked at Montgomery as she looked down at the baby.

Something tugged at him. Something deep.

Montgomery looked up and locked her eyes on him. "Sean, can I talk to you really quick?" she asked.

His eyes searched hers, looking for some clue.

Are we having our own baby?

"Yeah," he said, clearing his throat.

Lorenzo removed his coat and washed his hands before walking over for Montgomery to ease the bundle of joy into his arms. He claimed the seat she vacated to follow Sean out of the suite. He noticed she was carrying her briefcase and assumed it was work related. As she walked down to the end of the hall, his eyes dipped to take in the motion of her hips in the yellow slacks she wore with a matching V-neck sweater with blouson sleeves.

Montgomery turned to face him when she reached the lone window.

There was a look in her eyes. It was serious. More than usual.

And he knew before she even said the words.

More, Sean. Give me more, he remembered.

It seemed he had given her far more than either bargained for.

"I am pregnant, Sean," she said.

The news didn't weaken him as he thought it would. Perhaps because there had been time to get used to the idea. He nodded as she studied him even as his heart thundered. He looked down at her belly.

"It's yours," she assured him.

He jerked his eyes up to her face.

"And I'm having it," she continued.

Sean nodded again. Letting her guide the conversation because ultimately it was her body. Their life. But *her* body. That meant something.

"And I have a plan."

"A plan?" he asked, not hiding his confusion as he looked down at her, thinking the bright color she wore brought out the beauty of her bronzed skin and bright eyes.

Montgomery wore her hair up in a top knot, but she reached to twist a twirl at her nape around her finger.

She's nervous. Unsure.

She paced a little in front of him and when she stopped to face him again, gone was the hint of insecurity. She was Ms. Cool, Calm and Collected again. But Sean believed it a facade just like the steadiness he was showing her, even as he felt his own uncertainty.

"Okay, the plan," she said, her voice stern and professional as she reached inside her briefcase and withdrew legal documents.

Sean frowned as he took them.

"I propose a marriage of convenience," she said.

"What?" he exclaimed in total shock.

They both looked around them to ensure they were alone and unheard.

"Just hear me out," Montgomery said.

That took him back to the time she used that same phrase when she convinced him that a press junket was the correct course of action to defeat the scandal of the sex tape. She was in full crisis-control mode.

Ever the publicist.

"Marriage will provide security and legitimacy for our child," she began.

Our child.

"It will help me with the image of propriety on a business and personal level," Montgomery continued. "And help demolish the scandalous playboy image for you as you fight to head Cress, INC."

Sean looked down at the paperwork.

"I've laid out a full plan of marriage and eventual divorce after a year, a prenuptial agreement, a nondisclosure agreement and a promise that the marriage only takes place after a DNA test confirms paternity," she explained, her words crisp and concise. "I'm sure you're the father, but I understand you may need proof. I say let's do a quickie wedding in the next month—"

"Wait!" he snapped and then regretted his sharpness. "Please. Just give me a damn moment."

Montgomery licked her lips as she crossed her arms over her chest. "Sean—"

"Please," he asserted, the edge of the papers now creased in his fist. "Just give me a moment."

She nodded and took a step back from him.

Our child.

"Shit," he swore, turning and striding away.

He paused and turned to eye her. "When did you find out?" he asked.

Her eyes shifted away from his. "This morning," she admitted. With softness.

"You've had all day to wrap your brain around this plan and even draw up paperwork, so forgive me if I need some time, Montgomery," he said.

She nodded in understanding.

Sean looked down at the papers with a shake of his head.

A damn business proposal.

"How's the baby?" he asked, surprising himself.

He looked up and her eyes showed her surprise as well. "So far, so good," she said.

Sean smiled a bit. "Good," he said.

"Yes," she agreed.

"I'll be in touch. Soon," he said before turning and striding away as he rolled the paperwork up in his hands and slid it in the inside pocket of his coat.

He didn't go back to Monica's suite. Instead, he found the elevators to go up to the cardiology ward. When he finally entered his father's room, he paused in the doorway at the sound of his mother singing softly in French about loving him forever.

The sounds of sweet kisses echoed, and Sean backed out of the room.

"Come in, whoever's shadow is on the floor," Phillip Senior said in a booming voice and heavy British accent that seemed to echo in his barrel chest.

With a chuckle, Sean entered the room, closing the door as he stepped inside.

His tall and broad father lay on the bed in a designer bathrobe over his hospital gown. His mother sat on the edge of the bed beside him. They both gave him a look.

Feeling as if their love bubble was being invaded was a constant for Sean and his brothers growing up. His parents were forever lost in one another. They loved each other, their children and cooking. Together they had overcome difficulties, somehow strengthened their bond and built an empire from whose very existence their children all benefited.

Really, all any parent could do as they grew and matured was the very best they could.

A lesson to remember as a parent-to-be.

"And how was Delphine?" Phillip Senior asked.

"Amazing. And a surprisingly good cook," Sean said, pulling one of the few chairs that lined the pale gray wall to the other side of the bed before sitting. "Perhaps good enough for a cooking show of her own...on Cress TV."

"And is she still a beauty?" Nicolette asked.

Sean nodded. "Yes. She looks sixty or seventy. *Definitely* not ninety," he said.

"Good job getting her on *Tablemates*, son," Phillip Senior said.

Sean felt he sounded weak and tired. A glance at his mother showed her concern as well. "I can come back tomorrow," he said.

"No," Phillip Senior said emphatically before extending his hand. "Don't go yet, son."

Sean's eyes widened a bit as he clasped his father's hand.

Phillip Senior patted his hand. Affectionately.

Sean fought not to stare at the touch.

The Cress brothers were loved and taught to love, but shows of affection were Nicolette's commonplace. Phillip Senior had raised five sons and treated the job as a man raising future men. Tough. Loving. But not overtly affectionate.

There was a change.

Sean was stunned but tried to cover it well.

Nicolette leaned across the bed to pat the side of his face. "My son. I see your shock," she said. "Your father's condition has changed us both for the better."

Phillip Senior grunted. "Damn near dying has a way of doing that," he added.

"And seeing your love damn near die does the same to those who love him," Nicolette continued.

True.

The entire family had been rocked to discover their strong and formidable father passed out on the floor of the townhouse. Then the open-heart surgery, his recovery afterward and the waiting for the all-clear for his release from the hospital. All of it was daunting.

"To continue to do things the same after such an event is madness," Nicolette said. "For me, too."

"We surrender the fight, son," Phillip Senior said, closing his eyes.

"About the business. About the loves of my sons. About being so focused on where you boys lead your life that we stopped focusing on living our own," Nicolette explained as she leaned in to press a kiss to the cheek of her love.

Even with his eyes closed Phillip Senior smiled like a big cuddly bear.

Sean chuckled.

His father's grip on his hand weakened. Sean gripped his instead, wishing he could flood his father with his strength.

"Time to see the world and not just cook dishes from it, my love," Nicolette said.

Phillip Senior nodded in agreement, but it, too, was weak. *"À la nourriture. À la vie. À l'amour,"* he said in a whisper.

It was his mother's favorite saying in her native French tongue. To food. To life. To love.

It had become Cress, INC.'s brand used in some way in every division of the company.

Sean eyed his father.

"He's fine, superstar," Nicolette said. *"Je promets."*

I promise.

Sean released his father's hand as he nodded and rose,

replacing the seat back to its place, before leaving as his
mother began to softly hum.

"Nicolette, let's FaceTime Monica. I want to see Emme
before I go to sleep," Phillip Senior said.

"Yes! She gets more beautiful every day. Two grandchildren, my love. Can you believe it?" Nicolette asked.

"With the lot we have it'll be a dozen or better one day,"
Phillip Senior said. "Won't that be grand?"

Sean paused in the doorway.

And my baby will make three.

He stepped into the hall and closed the door before making his way to the elevator.

I'm going to be a father.

As the doors to the elevator closed, Sean leaned back
against the wall and pulled the papers from inside his
coat to unroll.

Montgomery was pregnant.

Deep in his heart, he had already known it was true.

Then nothing will ever be the same for either one of us.

He closed his eyes and tapped the papers against his chin.
A baby. Fatherhood. But marriage? The idea of that type
of union for any length of time was insanity. He was not
looking for love or a drastic change in his lifestyle. No more
partying? Or dates with any beautiful woman he chose?
Checking in with someone about his whereabouts? Not traveling to exotic locales on a whim? No more freedom?

Ding.

"Wake up, little brother."

Sean opened his eyes to find Gabriel and Lorenzo stepping onto the elevator.

"We're going down to enjoy a quick cigar," Lorenzo
said. "Join us."

Sean shook his head as he stepped off the elevator. "I
have a date with a beauty named Emme," he said before
turning to walk to Monica's suite.

He crossed her private waiting room and knocked on the door to her room.

"Come in," Monica called out.

He entered, finding that Montgomery was gone, his niece in her bassinet and Monica sitting her phone down on the bedside table.

"That was your parents," Monica said with a soft smile. "They told me you were probably on your way down."

Sean nodded, coming to stand beside the bassinet to tilt his head to the side as he looked down at the baby silently suckling on the side of her fist. "Can I hold her?" he asked her.

"Of course," Monica said. "I would never say no to any of the uncles. Her protectors. All of you."

Sean scooped Emme into his hands and held her in his arms with a glance at his sister-in-law. Her eyes were damp, but her smile was real.

"She will have the life I never had growing up in foster care. So much love and family," Monica said, swiping at a tear that raced down her cheek. "She'll never be alone."

"And neither will you. Never again." Sean promised this woman his brother deeply loved who had once been a housekeeper in their home and was now one of the family—fitting in like a perfectly cut puzzle piece. "We're family."

Monica nodded in agreement as she reached to squeeze his wrist. "And that matters so much."

Sean looked down into the face of the little brown bundle of joy. When she opened her eyes and then smiled, revealing a dimple so like his own, love for her swelled inside his chest. Just like the devotion he had for Collie. Family. Blood. A connection never to be broken. Love unbound. He *knew*, even with his doubts and hesitations, that his feelings for his child would run even deeper.

In that moment, as he raised his niece enough to snuggle his chin against her cheek and press a kiss to her forehead, Sean knew what he *had* to do.

Four

One month later

"Mr. Cress."

Both Sean and Montgomery looked up at the flight attendant standing between the leather sofas where they sat opposite each other.

"We are still not cleared for takeoff due to inclement weather," the woman who introduced herself as Lili said. "The pilot suggests continuing to wait it out on board so that as soon as he's given the all-clear we can immediately taxi for takeoff."

"Thank you, Lili," Sean said, setting down the tablet on which he had been reading something.

Montgomery eyed his profile. His square jawline and long lashes. The deep maroon cashmere sweater he wore looked delicious against his shortbread complexion and dark hair.

Lili handed each of them a leather-bound binder with

the Cress, INC. logo embossed on the front. "Here is the inflight menu, which as you know is catered by CRESS X in Tribeca," she said. "Please let me know if there's anything I can get for you."

"The future Mrs. Cress loves fresh pineapples," Sean said as he opened the binder.

Montgomery paused in looking at the selections, surprised he knew that.

"In fact, we do have fresh fruit," Lili said, looking at Montgomery. "Would you like me to make a plate for you?"

"Yes. Yes, I would actually," she said, looking down at the menu. She was thoroughly impressed. It far surpassed the fare offered on first class flights. "*And* the Caesar salad, sweet potato soup and lamb shank with grilled vegetables."

Sean bit back a smile. "Hungry?" he asked, looking amused.

"Very," Montgomery said as she handed the flight attendant the menu.

"I'll have the sea bass with mashed potatoes and grilled vegetables and black coffee," he said, handing over his menu as well. "And let's do the full setup at the table."

"Of course," Lili said before walking to enter the galley, leaving them alone.

Sean looked down at his Piaget watch. "Besides being ravenous, how are you feeling?" he asked.

"Cravings are cravings," she said. "And I feel fine."

"So we're in full baby mode," he said, his eyes dipping to her stomach.

Montgomery crossed her legs in the fuchsia virgin wool convertible sweater she wore with matching straight-leg slacks. "We woke up late in the pregnancy game, Sean. There's nothing to do but get on board," she said.

"Right," he agreed.

"We're having a baby," Montgomery said, still trying to wrap *her* brain around that as well.

"And getting married," Sean added.

They shared a look.

The feel of his eyes on her warmed her.

Montgomery looked away. She ran from her desire for him. It had gotten her into enough trouble.

Sean accepted her proposal. They completed the DNA test. Signed the papers. And were flying to Vegas to get married.

My father will be livid, but not as much as me being unmarried and pregnant.

"Two questions."

Montgomery cut her eyes over at Sean at his comment. "Fire away," she said, shifting on the seat.

"Is there a thing with the bright colors you always wear?" he asked.

Montgomery looked down at her outfit and then up at him. "My way to live out loud after growing up feeling unseen and unheard as a preacher's kid," she explained.

"A preacher's kid?" he asked, his beautiful eyes widening in surprise.

She nodded. "My father," she said.

"Is that why you wanted to get married?" Sean asked, his eyes studying her.

"Trust me, it's worth it for my peace," Montgomery said.

"Shouldn't I have asked for his permission to marry you?"

"Don't ask for permission. Plead for forgiveness," she said. "He wouldn't have approved it anyway."

Sean looked offended. "I'm a catch!" he spouted.

Montgomery shifted to the edge of the sofa to lean over and pat his knee. "Of course you are," she said consolingly.

Sean did not look appeased.

Reverend Morgan would have wanted months of courtship and a completed premarital course before giving his stamp of approval and there was no time for that.

"Next question," Montgomery said, hoping to divert his attention.

Sean leaned forward as well, placing an elbow on each of his knees and locking his hands in the space between them. "Once again we're stuck together with nowhere to go," he said.

His stare was so intense.

She fought the urge to lick her lips as her pulse raced.

This was the first time she had seen him since they met to do the DNA test. Nothing had changed. She was still affected by him. Turned on by him. He made her feel more alive in those moments just before he neared her.

Her eyes dropped to his mouth but then she shifted them away, only for them to fall on the queen-size bed in the sleeping area at the rear of the plane. When she looked back to him, his line of vision had followed hers. "Sex is not a part of the deal," she rushed to say.

Sean nodded as he looked back at her. "It can be," he said, his voice deeper than usual. More serious. "It should be."

Even as she shook her head she shivered. "You're free to live your sex life to the fullest as long as you're discreet," she reminded him as she sat back on the sofa needing space from his energy.

It barely helped.

More. Give me more, Sean, she had begged him.

Montgomery was thankful for the thickness of her sweater as her nipples hardened at the memory.

"Let's not pretend that night wasn't amazing," he continued.

Yes. Yes, it was.

For the first time in her life, Montgomery knew what it meant to be fully pleasured. Standing on wobbly legs in that elevator as she rushed to get dressed had been the most difficult of tasks to complete.

"It's up to us just how much we enjoy the next year, wife," he stressed.

"Not yet," she reminded him.

Sean fell quiet and picked up his tablet to swipe the screen.

Montgomery felt like a hypocrite. She was disappointed he had ceased his flirtation and seduction. She tucked her hair behind her ear and picked up her own laptop on the sofa beside her. She focused on the daily clippings of her clients in the press that her assistant emailed her. But her eyes kept going to him. Watching him. Remembering him.

Wanting him.

A year was a long time to live with a man and deny herself pleasure every day.

A very long time.

Being basically alone on the plane, as the crew kept out of sight, was a preview of their life to come. Working together always came with a team of people and tasks to help distract them. Here there was nowhere to hide or run from the attraction.

Just like the elevator.

And when Sean looked up suddenly and caught her eyes on him, his expression changed and his eyes darkened.

He did not hide his desire for her. It was there. Stirring her.

That all-too-familiar pulse charged the air.

He said nothing, but his eyes said it all.

Let's not pretend that night wasn't amazing.

The feel of his tongue circling her nipples. His hands stroking her back and buttocks. Whispers against her skin. Inches stoking deeply inside her.

Montgomery felt breathless and could not look away from him. The chemistry seemed to have a life all its own. With her eyes still locked on him across the short divide, she traced her bottom lip with her finger. His eyes dipped to watch the action before he moved to sit beside her.

The heat of his body and the scent of his cologne teased her.

"Montgomery," he said, low in his throat.

In just him uttering her name was a request to give in to the passion again.

She focused her eyes on her laptop but truly had no clue what she was pretending to read on the screen. She wanted nothing more than to fling the device away and turn to climb onto his lap. She closed her eyes and envisioned him raising the skirt of her dress up around her waist and his hands massaging her plump bottom as he pressed kisses along her neck.

The bud of her intimacy throbbed to life.

She released a little grunt and shifted away from the heat of him. The temptation. His appeal.

Sean Cress was a well-known playboy who seemed to run through women like tissues. His charm and beauty made him desirable. Having enjoyed his skill as a lover made him irresistible.

"Dinner is served," the flight attendant said.

Montgomery jumped to her feet, thankful for the interruption. "I'm starved," she said with a nervous laugh as she pushed her hair back from her face.

"Damn right you are," Sean muttered.

She looked back at him.

"And so am I but to hell with food," he told her.

What would his mouth feel like on me right now? Kissing those lips. Stroking my clit.

Montgomery faced forward and moved over to the table to take a seat. She rushed to pick up the glass of iced water for a deep sip that was cold but useless to douse the flame he stoked.

Sean pushed up the sleeves of his sweater as he took the seat across the table from her.

His eyes stayed locked on her as Lili set their steaming plates in front of them before stepping back.

"Let me know if there is anything else you need," the woman said.

Sean removed his napkin and snapped it open from its fold. "What I want only the future Mrs. Cress has," he said, giving Montgomery another intense look before dropping the linen atop his lap.

Lili bit back a smile and left them alone, closing the door to the galley.

"Sean," Montgomery said, hating that her hand trembled so badly that the water quaked inside the glass. She rushed to set it down.

"Do you want me?" he asked, sitting back in the chair as he stroked his fingers across the glossy top of the lacquered wooden table.

"What?" she asked, completely caught off guard.

"Te deseo. Quiero besarte mientras acaricio dentro de ti toda la noche. No he olvidado la primera vez. No puedo olvidarlo. Lo revivo, deseando que hubiera durado más," he said, his Spanish fluent and smooth.

And devastatingly sexy.

She knew he spoke French but not Spanish.

Montgomery minored in the language and dreamt of time to visit Spanish-speaking countries. So she understood him clearly and was shaken to her core.

I want you. I want to kiss you as I stroke inside you all night. I have not forgotten that night. I relive it, wishing it could have lasted longer.

This man. This man. This man.

"Te quiero en la cama debajo de mí con tus piernas envueltas alrededor de mi cuerpo mientras te monto. No había sitio para eso en el ascensor. Pero lo hicimos fun-

cionar. ¿Recordar?" he asked, taking a sip of his drink as he watched her over the rim of the glass.

Montgomery's heart pounded. Furiously so.

I want you on the bed beneath me with your legs wrapped around my body as I ride you. There was no room for that on the elevator. But we made it work. Remember?

How could she *ever* forget...

Desire conquered fear.

Their kisses and the touch of his hands undressing her released a fiery desire that was undeniable. The feel of the satin dress sliding down her body was like a second caressing hand. Montgomery shivered in pleasure as she clung to Sean, wishing she could see more of him hidden by the darkness. But her hands revealed all as she felt the hard contours of his body beneath his clothes. His broad shoulders. Wide back. Hard buttocks.

Standing in nothing but her strapless lace bra, matching thong and heels, Montgomery flung her head back and reveled in the feel of his tongue against her pulse. "Yes," she sighed with a moan of pure pleasure.

He walked them back until she felt the coldness of the wall against her back and buttocks. The shock of it only intensified their heat. She bit her bottom lip as he lowered his body to press kisses everywhere. That deep dip between the curves of her breasts as her chest rose and fell with each hot breath. A deep suck of her hard nipples through the sheer material covering them. Her belly. Navel. Each hip.

Each move sent a jolt of electricity through her body that arched her back from the wall.

"Sean," she whimpered as he used his fingers to ease her thong down over her buttocks and then her hips.

When they dropped atop her feet, she kicked them free.

"Damn," he swore, pressing his face against the clean-shaven plump mound of her femininity.

Lightly, he bit it.

Montgomery cried out.

"You smell good," he moaned against her flesh in the moments just before he slid one leg over his shoulder and opened her lips to taste her.

Her fingers dug into his shoulders and without a bit of control her hips arched forward.

She wished she could look down and see him taste her— enjoy her. His grunts of pleasure echoed in the darkness that was only slightly broken up by the phone that fell to the floor in the corner.

Over the years Montgomery had thought she experienced pleasure, but no one had ever tasted her in that way before. She cupped the back of his head, almost tenderly, as she looked out into the darkness and worked her hips back and forth as he suckled her. It was beyond anything she had ever felt before. So intense. So provocative.

What little restraint she had faded, particularly under the cover of darkness. She gave in. Fully.

Montgomery softly licked her lips. "Make me cum, Sean," she begged.

His body froze at her boldness. And then he went to work fulfilling her request. The rapid flicker of the tip of his tongue sent her right over the edge into bliss. Sweat coated her body and her heart raced as she cried out. Sean was relentless, locking her legs in place as he devoured her, caring nothing for her uncontrollable quivers of her body as she climaxed.

But she was not done.

"Now," she begged, pushing away his face. "Please."

With one last kiss, Sean rose in the darkness. She heard the rustle of his clothing as he undressed. When he reached out for her she met his touch and jerked him closer. He pressed kisses along her shoulder and up her neck to eventually reach her mouth. Their tongues danced against each other before she sucked his into her mouth with a deep moan.

Smoothly, he raised her leg up onto the crook of his arm.

Her hands explored his nudity. Reveled in it. He was so hard and fit.

The tip of his throbbing hardness stroked against her clit as she sought and found the base of his neck to suckle.

His moan of pleasure thrilled her.

The feel of him sliding his hard inches inside her fulfilled her in a way beyond the thickness of him.

With a smile she moved her head to deeply bite one of his shoulders as she raised the leg he held to now rest on his shoulder.

"Wait. Don't move. Don't make me cum. Not yet. Please," he begged, his deep voice evidence of his shivers.

She rolled her hips as she traced her fingers across the muscles of his back and gripped the strength of his buttocks.

"Montgomery," he warned in her ear before pressing a kiss to her cheek.

She turned her head toward him. "So be it. Cum then," she whispered against his mouth. As she worked her core up and down the tip of his inches.

"It's so tight. So wet and hot. Damn," he said in a low roar.

"More. Give me more, Sean," she begged, needing the rest of her climax she shifted her hips as he stroked inside her.

And he did.

Slowly. He filled her deeply.

Montgomery lightly tapped her head against the wall, sure she was slipping into madness.

They moved together. In sync. Honed in to each other. Lost in his strokes, the spin of her hips and the fever of their kisses. Sometimes they rocked together slowly as they breathed in the charged air between and around them. But then they would quicken the pace and clung to each other almost desperately and got lost in one another. His hardness. Her softness. Their cries filled the air and with each stroke, Montgomery's buttocks made a slight pounding noise against the wall.

Thump-thump-thump-thump-thump-thump.

The world seemed to spin off its axis as they fought together for their climax.

Sean's rough cries thundered against the walls of the elevator as Montgomery buried her face against his neck and held him tightly during the entire explosive ride that jerked their bodies and riddled them with a pleasure that craved infinity. And they sought the pleasure until both were still, panting and spent.

Montgomery blinked. She released her reverie to find him still watching her.

"Were you remembering?" Sean asked. "I see it in your eyes. The same desire I felt that night I see in your eyes right now. Why fight it?"

Montgomery fought for the control she treasured and ignored his temptation as she focused on her food. "The soup is just what I need on a cold night like this," she said. "How's your meal?"

Sean chuckled. "Lacking in comparison," he said.

Montgomery crossed her legs, hoping the pressure of her thighs would stop the steady throbbing of the bud of her intimacy—that fleshy button ready to be pushed. She refused to even look directly at him—be drawn to him and tempted by her desire.

Their marriage was her idea. Her machination. Foolishly, she had not calculated her lingering desire for him into the equation.

What have I done?

They continued their delicious meal with her keeping

their conversation focused on work. She was thankful that inquiring about his newest culinary show seemed to dull his sexual desire as he spoke of the program he completed that was to be aired the following year. And his excitement was infectious. She found herself asking questions and making suggestions to help promote it. She had assumed Sean Cress—the sexy A-list playboy chef—was in love with himself, but it was becoming clear that he loved the opportunity to share his love for cooking more.

Interesting.

"How was your meal?" Lili asked as she used a tray to remove their plates.

"Delicious," Sean said, sparing her a quick glance and thankful smile.

Montgomery could clearly see just why the man was a star. He was charming, smart, confident and exuded a warmth that made you want to be near him. Close to his vibe. Affected by his upbeat mood.

She covered a sudden yawn with her hand. "I think I need a little nap," she said, rising to her feet.

Sean did the same.

Ever the gentleman.

"You feeling okay?" he asked.

She nodded. "Yeah. A little tired," she said, coming around the table to move back to the sleeping area.

"Will you dream of us?" Sean asked.

Montgomery paused in removing her heels.

Inevitably.

She didn't dare look in his direction. Instead, she lay down on her side and pulled one of the plush pillows to her body to hold. With her eyes locked out the window at the movement of uniformed airport employees in the frigid cold rain, she wondered how the heat of Sean's body would feel beside her. Behind her with his strong frame outlining hers and his hand resting on her belly. His inches hard against her buttocks. His breath softly fanning the hairs of her nape.

And in the moments just before she closed her eyes and drifted to sleep she felt a warm cover draped over her body. "Thank you," she said softly, thinking it was their attentive flight attendant.

The scent of a warm masculine cologne proved her to be wrong.

Montgomery awakened with a stretch and a deep sigh as she rolled over onto her back. When she sat up, she found Sean at the conference table furiously typing away on his laptop. He glanced back at her.

"Hello, sleepyhead," he said.

She flung back the cover and swung her feet over the side of the bed. "Where are we?" she asked.

"We should be landing at the North Vegas Airport soon," he said, watching her as she slipped on her heels.

"I didn't think the weather in New York would ever clear up for us to take off," she said, rising to smooth and arrange her clothing that had twisted in her sleep.

"We took off about an hour after you went down for a nap," Sean supplied before closing his laptop.

She walked the length of the plane to pass Sean and reach the sofa where she had left her own work. Taking a seat, she began to pack her tablet and laptop in her monogrammed briefcase.

"Good thing we won't be sharing a bedroom," he said.

She gave him a curious look. "I agree, but what's your reasoning?" she asked.

"You snore."

Montgomery's mouth dropped open. "The lies you tell, Sean Cress!" she exclaimed.

He laughed and shrugged. "There's no way our baby will sleep well with all that rumbling going on," he quipped.

Montgomery snatched a piece of paper from a notepad and balled it up to fastball over at Sean. He ducked and caught it with one hand.

"Poor kid," he joked.

"Are you being serious?" she asked. "Are you really saying I snore?"

Sean rose to saunter over to the sofa. "Are you really saying you don't know?" he asked, slightly incredulous.

"Sean," Montgomery insisted, wanting to know.

He looked down at her. "Just a low purr and not a loud rumble," he said. "Thank God."

"If it would get you in bed with me you would lie right next to my loud rumble and like it," she shot at him.

"Sure would," Sean agreed with a wink.

Montgomery gave him a playful eye roll before focusing on gathering her things in preparation for their landing. She slid on her cream longline wool coat before sinking back down to the sofa. She was just an hour from becoming Mrs. Sean Cress and seven months from becoming a mother. She released a breath. A heavy one.

All of her plans—her perfectly constructed life—were off the rails.

Everything.

"Hey."

She looked up at Sean now standing beside her.

His eyes searched hers before filling with concern. "No need to panic," he assured her, reaching to grip her shoulder in comfort. "We're in this together and we're doing what's best."

Montgomery nodded in agreement and raised her hand to cover Sean's with her own before briefly leaning her head against his forearm.

"We're preparing to land, Mr. Cress," Lili said.

Sean reclaimed his seat and Montgomery instantly missed the warmth of his touch. The nearness of him.

They landed with ease.

"Enjoy your stay in Las Vegas, Mr. and Mrs. Cress," Lili said as they passed her to deboard.

Montgomery stopped for a moment at that before she continued down the stairs where Sean preceded her. He stopped to extend his hand. Again, she paused and looked around at the airport, the sleek black jet, the high-end SUV sitting on the tarmac and the handsome man awaiting to assist her. This was her life for at least the next year.

Mrs. Cress.

Most women would look forward to the wealth, the luxury and the glamour.

Montgomery did not.

She took Sean's hand as she took the final steps down off the plane. They walked together down the black carpet leading to the SUV as their driver opened the rear door for them to slide onto the heated leather seats.

Sean answered a call on his phone but Montgomery was lost in her thoughts. Her fears.

She didn't want to lose herself in the lifestyle of the wealthy and prominent Cress family. Not for herself or her child. Such affluence, without the proper guidance, love and support, could lead to the ruin of a child growing up in it. Her career as a publicist who helped clean up the messes created by spoiled celebrities made it clear what privilege could do to a person.

I won't let it ruin my—our—child.

Things moved quickly. They drove straight to the Clark County Marriage License Bureau to provide their identification for the license application they completed online. Next, they reached the luxurious five-star hotel resort directly on the Vegas strip and were quickly led to their private suite with marbled floors on the fortieth floor. Sean removed his coat as the hotel porter showed Montgomery around the massive suite. She was stunned by its opulent decor, luxury and size. Her eyes widened at the butler's pantry to her left and a full bathroom to her right. Two-bedroom suites were on either end of the wide hall. The center of the suite had 360-degree views with a living room, wet bar and dining area. She turned as she looked up at the towering tray ceiling with glass inlay.

"What size is this?" she asked the porter.

"The apartment is nearly thirty-five hundred square feet," the man replied.

Montgomery released a low whistle.

"Anything else, ma'am?" the porter asked.

She shook her head.

"Enjoy your stay," he said before exiting the suite.

"Thank you," she said, closing the door.

She turned to cross the hall, finding Sean standing before the apron window, seemingly in deep thought, with his hands in the pockets of the maroon wool slacks he wore.

After agreeing to a Vegas wedding, Sean told her he would take care of the arrangements. Montgomery had never expected this was his idea of a quick trip to Vegas.

"Sean—"

He looked back over his shoulder. "The officiant will be here in an hour," he said.

"At this late hour?" she asked, checking the time on her watch.

"It's Vegas," he said, splaying his hand as he gave her that smile.

Her heart skipped a beat.

"Which room is mine?" she asked, reaching for the handle of her carry-on sitting by the door. "I want to freshen up."

"The one to your left," Sean said. "And check your closet."

Montgomery frowned. "The closet?" she mumbled as

she made her way down the long, well-appointed hall to reach the bedroom suite. "What's in it? A chandelier?"

With a quick glance at the sweeping view of the brightly lit strip against the skies that seemed a dark blue, she crossed the spacious suite to seek out the closet, finally finding it in the entry to the en suite. Opening the frosted double doors, she was taken aback by the sight of at least a dozen white and off-white dresses with five pairs of shoes either satin or embellished with crystals.

"No way," she whispered, stepping in to quickly check the sizes of each one.

It was right.

She stooped to pick up one pair of shoes.

Dead on again.

That man. That man. That man.

She hadn't planned on anything special for the ceremony but it seemed Sean had plans of his own. A huge gesture to her probably was nothing more than a whim to a wealthy man like Sean Cress. Still, the dresses *were* beautiful and regardless of the circumstances, it was her wedding.

Maybe the only one I'll have the way things are going.

She kicked off her shoes and undressed as she made her way across the marbled bathroom to draw a bath. Once she loosely pinned up her hair and sank beneath the steaming depths of the water, she eyed the dresses that ranged from simple to sexy to sequined.

An hour later she emerged from her suite wearing a cream strapless linen-silk midi dress scattered with matching floral applique. The hem of the full skirt floated just across her knees and it fit her frame to perfection. Because the dress was so ornate, she went with a simple but beautiful strappy sandal embellished with gold crystals.

She paused at finding a trail of white rose petals down the hall. A bouquet wrapped with cream silk and a crystal adornment rested on the floor. The sound of a violin filled the air. A photographer stepped into the hall to begin silently snapping pictures.

"What?" she asked in surprise, reaching the bouquet and stooping to pick it up.

As she rose and turned, the lights dimmed and candlelight reigned from seemingly every available spot in the large living area. The trail of rose petals continued and led to Sean standing in front of the Vegas view in a tuxedo that seemed tailored to fit. She barely noticed the officiant take his spot as Sean turned and looked at her. His mouth fell open.

"Wow," he mouthed with an admiring shake of his head. "Beautiful."

And that reaction from him caused her to swoon.

She came down the path made of roses to stand before him, feeling a shyness at the way his eyes never strayed from her. Seemed to caress her. Praise her.

"I hope we have a girl and she looks just like you," he said, his voice warm and his eyes deep.

"Sean, you didn't have to do all this. It's too much," she said, before whispering, "It's not a real marriage. It's—"

He reached to lightly pinch her wrist. "Seems real to me," he whispered back. "Besides, don't we want it to look real?"

She shook her head, amazed that she felt weepy. She wanted nothing more than her Mr. Perfect to have surprised her with such a romantic gesture. Someone who loved her and wanted to spend the rest of his life with her.

"Do you like it?" Sean asked.

"I *love* it," she gushed.

"Then just enjoy it," he urged, reaching for her hand.

Montgomery looked around at it all, feeling nervous at the grandeur. The opulence. It was all commonplace for Sean. She made a good living as a top publicist—a very good living—but it was nowhere near the lifestyle of the Cress family.

"I guess this might be too much, too."

She looked at him.

Handsome charmer.

And then she looked down at a Tiffany-blue ring box he held with a wedding band and a perfect diamond solitaire ring inside. It was five carats. If not more.

Montgomery stepped forward and leaned in, her mouth to his ear. "I want us to stay at my house in Passion Grove for the next year," she said, needing balance. Wanting to feel more of herself and her life in the picture they were creating. "It's where I'll live with the baby after our divorce so let's set the routine for it now."

Sean looked confused and squinted his sexy eyes. "Okay," he agreed.

"Okay," Montgomery said, taking that step back forward.

As the officiant performed the ceremony, Montgomery could think of nothing else but the feel of Sean's hand covering hers. Its warmth was comforting. Its heat made her tremble in awareness of him.

"By the power vested in me by the state of Nevada, I pronounce you husband and wife," the officiant said with a smile. "You may now kiss your bride."

Before Montgomery could protest, Sean gripped her upper arms and leaned in. His soft kiss landed to her cheek. She forced a smile as her disappointment of not being kissed by her husband stung.

Five

I should have kissed her.

He took a sip of coffee and eyed Montgomery over the edge of the platinum-rimmed cup as they flew back to New York after an uneventful night in Vegas. Her hair was pulled back in a sleep ponytail with light makeup and she wore a cream wide-leg sweatsuit. She looked surprisingly refreshed. They had enjoyed a late dinner—ribeye, seafood soufflé and garlic broccolini followed by a complimentary one tier wedding cake adorned with fresh flowers—and then focused on work as they lounged on separate sofas before going to bed in the wee hours of the morning.

But even as he tried to focus on monthly ratings reports from Cress, INC. and more details on possible streaming services to acquire, he couldn't forget the first sight of Montgomery when he turned and saw her walking toward him in that dress. She had taken his breath away. It felt as if something clutched his heart, and warmth spread over his body.

And that shook him.

As Montgomery Morgan stood before him looking like something out of a dream, pregnant with his child and just proclaimed as his bride, Sean had been shocked at his hope that it all could be real.

And *that* scared him.

As badly as he wanted to feel the touch of her lips against his, Sean resisted because theirs was a one-year marriage of convenience brought on by an accidental pregnancy. The baby would tie them together for a lifetime, but the marriage would not.

In a year I'll be free again.

Still…

I should have kissed her.

He began to think that moment would be his biggest regret. And perhaps for her as well, because for a second, he thought he saw disappointment in the depths of her feline-like eyes.

"Oh no," Montgomery said, looking up from her laptop.

Sean shifted his eyes away so that she wouldn't catch him staring at her. "What's wrong?"

"Your insane popularity," she said before turning the device around for him to see.

"Celebrity chef Sean Cress weds his publicist, Montgomery Morgan," he read before looking down at the photo of them taken when they entered the hotel the morning of his press junket.

"It's *everywhere*," she said, rising to begin pacing.

Sean closed the laptop and set it on the sofa beside him. "It wasn't a secret, Montgomery," he said calmly.

She whirled to eye him with an incredulous expression.

"The purpose of the marriage was for it to be known to protect you professionally and personally. Remember?" he asked.

"But not like this," she said, coming over to pick up her

laptop and drop down on the sofa beside him. "The plan was telling our families first."

"The best laid plans of mice and men often go awry," Sean quoted the line of the well-known poem.

"That seems to be my life story lately," she muttered with a twist of her lips showing her annoyance.

He laughed. "No worries, wife," he said with teasing.

"Don't remind me," she drawled before leaning back against the sofa.

Sean just laughed.

Montgomery closed her eyes and massaged her forehead with her fingertips. "Think, think, Go-Go. Think," she said.

Sean eyed her profile. "Go-Go?" he asked.

Montgomery opened one eye to side eye him. "It's my father's nickname for me," she explained.

"It fits," he said. "Can I call you that, Go-Go?"

She sat up and locked eyes with him. "Absolutely not. When you say it, it sounds like it means something else entirely," she said.

"True," he said with a wink.

Montgomery reclaimed her leaning position and closed her eyes. "It's all about the spin," she said. "That's all. Spin it. Control it. Don't let it control you."

Sean furrowed his brows as he watched her give herself a pep talk.

"Okay," Montgomery said, sitting up straight again. "To beat back the frenzy of the press I'll secure an exclusive interview with *Celebrity Weekly*—they love you over there. I'll come up with a great backstory. We'll use the pictures from the photographer you hired. The *right* pictures."

"Ever the publicist," he said.

"Trust me, I've been working on presenting the right image my entire life," she said as she rose to her feet and crossed the space to scoop her phone up from the sofa where she had been sitting.

"Because of your father?" he asked. "That can't have been easy."

Montgomery looked up from her phone. "But it was fun," she said with a smile that was sad. "In those moments where I stole away and was fully me without him watching and judging and expecting…it was so much fun."

Both of their cell phones began to ring.

Sean looked down at his on the seat beside him. It was his mother.

And here we go.

Unlike himself, the majority of the Cress family hated the press, but kept on top of it nonetheless.

"My father," Montgomery said, tossing the phone back down onto the seat of the sofa.

Sean eyed her. She looked concerned.

Gone was the confident and in-charge woman he had come to know. As she sat there fretting like a child caught being naughty by their parent, Montgomery had revealed yet another side to her. He now understood it was her concern for her father's opinion of her that she got married to keep from being judged by him.

Sean sent his mother to voice mail.

"You want to deal with your father now?" he replied. "Or in person?"

Montgomery shook her head as she bit at her bottom lip. She rose to start pacing as she made calls to secure the interview and tackling the blowout from the news of their elopement. The shift from nervous daughter to confident boss was intriguing.

Which one is the truest version of her?

Montgomery released a long sigh as she sat on the seat next to Sean again. "My father has been calling back-to-back-to-back," she said, sounding weary. "I love my dad, but his energy just drains me sometimes. He never takes off the clergy robe. *Never.*"

"However you want to handle this is fine with me," he assured her.

With a shake of her head, she picked up her phone.

When she moved to walk away, he reached for her wrist to keep her beside him.

"Montgomery!" her father exclaimed. "What is the mess on the news about you getting married in Vegas? Is that true?"

"Hi, Daddy," she said.

"Answer me, Montgomery Elise Morgan!" her father roared.

"Yes, I got married last night—"

"Have you lost your mind!" Reverend Morgan yelled.

Montgomery held the phone away from her ear.

Sean winced. He could only imagine the size of a man with a voice so deep.

"I understand that our decision to elope caught you by surprise," she said.

"This is completely unacceptable, Montgomery!" the man exclaimed.

She sighed.

"I am disappointed in you," Reverend Morgan said. "And I am confused at your behavior. This not who I raised you to be. Honor thy father and thy mother—"

Enough.

Sean eased the phone from Montgomery's hand and placed the call on speaker. "Hello, Reverend Morgan," he said.

The line went silent.

"I'm Sean Cress, Montgomery's husband—"

"I have *nothing* to say to a man who doesn't have the respect for himself or for me to meet me before marrying my daughter."

Sean made a mock face of horror.

Montgomery actually smiled a bit.

"Well, let's correct that," Sean said, keeping his voice affable. "But we'll give you whatever time you need to adjust to the news because I understand that it can be hard to accept that your daughter is now an adult able to make decisions for herself—come what may."

"Listen here—"

"And I get that in the heat of the moment—after hearing that she made a decision as a grown woman, living on her own and running a successful business—that it might feel easier to choose your anger over her happiness," Sean said smoothly. "Parenting is tough—when they're kids, but once they're grown it *can* be easier. You've done your job to get her to adulthood so the training wheels needed in childhood can come off."

Montgomery's mouth and eyes opened wide.

The line went silent.

"If she does stumble and fall you can be there to support her through a life lesson," Sean continued. "But if she soars you choose to be happy for her."

"The nerve," Reverend Morgan muttered.

"I know for me, as her husband, I put Montgomery's feelings first," he said. "I'm sure as her father you do, too. Right?"

"I will not be disrespected by you or my daughter," her father continued, his voice hard and cold.

"*No one* wants to be disrespected, sir."

The line went silent again.

"She's happy, sir. At least I think she is—or she was," he added, looking to lock eyes with her.

Montgomery surprised him by leaning in close to the phone. "I am. I'm happy, Daddy," she said, her voice soft. "Please don't ruin it."

Does she mean that? Is she happy?

Sean reached to squeeze her hand, thinking it was the

first time she spoke up for herself with her father. He felt proud of her for that.

"Take all the time you need," Sean said. "And I look forward to finally meeting you and sharing some more good news—"

The call ended.

Sean handed Montgomery back her phone.

"I miss alcohol," she said before pressing a hand to her stomach.

"He'll get over it. Don't give up on him—"

"What if he gives up on me?" she asked.

"Then the foundation was shaky anyway, Montgomery," he told her.

She nodded in agreement. "And what about your parents?" she asked.

"Don't remind me," he drawled.

Upon their arrival in New York, they deboarded the plane and crossed the tarmac to his awaiting SUV. The cold winds whipped about them as snow began to fall. He was thankful to reach the vehicle.

"Colin," Sean said in greeting.

Montgomery gave the man a warm smile before taking the rear seat.

"Welcome home, Mr. and *Mrs.* Cress," Colin said with a wink before securely closing the door after Sean followed his wife's lead.

"Where are we headed, sir?" Colin asked, now in the driver's seat.

Sean looked over at Montgomery. She was looking out the window as she twisted her wedding rings on her finger. "Honey lover baby sugar," he said lightly.

She turned her head. "Huh?" she asked.

"Colin needs your address and I guess…so do I," he said.

"Right," she said. "It's 22 Belladonna Lane in Passion Grove, New Jersey."

"Got it," Colin said, typing the address into the GPS.

"*Belladonna* means beautiful lady in Italian," Sean offered.

"You speak Italian, too?" she exclaimed, turning on the seat to eye him.

Colin turned on his seat as well, looking back at them. "Excuse me, but do you two *know* each other?" he asked with a doubtful expression that was comical.

Sean and Montgomery faced forward to eye him and then looked at each other before breaking out in laughter. It was hard not to.

With a shake of his head, Colin turned on his seat and accelerated the vehicle forward to take the couple home.

Montgomery removed her tortoiseshell readers as she sat behind her desk in her home office. The sound of Duke Ellington and John Coltrane's "A Sentimental Mood" played from downstairs. She rolled her chair over to the window to see her vehicle parked in front of the house.

He's back.

Sean had dismissed Colin for the night and then driven her Jaguar to Passion Grove's small main street to grocery shop. She rose from her seat and crept over to the open door to listen to the sounds of him moving about the kitchen as he hummed to the popular jazz tune that had her feeling melancholy.

"You there, boss?"

Montgomery forgot she had been on the phone with her assistant. She walked back over to her desk. "Yeah, I'm here," she said, reclaiming her seat and replacing her glasses.

"I just sent the clip," Hanna said.

Montgomery opened the link in the email. She looked on at the video of Colin stopping the SUV at the end of the curved driveway where a small crowd of paparazzi was gathered in the street in front of her house. Thankfully, the oncoming winter storm had kept the crowd small. Sean lowered the rear window, revealing them together.

"Y'all look good together, boss," Hanna said via speakerphone.

Yes, we do.

She looked on as Sean flashed his winning smile. "We thank you for your interest in our marriage but we ask for privacy at this time and look forward to you learning more about our love story in our exclusive interview with *Celebrity Weekly* magazine," Sean said as scripted. "Now, get out of this weather. Be safe."

As questions flew at them, Montgomery and Sean gave a friendly wave before Sean raised the tinted window. Colin drove them up the drive where the press knew they were not allowed on private property.

The video ended.

They looked in love and happy.

And none of it was real.

"Thanks, Hanna," Montgomery said, reaching to end the call.

"Enjoy your night, boss. The weather is supposed to get really bad," Hanna said.

"Tell everyone to head home early. Be safe," she said.

"Done deal."

Montgomery replayed the video on mute and paused it at the sight of her and Sean smiling from the rear seat.

Earlier, the way he smoothly handled her father had made her feel relief because what she wanted with her father was an adult relationship with mutual respect. She had texted him earlier to say she loved him and he never responded. He was upset about the husband, but he would've been apoplectic about her getting pregnant before marriage.

Hell, I'm still dealing with it myself.

She tapped the touch screen of her computer to pull

up her vision board. On it was her ideal life including her dream wedding dress, engagement ring, vacation spot and list of things that made a man *her* Mr. Perfect.

"Loving—of me and God. Attractive. Mature. Faithful. Gainfully employed. Attentive. Loyal. Handy around the house. Great lover. Traveler. Doesn't complain. No bad breath. Good health. Doesn't argue. Doesn't use profanity. Doesn't drink. Never been married. No children," Montgomery read before pausing.

She frowned a bit. She had only made it midlist.

It's a little lengthy.

"No children," she repeated.

How could she expect that from her future husband when she no longer could offer him the same?

She closed the vision board and focused on finishing a press release for a bestselling author and reading through incoming reviews for the debut album of a new indie recording artist whose single was trending on TikTok. By the time she shut down work for the day the skies were dark and the snow was falling heavily.

She texted her father to be safe in the weather but again he didn't respond, although she could see that he'd read it. She hated the guilt she felt at his anger. It nagged at her. She wasn't used to letting her father down. To being less than perfect in his eyes.

It was clear he wasn't dealing with her fall from grace, either.

Montgomery left the office and went down the stairs. She paused at the sight of the fireplace lit and the lights dimmed. She made her way around the corner to the hall leading to the kitchen. She leaned against the wall and watched Sean moving about her kitchen that she upgraded with new appliances and paint but was still in need of the walls being removed to increase its size and create an open floorplan.

Sean was so lost in his tasks that he didn't notice her standing there watching him.

He was just as intense in his cooking as he was in his lovemaking.

Wait. Don't move. Don't make me cum. Not yet. Please.

Montgomery bit the inside of her cheek and crossed her arms over her chest as her body pulsed to life at the memory of Sean's heated words. Earlier, when they first arrived to the house, as she showed him around the space and to the bedroom he would stay in, she had felt so nervous. Brushing past each other in the hall or innocent touches had stirred her. The man's presence wreaked havoc on her peace, and Montgomery had fled to her office to get some relief from her desire, afraid she would grab him and strip away every bit of his clothing.

I wish he had kissed me.

All night in Vegas as they enjoyed dinner and then focused on work, she had constantly wondered why he hadn't taken the chance to kiss her again. And she had to face why it bothered her that he hadn't.

I want Sean Cress.

To kiss.

To taste.

To feel.

To have inside me.

She enjoyed his flirtations. It was flattering. And arousing.

And now they were living together.

I did not think this through on so many, many levels.

Sean looked up from chopping green onion. He did a double take at her standing there and then smiled. "Hungry?" he asked. "With the winter storm coming I thought a pot of stew would work for dinner."

Montgomery pushed off the wall and came around the counter to stand beside him as he removed the lid of a large black ceramic stockpot she didn't recognize. "That's new?" she asked, tapping a fingernail against the side of the pot.

"Yes. That gourmet grocery store on Main Street is amazing," he said. "And you needed new pots. Yours were…"

Montgomery arched a brow and waited for him to finish his thought.

"Thin," he said.

The nerve. It's true, but damn.

"I don't really cook," she said. "Food delivery apps are my friend."

"I'll try to cook as much as I can when I'm not traveling for work—"

"Or attending the newest movie premieres, A-list parties, or appearances on celebrity gameshows," she added.

"Really keeping up with my life?" he asked, looking amused.

Montgomery cleared her throat, feeling embarrassed at what she just revealed. "I'm your publicist. Remember?" she said as she moved back around the counter to put space in between them.

"Right," he said, drawing it out and teasing her in the process before he chuckled.

"What's for dinner?" she asked.

"Beer-braised oxtail stew with my brother Lucas's version of bacon, chive and cheese biscuits," he said. "Sound good?"

"Sounds delicious," she said, hoping her stomach didn't rumble loud enough for him to hear.

"Wanna try it?" he asked, reaching for a tablespoon to scoop some of the stew.

Montgomery leaned across the counter as Sean fed her. She chewed. The meat was so tender and well seasoned. "Give me more," she said with a grunt of pleasure.

They both stiffened and shared a look.

The sound of their mingled cries of passion on that elevator echoed in her head.

She was the first to look away. To resist and ignore their desire for each other.

One day down and three hundred and sixty-four more to go. God help me.

Sean focused on rolling out the dough for the biscuits.

"Have you talked to your family?" she asked.

"My brothers? Yes. My parents? Not yet," he said.

"And your brothers?" she asked, thinking of the call from Monica that she didn't answer.

"Shocked," he said, grabbing a handful of flour from a large bowl—also new—to lightly dust the top of the dough.

"Because?"

"I never wanted to get married," Sean said.

"Because," she pressed.

Sean glanced up at her. "I enjoy my freedom. I like my life," he admitted.

See? Not the marrying type. But here we are married.

"You? Did you want to get married?" he asked.

Montgomery paused. "Yeah, I did. I had it all figured out and then…"

"And then we got stuck on that elevator," he finished for her.

She nodded, covering her face with her hand. "I still can't believe—"

"How good it was?" he asked, using a new biscuit cutter on the dough before placing each piece on a parchment-lined baking pan.

God, yes.

"That I had sex with an acquaintance," she said. "Maybe I have lost my mind. Maybe *we* lost our minds."

Sean picked up his phone and looked at the screen. "With the time zones we did not make twenty-four hours," he said.

"No, we're in it now and I'm not ready to return you just yet," she said playfully.

"Thanks," he drawled.

"It's just we haven't really talked about the future," she said. "The marriage has an end date, but not the baby. Where are we on childrearing? School? Visitation? Financial contributions? Everything is so out of order! It should be A-B-C not A-1-Z-B-square or whatever."

Sean slid the sheet pan into the oven and removed another with a batch of biscuits perfectly browned. "Then let's talk," he said.

The lights flickered.

Montgomery went still.

"Maybe we should check on the weather," Sean suggested, looking around the kitchen. "Where's the TV in here?"

Montgomery eyed him in disbelief. "You cannot be *that* privileged?" she said. "If so, you on the *wrong* side of Passion Grove, Richie Rich."

"Ha-ha," he said, coming around the counter and striding past her to leave the kitchen.

She turned and leaned back against the edge of the counter as she watched his tall and fit frame. He moved with confidence, strength and the swagger of a man who knew he had good d—

The lights flickered again.

And then went out.

"Oh, *hell* no!" Montgomery wailed in the darkness.

Light illuminated from the living room before Sean appeared in the hall, carrying his phone with its flashlight leading the way.

"You okay?" he asked.

She nodded. "Yeah," she said. "We are always stuck in emergencies together. Are we cursed?"

"Most definitely," Sean said without hesitation. "Do you have any candles?"

"Candles didn't make the shopping list?" she asked with a bit of snark.

"Petty much?" he asked.

"There's some in the hall closet," she said.

Sean reached for her hand and held it. "Come on," he said.

She followed behind him ever aware of just how warm his hand felt against hers. They reached the closet and worked together to light the fireplace, then lit candles and placed them on the counter in the kitchen and in the living room.

"Let there be light," Montgomery said, walking over to the front window to look out at the snow now inches high on the ground with more falling.

Sean came to stand beside her. "Looks like we might get snowed in," he said.

Montgomery raised her head to look at the snowflakes swirling around the tip of the lantern out on the street. "It's beautiful," she said.

In their reflection in the window, she watched as Sean slid his hands inside the pockets of his cords. "To me, I see aggravation," he said. "It will become dirty. Cause accidents. And slow down everything."

Montgomery feasted on his handsome features in the glass. "Who will our kid take after?" she asked.

He looked down at her.

She didn't dare look up at him.

"Whoever he or she wants to be," Sean said. "No pressure to make either of us so happy that he has to pretend to be what we want."

She did glance up at him then. "Like me?" she asked.

"Listen, my parents aren't much better than your dad," Sean admitted. "We all left our successful chef positions behind to take executive positions in the company they created because it's what they wanted. We all made a success of it, but in truth we set aside our own dreams to help theirs grow."

"But I thought you wanted to be the new CEO?" she asked.

"I do, but mainly to get my ideas put through," he admitted. "And…"

His words faded.

"And what?" she asked, surprised by the conflict she saw in the depths of his eyes.

"I feel it's owed to me, to be honest," Sean admitted. "I do the same corporate work as my brothers *and* maintain a full schedule taping three shows a year that help build the Cress, INC. brand name. I am the hardest working of the Cress brothers. I am always working or thinking about working. So it bugs me when they berate me for my fame and think I'm ego tripping, but I use that fame to help promote the family business. I am more than just a pretty face and great body."

Montgomery arched a brow. "Did you really just say that?" she mused with a bit of a smile.

"What? Too much?" he asked, nonplussed.

She couldn't tell if he was serious or not and gave him a judging look.

Sean just shrugged one broad shoulder.

He's adorable.

"Should we eat while we wait out the storm?" he asked, picking up a candle before turning to cross the living room.

"Might as well. There's nothing else to do," she said, following behind him.

Sean suddenly stopped.

Montgomery walked into the back of him and felt nothing but strength.

"Oh, there's something else we can do," he said, looking back at her over his shoulder.

Montgomery visibly swallowed.

Sean turned. "We haven't spent one night in this house and this thing between us is already bouncing off the walls—just like in the elevator," he said.

"Except there's more walls," Montgomery whispered before releasing a little shriek of pure frustration.

Sexual tension was being stoked without them even trying. It was organic and pure.

And hard to deny.

So very hard.

"I suggest a caveat to our prior agreement—a healthy sex life," he said, his voice deep and serious as his eyes searched hers by the light of the candles and the lit fireplace.

Montgomery thought of their steamy encounter and was intrigued to have another taste of him.

"No promises. No expectations. Full steam ahead with the divorce in a year," he added. "But in the meantime, we enjoy the one thing that brought us together in the first place. Amazing sex."

Montgomery took a step back from him and all the intense pleasure he dangled before her.

Sean watched the move. "Why fight it?" he asked.

Because I might not want the sex to ever end.

"Listen, it's your choice. Think it over. Let me know. My bedroom door is open," he said. "Because I want you in a way that distracts me."

Same.

Giving in would be so easy.

And he would be so hard.

Montgomery released a grunt.

But he is not my Mr. Perfect. Far from it.

Sean's expression became curious as he watched her.

But this isn't about my happily-ever-after.

Montgomery forced a smile she was afraid looked freakish when he frowned.

She stopped smiling. "Sean, I can't," she said.

Why waste time when I know we're not meant for each other?

He nodded in understanding. "It's up to you, Montgomery," he repeated before turning to make his way to the kitchen.

Give me more, Sean.

Montgomery went from begging for *it* to running away from *it*, when she knew she desperately ached for *it*.

To touch.

To stroke.

To taste.

To ride.

Saying yes would be easy. It's denying myself that's so very hard.

Six

Sean stood at the window of his bedroom at Montgomery's house, looking out at the snow continuing to heavily fall. Two tall and fat candles by his bedside gave the room a soft glow but it was the phone that lit upon his face as he looked at his parents on the screen. His father had been released from the hospital and they were in the movie theater at the townhouse.

"Look, husband, our son has remembered we exist," Nicolette said, her annoyance seeming to deepen her French accent. "Since we didn't get an invite to the wedding and weren't told he was marrying The Pretty Publicist."

"All done, *Maman*?" Sean asked.

"All done? I've only just begun," she snapped, her blue eyes blazing with angry fire.

"With?" he asked.

"With trying to figure out at just what point did you lose your mind? Do you even have a prenup? Just when did you decide marriage was for you because you have never shown a desire to be locked down as you say. I am confused by the decision, Sean."

"Montgomery changed my mind," he said, knowing it was a half-truth.

Nicolette paused, surprised by his answer.

"Dad?" Sean asked, giving him a chance to have his say as he eyed his father frowning as he sipped some steaming brew from a cup.

Phillip Senior cut his eyes up. "Prenup?" he asked before taking a sip that brought on a swear as he frowned some more.

"Yes—at Montgomery's suggestion," Sean assured him.

"Good. Right now I'm more concerned with what *is* this?" he asked, his English accent clipping his words.

"Seaweed tea," Nicolette said. "It gives you energy, immunity and a healthy heart."

"Bloody late for *that*," Phillip Senior snarked.

His mother patted his father's cheek and blew him a soft kiss before turning to eye Sean.

"Où est exactement votre nouvelle épouse?" Nicolette asked.

"Asleep." Sean answered her question of where exactly was his new bride.

Phillip Senior chuckled and raised his cup to him in toast. "A Cress man through and through," he said.

Anything but because Montgomery offered to be my wife in this marriage of convenience but does not want to be my lover.

"I'm ready to go to bed," his father said, his voice showing his fatigue.

It would take six to eight weeks for him to fully regain his strength and heal the wound on his breastplate from the surgery.

"As soon as the weather permits, I'll be by the townhouse to collect my things and check on you," Sean said.

"Bring the new Mrs. Cress," Nicolette said.

"If you agree to surrender the fight and not corner her with one of your bullying sessions," Sean said, well aware that his mother had tried to scare off each of the wives or girlfriends of his brothers. "Besides, your stunt doesn't seem to work."

Nicolette made a face of distaste that amused him.

Raquel, Monica, Jillian and Bobbie were each officially a Mrs. Cress.

"One day when you become a parent you will understand my motivations, Sean Pierre Cress," Nicolette told him.

That will be sooner than you think.

He was surprised at his desire to tell them the news but stuck to his agreement with Montgomery to keep the news until they were in their second trimester.

"Bonsoir," he said, wishing them a good night in French.

"Bonsoir," they said in return.

He ended the call and tossed the phone onto the middle of the bed. As he turned from the chill of standing near the windows in need of upgrading, Sean noticed cold permeated the entire room. With a frown he rubbed his bare arms and walked over to press his hand to the radiator. It was frigid.

The heat is off, too.

The thin cotton sleep pants he wore did nothing to shield him, but his thoughts went to Montgomery. He hurried to grab his phone to turn on the flashlight before blowing out the candles and crossing the carpeted floor to fling the door open and rush down the hall to her bedroom. It was dark but his light showed Montgomery was in the middle of her bed, huddled under the covers and curled into a ball.

His heart pounded as he went to her side to ease back the comforter. She was asleep but shivering from the cold. "Montgomery," he said, gently nudging her shoulder to awaken her.

He noticed that her lush lashes were naturally fuller at

the outer corners as she blinked before opening them to look up at him. "Hey," he said.

Such beautiful eyes.

"It's cold," she said, resembling a turtle as she ducked her head back under the covers as if it was a shell.

"The heat went out," he said, reaching to gather her and her bedcovers into his arms to lift with ease.

"That damn boiler," she muttered, snuggling her face against his neck.

Sean's body reacted to that as he used his phone to guide them out of the room, out to the hall and down the stairs. He felt her trembles and they reminded him of the feel of her when they climaxed together.

It feels good to hold her.

When they reached the living room, he regretted having to place her on the sofa. "Hold tight," he said.

"Okay," she said, sounding as if her teeth chattered.

He moved over to the fireplace to relight the wood stacked inside it.

After they ate an early dinner by the fire and decided to go to bed, he had doused the fire to ensure safety. Now they needed it badly to fight off the frigid cold created by the winter storm still raging outdoors. Soon the crackle of fire echoed. He moved the coffee table from in front of the sofa and then pushed the furniture forward to be closer to the heat before he lay down on the sofa under the covers beside her.

She was still trembling as he gathered her close with his head atop her head. He was surprised—and pleased—when she didn't protest.

"Still love the winter?" he asked.

"N-n-n-no," she stammered.

Sean chuckled.

The side of Montgomery's face lay against Sean's chest and the sound of his chuckle that seemed a second nature to him was deep. The light spray of flat hairs on his chest was soft. His muscles hard.

And the smell of him.

Something warm with woody notes.

She fought the natural urge to ease one of her legs atop his. Or to let the hand lightly resting on his muscled arm slide down to slip beneath the elastic waistband of his pajama bottoms.

Why fight it?

"Are you warming up?" Sean asked.

Am I.

Her body was on high alert from being pressed against him. Everything either throbbed or raced. One of his brown nipples was in her line of vision and she wanted so desperately to trace it with her tongue. Until it hardened. And he moaned in pleasure.

"Try to get some rest," he said, sounding as if his own voice was heavy with oncoming sleep.

When he pressed a kiss to the top of her head it felt the most natural thing in the world.

She stared into the embers of the fireplace, imagining giving in to her desires, until soon her eyes closed as she drifted to sleep as well.

Montgomery was awakened as her body was jostled. "Huh?" she asked, raising her head from Sean's chest.

"I didn't mean to wake you," he said as she looked up at him. "I was getting up."

Their eyes locked.

"Why?" she asked, still half-asleep and wondering just how much time had passed.

"Because I am a man with only so much control, Montgomery," he said, notching his chin up a bit.

She turned her head and looked down to find him aroused and his inches standing tall against the comforter.

"Ooh," she said as the core of her womanhood pulsed to life—like it applauded him.

It's up to you, Montgomery, Sean had said.

"Sorry. I was trying to get up before—"

She reached her hand inside his pants and gripped him with a deep moan from the back of her throat.

It was his time to tremble.

"Montgomery," he warned, his voice strained.

"It's up to me. Remember?" she said, looking up at him and loving the heat in his eyes. "New deal?"

"Name it," he said.

"We can add sex to our marriage but I need fidelity," she said as she began to stroke his hard inches from root to tip. Slowly. "No scandals. No mistresses. Deal?"

"Deal," he answered firmly as he placed his hands under her arms to drag her body atop his.

Her face was above his. In his eyes she saw the flickering embers of the fireplace mixed with his hunger. She felt the thundering beat of his heart. And his hard inches pressed against her belly. "I'm serious, Sean," she stressed, her eyes searching his.

"So am I," he promised just before he raised his head to capture her mouth with his own.

Montgomery's moan was filled with hunger as she gave in. Fully.

Their kiss was slow and sensual. Meant to heighten their desires. To tease with promise for more.

She pushed the cover to the floor beside the sofa and brought her knees up to rest on either side of his body, pressing the length of his hardness against her core. With a grunt she rolled her hips.

"Yes," Sean moaned into her mouth as he brought his hands beneath the satiny gown she wore to grip her buttocks.

She gasped at his heated touch, ending their kiss with

a lick of his mouth and soft suck of his bottom lip before sitting up with her hands pressed to his chest. He eyed her in wonder as she gripped the edges of her gown to raise it over her head. She felt the heat of the flames in the fireplace against her nudity as she brought her hands up to cup her own breasts.

"Montgomery," Sean moaned.

"Huh?" she asked with a tease.

That door inside her where she succumbed to her passion was opened again. Just like that night they were trapped together in the elevator. It was a part of her she never knew existed. Where she found power in her sexuality. Where there was no shame or inhibition. No desire to be a "good girl" and present the image of perfection. Where she did not put the wishes of others ahead of her own. Be shy? Pretend?

No.

She raised her arms above her head.

"I love your body," Sean marveled. "I *love* it."

"Now we can see each other," she said.

"Damn right," he agreed.

She dipped down to suck one of his nipples to hardness before shifting over to do the same to the other.

He hissed in pleasure.

Montgomery lightly licked a trail down the hard ridges of his abdomen as she moved backward to sit atop his knees. With a look up at him, she freed his hardness from his sleep pants to stroke. His hips arched upward at her touch. She eyed the dark length of him and his thickness before stroking the smooth tip with her tongue.

Sean cried out.

She sucked him—slowly and deeply—enjoying the feel of him against her tongue.

His hands entwined in her hair.

She took in all of him until the soft hairs surrounding the root of his shaft tickled her lips and the scent of his soap filled her nose. With patience she continued to taste him by firelight, enjoying its heat as the one inside her rose. Just the sight of Sean's face twisted in pleasure fueled her.

"You like it?" she asked before giving his tip another lick.

"Too much," he said, easing her head back to free himself before he reached to pull her body up against his again.

He shifted them on their sides on the sofa. Facing each other. Eyes locked.

She raised one leg to drape over his hip as she settled her head atop one arm and gripped the strength of the other. The feel of his hardness was there between their bodies, reminding her that he was more than ready to fill her with it. The soft hairs on his chest teased her hard nipples, and Sean used his fingertip to softly trace her body from shoulder to thigh.

She took a deep inhale.

When he raised her leg to place it on his shoulder, she gripped his arm and rolled her hips as he softly stroked her pulsing bud. It danced for him and his eyes devoured the expressions of her face as he brought her to the edge of a slow but intense climax.

Yes. Yes. Yes. Yes!

The anticipation of her release made her ache.

"Do you want it?" he asked, his voice thick. "Do you want to cum?"

Her fingernails dug into his arm as she quivered. "Y-y-yes," she whispered.

Sean smiled and used the arm she lay on to grip her body and pull her closer to kiss her deeply as he did indeed make her climax. He swallowed her cries of pleasure and was relentless in massaging her bud as she shook from the white-hot spasms that controlled her.

And just when she thought she could take no more, Sean

freed the bud and gripped his dark inches to guide his dick inside her tightness with a thrust of his hips.

Together they broke their heated kiss to release rough cries in the space between their open mouths. It blended with the crackle of the firewood.

Slowly, he stroked inside her as he gripped the soft flesh of her buttocks. She reached to do the same to him, enjoying the flex and release of his muscles with each thrust that pushed her into such a deep climax that she felt her inner walls clutch his inches. Again and again and again. A fine sheen of sweat coated their bodies as he quickened his pace.

"Sean," she gasped. "Don't stop. Don't stop."

He didn't.

Even once she was weak and sure she didn't have the strength or the will to walk, he held her tightly and continued his onslaught.

She felt his inches get harder—like steel—and his body stiffen. The look in his eyes changed in that moment just before he flung his head back and released a long roar that echoed. Gripping his face, she jerked his head forward and kissed him, seeking his tongue with her own to suckle it as she worked her inner walls to drain him of every bit of his release. She didn't stop until he was trembling, releasing small whimpers and spent.

"Damn," he whispered in the aftermath as he pressed kisses to her sweat-dampened face. "Damn."

Montgomery pressed her hands to his chest, feeling the hard pounding of his heart, and couldn't find one regret for the choice she made to have him. Not one.

Ding-dong. Ding-dong. Ding-dong.

Sean awakened from the steady ringing of the doorbell. Montgomery was still asleep where they lay on the floor atop a pallet he made from comforters and blankets. The intensity of the fire had died down and during the night they had snuggled closer for more warmth.

Being sure to cover her nudity with more blankets, Sean searched for his pajama bottoms to pull on and grabbed a throw cover to wrap around him. He was pleased to see the lights were back on as he made his way to the front door to ease it open. The winter winds still were brutal and circled around the tall and thin man standing there with a scowl on his face. "Good morning. Can I help you?" he said.

The man shook his head. "I guess you're my daughter's...*husband*," he said, his voice deep and filled with his annoyance.

Montgomery's father.

Sean stepped back and opened the door fully. "Yes, I am, Mr. Morgan. It's nice to meet you," he said, looking over at Montgomery still sleeping on the floor.

"*Reverend* Morgan," he corrected him, knocking snow off his boots before stepping inside. "You would know that had you bothered to meet me."

"I see neither time nor the cold has cooled you off yet," Sean said with a smile.

"And freezing in here all night didn't teach you any manners," the reverend countered.

"Let me wake up Montgomery."

"Don't," the man demanded as he crossed the living room. "I don't have anything to say to her. I just came to check on the boiler."

Sean followed behind him. "That's good of you considering you're not talking to her," he said as the man opened a door leading down into the basement.

"I want her to respect me, not suffer," he said before descending the stairs.

"Thank you for thinking of us," Sean offered, dodging a spider web that almost covered his face like a palm.

The reverend paused and looked back. "I said *her*," he said with emphasis before turning around.

"Sir," Sean said.

"Good start," Reverend Morgan drawled.

Why am I even trying?

Sean released a heavy breath.

For Montgomery. And this man will be the grandfather to my child.

"Sir," Sean repeated with emphasis. "I'm from a good family. I have a great career—"

"Oh. I *know* who you are," the man said before opening the electric panel on the wall to turn off the electricity.

"Great!" Sean exclaimed.

Reverend Morgan snorted in derision.

"Is that good or bad?" Sean asked. "Listen, the sex tape was from years ago—"

"The sex tape!" Reverend Morgan exclaimed, his voice booming against the walls.

Uh-oh.

Sean felt out of sorts. He had never met anyone who disliked him.

"Listen, Reverend Morgan, not speaking to Montgomery is—"

His temporary father-in-law was bent down near the boiler, but paused to look back over his shoulder at him. "Is what?"

"A move meant to make sure she does what you want instead of what she wants," Sean continued. "Whether you mean it to be or not, it's emotional blackmail. Sir."

Another grunt.

"Where was all this wisdom when you made a sex tape?" Reverend Morgan asked with snark. "Oh, wait. There was none."

Sean nodded. "As men we all make mistakes. No one is perfect…or should expect perfection," he finished.

Reverend Morgan waved his hand at him dismissively and focused on working on the boiler.

Sean hoisted the dragging blanket up higher on his shoulders to keep it off the floor as he looked around at the basement. It was unfinished, stacked with containers and had a slightly damp scent to it. When he thought of the finished basement at the Cress family townhome, complete with the housekeeper apartment, wine cellar, laundry room and storage, the space left a lot to be desired. There was size but no function.

At the sound of the metal gate of the boiler closing, Sean turned to find his father-in-law wiping his hands on a cloth he shoved back inside the overalls he wore under his leather winter coat.

"That boiler needs to be replaced, man of the house," Reverend Morgan said with sarcasm.

"No problem," Sean assured him.

The man breezed past him and climbed up the stairs. The scent of the heat rising in the radiators already began to fill the air.

"Reverend Morgan," he called up to him.

The man paused.

"I know it couldn't have been easy raising a daughter alone," Sean said. "Montgomery is proof you did a good job."

"And your recipe for Bolognese is salty," Reverend Morgan said sarcastically, leaving the basement and closing the door.

"What the—!" Sean said in indignation before taking off to climb the stairs two at a time, relieved the man hadn't locked the door.

He reached the living room just in time to see Reverend Morgan leave the house, closing the front door behind him. Not a second later Montgomery's head popped up from the floor. "Were you pretending to be asleep?" he asked her in astonishment as he crossed the room to stand beside their pallet.

Montgomery lay back down and rolled over onto her back to look up at him. "I knew it was my father at the door," she admitted. "I just swore he was coming to preach a sermon. Trust me, pretending to be asleep has gotten me out of a lot of *long* conversations."

Sean let the blanket around his shoulders fall to the floor. "Or you could have talked to him the same way I did," he said.

She sat up. "What did he say?"

"Same-o-same about respect," Sean told her. "And that one of my recipes was too salty. Can you believe that?"

Montgomery looked taken aback. "He said that?" she asked.

"Is he a fan of one of my shows?" Sean asked, sitting down on the sofa watching her think about the question.

"I don't know," she said. "I left home for college and never moved back. I don't know what my father does in his free time. I honestly don't know. I never thought about it."

"Montgomery, a part of your father seeing you as more than his little girl is you presenting yourself as more than that," Sean said.

She looked doubtful. "Easier said than done."

"I'm going to finally clean up the kitchen," he said, rising to his feet and ignoring the distraction of the covers having fallen down to her lap as she stared into the dying embers in the fireplace.

Seven

One month later

Montgomery sat behind her desk at the midtown Manhattan offices of Montgomery Morgan Publicity. She looked around at the modest offices housing her six-member team made up of two public relations specialists, her executive assistant, Hanna, an account manager, graphic designer and college intern. She took pride in her accomplishments and the success of the business she built from the ground up, starting her career as a college intern and working her way up through the ranks in positions at public relations departments at publishing houses, music companies, fashion designers and corporations. Twice she had been named on *Ebony's* Power 100 list and been featured in *Essence*.

It was quite a feat at just thirty-three.

But with every passing day, her focus was far less on her business.

She turned her clear office chair to look out the window.

But it was not the view of the metropolis showing signs that winter was ending and spring was soon to begin that she enjoyed. It was her reflection against the glass as she pulled the turquoise dress she wore close around her belly swollen with Sean's child. Her days of being able to hide her pregnancy were drawing to an end.

With each kick and flutter of the baby's movement, every doctor's appointment that showcased a new milestone, every purchase in preparation of its arrival and the steady growth of her belly, her love for the baby grew and her fear of motherhood lessened.

She reached for her phone from atop the modern black L-shaped desk with bronze accent legs that matched the decor of the entire office suite. She pulled up her father's number and called him, hating how nervous she felt to reach out to her own father. After three weeks of attending church every Sunday and being ignored, Montgomery had stopped going. Still, every day she left a voice mail or text message hoping one day he would close the divide between them.

She needed to be forgiven.

For so long, she feared outright disobeying him but never had she imagined him cutting her out of his life completely. Not for getting married.

Her call went straight to voice mail. "Hey, Daddy. It's me. Montgomery. As always, I hope you're okay," she said, her voice shaky with her hurt. "I have some good news and I wanted you to be the first to know that Sean and I...are having a baby, Dad."

Sharp pain radiated across her chest and she pressed her eyes closed as tears threatened to fall. *Damn it.*

"You're going to be a grandfather," she said, her voice soft with her hurt. "I love you."

She ended the call and released a heavy breath.

Knock-knock.

Montgomery released the dress to billow about her frame

again before she turned. "Yes, Hanna?" she asked at the sight of her assistant standing in the doorway holding an enlarged copy of the upcoming cover of *Celebrity Weekly.*

"This just arrived," Hanna said, wiggling her eyebrows as she crossed the room and set the posterboard atop her desk—and close to her boss's face.

Montgomery leaned back to take in the photo of herself and Sean posed together for their exclusive interview on the surprise nuptials. The photo was taken during the wedding ceremony.

The digital edition had been released online last week.

"Y'all look great together," Hanna said, still holding the corner of the large 16x20 foam board as she came around it.

We do.

She remembered the shot well. It was the moment just after they were pronounced husband and wife. The glow of the candlelight against the night views of Vegas in the background was spectacular. Her dress truly seemed whimsical and romantic in the setting. The photo had quickly gone viral to rave reviews.

Her heart pounded a little as she leaned in to study her face. And the look in her eyes.

She gasped at the discovery.

There, in the brown depths of her feline-like eyes, was her hunger for his kiss. The one that landed on her cheek instead of her mouth, filling her with such disappointment.

Not that they hadn't made up for it.

She had lost count over the past four weeks how often one of them would leave their bedroom to seek out the other in theirs. Whether long, slow and sensual or fast and hard, they would get lost in each other for minutes or hours.

They would disagree over any and everything. And their lives were lived separately with them only making joint appearances for his family or a public event. There were even a few nights he would go out alone and return in the early hours of the morning. She never questioned him. She felt she had no right—even though she would wait up for his safe return in her bedroom without him knowing.

Between those sheets, nothing mattered but their pleasure.

Nothing at all.

With the hint of a smile, she tilted her head to the side and wrapped the end of her ponytail around her finger.

Just that morning, after being away for a week to tape a new special in the Swiss Alps, Sean returned and knocked on the door to the bathroom before peeking his head inside to ask to join her in the shower. She agreed and through the steam, she saw that he was naked. Without hesitation, she had pulled the curtain back and reached for his wrist to pull him under the spray of water with her.

As her body grew with their child, she assumed his desire for her would wane.

She was so very wrong.

She licked and bit down on her bottom lip, remembering the feel of his body lightly pounding against hers as he stroked inside her from behind as the water sprayed down against them, plastering her hair to her scalp and ruining her silk press.

Well worth it.

The man had climaxed twice with a rough cry as the muscles of his body tensed and his hardness pulsed with each shot of his release inside her.

She grunted at the electric memory.

As Hanna gave her an odd look, Montgomery cleared her throat and sat up straight to regain her cool and composed decorum as she almost figuratively melted in her chair.

Because of Sean Cress, she had added exquisite lover to her list for her Mr. Perfect. Although she wondered if there was anyone who could best him physically.

Perhaps love will give my future husband the upper hand.

Over the weeks they had developed a friendship and were comfortable with each other but theirs was no love match. Being with Sean had taught her that there could be great passion without love.

And it was that element she wanted in her life. Still.

A loving relationship with a man with whom she was compatible and had more in common than amazing sex.

Bzzzzzz. Bzzzzzz. Bzzzzzz.

Montgomery turned her phone over and her heart raced to see a photo of her father's face. "That's it for now, Hanna," she said, picking up the device to answer the call.

Hanna quickly left and closed the door behind her.

"Hi, Daddy," she said, letting her emotions swell in her voice and hoping he had set aside his anger at her. Finally. That he was able to just be happy for her.

"Congratulations, Go-Go," he said.

She closed her eyes and then pressed the bridge of her nose between her fingers. "Thank you," she said.

The line went silent.

"Daddy?" she said, not sure he was still on the line.

"I'm here," he said.

It felt so awkward. So forced.

Not what she hoped for. No joy. No excitement.

Her father's silence was just as heavy with his judgment as were his harsh words.

Montgomery pressed a hand to her belly, praying she had more forgiveness and grace in her for her child than her father had given her. "It's good to hear from you. Why don't you come over for dinner," she offered. "Sean can make some less salty Bolognese."

That did get a grunt.

Montgomery felt exasperated and clutched her free hand into a fist. But what surprised her above all was the desire she had to talk to Sean. He had proven himself able to lift her spirits by making her laugh or offering sound advice.

"Am I welcome back to church?" she asked.

"I never once said you weren't welcome, Montgomery," he said.

No, you made me feel unwelcomed—unwanted—and actions speak louder than words.

But she did not say that. She couldn't bring herself to do it. Old habits seemed hard for her to break.

Montgomery, a part of your father seeing you as more than his little girl is you presenting yourself as more than that.

Sean's words resonated.

"Daddy, can I call you back?" she asked, wanting freedom from his judgment.

"I expect to see you Sunday at church," he said, his voice demanding.

Montgomery held the phone from her face to stare down at it in shock. Anger at her father sparked in her. He denied her very presence in church and then made her feel like she was not justified in no longer attending.

What in the hell?

"Okay," she said, setting the phone down and letting her finger hover over the red button to end the call.

"Go-Go," he said.

"Yes?"

"Be safe," he said with more warmth than she had heard in his tone in months.

"I will, Dad," she said.

He ended the call.

Montgomery released a long sigh and leaned back against her chair with her eyes closed.

Bzzzzzz. Bzzzzzz. Bzzzzzz.

She opened one eye to look at her phone. With a shake of her head, she smiled at Sean's name on the screen. She reached to answer the call and placed it on speaker. "Mr.

Cress, how may I assist you, sir?" she said, her hands splayed against her belly.

"Mr. Cress?" he asked, his deep voice amused. "I think I would like you to call me that next time I'm sexing you."

Her heart pounded. "Really?" she asked.

"Definitely," he countered.

Montgomery chuckled. "Mr. Cress, if you're nasty?" she asked, a play on the lyric from the Janet Jackson song "Nasty."

That made Sean laugh from his belly.

And she enjoyed doing that because his laughter was infectious.

"Listen, I'm still at the house and the lights went out," Sean said. "I had an electrician come out and the house needs massive rewiring."

Cha-ching. Cha-ching.

"What's the estimate?" she asked with a shake of her head. "And how soon can they repair it?"

"He's still working on that, but it's going to take close to a month to complete," Sean said.

Montgomery released a heavy breath. "I love my house, but it's becoming a money trap," she said.

Over the weeks she had shared with him her wishes on how to completely update the home to be a showcase again.

"Listen, we'll stay at my condo in Tribeca until all of the work is repaired and I'll pay the bill so don't worry about it," he said.

"No," she protested. "It's my home. My bill."

"And you're my wife," he stressed.

"For ten more months," she countered.

"I live there," he continued.

"For ten more months," she repeated.

"And staying at my condo? Can I offer that or does that offend your sensibilities as well?" he asked. "Or maybe you want to pay rent?"

"Is that sarcasm, Mr. America's Favorite Chef?" she asked.

"I'm nice, not perfect," he said.

At least not for me.

"You know I'm leaving next week for work and I would feel better making sure you are good before then, Montgomery," he said.

"But that's not your responsibility."

"Untrue. You are my wife—no matter the end date and you are pregnant with my child," he said. "That makes you my responsibility. I can't change who I am."

A wealthy playboy married to a woman he doesn't love.

"Listen, we have dinner tonight at my parents'," he said. "We'll go by the condo first and you can see if you like it."

"Okay, Sean," she acquiesced, releasing the nervousness she had of stepping deeper into his world of wealth and luxury.

Sean looked out the apron window of his condo at the view of the waterfront in the Tribeca section of Manhattan. He considered this an investment property and a second home from the Cress family townhome. At times he allowed out-of-town guests to use it, threw parties, or found the solace unavailable in a family home. No one in the family except Lucas knew about his luxury hideaway in a building exclusive enough to draw the likes of other high-profile celebrities and athletes.

For Sean, being in a large, well-known family, and a frequent subject of the press meant having something that was just for him. His parties were legendary and Sean took great pleasure in having a part of his life not wrapped up in being a Cress.

He glanced back over his shoulder at Montgomery standing and looking up at one of the many large paintings of himself that he'd been gifted over the years by fans of his shows who were extremely talented. There were also many photos of himself with other celebrities and dignitaries—including a couple of presidents of the United States. It was also in the condo where he kept all of the awards he'd won over the years.

He eyed her profile, again struck by how beautiful she was to him. He loved the way she had cleverly hidden her pregnancy from the world. Another secret.

One he felt himself get more excited about with each passing day.

The first time Montgomery grabbed his hands and pressed them to her belly as the baby kicked—or maybe even did flip-flops—his heart had burst with love for the baby. His child.

Our child.

He let his eyes enjoy the sight of her in the black ruffle trapeze dress she wore under a black satin tuxedo blazer with high heels. Time had not dulled his attraction to her. In fact, it was stronger. He couldn't get enough of her. And when he would go to her bedroom seeking the pleasure he craved, she never denied him. Whether sleeping, working or reading, she would welcome him into her bed. For him, there was nothing better than being awakened from his sleep by Montgomery climbing into his bed beside him, naked and ready.

But it was more than just her body.

Montgomery Morgan—she hadn't changed her name—was intelligent and witty when she wasn't hiding behind one of her facades—cold and formal for business; innocent and fragile for her father.

Suddenly, Montgomery looked over at him with a smile, with her ebony hair in loose curls pulled back from her face with a thin elastic band with a crystal adornment that rested just above her ear. His gut clenched.

"Will our child have its father's ego?" she mused, walking over to stand beside him. "Because *this* is a shrine. And clearly a bachelor pad."

Sean chuckled as he looked around at the sleek and modern decor in black and charcoal. There was no softness to be found. It was the space of a man. "We'll only be here until the house is ready," he reminded her.

"It's a beautiful space," she said, looking out at the view of the water as the sun began to lower. "Well worth every million, I'm sure."

Sean didn't miss the hint of contention in her voice. It was there any time his wealth came up. The elephant in the room he chose not to address. He wasn't a classist, but he couldn't pretend he didn't enjoy the trappings of wealth. And just by the very existence of their child, he or she would automatically become an heir to both the Cress family fortune and the prosperity he had garnered in his own right.

"There's a pool, spa and library in the building," he shared, easing his hands into the pockets of the black suit he wore. "Security, doorman and concierge."

She looked up at him. "Stop selling me, Sean," she said. "Thank you for letting me stay here while my house is being worked on. I promise I'm not ungrateful."

He bent his head to press a kiss to her forehead.

Her gasp was crystal clear.

He looked down at her eyes finding the same surprise he felt at the tender gesture.

I couldn't help myself.

"Ready?" he asked, stepping away from her.

"To tell your family I'm pregnant?" she asked, the click of her high heels indicating she followed behind him to the door. "Definitely not."

Sean opened the front door and held it for her. "They're not that bad," he insisted.

Montgomery gave him a look as she passed him out into

the hall. "Just keep an eye on your mother," she requested. "I heard she likes to corner newbies."

True.

It really was a trait he wished his mother would stop. Although he was sure she was just being a mother bear to her cubs, he knew the optics were not great. Serving as a gatekeeper to their family barked of elitism.

"To be fair, I didn't hold back giving your father my opinion of how he treats you, so feel free to politely put her in her place," he said.

Montgomery looked surprised. "What did you say?" she asked as he closed the door and pressed his thumb to the biometric lock to secure it.

"Huh?" he asked as they walked down the ornate hall to the elevator.

"What did you say to my father?" she asked.

"That whether he meant to or not, the way he was treating you was emotional blackmail," he told her with a shrug of his shoulder. "It's a way to control someone. Do what I say or I will withdraw my love, my attention, my support."

Montgomery frowned.

"Did I overstep?" he asked.

She shook her head. "No. I just never looked at it like that and I wish it wasn't true," she said, her sadness so evident as she looked down at her feet in deep thought.

"Hey, hey, hey," he said, placing his hand to her chin to raise her head. "You guys talked today. Right? Things are beginning to thaw with you and your dad. It will get better."

She gave him a smile that was forced.

As Sean drove them to his parents' townhouse in his Bentley Continental, he noticed Montgomery remained silent as she looked out the window. He found his eyes kept going to her and he had to fight not to reach for her hand just to assure her. Comfort her. Be there for her.

And when he thought he saw the glimmer of a tear on

her cheek, Sean did reach across the seat to take her hand into his own. She instantly squeezed it with her fingers and looked over at him with a soft smile of thanks.

At the townhouse, after Sean parked on the street outside the home and helped Montgomery out of the vehicle, she paused on the street to look up at the towering Victorian-era structure. It was impressive, particularly during the inky night, and the up-lighting made it seem like a beacon in the darkness. His eyes studied her face, looking for more of her unspoken disdain for affluence, but she just smiled at him as he opened the gate of the wrought iron fence lining the front of the property and they climbed the steps together.

"Careful in those heels," he said, feeling protective.

"I could outrun you in these," she said with confidence.

"All I ask is you wear them later—with nothing else on," he said as they reached the top step and he pressed the doorbell.

The door opened, not giving her a chance to answer, although he caught the light of interest spark in her eyes.

"Good evening, Mr. and Mrs. Cress," Felice the house-keeper said, stepping back to hold the door for them.

"How are you doing, Felice?" he asked, giving her a warm smile.

The middle-aged woman gave him a wink. "Better now that my favorite is back home—for a little while anyway," she said.

Sean clasped his hands and laughed. "Good to see you, too, Felice," he said.

"Charmer," Montgomery whispered to him after they passed the woman, crossed the marbled entryway and then stepped through the open foyer door into the living room.

"Here are the newlyweds," Nicolette said with a large smile from her seat on the sofa beside his father.

Sean creased his brow at his mother's insincerity. She wasn't acting for a performance, just politeness. But that was Nicolette. To anyone outside of their inner circle, life was grand and there were no worries. He didn't doubt that keeping up appearances had her nerves stretched thin.

"Hello, everyone," Montgomery said as Felice took their coats.

With his wife at his side, Sean made the rounds. The entire family was in attendance. Lincoln and Bobbie, Phillip Junior and Raquel, Gabriel and Monica, Coleman and Jillian, and Lucas—the lone unmarried Cress brother.

"Where are my nieces?" Sean asked as he accepted the snifter of thirty-year-old brandy from Phillip Junior.

"In the nursery with the au pair we hired for the night," Nicolette said, her hand clasping his father's knee. "I'm giving my daughters-in-law a little respite for a few hours while we celebrate my love getting a good checkup at the cardiologist."

Phillip Senior turned up his lips at the soda water he was drinking as he eyed the liquor his sons were sipping.

"What's your drink, Montgomery?" Phillip Junior asked.

"I have it, Mr. Phillip," Felice said as she entered the room carrying a tray and walked up to Montgomery sitting with his sisters-in-law—completely fitting in. "Mr. Sean asked for Chef to be sure to have this for you whenever you visit."

Over the rim of his glass, Sean watched Montgomery's surprise at her favorite drink, pear-flavored sparkling water topped with fresh slices of the fruit.

She looked over at him across the living room and mouthed, "Thank you."

"My sons are in love," Nicolette said, her eyes slightly reserved. "All of you are staring at your wives."

Sean looked around him and it was indeed true.

Lincoln eyed Bobbie and her wild mane of loose curls.

Phillip Junior was taking in the length of Raquel's leg exposed by the slit in her dress.

Gabriel seemed intrigued by Monica innocently stroking the base of her throat as she talked to the other women.

Coleman had just motioned for Jillian with an incline of his head toward the kitchen.

Unlike his brothers, his marriage to Montgomery was no love match and, at that moment, he was well aware that they believed it to be.

More deception.

"My turn is coming," Lucas assured them.

All the brothers reached to give him light and playful punches. Although Lucas was thirty years of age, he was undeniably the baby of the family.

"Je ne suis pas pressé, mon petit garçon," Nicolette said, telling him she was in no rush, my baby boy.

Lincoln, their half brother whom they had come to love, chuckled as the other Cress brothers threw their hands up in exasperation at their mother's insistence on babying a grown man.

Lucas just shrugged and looked pleased because he knew being the "favorite" was a playful bone of contention with his brothers.

Montgomery excused herself and walked over to him, lightly touching his arm. "Can we go up and see the children?" she asked.

He finished his drink and handed his glass to Phillip Junior "Sure. And I'll show you my old room," he said, taking her hand in his and leading her down the hall and into the bustling kitchen.

"Wait," he said, stopping before they reached the elevator in the corner. "You okay with this?"

"I use them at work all the time," she said. "Plus, in the end, I wasn't scared anymore. Remember?"

More, Sean. Give me more.

"Oh, I remember," he said as they continued to the elevator.

"Your mother hasn't said much to me," she said as soon as he closed the gate and pressed the button for the fifth floor.

"I thought you wanted her to keep her distance?" he asked.

"I do," she said, playing with her ear.

Something she did when she was nervous.

"No worries, Montgomery," he said as the elevator slid to a stop.

They crossed the massive den to reach the nursery. The au pair held a finger to her mouth from where she sat rocking Emme to point to Collie, who was snuggled under the covers in the middle of the bed with her mouth open and her glasses on the bedside table as she slept.

Montgomery continued forward to quietly look down at the baby—now three months old.

"Would you like to hold her?" the au pair asked with the hint of a German accent.

"Yes," she stressed.

Sean remained near the door and looked on as Montgomery bent to scoop the bundle of joy into her arms. Back and forth she slightly swayed as she looked down at Emme, who cooed causing Montgomery to smile so brightly that it lit up her face.

That tugged at him.

"I'll leave you alone," the au pair said before exiting the suite.

"Can you believe we're going to have one of our own?" she whispered, looking over at him.

"I can't wait," he admitted.

Patiently, he leaned against the wall and watched her enjoy those precious moments bonding with his niece—*their* niece.

She's my wife. For now anyway.

When Montgomery finally placed the baby in her crib it was with obvious reluctance.

Neither of us thought we wanted a child and now we're anxious for its arrival.

Sean and Montgomery stepped out into the den and the au pair reentered the suite, closing the door behind her. They both paused to see Nicolette exit the elevator with her silver chiffon dress trailing behind her.

He felt Montgomery stiffen beside him and he placed a hand to her lower back.

Nicolette gave them a smile that didn't reach her eyes. "Sean, may I have a moment alone with your wife?" she asked, her hands clasped in front of her.

"No, most definitely not," he said.

Montgomery glanced up at him as he continued to eye his mother. "No more of your covert mission to lay down the law to new members of this family," he said. "Montgomery is pregnant and I will not let you aggravate her with that nonsense, *Maman.*"

Nicolette released a gasp of surprise—a momentary lapse before she quickly regained her composure.

"I suggest you take this time to prepare yourself to act appropriately, *Maman,*" Sean said. "And when you join the rest of the family be prepared to show happiness when we reveal we have a baby coming."

His mother's blue eyes dropped down to Montgomery's belly. "Congratulations," she said, stepping forward to press a kiss to both of their cheeks. "A baby is always a blessing. Let's go share the good news."

He kept his hand on Montgomery's back, wanting to reassure her as they all stepped onto the elevator and descended back to the first floor. As soon as they stepped into the living room, the entire Cress brood surrounded them with joy.

"Congratulations!" everyone exclaimed.

His mother quietly regained her spot next to Phillip Senior, reaching to take his hand in hers to grasp tightly.

"How did you all know?" Montgomery asked as the women all pressed hands to her belly.

Monica held up the video baby monitor.

They had overheard the news.

As the women whisked her away to start chattering about baby names and clothes, Sean eyed his father, who raised his virgin drink to him in a toast before leaning to whisper something to his wife.

Nicolette rose and crossed the room to leave the living room. She returned after a while with Felice carrying a tray of champagne-filled flutes, which the woman quickly distributed before giving Montgomery a flute with more flavored sparkling water. His mother reclaimed her spot next to his father.

They all looked on as Phillip Senior slowly rose to his full height from his seat on the sofa—a clear effort on his part.

"As my days feel counted, I am pleased to be able to see and hold another Cress baby," he said with emotions rarely shown by him brimming in his eyes. "I have many regrets, my sons, but never the birth of any of you. Never."

Sean was surprised by their father's impassioned emphasis.

Phillip Senior raised his flute of champagne. "For this I will drink with you all, my family. *À la nourriture. À la vie. À l'amour*," he said, resting his eyes on Sean.

To food. To life. To love.

"*À la nourriture. À la vie. À l'amour*," they all said in unison.

Eight

Montgomery bit the tip of her stylus as she looked up from her tablet at the light rain drizzling against the windows of Sean's condo. She had been swiping through press clippings of all her firm's clients over the past week. The hour was late and she was home alone.

Sean had left right after their dinner of homemade pizza.

Was she curious where he was and what he was up to? Definitely. Did she ask him for an explanation? Definitely not.

Still, I'm curious.

Had he gone back on his word and was with another woman?

Somehow, she didn't believe that, plus, a lot of the time the press followed his movements so closely that it took a cursory check to discover his activities. Still, it was evidence that Sean Cress was not prepared to settle down. He was a certified bachelor at his core and when their marriage of convenience was over, she was sure he would kick it back into high gear. Women. Parties. Jet-setting.

She had resolved herself to take on the majority of the work of parenting as her ex enjoyed his lavish lifestyle.

And in time, once things were settled and she made a new routine for being a single working mother, she would find her Mr. Perfect—who was interested in being a stepparent. What does that look like? Curious, she opened up her old dating app. She hadn't logged in since she discovered she was pregnant. As she swiped through possible matches, she read the bios of each. Some men unequivocally stated they were not interested in women with children. She paused at the sight of a handsome bearded man with a toothy smile.

"Charles Yaeger. Private school principal. Man of God. Father of one daughter I adore. Looking for a single parent who understands the importance of family, not just dating—although romance is *always* important," she read.

He seemed…perfect.

The lock on the front door disengaged as she closed the app and put to rest any concerns over Charles Yaeger still being available two years later. With a glance back over her shoulder, she eyed Sean entering wearing a tuxedo with his bow tie undone.

He paused at the sight of her as he took off his shoes. "Still up?" he asked.

"Just working and enjoying the view," she said, holding up her tablet.

He walked over to lean against the back of the couch and look down at her with a yawn. "Don't forget I leave tomorrow," he said.

He was doing a new series, highlighting his travels across the continent as he feasted on local cuisine indigenous to the area. He was excited about it and had been preparing by reading up on each country to which he was traveling. It was all he'd talked about for days.

"I didn't," she said. "For a few weeks, right?"

He nodded. "By the time I get back the house should be ready," he said.

"Thanks for overseeing that for me," she told him, tilting her head back on the couch. "And for paying half the bill."

Sean's eyes studied her face. "No problem," he said. "You should turn in, too. Your eyes look tired."

True. He was always so observant.

Montgomery rose, leaving her tablet on the sofa as she followed a yawning Sean across the expansive living space and chef's kitchen to reach the rear where there were four bedrooms.

"'Night, Montgomery," he said as he continued to the master bedroom.

"Sean," she softy called behind him.

He looked over his shoulder.

She beckoned him with her finger. "Three weeks is a long time," she said.

Sean raised both brows as he turned.

Montgomery undid the satin robe she wore and it slid o a puddle at her feet as she turned and leaned in the open loorway with the light of the bedroom outlining her frame.

"Damn," he swore from down the hall.

She smiled.

Moments later his arms were around her and his lips pressed to her neck. She sighed and shivered as she led him into the bedroom. The rustle of fabric let her know he undressed and left a trail of clothing. When they reached he bed, he pressed the length of his hard inches against he groove of her buttocks, naked and warm. He sucked her ape as his hands cupped her breasts and teased her nipples.

No words were needed. Passion spoke.

He kissed her from her shoulders to the back of her

knees, pausing to lightly bite each of her soft butt cheeks. And when he rose his hands massaged the length of her back before applying enough pressure to guide her to bend over. She felt him blow a cool stream of air against her pulsing core just before he buried his face to suck her throbbing bud into his mouth from behind.

Montgomery took a deep breath and jerked her head up, causing her hair to fling back from her face. In the round mirror over the dresser, she watched her reflection as she pressed her hands down into the bed and gripped the coverlet as Sean tasted her slowly and with reverence. Her first climax brought tears to her eyes. "Sean!" she cried out in a whimper as she let her head fall back.

He came around her to sit on the bed, gripping her hips to pull her forward to continue his feast as he deeply sucked her taut nipples. With a shudder, her hands gripped his broad shoulders as he brought her to yet another climax.

With her knees already weak and her pulse racing, Sean turned her body and held his inches as he guided her down onto its steel-like hardness. With a lick of her lips, she circled her hips until nearly all of him was inside of her. She felt his thickness. His strength. His heat.

With his face pressed to her back and his arms wrapped around her breasts as he rocked up inside her, Montgomery covered her face with her hands and let her head lay back on his shoulder as he brought her to a third blazing explosion. "Montgomery!" he roughly cried out as he joined her in the rapture.

Sean stood on the balcony of the villa in Rabat, the capital city of Morocco, overlooking the hotel's garden as he sipped a cup of Moroccan coffee brewed with orange blossom water, spices and topped with warm milk. He was enjoying the food and culture of the North African country. With this show, he had a costar who focused more on he sights to see in the beautiful country rich with history. He had taped his conversations with locals as he explored markets and learned more about the spices and local dishes. Tomorrow the chef from the four-star hotel where they stayed was going to walk him through making mint tea, roasted eggplant dip with naan and then a chicken tagine with olive served with seasoned couscous.

It had been a week since he left New York and outside of the hours they taped, he was feeling bored. Restless.

Alone.

That was surprising.

Sean usually sought solace after long days of filming or being socially outgoing. He would enjoy the comfort of his bedroom suite at the townhouse or the quiet of his condo. To think. Read. Sleep.

Now it felt unsettling.

Knock-knock.

With another sip of his drink from the aged bronze cup, Sean crossed the bedroom and opened the door to the hall. It was his cohost, Sara Paul, an Indian beauty with waist-length hair and pert breasts that were currently on display in a sheer nightshirt. She was barefoot, probably sans pant-ies—he couldn't tell—and carrying a bottle of champagne.

Sean eyed her in amusement as he leaned in the door-way, still fully dressed. "And exactly what part of the show is this?" he asked before taking another sip of the brew.

Sara smiled. "Just a little entertaining in the downtime between shoots," she said.

Sean leaned forward to look left and then right down the length of the hall. "People are coming," he advised her.

Sara hid her face with her hands as a middle-aged couple passed by.

"She doesn't have any panties on!" the man whispered.

Welp, that answers that, Sean thought.

The stranger glanced back at Sara, earning him a pinch from his wife.

"Sara, I'm here to work not play," he told her, already stepping back and closing the door.

She looked disappointed and pouted. "What happened to the Sean Cress I've heard so much about? The one I saw in the sex tape?" she asked with sultry eyes. "You were.. impressive."

"Good night, Sara," he said in a singsong fashion as he closed the door.

"No woman has ever made you weep," she said, pressing her face to the slowly narrowing space between the door and the frame.

Sean closed the door, hoping the woman had stepped back before she was hurt in any way. He had no regrets for turning down her charms.

She was no match to Montgomery.

"I miss your father. I really do," Montgomery said as she looked down at her steadily growing belly.

She knew she shouldn't. It made no sense to get used to him in her life every day when their time being married and living together would end. It was foolish.

But still true.

He called every few days to check on her, but it felt more perfunctory than due to missing her as well.

She attributed her longing for him to craving his sex but it was more than that. He wasn't there in the morning to fix breakfast or drop her off at work. Attend doctor's appointments. Cook dinner. Make her laugh. Regale with stories from his adventures in celebrity.

Or even to disagree.

On schooling for their child. Private versus public.

And the use of nannies. She was against it.

Even how much child support he should pay. The week

amount he offered was insulting—as if she could not provide a good enough life for their child. Or at least good enough in the eyes of the mighty Cress family.

They were so different.

Still...

Montgomery missed the affable charmer.

Using her thumb, she swiped across her phone to scroll through his social media feed. He was in Greece. Living life to the fullest with a smile bright enough to replace the sun.

"You okay, Go-Go?"

She looked over at her father across the dining room table of his home. They were enjoying dinner together after the Sunday church service. She'd been surprised that he cooked the meal of pot roast and roasted sweet potatoes.

"I'm good. Just wondering when *you* started cooking," she said, being honest.

"Your hubby sent me a care package," he said, using his fork and knife to slice through the tender meat.

"What?" Montgomery exclaimed.

Reverend Morgan shrugged his thin shoulders. "After the storm," he said.

She stood and moved past him to enter the kitchen. It resembled a Cress, INC. showroom. There was a colorful array of pots, bakeware, spices, cookbooks and other accessories. It was an incredibly kind and generous gesture—particularly to a man who openly disapproved and insulted him. She picked up one of the cookbooks to find Sean's smiling face on the cover. She pressed a hand to it.

Sean never said a word.

She returned to her seat in the dining room. "You like the stuff?" she asked.

"It'll do," he said.

Montgomery stiffened. "It'll do?" she repeated with a tinge of annoyance before she could catch herself.

She felt defensive of her husband.

Reverend Morgan picked up the napkin from his lap to wipe both corners of his mouth. She leaned in to see the tag with the Cress, INC. logo on the linen. "My forgiveness is not for sale, Montgomery," he said sternly.

"But it shouldn't be held for emotional ransom, either, Daddy," she muttered before taking a bite of the meat.

"What's that you said?" he asked.

Just then she remembered how Sean had respectfully put his mother in her place and stood up to her foolishness. She admired him for that and wished she had the same courage when it came to her father.

"Nothing, Daddy. Just nothing," she said, focusing on her meal.

Sean dived into the tranquil turquoise waters of the island of Upolu in Samoa, a Polynesian island country. He enjoyed the clear waters and its warmth against his body as he swam what seemed like infinite laps before circling back to his thatched-roof bungalow—one of a dozen on the private beach. As he left the lagoon and climbed the stairs of the over-the-water structure, he knew Montgomery would enjoy such a place.

He paused in drying off with a plush towel at the thought of her. It seemed a constant—particularly with each passing day he was away from her.

What's she doing?

Is she being safe?

Is she working too much?

Is she staying calm to get her blood pressure lowered the way the doctor ordered?

They didn't speak as often as he would like because of filming and the time difference. Samoa was nineteen hours ahead of Eastern Standard Time.

He checked the time on his phone and did the calculations. It was roughly two in the morning in New Jersey.

Although he longed to check in on her, he didn't have the heart to awaken her. With her full work schedule and the pregnancy, she needed all the rest she could get.

Sean did call his brother Lucas.

"Seriously, bro," Lucas said in irritation, his voice filled with sleep.

"My apologies. I need you to do me a favor," he said, tucking the phone between his shoulder and ear as he worked his wet swim trunks down his body to step out of them.

Nude, he crossed the hexagon-shaped bungalow to reach the frosted glass bathroom.

"Check on Montgomery for me?" he asked as he turned on the square rain showerhead.

"I can do that," Lucas said.

"What's wrong, baby?" a woman's voice asked.

"It's just my brother," Lucas said to her.

Sean instantly pictured someone buxom and not too bright. It was his brother's type. Of all the brothers, Lucas was the most active with the ladies. Since his weight loss several years ago he was definitely making up for his days being the chubby kid who craved snack cakes more than the attention of girls—just the way their mother liked it. "You home?" he asked.

"Yeah."

"*The* Nicolette Lavoie-Cress is going to flip if she catches another overnight guest in her precious abode," Sean warned, remembering the fit their mother had the last time it happened.

Lucas just laughed.

"The future Mrs. Lucas Cress?" he asked as steam filled the bathroom.

"Definitely *not*," his baby brother stressed.

Sean could only shake his head.

"Did you try the pani popo?" Lucas asked.

Although Lucas was now built tall and lean, the kid who loved sweets was still there. "Yes," he said of the Samoan bread rolls baked in coconut milk sauce. He was the one to tell his acclaimed pastry chef brother about the local delicacy he heard about but hadn't tried until earlier that day during lunch. "Delicious. I damn near ate a pan by myself."

"Great. Now I'm hungry," Lucas said, sounding disgruntled.

"Eat what's in bed with you. No calories," Sean quipped.

Lucas laughed. "I'm in the den so I can talk freely."

"Listen, don't forget about Montgomery," he insisted, returning to the reason for his late-night call.

"Looks like you can't forget about her," Lucas said.

His brother was the only one who knew that his marriage to Montgomery was arranged.

"I do miss her," Sean admitted.

"Maybe the marriage is more real than you want to admit," Lucas offered.

"Noooo," Sean said with a definitive shake of his head. "I like her. We have fun. And she's having my baby—"

"Your *ba-by*," Lucas interjected, obviously still shocked by that.

"Right?" Sean agreed. "But this is not for forever. I need my freedom. This year of marriage is enough for me."

"And Montgomery?"

Sean thought of her. "This whole marriage of convenience was her idea, remember?" he reminded.

"Things change."

Sean shook his head. "But I don't want them to," he insisted. "I've come to grips with fatherhood. I'm ready and eager. Marriage? *Never*."

"Who are you trying to convince? Me? Or yourself?" Lucas asked. "I know you, big brother, and you've changed for the better since you've been with Montgomery."

"Changed? In what way?"

"Settled. More focused. Less caught up in yourself," Lucas quickly supplied.

Too quickly for Sean, who frowned. "Well, damn. I didn't know I needed changing," he drawled.

"I didn't, either, until I saw the changes."

"It's just me being sure not to embarrass my wife in the press so I'm chilling," Sean said. "But as soon as I'm free I will be living it up again. Watch."

"I hear you."

"But do you believe me?" Sean asked.

"Nope."

Sean chuckled. Lucas was always the most honest with him. Always. "Let me wash my ass and you go enjoy your late-night snack. And strap up," he added. "You see the situation I'm in."

"I got a drawer full."

"'Night, bro."

"'Night."

Sean ended the call and sat the phone on the edge of the semi-recessed sink before opening the glass door and stepping under the spray of water.

Montgomery looked at the pan of rolls then up at Lucas. She took a deep inhale and released a grunt of pleasure. "What are these called?" she asked.

"Pani popo," Lucas said with a smile that reminded her far too much of his older brother.

Lucas Cress, like the other five brothers, was undeniably handsome. He favored former *Bridgerton* actor, Regé-Jean Page, with a shortbread complexion, slashing brows and smoldering eyes.

With a smile, she reached and picked up one of the sticky rolls from the pan to take a bite. It was light in texture and sweet. Her eyes widened. "That's so good," she sighed with a shimmy of her shoulders.

Lucas moved about the kitchen of the Tribeca condo with ease, gathering saucers, utensils and linen napkins with the comfort of a person who had been there before. "Sean told me about them and I looked up the recipe," he explained where they sat at the island.

"You heard from Sean," she said lightly, trying not to show her disappointment that she had not.

"Yes, at two in the morning," Lucas told her. "He asked me to check on you."

Montgomery smiled.

Lucas chuckled. "He's in Samoa this week and it's nineteen hours ahead," he explained on behalf of his older brother and best friend. "Trust me, you were on his mind."

Montgomery focused on eating more of the roll she held, although her heart wildly pounded.

"How are you feeling?" Lucas asked, his voice serious.

"Good," she told him, picking up her cup of mint tea to sip. "My blood pressure is higher than my doctor likes so I'm working on destressing and cutting back on salt. In fact, I have an appointment tomorrow afternoon."

"Does Sean normally go with you?" Lucas asked.

Montgomery nodded. "Tomorrow is the first he'll miss."

"Then I'll take his place," Lucas declared.

"You don't have to do that," she said, fighting the temptation for another of the sweet rolls as she kept in mind of gestational diabetes.

They are good, but not that good.

"Yes, I do because you're family and we stick together, especially since you are carrying my niece or nephew," he said.

The wealth of the Cress family made her nervous. She worried that their influence and affluence would have a negative effect on her rearing of a child, but one thing she took comfort in was their closeness. She had come to learn that the Cress brothers were close, loving and supportive.

Her child would have the best uncles in the world—especially since she wasn't quite sure how involved Sean would be, once they were divorced.

"Okay," she agreed as she pushed the pan of tempting rolls away.

"You done?" Lucas asked with a frown similar to that of his brother.

"If I eat that it will shoot up my blood sugar," she said, using a linen napkin to free her fingers of sticky crumbs.

"And if I eat it, I won't stop and I'll soon be back three sizes bigger," he countered.

They eyed each other and then eyed the rolls.

"Just one won't hurt," Montgomery said.

"And then we'll freeze the rest," Lucas offered, turning to retrieve a box of freezer-safe Ziplocs.

Montgomery eagerly reached to pick up a roll.

Lucas followed suit.

With eyes twinkling with mischief, they touched the pieces of bread together in a toast before devouring them far too quickly.

It had been three weeks since Sean Cress had been home.

He was exhausted, hungry and slightly out of sorts from the varying time zones across which they traveled to complete the three episodes his producers hoped would lead to a full series order. Sean wasn't so sure of the project anymore. Sara was still far too aggressive in seeking out sex with him, and he spent more time watching other chefs prepare meals than digging in himself.

With a yawn and stretch, he entered his Tribeca condo, letting the leather duffel he carried slip from his shoulder to the floor.

The house was dark and quiet with pockets of lights. In the air was the light scent of Montgomery's perfume. She liked to work in the living room instead of using one of the empty bedrooms during their stay at the condo. Next to the sofa were a pair of the fuzzy slippers she wore around the house. And open on the low-slung living room table was a book on what to expect during pregnancies. He smiled at her laptop on the kitchen island. Next to it, he found a note and a roast beef and provolone sandwich with arugula, sun-dried tomato and red onions on fresh-baked bread.

"Welcome home, Sean. It hasn't been the same with-out you. Montgomery," he read before looking around the space again.

Somehow the cold and modern bachelor-pad condo felt like home.

He removed the hiking boots he wore with olive cargo shorts and an orange long-sleeve tee. He went down to the sleeping area and paused at the entry to Montgomery's room. She was in the middle of the bed. He smiled at the sounds of her soft snores. His eyes dipped to the swell of her belly through the covers with her hand resting on it. The urge to undress and climb in the bed just to hold her was strong. And surprising.

I know you, big brother, and you've changed for the bet-ter since you've been with Montgomery.

Sean moved away from the doorway and continued down the hall to reach the owner's suite. He undressed, leaving the clothes in a pile by the door, and strode naked to his en suite. He was fatigued but he knew he couldn't properly rest until he washed away the forty-eight hours of filming and then the traveling to get back to America.

"Shower *and* shave," he said, looking at himself in the mirror. His beard was nearly full grown. "Then sandwich and sleep."

With instrumental jazz music playing from a playlist on his phone, Sean made quick work of the beard, using clippers to cut it down to a light shadow. In the shower the feel of the heated water beating against his aching muscles was therapeutic. With a towel draped around his waist, and another quick look at Montgomery asleep in her bed, he made his way to the kitchen to devour the sandwich. It hit the spot.

"Hey."

Over the edge of the glass of milk he poured for himself, Sean eyed Montgomery walking into the kitchen in a pink satin shirtdress and matching fur slippers with her hair up in a ponytail. She looked adorable.

"Hey," he responded, coming around the slate island to pull her in for a hug as he lightly settled his chin atop her head.

Montgomery wrapped her arms around his waist. The baby kicked and they both laughed but continued to hold on to one another.

Fighting his fatigue, Sean swung her body up into his arms. As Montgomery settled her head on his shoulder, he carried her back to her bedroom to lie on her bed. When he stepped back, he felt a draft across his buttocks as she tugged at his towel before dropping it to the floor.

He climbed onto the bed and lay down on his back as he eyed her.

"Tired?" she asked as she climbed onto the bed beside him on her knees.

"Yes," he stressed, easing his hand under her shirtdress to lightly caress her soft breasts.

Montgomery purred as she sat atop his strong thighs.

Sean gasped when she reached to stroke him. With a moan and a lick of his lips, he worked his hips as she massaged him from root to tip until he was hard. She rose up on her knees and held his dick as she eased down onto him until he filled her.

She was hot and wet and tight. So tight.

Slowly, Montgomery rode him as she pressed her hands down on his chest. He watched her in wonder, amazed at her passion and her stamina. He fed on the pleasure on her face. He reveled in their connection. Their chemistry.

As he felt his release build, Sean reached up to grip the headboard. He felt the muscles of his arms tense. His explosion came and shook him as she continued to ride him through it. It was made all the more intense because she climaxed as well. The clutch of her walls. Her nails digging into his flesh. The pleasure on her face. Her trembles.

"Welcome back," she whispered down to him.

"It's good to be back," he told her in between harsh breaths.

When she tumbled on the bed beside him, Sean turned on his side to gather her body close to his. He pressed a kiss to her nape and settled in to sleep with her in his arms for the rest of the night. He didn't have the energy or the desire to leave her bed.

Nine

"That was delicious, Sean."

Montgomery fought the urge to drag her finger in the drippings left from the salted caramel, pear and walnut Tarte Tatin. Well aware they were in CRESS X in Tribeca, a fine dining establishment, she resisted. Instead, she picked up her margarita mocktail. "Wonderful selections," she said, raising the glass to him in toast of the tasting menu.

He touched his glass to hers before they both took sips and eyed each other over the rims with the hint of flirtation.

In the days since his return, things were different between them.

More lingering touches.

More caresses.

More talking.

More laughing.

More time spent together.

More lovemaking.

It was nice.

Very nice.

Montgomery didn't believe there was anything better than Sean rubbing her entire body down with oil. What started as therapeutic slowly became erotic when his fingers glided over her rounded belly and down in between her thighs to spread them before he stroked her plump mound and teased her pulsing clit.

Memories of her cries of pleasure echoed as she remembered trembling and arching her back off the bed as she gripped the sheets into her fists.

"How is the acquiring of the streaming service coming along?" she asked, purposefully guiding her thoughts away from naughty things with Sean.

He clasped his hands together. "It's a go," he said, his eyes filled with his excitement. "CressTV is happening and will be incorporated under my duties at Cress, INC."

"Congratulations, Sean!" she softly exclaimed.

"There's a lot to figure out with my current contracts to do shows and we're considering whether to delay the launch until those shows have aired or not. Or should we buy out the contract or acquire the rights to the shows," he explained. "There's a lot to consider and to learn. I'm excited."

"And will this secure the CEO position?" she asked just as their server appeared and set glass bowls of beautifully cut and arranged fresh fruit before them.

My favorite.

She selected a grape to pop into her mouth and moaned as she found it to be sweet like cotton candy.

"To be honest, the launch of the streaming service and my current duties will be so time-consuming, that I'm not sure I want the position anymore," he admitted, selecting a star-shaped piece of melon to bite. "As the CEO I would have to appoint a new president to take over my duties supervising the cooking shows. I feel the most excited about CressTV right now."

"And your baby," she reminded him.

Sean smiled. "Of course. I meant work, not personal, Montgomery," he said.

"My mistake," she replied, picking up another grape.

"No worries. You don't make many," he reassured her.

"And some of them turned out for the best," she said, pressing her hands to her belly.

"We're having a baby," Sean said.

"We. Are. Having. A. Baby," she said in mock disbelief.

"A girl with your eyes."

"Or a boy with yours."

They finished their fruit and took their leave, holding hands and talking as they awaited the Bentley at the valet. As they drove home, Sean's phone began to ring. He reached for it. "Yeah."

Montgomery reached into the clutch she carried for her compact to check her makeup and hair.

"We're on the way back from dinner but if you have your key just go in and get it," Sean said.

Just go in and get it?

"Okay," Sean said, finishing the call and setting his phone back on the console.

Montgomery eyed him with curiosity.

"That was Lucas," he supplied. "He needed something out of the condo."

"Something?" she asked, her interest piqued.

"A case of champagne."

"Where?" she asked.

Sean gave her a look as he used one hand to turn the corner. "In the last bedroom," he said.

I never went in the other bedrooms.

"And Lucas has a key?" she asked, thinking of Lucas's familiarity with the home when he came to visit her that day while Sean was in Samoa.

"Yes," Sean said. "Is that a problem?"

Montgomery shook her head. "Of course not. It's not my place. It's yours. I'll be home this week," she said.

Sean reclaimed her hand in his and raised it to press kisses to her fingertips.

But her thoughts were not on seduction.

Champagne in a bedroom?

As they rode up in the elevator, Montgomery leaned back against Sean's chest as he pressed kisses to her temple. "What if we miss each other after the divorce?" he asked, his voice deep and low in her ear.

Montgomery trembled, remembering their first steamy time on an elevator together. "Then we will get over it," she said, turning to look up at him. "Our deal ends with our divorce."

Sean pressed his hands to her face and bent his head to kiss her mouth.

Montgomery gasped in between each one. She reached up to clutch his elbows as her knees weakened when his kisses shifted down to her throat.

"You sure?" he asked with some of his old bravado.

"Unlike you, Mr. Cress," she said as she leaned back from his heat. "I have every intention of one day finding the man meant for me and walking into marital bliss."

"Mr. Perfect," he said with a hint of sarcasm as he stepped back from her.

"Mr. Perfect for *me*," she stressed, turning as the elevator slid to a stop and the doors opened.

He inclined his head and said nothing, but Montgomery was curious about his thoughts. As they made their way down the hall, their mood had shifted. Their hands were not entwined and the flirtatious warmth with hints of heated passion to come had cooled.

When they entered the already lit condo, Montgomery felt relief to step out of her beloved heels with a sigh. She walked into the kitchen to open the fridge and pull out a bottle of her pear-flavored sparkling water.

Sean settled on the sofa and used the condo's assigned tablet to turn on the television.

The silence was awkward.

Montgomery eyed him, wondering just why his ardor had cooled because she mentioned her intention to re-marry. For a second she thought of jealousy but then quickly pushed that aside. Sean's interest in her went only as far as sex and the mothering of his child.

He looked up and caught her eyes on him. He shifted his gaze back to the television screen.

It felt like a rebuke and that stung.

"No late-night parties to attend?" she asked.

He gave her another glance. "If my presence suddenly bothers you, I'm sure I can find something to get into," he said.

"I bet you could," she snapped.

Now he locked his eyes with hers and they were heated. Not with desire but annoyance.

"You probably been finding something else to get into the whole time," she said.

"I'm not the one who pretends to be something I'm not. I don't lie," he shot back.

It landed and emotions pierced her.

"Let me warn you, Sean Cress, I am not the one to ver-bally spar with," she said, her voice cold.

"Unless I'm your father and then suddenly you'd be *mute*," he said, his voice dripping with sarcasm as he con-tinued to flip through the channels.

That hurt.

"When you're nice, you are very nice, Sean Cress," she said, hating that her voice trembled. "But that was very nasty. And cruel. I guess I was a fool to think you were above that."

She turned and walked away.

"Montgomery," he called behind her.

She ignored him, although she heard his contrite tone.

When she reached the end of the hall leading to the bedrooms, she looked to the right at the door she had never opened in the past month. She closed the distance and wrenched the knob before pushing it open.

"What?" she exclaimed, seeing the cases upon cases of liquor that lined the walls.

She stopped counting at more than two dozen different brands. She turned to see him standing in the hall with his hands dug into the pockets of his tailored black slacks. "Sean," she said with concern. "Was this your party pad?"

"I've had parties here, yes," he admitted.

"So much so that you keep inventory for a liquor store on hand?" she asked, unable to hide her astonishment.

Sean chuckled. "I'm a grown man, this is my home and this is not Prohibition, Montgomery," he said.

She looked back at the abundance of alcohol and then at him. "You gave me the impression that you barely stayed here. Like it was an investment property," she said.

"Both are true."

She frowned.

"Why are you spoiling for a fight?" he asked before stepping back to lean his tall frame against the wall as he continued to watch her.

"I don't want to fight," she said.

"What do you want, Montgomery?" he asked.

"To know if you ever had women here?" she asked.

He shifted his eyes away.

Montgomery winced. "Sean," she said, awaiting an answer.

He looked back at her. "Yes," he admitted.

"Flings?" she asked as her heart pounded and she felt anger she couldn't explain.

No, he wasn't her husband at the time.

No, their marriage wasn't meant to last.

No, he owed her no explanation.

Still...

She eyed him, not hiding the hurt she felt even if she couldn't fully grasp the reason for it.

His silence was telling.

With a nod, she licked her lips. "Feels great to be one of the number of women you screw here," she said, her voice low and numb as she leaned in to close the door and then came down the hall.

He stepped in her path. "I never looked at you that way, Montgomery," he said with earnest.

"The idea of living here now feels the same as me visiting the Playboy mansion," she said with a shrug of her shoulders. "It's a no for me."

He reached for her and she shirked away from his touch before continuing down the hall to enter her room and close the door behind her.

Knock-knock.

"Montgomery, let's talk about this," he said through the wood of the door.

She locked it and moved to lie across the foot of the bed. When she heard his footsteps echo as he moved away from the door, she felt relief. As she lay in the darkness and clutched one of the throw pillows on the bed to her chest, Montgomery wrangled with her emotions.

Foremost was her confusion.

She was well aware of Sean's past—she served as his publicist/crisis manager for the release of a sex tape—but still, it bothered her. It burned in her gut. It kept her from getting a restful night of sleep. Anytime she closed her eyes, visions of Sean and a bevy of women enjoying a late night of lascivious partying in the condo plagued her.

And she hated it.

She wasn't quite sure why in her visions Sean was wearing chaps sans pants and standing atop a table as he poured magnums of champagne upon the exposed breasts of the women looking up at him in adoration.

"Go, Sean! Go, Sean! Go, Sean!" the women chanted in her visions.

I have a headache.

She was thankful for sleep although it was restless. Her thoughts remained troubled even at work the next day.

With a sigh, Montgomery entered her office and closed the door, momentarily leaning against it before she continued across the space to her desk. Hanna had ordered lunch but she ignored hers as she reached for her phone to pull up the contact information for the electrician working on her house.

As the phone rang, she picked up the clear plastic container of grilled chicken atop arugula salad only to sit it back down before tapping the tips of her nails against the desk.

"Hello," Ernesto said loudly with the sound of drilling in the background.

"Hi. This is Montgomery. I know you've been in contact with my husband, Sean Cress—"

"Yes! Great guy," Ernesto said.

Montgomery held back on making a snide comment on just how friendly that great guy was. "I was just wondering when the electrical work would be done," she said.

"We wrapped up two weeks ago, Mrs. Cress," Ernesto said. "Hold on. One sec."

She tensed.

Ernesto gave orders to his crew.

Two weeks ago?

"Mrs. Cress, we have an emergency here, but I assure you the job is complete. My bill was paid in full and I hope you both will call on me again if you need further electrical work," he rushed to say.

"But I have questions," she insisted.

"Okay. Can I call you back? Please," he stressed.

"Yes," she said.

He ended the call.

This makes no sense.

She started to call Sean but decided against it because he had lied to her about the status of the house. "Why?" she asked herself aloud.

One thing was true about Sean Cress. He was no liar. At times he was too honest.

Or was he too good to be caught?

Montgomery quickly gathered her keys, her bag and her briefcase before she strode out of her office. Hanna paused in taking a bite of her own salad. "Finish your lunch. I have to make a run and I'll be back in an hour. If that changes, I'll call and update you," she said, quickly moving past the young woman's desk.

"Is everything okay?" Hanna called behind her, drawing the curious stares of Montgomery's other employees.

She glanced back over her shoulder. "I hope so," she said, pushing the front door to leave the offices on the fifth floor of the thirty-story building.

Even last night as they argued he could have told her the electrical repairs were complete.

Did something go wrong?

Did he have to hire someone to come behind Ernesto?

Once in her car, Montgomery made good time getting from Manhattan to Passion Grove. As she drove up the drive, it felt good to see her home again—and it would even be better to be back in it again.

She unlocked the front door and stepped inside but paused. "Oh my," she sighed.

The smell of paint was strong and absolutely nothing

about the house looked recognizable. She felt like she was on a home makeover show and it was time for the big reveal. With her mouth open, she moved about the entire home, amazed at all of the renovations and upgrades. She gently touched it all. Walls removed. New floors and paint. Updated fireplaces. Reconfigured kitchen. Her bedroom was now made into an owner's suite with its own attached bathroom. Even the basement was now finished and fully decorated as a theater room with its own bathroom and pantry.

It had to be the work of Sean.

"Oh, Sean," she sighed, pressing her hands to her cheeks and finding them flushed with heat.

Over their months together she had briefly mentioned plans she had for her 1940s home but never had she guessed he would take those ideas and make them a reality. With the same attentiveness he gave to remembering her love of fruit on their airplane ride or being sure her favorite drink was stocked at his parents'—she never even knew he was paying such close attention.

And then truth settled in. The reason she was so annoyed by the thought of him with other women. Why she missed him so much. Why their lovemaking shook her to her very core. Why his smile brought her so much joy.

Tears welled and she didn't contain them. They wet her fingers.

I love him.

But her heart was broken.

As much as she longed for love in her life, never did she want it to be unrequited.

And the man made it so very hard *not* to love him.

To want him.

To have him.

Montgomery sank on her sofa, wishing he was everything she envisioned for herself. Her Mr. Perfect. The love of her life.

But he wasn't and he didn't want to be.

What am I going to do?

Sean drove up the drive of Montgomery's house and parked behind her vehicle before exiting and making his way to the front door. It opened and there she stood.

Her eyes were red and puffy. Her arms were crossed over her chest as if consoling herself.

That tore at him.

"How can I thank you for the house?" she asked, her voice soft. "It's beautiful. It's perfect."

A tear raced down her cheek before she lowered her head.

"Montgomery, what's wrong?" he asked, stepping closer to wrap her in his arms.

For a moment, as he massaged her back, she leaned her head against his chest.

"You're killing me. Tell me what's wrong," he said, pressing kisses to her temple as he held her tighter. "How can I fix it if I don't know what's wrong?"

She stepped back out of his embrace and wiped her tears with the sides of her hands. "You can't fix it," she said, running one hand through her hair as she looked over at him.

Sean slid his hands into the pockets of the slacks of his tailored suit. It was to keep from reaching for her.

"I love you," Montgomery admitted before another round of tears. "And that was not a part of the plan."

He was stunned. His heart pounded. Hard and fast. He freed his hands to use one to wipe his mouth as he eyed her and saw in the depths of her eyes her feelings for him.

But he didn't know what to say.

He didn't know what she wanted him to say.

All he knew was she was hurting and that pained him.

"Montgomery," he said, taking a step toward her.

She held up a hand to stop him. "I'm in too deep and I gotta get out," she said, beginning to slowly pace in the area between the living and dining areas. "The sex. The closeness. My jealousy over your past. All of your nice thoughtful gestures. I need space. I need to get over this because we have to raise a child together."

He watched solemnly as she pressed her hands to her rounded belly and let her head fall back with her eyes closed as more tears fell.

"Montgomery, please," he begged, taking steps toward her.

Needing to hold her.

With a shake of her head, she denied him before releasing a shaky breath that seemed to reverberate.

"I'll repay you for this," she said, looking around at the house.

"No," he said sternly. "I did this for you and the baby. I never expected you to repay me. I never even cashed the check you gave me for the electrical work."

"Of course you didn't," she said.

That made him smile a little.

"It's perfect. It's everything I wanted for my home and more," she said, walking over to grip the back of one of the new tufted dining room chairs before she looked back at him over her shoulder. "How can I not love you?"

His chest tightened.

"But I gotta get over it. I have to get over you," she said, trying to sound practical as she looked away from him.

Sean looked around at the house, curious what brought her back to it early. The final work to be completed before he wanted to surprise her was painting the exterior. For weeks the excitement of surprising her had him delirious with anticipation. Over and over he would imagine the look on her face. He had been distracted with pleasing her.

"New plan," she said, clasping her hands together. "We live separately but make appearances together to keep up the ruse."

No.

"Whatever you need, Montgomery," he said, walking over to lightly grip the back of her head as he pressed a kiss to her cheek.

She looked up at him.

They locked eyes.

That undercurrent of awareness and desire that constantly throbbed between them was just as present as ever.

It was tempting.

God, she's beautiful.

The *very* last thing Sean wanted to do at that moment was release her and leave.

But he did.

He *had* to.

Two weeks later

Sean stared down into the brown depths of his drink as he leaned against the wall of the superyacht. When a vision of Montgomery appeared instead, he swirled the alcohol to make it disappear, sending some of the brandy over the side of the snifter.

But I gotta get over it. I have to get over you, Montgomery had said.

"Shit," he swore, gripping the glass.

With a breath he looked around at the celebrity-filled party. Loud music. Gyrating bodies on the dance floor. The loud chatter of talking voices. Flashing lights.

In the past he would have been making his rounds, talking to celebrity friends, posing for pictures and having one hell of a good time. Now that seemed impossible for him.

I love you, Sean.

During the past two weeks, he had tried everything he could to forget the last time he saw Montgomery. Parties during the Cannes Film Festival on the French Riviera. Movie premieres. Club openings. All the while fending off questions about the whereabouts of his new bride.

What he'd learned was his taste for the fast-paced celebrity life was over.

The music too loud.

The conversations too trite.

The hour too late.

I know you, big brother, and you've changed for the better since you've been with Montgomery.

With a scowl, Sean finished the drink in one gulp before making his way through the crowd to the bar to have another.

How can I not love you?

She haunted him.

He missed her and in his own way, he had to get over her, too.

Her smile.

The scent of her perfume.

The sound of her laugh.

The sweetness of her kiss.

Even her soft snores.

And once he returned from traveling, they had slept together. Holding her and having her near while he slept gave him the best rest. He hadn't had another since she returned to Passion Grove. Tossing and turning had become his nightly ritual.

With another curse Sean finished his drink and made his way off the yacht. He was thankful for Colin as he felt the effects of the alcohol.

"Home?" Colin asked from the driver's seat. "Or another location, sir?"

"Tribeca," Sean said, leaning his head against the rest. "Thanks, Colin."

"Everything okay?" the driver asked.

Sean stared out the window of the moving vehicle. "No," he said, sounding as disgruntled as he felt.

The men rode in silence until Colin pulled to a stop outside Sean's Tribeca apartment building. With effort, Sean left the rear of the vehicle.

"Flowers and a nice night out together usually get me out of the dog house with the missus," Colin offered.

Sean just gave him a smile of thanks and closed the door. The night doorman of the postwar building held the door for him. As he crossed the lobby, he checked the time on his phone. It was nearly two in the morning.

When Montgomery lived with him and he had a late night out, she would be waiting up for him—pretending to work or to read, but up. Like she made sure he got home safely.

As he unlocked the front door of his apartment and entered, his eyes went to the empty sofa. Gone was any sign that Montgomery had once lived there. Now the silence he once sought felt mocking.

I need to get over her, too.

That was turning out to be easier said than done.

"Come back to bed."

Sean frowned at the woman's voice that echoed from down the hall.

Montgomery?

With his heart seeming to slam against his chest from the rush of surprise and happiness, Sean took long but quick strides down the hall to Montgomery's old bedroom.

He frowned at the woman sitting in the middle of the bed, her nudity evident under the sheet clinging to her frame. "Who the hell are you?" he barked.

The woman shrieked. "Oh, my God. It's Sean Cress,"

she said, clapping her hands together and causing the sheet to fall to her waist.

Sean turned his back to her before he caught sight of her breasts.

"My bad, bro."

Lucas.

"Is your *date* covered?" he asked.

"I don't have to be," the woman said in a girly-like voice that would shred his nerves.

Sean worked his shoulders. "Let me say I now see how *Maman* feels, Lucas," he said, hearing his own annoyance.

"See. You changed," Lucas said in an "I told you so" tone.

"Sean, can I have an autograph?" the woman asked with a giggle.

"Kimmie, my brother is *not* signing your breasts," Lucas drawled.

"Why?" she wailed.

With a shake of his head, Sean left the room. He'd taken a few steps but backtracked to lean in backward to pull the door closed on their shenanigans.

Ten

One week later

Montgomery sat in the middle of the bed with her feet propped up on pillows. Per her doctor's orders, she was on bed rest due to the risk of preeclampsia. She looked at her swollen ankles and feet that had her in flat shoes. It felt odd walking in them, but she had no choice because her beloved heels were no longer comfortable or practical.

"You owe me," she said, looking down at her belly that nearly blocked any view of her upper thighs.

She looked to her open front door at the sound of noises echoing from the kitchen. She knew her father was in her new kitchen, wearing his Cress, INC. apron and cooking something from one of his cookbooks.

Montgomery sighed.

When he called to reprimand her and Sean for missing church, Montgomery told him Sean was traveling for work and her activities had been limited by her doctor. Her father had made it his duty to stay with her until Sean's return—which only she knew was never going to happen.

She was tired of half-truths.

Lies.

To her father.

To herself.

To the world.

To Sean.

Although their new agreement was to put up a front for their families, Montgomery was nowhere near ready to be under the same roof with Sean again. Her love for him was still strong—maybe even stronger from missing him so much. And so when he called her to ask if he could still attend doctor's appointments with her, Montgomery had begged off. Then he called afterward to see how it went and she told him everything was going well.

Yet another lie.

She shifted to find comfort in the bed and then leaned back against the plush pillows stacked behind her. She felt weepy and took a deep breath hoping to defeat her poignant sadness. All of her plans and she'd left her heart unprotected. Not once had she factored love into the equation.

The best laid plans of mice and men often go awry.

She softly smiled as she remembered Sean's words.

"I still can't believe how good this house looks," Reverend Morgan said, walking in carrying a tray. "Your grandparents would be proud. It's a showcase."

"Sean did it all," she reminded him for what seemed the dozenth time.

"He's all right," her father said begrudgingly, setting the tray on the bed beside her.

He's more than all right.

She looked down at the bowl of grilled chicken fettuccine Alfredo with a side of steamed broccoli. "That looks good, Daddy, but I'm not hungry," she said. "I feel a little nauseated and my back hurts."

"Anything I can get you?" he asked, moving the tray to sit on the bedside table.

She shook her head as she smoothed her hands over her belly.

Her father frowned. Deeply. "Your husband should be here with you," he said. "Not gallivanting over the world. What kind of father will *he* be?"

One who lets his child be who he or she wants to be. Who takes care of his child the way he takes care of strangers. And loving, like he is with his family.

"Daddy, I'm going to take a nap," she said, shifting down on the bed.

"What type of future will the two of you have if he's not here when you need him?" Reverend Morgan continued, his voice rising.

Montgomery closed her eyes. "Daddy, please," she stressed, feigning a yawn and hoping he took the hint.

"This is what happens when you rush into a marriage with someone you don't know," he continued.

"Daddy—"

"This house is beautiful but it's a thing. A possession. What you need more than his money is his presence! And he has the *audacity* to tell me I'm holding you emotionally hostage," her father said, his deep voice dripping with sarcasm. "And about expecting perfection."

Montgomery sat up again—with effort. "What did he say about perfection?" she asked.

Reverend Morgan looked confused. "What?"

"What did Sean say about perfection?" she repeated.

Her father frowned. "Something about all men making mistakes and that no one is perfect or should *expect perfection*," he said, mimicking Sean and using his hands to do air quotes.

No one is perfect.

Like I tried to pretend to be for my father.

Or should expect perfection.

Like I expected from Sean—or any other man to be a part of my life.

The weight of the irony—and her hypocrisy—settled in.

"Emotional blackmail," her father snarked.

Montgomery, a part of your father seeing you as more than his little girl is you presenting yourself as more than that, Sean had said.

"It was," Montgomery said softly, her eyes downcast on her belly and not on her father.

"What?" he asked.

"You cut me out of your life because you didn't approve of a decision I made for *my* life," she said, her tone strengthening as she raised her eyes and locked them with her father's. "That hurt…and it made me so angry with you."

Reverend Morgan scowled. "Angry?" he asked, appearing astonished by her revelation. "Did I dishonor you?"

"No. I dishonored myself by pretending to be perfect to make you happy," she said. "I got good grades. I never talked back. I agreed to your every wish—like giving up swimming even though I used to love it. I made sure to never rock the boat and displease you."

"I never asked you to be perfect, Go-Go," he said, sinking down to sit on the foot of the bed.

"No, but you implied if I didn't you would judge me," she said. "And the one time I made a mistake that you *know* about you did even more than judge. You amputated me from your life for weeks."

She was surprised he showed regret at his actions.

"I was hurt and angry with you," he explained.

"I have never completely felt like myself around you because I never let you know who I am—which is *far* from perfect," she said.

His stare became accusing.

"Dad, my desire to have your approval was so strong that when I got pregnant by Sean, I asked him to marry me for a year so that I wouldn't have to admit the truth," she told him, even as her stomach seemed to flip-flop.

Reverend Morgan jumped to his feet and stepped back from her as if repelled.

"So what now, Dad? Are you going to block me out of your life again?" she asked, her eyes filling with tears. "Your grandchild, too?"

His eyes went down to her belly and then up to her face again.

"I never wanted to be anything less than perfect for you," she continued. "And without even knowing I sought that same perfection in others. I was wrong on both accounts."

Perfection in any one person doesn't exist.

"I became what I…" She let the words trail.

"That you what?" he asked.

"I became what I resented," she finished.

His face contorted with pain. "You resent me?" he asked, his deep voice a harsh whisper.

"Although you preach about forgiveness and grace, you offered me none," Montgomery countered.

Reverend Morgan picked up the tray and turned to leave the room, the slope of his shoulders dejected.

"Dad, I love you and some of this dynamic between us is my fault for not ever being honest with you," she said, feeling pain for causing him any. "I forgive you and I want us to have a better relationship. A real one with flaws and all. I hope you want the same and can forgive me, too."

He paused in the open doorway and gave her a brief look back before he left the room and closed the door.

The Cress brothers as a collective drew nearly every eye of the women—single and taken—at CRESS IX in Washington, D.C. Sean paid the attention no heed as he reached forward to refill his wineglass. Once they decided to catch up with each other over dinner and drinks, they agreed to do a pop-in of one of the family restaurants and hopped on the jet. He was thankful for the company of his brothers as he fought to deal with not seeing Montgomery. Her need for distance was so great that she hadn't wanted him at the most recent prenatal appointment.

That had hurt him.

He had come to enjoy seeing the growth of their baby and learning of its milestones while sharing in that with her.

And how much time would she need? Will I be able to see my child?

"What's going on with you, Sean? You're not your normal charming and happy self."

He eyed Coleman as he tipped his head back to drain the goblet of the wine he just poured.

"I'm fine," Sean said, turning in his seat to motion with his fingers for their server.

He didn't miss that his five brothers shared looks as he ordered a round of drinks—harder than the award-winning wine they had been enjoying.

"I've never seen you miss a chance to flirt with a woman and you've ignored about a dozen since we arrived," Phillip Junior supplied as he reached for handmade chocolate they had for dessert.

Flirtations?

He hadn't flirted, dated or sexed another woman since Montgomery and had no desire to.

"Not even photos or autographs with his fans," Gabriel added.

Sean ignored them, thankful when the server returned with a tray of six drinks.

"Talk about it. Maybe we can help," Lincoln offered.

Sean said nothing and the normal ambiance of the restaurant echoed.

"He misses his wife," Lucas supplied, drawing a hard look from Sean. "And is miserable because of it. Trust me, we all miss the life of the party."

The brothers toasted to that, causing Sean to deeply frown. "Jerks," he muttered.

But they weren't. These were his brothers. Four he grew up with and one he had grown to love just as much as the rest. Some older. Most were younger. None meant him any harm.

"Marriage is not for me," he said.

"Is it marriage or Montgomery?" Lincoln asked.

"Marriage," Sean asserted without hesitation.

If he ever had the inclination to share the rest of his life with someone it would be Montgomery.

"To hell with being alone," Coleman said. "For me, there is nothing better than sharing my life with Jillian."

"Damn right," the other married brothers agreed.

"After all the years we've been together, Raquel and I have our own language," Phillip Junior told him. "What would take fifty words to explain to everyone sometimes just takes a look with my wife."

Gabriel took a sip of his brandy. "There's nothing better than climbing into bed next to Monica—especially now with Emme lying there between us," he said. "For me, it's the best part of my day."

Sean thought of doing just that with Montgomery and their child.

"I like my freedom," Sean said, more to himself than them.

"*Listen,*" Lincoln said, drawing the eyes of all his younger brothers. "Give up whatever burden you believe marriage to be and get rid of your fear about losing your independence. Realize life can be just as good with someone as you *think* it is without someone."

His brothers all agreed—even single Lucas.

Sean fell silent as he sipped from his drink. There was only one thing he knew for sure. When he had the Passion Grove house remodeled for Montgomery—paying whatever cost to ensure it was done efficiently and quickly—he had envisioned living there *with her*.

Bzzzzzzzzz. Bzzzzzzzzz. Bzzzzzzzzz.

All of the men reached for their phones to see if it was theirs that vibrated.

Sean frowned at the unfamiliar New Jersey number. "Hello," he said after answering.

"Sean? Sean, this is Montgomery's father. Reverend Morgan," the man said, his voice trembling.

He sat up straight. "What's wrong?" he asked.

Five pairs of eyes settled on him.

"It's Montgomery. She went into labor early. We're headed to the hospital. She wants you there," he said. "No. She says to tell you she *needs* you there."

I love you, Sean.

"I'm on the way. Which hospital?" he asked, already rising to his feet.

Fear and panic nearly weakened him. She was over a month early.

Father God, please look out for Montgomery and our child.

Sean strode through the restaurant at full speed, but it still didn't stop the hard pounding of his heart.

"Sean!"

He stopped and turned. His brothers stood standing around the table staring at him in bewilderment. He'd forgotten them. He reached for his wallet as he made his way back to them. He threw a wad of hundred-dollar bills on the table. "We have to get to New Jersey. Montgomery's in labor," he said.

"Already?" Gabriel asked.

Sean nodded and hid not one bit of his fear from his eyes. "It's early," he said.

Lincoln signaled for the server and handed him all of the cash.

The Cress brothers walked out together and quickly made their way to the three-row chauffeur-driven SUV awaiting them. Sean said nothing as they climbed in. He sat on the middle seat between Lucas and Lincoln. As Lucas urged the driver to get back to the airport as quickly as possible, Lincoln called the pilot to reroute their flight to New Jersey instead of New York and the other brothers all called their wives to tell the news, Sean clutched his hands together tightly in the space between his knees to keep them from visibly trembling. He was acutely aware he was not just surrounded by his brothers, but also supported by them. He was grateful. Without them, as his fears and concern about Montgomery and their baby consumed him, he knew he would have felt more alone than ever before in his life.

During the entire trip back, the mood was solemn.

Sean tore through the hospital, leaving his brothers behind, to reach the maternity ward. Reverend Morgan sat in the waiting room wringing his hat in his hands. He stopped with his chest heaving. "How are they?" he asked in between pants.

The man rose to his feet, his face despondent and his eyes brimming with tears. "It's M-M-Montgomery," he stammered. "They don't know if she's going to make it."

Sean shook his head, denying the words. And then he thought of a world without Montgomery in it.

I love you, Sean.

He could picture her so clearly wearing her heart on her sleeve and proclaiming her love for him with no shame.

Will that be the last time I saw her alive?

"No. No," Sean whimpered as he dropped to his knees and covered his face with his hands, feeling completely shattered.

Somewhere in the midst of his grief, he felt strong hands lift him to his feet.

"Sit him here," one of his brothers said.

Lincoln.

"We're here, bro," another said.

Lucas.

Sean looked up at his baby brother, his best friend, as his eyes burned with his tears. "She might not make it," he said.

"Have hope," Lucas said, pushing napkins into his hand. "Don't give up."

I love you, Sean.

"I need her in my life," Sean said, unable to deny his feelings any longer and regretting that he hadn't admitted that to her or himself. "And the baby."

"Trust me," Lucas said, taking the unused napkins to brush the tears from his brother's face. "We all know you do."

Two weeks later

With tenderness, Sean stroked Montgomery's cheek as he looked down at her face. She appeared peacefully sleeping, but all of the medical equipment being used on her was evidence she was in a medically induced coma to give her time to heal from the seizures and stroke brought on by eclampsia. As he worshipped her with his eyes, the sound of "Dream a Little Dream of Me" by Ella Fitzgerald and Louis Armstrong played from his phone. Every day he came to the hospital, sat at her bedside, talked to her and played that song while he was there.

"While I'm alone and blue as can be, dream a little dream of me," he whispered into her ear along with the song.

He could only hope that she did just that as she rested.

Sean pressed kisses to her face as his heart swelled with emotions he could no longer deny. Not anymore. "Come back to me, Montgomery," he begged of her.

He longed for the day she looked up at him with those most beautiful eyes and said the words he needed to hear.

I love you, Sean.

With his hands pressed to her cheeks, he pressed his mouth to the side of hers and let his forehead lightly rest atop hers before he reclaimed his seat beside the bed. He gathered one of her hands between both of his and listened to the jazz classic as he willed her to awaken and return to him.

To us.

Their son was born premature but healthy. Morgan Sean Cress. Just the way Montgomery wanted it.

"He's beautiful," he told her with a smile. "You got your boy with my eyes. And my dimples. But he has your chin."

He eyed her and ached that she had never seen or held their son.

"Dream a little dream of me," Ella Fitzgerald sang.

He winced and looked away from her. At times, seeing her in that way felt like pure torture.

"How is she?"

Sean looked to the door to find Reverend Morgan walking in, hat in hand. "The same," he said. "But the doctor said there's been improvement of her vitals. She's hopeful."

"Then we'll be hopeful," his father-in-law said.

Sean nodded as he rose to his feet and stood by the bed to look down at his wife. His everything.

I know that now more than ever.

"It's high past time I thanked you."

Sean looked across the bed at the older man. "For?"

"Take your pick. The gift from your family's company. The talks even when I didn't want to listen. For loving my daughter. My grandson," he said before clearing his throat. "She told me the truth about the baby and the marriage."

Sean looked down at Montgomery, feeling proud of her.

"I just want my daughter back," the reverend said. "I have so many regrets. I want things to be different between us."

Sean gave him a smile that still had a hint of his sadness. "Same," he agreed. "If she'll let me."

"Same," her father agreed before bending to press a kiss to her forehead.

Soon, Sean took his leave with one last look back at her. As they did every day, the men took shifts sitting at her bedside. Sean would go home and then make hourly calls to the nurses' station for updates on Montgomery's condition. Outside of handling the business side of Montgomery Morgan Publicity while her staff stepped in to cover her PR duties, that was his life for the past two weeks. Everything else had come to a halt. No filming. No meetings. No work.

Things had changed. *He* had changed. For the better.

Sean drove to the Passion Grove house, but when he unlocked the door to enter, he felt the way he always did without Montgomery being there. It was just a house and not a home.

Bobbie and Lincoln looked up at him from where they sat on the sofa together.

"Thanks," Sean said, dropping his keys on the metal table in the foyer and using the large bottle of sanitizer on his hands before moving over to the smart bassinet to look down at his son swaddled and sleeping away. "How was he?"

"Perfect," Bobbie said, pushing her wild curls back from her face before leaning forward to look down at Morgan as well. "There is nothing better than the smell of a baby."

Lincoln eyed his wife with love and indulgence.

In the past week since Sean had brought the baby home, his family rotated sitting with the baby while he visited Montgomery in the hospital, but he took care of Morgan by himself. The nurses at the hospital had prepared him for caring for the baby before he was released to him. With every passing day his nervousness of his son's small size faded. His hands shook a little less as he fed him by bottle, bathed him, changed his diapers and swaddled him. All while talking to him softly about his mother.

"You sure you don't want a nap before we go?" Lincoln asked.

Sean shook his head as he bent to scoop the baby up into his arms. "Morgan and I need to have a man-to-man talk about his mom doing much better today," he said, raising the bundle to press kisses to his brow.

"I made you a seafood lasagna," Lincoln informed him as he followed Bobbie to the front door.

"I appreciate that," Sean said, meaning it.

The help of his parents, his brothers and his sisters-in-law touched him deeply. He wasn't sure how he would ever repay them except to be there in the same way if they ever needed him.

Once they left, he locked the door behind them and warmed one of Morgan's bottles before carrying the baby upstairs to his nursery decorated in shades of cream and deep blue. He settled on one of the matching gliders of navy with cream trim, propping one leg up on the matching ottoman as he gently swayed back and forth.

Morgan opened his eyes and smiled, revealing his dimples. Although he knew his son could only see blurry images, he still smiled down at him as love warmed his entire body. "Hey, little man. You hungry?" he said, introducing the nipple into the baby's mouth the way the nurses taught him. Soon, the gentle sounds of his sucking could be heard. "How are you? You miss me? Because I missed you. Guess who else misses you? Your momma. And I know she's just as ready to wake up and see you as you are to see her."

Sean fed his son, careful to burp him in between, and then changed his diaper not long after. As he rocked him back to sleep, he eased his pinky against Morgan's palm and softly hummed "Dream a Little Dream of Me."

Eleven

One week later

It was a standoff.

As Sean sat across from his parents, Nicolette and Phillip Senior, his eyes fell to his son being held by his mother. He fought an urge to take Morgan from her arms.

"What part of living your own lives is this?" Sean drawled.

Nicolette and Phillip Senior shared a look. "Sean, what if Montgomery doesn't...recover?" she said, casting her solemn gaze on him as she slowly shifted her knees back and forth to rock Morgan in her lap. "You can't continue to raise him alone like this, son. Come home."

The thought of losing Montgomery forever was his constant fear and it tore at his gut like claws. He also worried if he would be able to do it alone, but he couldn't deny that he knew Montgomery's issue. "No," he said with finality.

"Montgomery did not want our child raised like *that*—the wealth."

Nicolette looked disbelieving. "Who would deny a child such privilege?" she asked.

"One afraid that it may shape him to be entitled, my love," Phillip Senior said. "It's the same reason I made the fight for CEO so hard for our sons. I wanted them to work for it and not feel entitled to it—especially Phillip Junior."

That surprised Sean. It was a revelation he hadn't anticipated. The missing link to the puzzle of why the same parents who raised them to be close-knit, loving and loyal, had then pitted the brothers against each other to claim the prize of CEO. And in the beginning, the race to the finish had put a strain on their closeness—something they were still working to repair.

Sean looked into the unlit fireplace, squinting as he fit all of the puzzle pieces together. He shifted his gaze to his father, who was smiling down at his grandson. "Phillip Junior will be appointed CEO," he said.

Nicolette and Phillip Senior shared another of their furtive glances—they'd shared many over their decades together—but neither confirmed nor denied his theory.

Sean thought of his own ambivalence over the CEO position. That plus his concerns about Montgomery's recovery made whether or not Phillip Junior had been victorious in securing the position of little importance to him.

Nothing mattered but bringing Montgomery home to our son.

"Please think about our offer, Sean," Nicolette said, raising the baby to snuggle her nose against his cheek. "Let your family help you."

Sean stood up and gave them a forced smile as he crossed the room to press a kiss to the top of his mother's head. "Thank you for helping me by watching your grandson while I go visit his mother," he said, eyeing his sleeping son with adoration. "That is all the help I need."

"But Sean—"

His father's hand to his wife's arm stopped her words.

"Let him be, my love," Phillip Senior said.

Sean raised his chin toward the baby station he set up in the living room for them. "There's bottles, diapers, wipes, a few extra outfits—"

Nicolette laughed. "I raised five sons and nothing in childcare has changed since then," she said.

Sean chuckled. "Right. Okay," he said. "And don't call in a nanny or au pair. Montgomery wouldn't want that. If he gets to be too much or you have something to do, I have Jillian on standby."

His mother looked slightly offended but thankfully said nothing.

After ensuring Montgomery's bedroom and office were locked to prevent his mother from snooping, Sean left them to be driven to the nearby hospital by Colin. His hand gripped Morgan's empty car seat. Missing him already and wondering how he could have ever thought fatherhood would be a burden to his life. For the past few weeks, his life revolved around his son and he couldn't imagine it being any different anymore.

But it can.

When—not if—Montgomery awakened he was aware she may not want him around as much. He could be relegated to a part-time father. A visitor in his son's life. She may still want time to get over him and meet her Mr. Perfect one day. She may not forgive him for not returning the love she professed.

All he knew was he enjoyed waking up every morning and standing over Morgan's crib as his son awakened at the same time each day.

All of that could go away.

Still, to have Montgomery back beautiful and lively as ever in her beloved heels and brightly colored wardrobe was the greatest desire.

I want her back.

He picked up his phone and pulled up the email from the Vegas photographer with all of their digital photos from the wedding. He swiped through them, ending with the one they used on the cover of *Celebrity Weekly*. It was the moment he didn't go for the kiss. The one he had regretted— and still did. She looked so beautiful that night.

It was a huge contrast from the woman constricted by medical equipment.

He set the phone down on the seat beside him.

"Everything okay?" Colin asked.

He forced a smile as he looked at his driver eyeing him in the rearview mirror. "Just thinking of my wife," he admitted, his sadness feeling like a second skin.

"You two came a long way from that first car ride," Colin said. "And you've got even further to go."

I hope.

"Thanks, Colin."

At the hospital, as the sounds of New Jersey in the summer echoed loudly around him, he exited the vehicle and accidentally knocked his phone from the seat and down onto the concrete pavement. "Damn it," he swore, bending to pick up the device. The screen was shattered.

"Great," he muttered, sliding it into the back pocket of his denims before entering the hospital already.

As he did every day, Sean stopped at the gift shop and purchased a fresh bouquet of flowers before he would make his way up to the intensive care unit. "May I use your phone?" he asked the sales clerk, who looked at him with flirty eyes that he ignored.

"Of course," she said.

With a warm smile of thanks, he called his executive as-

sistant at Cress, INC. to purchase him another phone and
have it couriered to the hospital.

"Thank you," he said, handing her the phone back.

Her fingers stroked the back of his hand as she took it.

"I'm going to take these to my wife now," he said.

Thankfully, the woman took the hint.

As he rode the elevator upstairs and walked down the
hall, Sean hated that he couldn't play—

"Dream a little dream of me."

His steps faltered at the music filtering from Montgomery's room. Curious, he made his way to stand in the doorway. The curtain around her bed was pulled but he could
tell doctors and nurses surrounded Montgomery's bed. He
stepped into the room just as the curtain opened and the
doctor emerged.

"Mr. Cress!" Dr. Schultz, the vascular neurologist, said
with enthusiasm. "The nurse tried to call you—"

"Sean?"

The sound of Montgomery calling his name made him
take a small step back in surprise before he dropped the
flowers he held and rushed past the doctor to yank the curtain back. She sat up in the middle of the small bed as the
nursing staff continued to remove the majority of the medical equipment. She still looked a bit weak and her eyes were
glazed, but she was awake and looking at him as she gave
him a loopy smile that was clearly drug-induced.

"Hey," she said, sounding a bit hoarse.

"Hey," he told her, feeling elated with relief.

He wanted to kiss her so badly but the staff prevented
him from getting closer as they continued to work on her.

"Dream a little dream of me," Louis Armstrong sang.

"Mr. Cress."

He turned, hating to take his eyes off her. He listened
on as the doctor explained that they had awakened her
from her coma and all indications were she had suffered

no major loss of brain function during the stroke. Sean felt like falling to the floor again in relief but stiffened his legs and listened to the doctor's plan for her continued recovery.

His phone arrived—already activated and programmed by his assistant—and he only stepped out of the room to call her father—who wept—and his family—who rejoiced. Sean felt a little of both.

Claiming a spot near the back wall and out of the way of the staff, he watched on closely as they worked, adjusting her bed, giving her medicine via her intravenous line and offering her slow sips of water. By the time they were done and left them alone, she had fallen asleep.

"Excuse me," he said.

One of the nurses stopped.

"The music?" he asked, unable to fight his curiosity.

"When she awakened, she was singing it," the nurse said with a smile. "So we put it on for her. We thought it was adorable."

"Wow," he said, stunned by that.

"We also let her know you've been here every day and that the baby is fine," she assured him. "Just sit tight, let her sleep and get the rest of the sedatives out of her system and then you two can catch up. Okay?"

"Okay," he said, already looking past her at Montgomery.

When they were alone, he pulled a chair close to her bed and held her hand. Never letting it go even as the nurse came in to monitor her. Not even when her father arrived to sit with her as well. And when the skies darkened with night, still he sat by her side, thankful that his family could watch over Morgan as he watched over their Montgomery.

His doubts resurfaced.

Under the haze of medicine, she had seemed pleased to see him.

But what would be her reaction once free of the medicinal drugs?

I love you, Sean.

He eyed her as his heart pounded.

Still?

He closed his eyes and when sleep came, he welcomed it.

The sound of something toppling to the floor startled him awake. Sean sat up straight and looked around at the night nurse assisting Montgomery back into the bed before raising the blankets to cover her legs.

"Anything I can get you?" the nurse asked.

"No, nothing at all," Montgomery said with only the light above the bed breaking up the darkness of the room.

Sean felt nervous as she looked at him.

"Tell me all about our baby," she softly demanded.

"It's a boy and he's such a good baby," he told her with eagerness.

"Morgan Sean Cress?" she asked.

Sean nodded. "Just the way you wanted."

She smiled in thanks.

His heart tugged at the sight of it as he filled her in on every detail he could think of about their son. Every little thing.

And her eyes were eager as she soaked it all up.

"I just want to hold him," Montgomery said. "And kiss him. And get to know him so he can get to know me."

"He'll know you," Sean assured, rising to sit beside her legs on the bed.

"How?" she asked in disbelief.

He smiled.

Her eyes dropped down to take it in.

His heart skipped a beat.

"Because you're his mother...*and* I had a shirt with

your scent on it that I wrap him in under his blankets," he told her.

"You did?" she asked, reaching to cover his hand with her own.

Sean looked down at her touch. She tried to ease her hand away but he clasped it tightly. "I thought I lost you again," he said.

"Again?" Montgomery asked, shifting her eyes away.

"Those days after you—"

"Confessed to loving you?" she asked, now successfully tugging her hand away from his.

He reclaimed it, using his thumb to lightly stroke her inner wrist. "I was miserable without you. I need you—"

"No," Montgomery said, shaking her head. "Let's not do this now, Sean."

"But I—"

"My focus is getting stronger to get out of here and hold my son," she said, imploring him with earnest eyes. "Let me get home to him and have a moment to breathe after being in a coma for weeks. Then we can talk about what exactly *this* is."

"*This* is a marriage," he stressed.

"Is it?" she asked with a shake of her head as if to answer her own question.

He released her hand and his hopes. Rising from the bed, he strode over to the window to look out at the Jersey night. He was plagued with regrets over not accepting her love and returning it without question.

"Dream a little dream of me," Montgomery sang softly.

Sean looked back over his shoulder to find her lying on her side with her hands tucked under the pillows and her eyes closed as she drifted back to sleep. He lightly chuckled and smiled before turning to lean against the window with his arms crossed over his chest. When her light snores filled the air, he pushed off the glass and walked over to press a kiss to the spot just below her ear.

"I have all the time in the world, Montgomery," he told her, low in his throat, before leaving to go and pick up their son.

Two weeks later

Montgomery pressed kisses to Morgan's belly, enjoying his sleepy smiles as he wiggled his feet and hands while she attempted to put him in his sleeper. "That's Mama's baby," she cooed before picking him up to lay him against her shoulder to finish rocking him to sleep after a nice warm bath. "I love you with all of my heart. Every bit of it."

You and your father.

She could already see that Morgan would be the second coming of Sean.

Just as handsome and probably twice as charming one day.

"And some girl will love you just as much as I love your dad," she said, stroking his cheek with her finger.

"If only I could check all the boxes to be your Mr. Perfect."

At the sound of Sean's deep voice, Montgomery felt the hairs on the back of her neck stand up like she touched clothes with a static charge. With her heart suddenly pounding, she glanced over at him leaning in the open doorway looking handsome as ever in a crisp black shirt and denims.

Their eyes locked.

Love for him warmed her entire body. It was raw and pure. And so very deep.

How did I think I would ever get over him? That I ever could get over him?

The love she had for Sean Cress would last a lifetime—

even if she remarried and moved on, she knew she would always yearn for *him*.

"I didn't know you were getting home—back. I meant, I didn't know you were getting *back* so early and he just went to sleep," she said, rising with the baby in her arms.

Sean strode into the room to stand beside her as she placed Morgan in his crib on his back. They both looked down at him. "It's okay, I'll do his night bottles," he said. "We'll catch up on our day then."

She eyed his side profile, loving the devotion for their son in his eyes.

She had sworn he would run from fatherhood, but instead he stepped into it fully. She was incredibly moved and impressed that Sean not only took care of Morgan alone, but did an excellent job at it right here in her home, earning high praise from her father and the Cress family about his insistence on doing it himself—and in keeping with what he knew she would want. Not the type of sacrifice she thought a man like Sean Cress would make. She would have bet money that he would shift the duties off onto a nanny or the like.

In the time since she returned from the hospital, she had acquiesced when he asked to remain living in Passion Grove because he wasn't ready to be away from Morgan. And apart from the addition of their child, it all felt so familiar. Hungering for him, but pretending not to.

I have all the time in the world, Montgomery.

She hadn't been in that deep of sleep when Sean whispered near her ear in the hospital. The words seemed to haunt her because she didn't want him to give up, but she feared that any newfound feelings he had were brought on by her near death and in time they would fade, leaving her heartbroken again.

She looked away when he looked at her.

"Montgomery," he said, low in his throat with hunger and pleading. "I love you."

She pressed her eyes closed, feeling the impact of his declaration surround her. And felt thrilled to imagine for a moment that he truly did. Just as deeply as she adored him.

"I love you so much," he repeated, grasping her arms to turn her to face him.

And I love you.

With all the courage she could muster, Montgomery looked up at him.

Morgan stirred in his sleep and they looked down at him until he quieted again, before Sean took Montgomery's hands in his and led her out of the room to descend the stairs to the living room. She eased her hands from his and walked over to sit on the sofa. As she stared into the unlit fireplace, she remembered the night they shared in front of it during the winter storm.

"Dream a little dream of me," she sang softly, smiling a bit as she touched her lips with her fingertips.

"Did you?" he asked, coming around the sofa to sit on the opposite end.

"Did I what?" she asked.

"Dream of me."

She eyed him before she closed her eyes as a memory from her stay in the hospital nudged itself forward.

Dream of me, Montgomery.

She stiffened.

You're the best thing that ever happened to me.

Her eyes widened a bit.

Come back to me, Montgomery. Please. I love you so much.

Those and a dozen more memories of Sean's heartfelt words to her during her coma resurfaced. She eyed him with a lick of her lips. "Because I almost died?" she asked, speaking to her newfound fears about them.

Sean looked shocked. "Montgomery, this is my love for you. No pity," he said. "I was already wrangling with my feelings for you before I got the call you went into labor."

She allowed her hope to fill her eyes. And her heart.

"You have changed me for the better, Montgomery," he said, easing a bit closer on the sofa. "I want to spend my life with you. I want to grow old with you."

Could it be?

She dropped her head and smiled when he inched over a little more.

Love me.

"I want my family. Me, you and Morgan," he said. "I know you're caught up in the idea of the perfect man—"

She shook her head. "Not anymore," she said, now inching a little closer to him on the sofa.

Sean eyed the move and smiled. Slowly.

"Someone really smart—and sexy as hell—once told my father that all men make mistakes and that no one is perfect or should expect perfection," she said, reaching to stroke the top of his hand.

We can love each other.

Sean quickly turned his hand to grip hers, tugging her over a bit as he shifted as well for them to meet in the middle. He leaned in and pressed a kiss to the base of her throat.

They *both* shivered.

This thing between us is deep. Undeniable. And lasting.

"I was wrong to expect perfection when I resented perfection being expected of me," she explained.

Sean raised his head to lock eyes with her. "Insightful," he said with commendation.

"Right?" she asked.

They leaned their faces in close, touching noses as their eyes met and held.

"My life is better with you than it could *ever* be without you," he said softly, his words breezing against her lips.

She freed her tongue as if she could catch them like snowflakes.

He chuckled at the move.

Montgomery gave him a soft smile. "You are not perfect, neither am I, but you, Mr. Sean Cress, are perfect for me," she confessed.

He captured her mouth with his own as he wrapped his arms around her body to lift her over his lap to straddle. She eased her arms around his neck as she returned his kisses and gave in to the passion.

"Let's go to bed," she said in between kisses before rising to extend her hand to him.

Sean leaned back against the sofa as he looked up at her with legs spread wide, giving off the energy that he was equipped and ready to please her. "Yours or mine?" he asked.

Montgomery tilted her head to the side with one of her brows risen. *"Ours,"* she answered definitively.

He leaned forward and wrapped his arms around her thighs, picking her up over his shoulder as he rose to his full height. She bit down on her lip to keep from squealing in delight as he carried her up the stairs and into *their* owner's suite.

Epilogue

Five months later

Montgomery bounced a plump and happy Morgan on her hip as he played with her ear as she looked out the window of the nursery at the snow falling outside. She could hardly believe it had been a year since she first discovered she was pregnant. She chuckled, remembering how freaked out they both had been by the idea of becoming parents.

And just as they thought nothing had been the same for them again.

It's all spectacularly better.

They had settled in as a family in Passion Grove with plenty of love and passion. Communication and compromise. And lots of humor—especially about her exploits as a single woman searching for a husband.

They weren't perfect. That was impossible. But they were good. No major hassles that they hadn't faced together.

Montgomery had even acquiesced on the use of a part-time nanny only during those days it wasn't feasible to take Morgan to work with her. He made plenty of use of the nursery Sean had set up for them there—another Sean surprise.

Sean limited his traveling schedule and was focused on setting up the CressTV streaming service, including securing Delphine Côté for her own cooking series. The show was just in early development and was already heavily anticipated in the foreign markets. Still, as busy as he was, Sean was home for dinner every night, and lying on his belly on the floor watching Morgan play seemed to be his favorite pastime.

Well, except for making love once Morgan was asleep in his nursery for the night.

Montgomery pressed a kiss to Morgan's soft curls that were scented with his baby shampoo. She left the nursery and walked to the home office she and Sean now shared.

"No, I'm not missing a thing about nightlife," Sean said.

"The wife has the shackles on you pretty good," a male voice said via speakerphone.

Montgomery paused.

"Yup, and I love it in every possible way you can think of," Sean said without hesitation. "My life has never been so good. But enjoy the condo. Montgomery and I are happy to have it off our hands—and turn a good profit off the sale to you."

Damn right we are.

Montgomery moved away from the door and continued down the stairs, hating to snoop. It wasn't needed. Still, it felt good to hear the partying A-list playboy rebuff his former wild lifestyle.

When she reached the living room, she settled Morgan in his playpen where he instantly bent over to gnaw on one of the attached plastic objects. She poured herself a glass of wine in the kitchen and claimed a seat on the sofa. Beside her on the end table was a photograph of her little family surrounded by her father, his new lady friend from church and the entire Cress family clan.

Family.

Perfectly imperfect.

She was enjoying the adult version of her relationship with her father who had finally admitted that he had been a fan of Sean's cooking shows for years. They both enjoyed teasing her father about that.

Her eyes landed on Nicolette in the photo.

Montgomery was still recovering from the scare of the woman's sudden fascination with Passion Grove once she discovered the small town was home to a few billionaires, celebrities and a famous writer. Nicolette was trying to talk Phillip Senior into purchasing a weekend estate there. Thankfully, her father-in-law had no interest in living in New Jersey.

Sean came down the stairs and Montgomery looked back over the sofa to eye him as he soon lay on the couch with his head in her lap. "Do you think we'll get snowed in again this year?" he asked, looking up at her.

"You know our track record for getting in jams together," she said with a naughty twinkle in her eye.

"Yeah, and now we're stuck together for life," Sean said, his eyes warm with love for her.

"And *that* is perfect," she whispered down to him before kissing her husband deeply.

* * * * *

MILLS & BOON

THE HEART OF ROMANCE

A ROMANCE FOR EVERY READER

ODERN

Prepare to be swept off your feet by sophisticated, sexy and seductive heroes, in some of the world's most glamourous and romantic locations, where power and passion collide.

STORICAL

Escape with historical heroes from time gone by. Whether your passion is for wicked Regency Rakes, muscled Vikings or rugged Highlanders, awaken the romance of the past.

EDICAL

Set your pulse racing with dedicated, delectable doctors in the high-pressure world of medicine, where emotions run high and passion, comfort and love are the best medicine.

ue Love

Celebrate true love with tender stories of heartfelt romance, from the rush of falling in love to the joy a new baby can bring, and a focus on the emotional heart of a relationship.

Desire

Indulge in secrets and scandal, intense drama and plenty of sizzling hot action with powerful and passionate heroes who have it all: wealth, status, good looks…everything but the right woman.

EROES

Experience all the excitement of a gripping thriller, with an intense romance at its heart. Resourceful, true-to-life women and strong, fearless men face danger and desire - a killer combination!

To see which titles are coming soon, please visit

millsandboon.co.uk/nextmonth

LET'S TALK
Romance

For exclusive extracts, competitions
and special offers, find us online:

 facebook.com/millsandboon

@MillsandBoon

@MillsandBoonUK

Get in touch on 01413 063232

For all the latest titles coming soon, visit
millsandboon.co.uk/nextmonth